I0557780

SADDLEBAG DISPATCHES MAGAZINE PRESENTS

ACES, EIGHTS AND UNMARKED GRAVES

LEGENDS OF THE BLACK HILLS

Saddlebag Dispatches, LCC
A Subsidiary of Oghma Communications
Bentonville, Arkansas
www.saddlebagdispatches.com

Aces, Eights & Unmarked Graves:
Description: First Edition | Bentonville: Saddlebag Dispatches, 2025
Identifiers: ISBN: 979-8-89299-089-9 (trade paperback)| ISBN: 979-8-89299-090-5 (eBook)
FICTION/Westerns | FICTION/Action & Adventure |
FICTION/Thrillers/Historical

Trade Paperback edition August, 2025

Cover Design and Interior Design by Casey W. Cowan
Editing by Anthony Wood, Dennis Doty, Don Money & Benjamin Bailey

SADDLEBAG DISPATCHES MAGAZINE PRESENTS

ACES, EIGHTS AND UNMARKED GRAVES

LEGENDS OF THE BLACK HILLS

Holdup (20 Miles to Deadwood by Charles Marion Russell

TABLE OF CONTENTS

Voice of the HIlls by Frederic Remington

LIST OF ILLUSTRATIONS

Ranchero by Frank Tenney Johnson

PREFACE

———⊰⊱———

COME ON IN out of the gunsmoke and gold dust. Hobble your mount and find yourself a spot near the pot-bellied stove. Tip back your hat, shake off the trail dust, and pull out *Aces, Eights, and Unmarked Graves: Legends of the Black Hills* for another round of the best Western short fiction this side of the Missouri.

Grab your blanket and join Ben Henry Bailey, Lee Clinton, John Sanders, Bruce Hartman, Derryl York, Laura Rodley, M. F. McDonnell, Matthew Watson, and John Mort as they tell tales of the Old West under a moonless night.

Follow along with Calamity Jane as she leads a wagon train to Deadwood through desperate country with the help of Wild Bill Hickok and his old pard, Charlie Little. Follow two washed up miners who want a glimpse of "Sin City" instead rescues one of their sisters from Al Swearingen's brothel in Deadwood. Take another sip of steaming coffee and hear the story of Jesse James's notorious cousin, Jezzebelle. Do your best to tend to a rattlesnake bite that leaves the bones of a simple miner atop one of the biggest gold strikes in the West. Hop a train and track down a bank counterfeiter alongside a marshal with an unjust tainted reputation and his former lover. Watch as a nurse in a cancer ward inspires a writer to create a world in the Old West where both become heroes. Get the "story behind the story" about a sky blue ribbon that leads up to Jack McCall murdering Wild Bill Hickok. Play poker with a gravedigger bent on making his fortune off of other men's deaths at the card table who's luck run runs out playing the Dead Man's Hand.

You just never know who'll meet in *Aces, Eights, and Unmarked Graves: Legends of the Black Hills,* but you certainly will not be disappointed. And it's all brought to you by the award winning *Saddlebag Dispatches* Magazine, home of all things western.

—Anthony Wood
Managing Editor, *Saddlebag Dispatches*
August 7, 2025

SADDLEBAG DISPATCHES MAGAZINE PRESENTS

ACES, EIGHTS AND UNMARKED GRAVES

LEGENDS OF THE BLACK HILLS

The Trusty Knaves by W.H.D. Koerner

"WHAT KIRA INSPIRED"

THOMAS WHITE

DEADWOOD, DAKOTA TERRITORY
1877

BECK STANTON RODE into town an hour before noon. The blood-stained bandage below his right knee was another reason to track down Blake Mumford. Mumford tried to ambush him not long after Stanton crossed the railroad in Nebraska.

Stanton was trailing Mumford because Conway Brune, owner of the Brune Ranch in Colorado, wanted the runaway thief returned. Brune had trusted Mumford as one of his top hands, but Mumford had been privately selling Brune's stray cattle for over a year. Stanton would be well paid when he returned with Mumford, regardless of Mumford's condition.

The sky was overcast as Stanton walked his horse on Main Street. Some men were standing and walking about, some trying to evade the mud and piles of wood, and some drunk and stumbling. Money in his pocket meant Stanton could empty an eye-raising number of glasses in one of the many saloons, be it building, tent or dugout. Then he would walk, not stumble, to his horse. But Stanton wanted Mumford tied to ride as soon as possible.

Stanton blinked his keen eyesight from the men and ramshackle buildings on one side of the street to the other.

I'll find him. Even if I have to walk him down.

He trotted his horse to let a drunk stagger behind him.

Mumford shot off his mouth about this town, Stanton continued, walking his horse once again. The money from mining in Deadwood was just waiting for him.

You'd think he'd know enough not to ride to Deadwood after being branded a thief at the ranch... and after he took a shot at me. But if he didn't ride for the money he wouldn't be Mumford.

And when I find him, it won't be long before I lead him out of town... upright in a saddle or draped over one.

Stanton trotted his horse once again, but this time it was to let an irate man fall behind him. The man rolled once before he leapt to his feet and tried to strike another irate man who launched himself at him. The second man took a fist to the jaw, but did not fall back. He only set his feet in the dirt and threw a shoulder into the first man's midsection. They rolled to the other side of the street, cursing and pummeling the other. Stanton returned to what was ahead of him.

Ahead was a hotel, and near the hotel was a young woman dressed for travel with a lone bag at her feet. Pretty but weary, she had a face framed by the strands of blonde hair no longer secure beneath her hat. She listened to three young women standing with her, each also dressed for travel, and just as pretty, but not as weary. The three seemed intent on resolving some dilemma.

Stanton was astonished. Kira Smyth? In Deadwood? Why would a daughter of Croft Smyth be in Deadwood?

"Hey, statue. Pick a side of the street."

Realizing only then that he had stopped his horse in the middle of Main Street, Stanton turned to face the impatient order.

A scowling man with a dusty, wide-brimmed hat and a stained, fraying jacket sat on a buckboard with a stack of timber in the back. He glared at Stanton as if he had said all he would.

Stanton glared back momentarily, and then walked his horse to the side of the street opposite the young women. From there, he continued to walk his horse until he saw a space where he could stop and turn back to the young woman he recognized.

But just as he was about to return to Kira Smyth, he was held in place once again, only this time at the sight of a man not far ahead of him who was walking with a graver scowl and far more dust and stains than the buckboard driver.

The man Stanton watched walked up to two men, also land worn, but not with the same air of desperation. The two men looked briefly at one another and then back at the other man as if they only continued to find him wanting.

Stanton nodded with a solemn expression. Mumford.

Then he smirked. The money from mining was just waiting for him. He looks like somebody was just waiting at a mine to bury him, and that somebody did.

Mumford was already talking rapidly, even talking with his hands, as he stopped next to the two men. One of them took a step back and they both grimaced as if Mumford stank of something.

Nearly unblinking, Stanton watched his prey.

As he explained himself, Mumford was alternating from one man to the other, and twice he turned behind him and pointed at something beyond the buildings across the street. Only moments after Mumford's second turn, one of the men walked away as if his stomach was churning.

The second man was about to follow him, but Mumford grabbed him by the arm to hold him in place, nearly tearing his shirt sleeve. Mumford's eyes were now wild with insistence. He pointed once again beyond the buildings and, nearly screaming, stamped his feet.

The man tore his arm from Mumford's grasp with his other hand on his Colt. His sneer enhanced his threatening words, words Mumford did not seem to believe.

But believe them he did the moment after his hand landed on the departing man's shoulder. The man spun and struck Mumford on the cheek bone with the butt of his Colt. Mumford fell face flat in the dirt.

And when he dragged himself to his hands and knees, blood trailing down his face and neck, the now wheezing Mumford looked up, and recoiled as if stung by a scorpion.

He eyes now locked with the ominous Stanton, who walked his horse toward Mumford as if they were the only two men on Main Street.

Though still wheezing, the cattle thief leapt to his feet and ran as if all of his sins were ghosts at last descending on him.

He leapt over a crate at the feet of a man he simultaneously knocked out of his way, and moments later felt a searing pain below the knee of his right leg. Falling and rolling only twisted deeper the Sheffield Bowie knife the man had thrown.

Mumford could only writhe in the dirt as he tried to extract the knife with his badly trembling hands. Stanton rode up and dismounted. Time was the furthest of his worries.

After nodding to the man who had thrown the knife, Stanton returned to Mumford who wheezed because he no longer had the strength to cough.

"If you're worried about staying in Deadwood," Stanton said, his voice cool and measured and therefore even more threatening. "Don't be. You're going home."

Mumford stammered almost inaudibly, "How much do you want to leave me here?"

"How much do you have?" Stanton asked, his voice no less threatening.

Mumford's stammer was now a rasp. "I know I'm right this time. I know it. I only need...."

Stanton cut him off when he picked him up with one hand and knocked him out with the other. The sound of dry fist on flesh echoed the earlier sound of handle butt on flesh.

Stanton threw Mumford to the dirt, extracted the knife from his leg, wiped it clean on Mumford's other pant leg, and then threw the knife back near the owner. The knife stuck in a wall at a safe distance. Stanton and the man exchanged respectful nods.

As the man sheathed his knife, he watched Stanton securely tying Mumford's hands and feet.

WHEN STANTON WALKED his horse and his unconscious cargo back near the hotel, he saw Kira Smyth still outside, but standing alone. Stanton did not like the way the two grimy men closest to Kira were watching her.

Both men saw Stanton before Kira saw him, and they seemed to agree that there was a better place for them to be. They walked away as Stanton stopped his horse. Kira looked at the buildings down the street.

"Hello, Miss Smyth," Stanton said.

Kira turned as if grabbed by the arm, but then she nearly smiled. "You're Beck Stanton. One of Conway Brune's men."

"Yes, ma'am."

"Why are you in Deadwood, Mister Stanton?"

Stanton walked closer with his horse's reins tight in his hand. "Beck. And it may not be my business, Miss Smyth, but why are you in Deadwood? You didn't look so good until you saw someone you recognized. And I'd be obliged if you don't say you asked me first."

She looked about her momentarily as if there had to be a better place to answer the question. But without one, she just returned to him, her eyes red. "If you're Beck, I'm Kira."

Stanton nodded. "Kira."

"I married Stark Mantle, one of my father's ranch hands. My father wanted us to stay on the ranch, but Stark wanted to live in the Dakota Territory. He said where there were miners there was money to be made, and he knew how. I thought he knew what he was talking about, and I thought I knew him."

She paused and wiped her eyes with a handkerchief from her sleeve. Stanton waited.

"I knew his temper, but it got worse the further we were from the ranch. Before we crossed the railroad in Nebraska we were invited to ride with a group also riding for the territory. Stark said we'd be all right alone. But after words with some of the men who said they were only worried about us, Stark agreed. Then it wasn't long before he crossed one of the men in a way he shouldn't have, and I was a widow. There wasn't much grieving at Stark's burial, but no one punished him through me for the trouble he caused. They looked out for me. Some of them are from the Eastern States."

Once again she wiped her eyes, and Stanton waited.

"Some of the women said we could stay together. They're here to find work."

Stanton tried not to scowl, but he could not prevent it. "Work?"

There was no mistaking the scowl, so Kira paused before she nodded. "Did they say what type of work, Kira?"

She looked down the street. "There at the Gem. They said there's a man. He's well dressed and well spoken. He has work and new lives for women. I don't know if I have the name right. It's like swearing hen."

"Swearingen."

"Yes. Do you know him?"

"I've heard of him," Stanton said, his eyes locked on hers. "How'd you like to go home instead? You can ride out with me today."

Kira considered him. "Of course I'd like to go home, but can I trust you?"

"More than you can ever trust Swearingen."

Her eyes narrowed suspiciously. "How do you know that?"

"I'll answer your question and the one you asked me before. Just understand that I'm not one for many words."

"I'm listening."

Without turning, Stanton nodded at the still unconscious Mumford. "He was stealing and selling cattle. When Brune found out, he sent me after him. I'm bringing him back. And my leg is another reason."

She only blinked a look at his bandaged right leg.

"This side of the railroad he saw I was trailing him, and he took a shot at me. I fell off Gray Smear and landed on a shoulder. A doctor in Cold Brand took out the slug and set the shoulder. He had a nurse. She was good. All nurses should be as good. She told me about Swearingen when I told her I was after Mumford and riding for Deadwood."

"And what she told you would tell me to leave now."

"As sure as I'm standing here."

She considered him for a long moment and nodded. "I can pay for horses."

"I'll pay for the horses and a buckboard. We ride out as soon as we can. But there's time to warn those three ladies, if you can speak to them outside and away from anyone else. I'm sorry for all of them. But, as much as I'd like to see him shut down and run out, don't step on the... swearing hen, or any of his men."

She seemed to understand that he did not intend any humor. "I'll find out if I can speak to them as you say. I'm sorry for them too, and I won't step on anyone."

Still without turning, Stanton nodded at his unconscious cargo. "Don't worry about Mumford or the ride back to Colorado. I can protect you."

At last Kira smiled. "I know you can."

DEADWOOD, SOUTH DAKOTA
2021

BECK STANTON SET the last page of his short story, "What Kira Inspired," facedown on the other pages. He was sitting up in a hospital bed with a tray table as his desk. It was just after midnight.

Kira will be on duty after the shift change later this morning. But I will not give her the story until I am released to return home.

Before she left Friday, she said her weekend would be for riding and roping and the outdoors she loves. Not just a nurse, she's also a cowgirl, born and raised in South Dakota.

I was only here from New England on vacation. But here I stayed as a cancer patient. And here I recover from surgeries below the knee of my right leg.

He looked at the walker next to his bed and then back at the short story. Kira Smyth is my hero in fact, but I am only her hero in fiction.

She is helping me reestablish my life, so I help her reestablish her life in one of my amateur short stories. And when she reads the story, she may not like the details, but she may understand the sentiments. I can only hope.

He returned to the walker. *When she walks with me today, I'll use the cane. The walker stays here. She said the time for it is up to me.*

Then with the same conviction, he looked out the lone window at the moonlit sky and the land beyond the hospital.

At last Beck Stanton spoke, "By this time next week, I will walk without the cane."

———⊗———

—Thomas White wrote this short story as his second Western submitted to a publication. For many years, he has written pulp short stories for the sake of writing them. His first Western short story was published in the fifth anthology from Saddlebag Dispatches. He received a Ph.D. in the social sciences. A former general education college professor, he taught undergraduate survey courses and included introductory film studies in many of his courses with emphasis on classic feature films spanning the silent era to the early 1960s. Westerns and noir films were prominent. With no claim to being a film critic or historian, he nonetheless included film as a noteworthy resource for providing examples of curricula beyond textbook examples. His unpublished nonfiction includes explanations of such examples in Westerns directed by John Ford, Howard Hawks and Anthony Mann. He was born in Massachusetts, but is a lifelong resident of New Hampshire.

A NEW MOTHER FOR LEAH

BLANCHE DESCHAIN

AUTUMN WAS HEAVY on the land and pigs snuffled for nuts when Leah's ma took sick. She went to her room, and Leah watched the door close. Later the hogs came in, fat for winter, but she never saw her Ma leave the room. Not long after, her father rode away on a big black horse with soft-feathered hocks. When he returned, he wasn't alone.

It was winter when he pushed inside on a rush of cold air. Leah shrank herself small. He was carrying something in his arms. When he turned to the fire, the covering blankets fell back and she saw a slight woman.

"I've brought your ma. Heat some water, girl."

Leah rushed to fetch a bucketful from the icy well. Inside, she pushed the heavy iron pot over the coals, poking up the fire. She tried to hide how her hungry gaze raked the woman her father held. For his part, he stood there, watching her, clutching the woman to his chest. His eyes dead-flat, like a snake.

The woman had dark hair like her Ma, but the girl saw sharpness in her pale face. Her ma's had been round. Her eyes were blue where Leah had loved Ma's warm brown eyes. The woman looked sick as her mother had, and Leah feared this woman would die too.

In a quiet voice, Leah pointed out the differences she saw to her father. Her father's face drew tight with anger, this woman was her mother he thundered. She was only to address her as Ma. He dumped the small, shivery-thin woman on one of the wooden chairs. Her head fell back with a thump that made Leah wince.

Her father bid her go and air out her mother's trousseau. Leah tried to ask more about this strange woman. She would not call her ma. Her father lunged for her, chasing her away. Leah rushed up the stairs like hell itself was baying on her heels.

Leah came back down with an armful of clothing, hoping her father had calmed. Her da had filled the knee-high copper tub with steaming water. Without a word he dumped the woman into the water, fully clothed. Leah watched as she slipped beneath the water with nary a ripple.

When her father didn't move, Leah rushed to pull her up. The woman sputtered, choking on air, like a fish pulled from a river. He told Leah to wash her and make sure she didn't drown. He took a bottle in his fist and went outside.

Leah pulled off the woman's wet clothing, put it in a pile by the fire. The woman was bones, held together by sallow skin. Her body covered in bruises and scrapes, her skin marred by angry welts running down her arms.

After an hour, the woman was clean, and the water was cold and filthy gray. Her father had still not returned. Leah needed to get her out of the dirty water and into bed. Outside, the big horse was gone from the hitching rail.

Fear shivered through her, her Da often had a habit of leaving for days, and once, for a few weeks. She tried to wake the woman, started by talking to her, then calling to her loudly. When Leah panicked and started to shake her, the woman stirred—her eyes struggling to focus.

The woman tried to speak, but her teeth were clacking with cold. She looked panicked, her hands gripping the sides of the tub in a white-knuckled grip. Leah told her Da was gone and wouldn't be back, so they needed to get her out. The woman seemed to hear her, and they struggled in the sloppy mess of dirty water. They pulled together until she collapsed on the floor in a puddle of wet and cold.

"That bastard drugged me. My head hurts like it's going to split. He musta put something in the liquor, dirty bastard." She slurred her words. Leah helped her to the chair by the table where they both rested for a bit.

"Your room is upstairs. Don't sleep yet." Leah was apologetic, but there was nothing to be done. They made it up the stairs, and the woman collapsed on the bed. She banked the fire for the night and fell asleep by the ashes. When she woke at dawn, she heard the sound of shuffling feet upstairs.

When Leah opened the door, the woman asked where she was, and Leah tried to explain. When she begged for something called opium, Leah didn't know what she meant and the woman got angry. She flinched when the woman lunged at her. Weak as a kitten, she collapsed to the floor.

Leah got scared and shut the door. She sat outside and listened to the woman scream and curse as the sun passed noon, then moved on to sunset. She heard muttered stories about a dark man, about hawks, and sharp knives in darkness. This dark man sounded like a boogie man, the type Ma used to name in her stories.

When she opened the door later, the woman was still on the floor. Leah put the tray down and rushed to her. Beneath her palm, the woman's heart was racing, her skin pebbled with goose-flesh. Leah tried to drag her to the bed but couldn't get her far. Eventually, she put a pillow under the woman's head and covered her in her mother's quilt.

The woman shivered with chills but was covered in sweat all the same. Leah didn't know how to help. After a while, she lay down beside the woman. She put the woman's arm across her chest and tried hard to pretend it was her Ma. She tried to ignore the smell of sickness and the sharp bones that stuck out from her sparse flesh.

That night, Leah tried to spoon broth down her, but the woman couldn't hold it down. Her pupils were dilated like black pits, tears ran down her cheeks. She yawned constantly, cracking her jaw painfully. Leah worried she wasn't drinking enough water, but she choked when she tried to give her more. She wondered what she would do if the woman died.

A few days later, Leah woke from her spot by the fire and was sure the woman was dead, cold and still on the floor. She shook her, pounded her small fists on the woman's chest and suddenly the woman started to cough. When she caught her breath and Leah finally managed to get her into bed, they fell asleep against the headboard, exhausted.

It was seven more days before the woman woke, coherent. When she started to talk, the woman told Leah that her father found her in an opium den. The woman told her opium was a bad medicine that caught people in coils round the neck like a big snake and choked them to death.

Her father had checked her teeth and eyes like a horse and said he figured she would survive what was coming. Nobody would miss her. She told Leah she refused to die here in some backwoods cabin, stolen away by a crazy man.

After she could walk, Leah helped the woman to the big copper tub, her legs wobbly as a colt's. She was sure now the woman was going to live, and she allowed herself a spark of hope. The woman began to hobble around the dirt yard after that, prowling like an animal caught in a snare. She ate the food Leah cooked, and they settled into a routine. One day, they heard hooves and her father came home.

Weak as she was, the woman took a run at him, spitting and hissing like a wild cat. He pushed her down in the yard and went inside. The woman went to bed while Leah did chores. On the third day, her father ripped the woman out of the bed she had not risen from. When Leah tried to protect the woman, her father knocked her flat in the hallway with a hard fist.

He pushed the woman into the room, and Leah listened as he beat her. That night she crept in and found the woman had hidden a sharp paring knife beneath her pillow. Leah reminded the woman she was still weak and promised she would protect her until she was strong.

When they woke in the cold dawn light, her father had left for parts unknown again. Leah helped the woman to bed and went to care for the animals. Her body was used to this treatment, her face ached and she cried a little, but she was glad not to be alone. A sound behind her and she saw the woman lifting a fork from the barn wall to help her.

Leah made them lunch and when the woman smiled at a silly joke, Leah's heart grew wings. The woman still spent days in bed, until one day her luck ran out. Leah heard hooves and rushed upstairs to get the woman out of bed, but she wouldn't move to even her most desperate plea.

Her father came in and locked Leah out of the room. She sat outside the door and probed her fear like a bad tooth, afraid her father would finally kill one of them. She woke that night to a sound, from her spot asleep in the hallway, saw the woman slipping out the door.

"Please take me too. I can help you, I won't be trouble." The woman paused, half out the doorway, stood for a long time.

Finally, the woman stepped back inside, closed the door. She told Leah to go back to bed. Leah worried she would leave, but did as the woman told her.

When Leah woke, the woman was making breakfast over the fire. She was a terrible cook but Leah ate the food happily. They shared a smile when her father came in and choked down the burnt corn cakes. Chores were done quick now, with two sets of hands, the house was spotless, scrubbed clean.

As the years passed, Leah's love for this new mother grew, but sometimes she noticed things about her that weren't like her first ma. Her new ma could catch a dropped knife, snatch it up by the hilt so fast Leah didn't see her hand move. Late at night she crept out and watched her practice knife throwing when her Da was gone on a bend.

One day, Leah brought her a recipe book and she flushed a deep red, shyly telling Leah she couldn't read. After that Leah taught her to read. Once Leah came home from playing with kids on a nearby farm sporting a black eye. That night her ma took her down behind the orchard and taught Leah to hold a knife and dodge a punch.

Leah liked the stories her new ma told when they sat before the fire after chores. Sometimes about the man who taught her to shoot. The man was good at hunting and tracking but had a rotten heart. He was a bad man, but she had loved him in her own way.

Leah asked why she didn't leave her father now that she wasn't sick. Leah wished the woman would take her to the city with her. Her ma said she only learned what real love is just now, since she came here to the cabin. Leah couldn't imagine how her ma could love anything about this place, but she was glad of it.

Leah kept up her visits to the farm where she earned the black eye. Things happened as they did, she fell in love with the youngest son of the family. He had golden curls and pretty brown eyes. When he laughed, she swore birds chirped sweeter. The boy grew to a man and asked her father's permission, and they married in the spring.

One day, Leah and her ma went shopping in town. As they rode, her ma shied at the harsh cry of a hawk, her face going shock-white. Twice more they heard a cry as her ma turned them in a mad dash home. They returned to find her golden-haired husband face down in the dirt—shot dead.

Leah rushed to him. Behind her, Ma kept her seat on the palomino dancing nervously beneath her. Her hands were tight on the reins, and she looked like she might ride away. Fear filled Leah's gut. She shot her Ma a desperate gaze, watched her back straighten as she stilled her mount.

With a wild yell, her father ran around the house waving a rifle. He was thin and old now, bony in his stained-cotton long-johns, hair was wispy and sparse. He pointed the gun toward the porch where a hawk sat on the roof watching them with great golden eyes. A tall, dark man stepped from the shadow of the porch and looked to her ma.

"Howdy, my girl, I've been looking for you for a long time, my sweet." He smiled and it made Leah's blood run cold. "My Patty girl, I've missed you." Leah was surprised to hear her ma's name, realizing she had never asked.

The dark man was still handsome after all this time. Even now, his dark hair was threaded with silver. He still wore that devil's smile. His eyes glinted with anger and amusement both. But he would change, like quicksilver. Everything was a joke, until suddenly, it was deadly serious.

The man turned to Leah's old father and laughed. "This who you married, sweet? I'm 'fraid to be the one to tell you this, old fool, but Pat's been married to me since she was eighteen. You stole my wife."

"Hells, do I care! She's been a good wife and mother." Her father was foaming mad, little flecks of spit on his grizzled chin.

The man lifted his gun and shot her father dead in the gut. He curled over the wound and screamed like a child. Neither Leah nor Pat moved to the old man. Instead, Pat moved slowly over to Leah, pulling her up from her husband's body. She put herself in front, between Leah and this dangerous man. All the while, the man just watched them.

"Come now, sweet, how can you think I'd hurt your kin, she's yours right? A kid you got from whoring around, while you was still married to me? Now, I'd have probably left it all alone if you hadn't stolen from me, but you did. I'm here to take back what's mine." He raised his pistol toward her.

"You're the one that left me, Elmer. I just wasn't there when you came back. As far as the other, I don't have anything of yours, that silver claim is mine, it came to me from my father, you son of a bitch." She tried to push Leah toward her horse, but the man thumbed back the hammer. Pat paused knowing he would shoot the girl if the fancy took him.

They heard the sound of hooves, and a gang of men rode up—horses sweating and snorting beneath them. A wave of thrashing hooves, they rode a ring around the women, screaming and hollering. A woman split off from the group, the only silent rider. She rode near the porch and the hawk lifted from its perch to land, claws deep, on her shoulder. The woman rolled a cigarette as the men slid down from horseflesh to surround the women.

With ungentle hands, they tied them up, ransacking the house, and burning everything they owned in a bonfire. The cows were lowing, wanting to be milked when the men set the barn on fire. Leah and Pat watched in horror as the flames sent up thick, oily smoke into the night sky.

Hours later, in the deepest part of night, her husband's kin rode up, three abreast. They had seen the smoke and rushed to help. The old father and two strapping brothers, all with her dead husband's eyes.

They saw her man's body in the yard and tripped over their feet to kneel beside him. The two women watched, gagged and bound about the oak tree, straining their ropes but could do nothing.

The dark man shot the old father in the chest. Both sons froze in horror, fingers useless on their guns. When they came to their senses, both shot like mad, but luck-kissed, all the bullets missed the dark man. He walked toward them, shot one brother in the head and the man crumpled. The last brother fired off a round close enough to make the dark man hiss. He fell when the woman with the hawk stuck him in his kidney from behind.

After the commotion died down, the dark man took a squat by the oak tree and began to ask Pat questions he felt long overdue. He pulled the gag from her mouth, and she licked split lips.

"Where's the papers to my mine?" She pointed to the house, and laughing, told him he'd burned them. She saw his eyes go flat-black and felt a ripple of fear in her gut.

He hit her open-hand across the face and winced. She realized he'd been shot in the shoulder. Only nicked, the wound didn't seem bad. They watched him probe for the bullet with dirty fingers. The group mounted up and tied both women to a saddle.

That night at the fire, they let Pat free. From across the fire, Leah watched her become the woman she had seen glimpses of during their life together in the little cabin. Pat's words became cutting and clever, her voice was deeper, her laugh rougher. The rowdy group played a game of poker with bullets, she threw down her wedding ring as a chip. By the end, she pocketed both the ring and a handful of bullets. After the others had passed out, Leah watched Pat talk to the quiet woman by the fire.

"Adelita, please, you have to let us go," Pat whispered as she watched the flames of the campfire leap and spark, reflected in the other woman's sloe-black eyes.

"You know I can't do that, Pat." The woman shook her head sadly, feeding a bit of meat to the hawk. "We obey for now and must do so a little longer. I'm sorry. It's for a reason you would consider worth it, if I told you."

"My life and an innocent girl's? I doubt it."

"One life is innocent, even if mine isn't," Adelita put her pistol on her knee and turned her face to the shadows.

In the next few days, the dark man started to slump in his saddle, his arm starting to stink. They continued on the trail, and by sunset, he fell off his horse.

Adelita called for a halt. The gang started to get rebellious, muttering that he was slowing them down. The law would be on their trail, baying for blood, wanting death for the murders they had done at the dark man's command.

Adelita stuck close by as he slipped farther from lucidity and began to babble. Adelita was oiling her pistol, the hawk on a limb above her, when the men started to harass the dark man. They wanted to know why he hadn't tortured Pat for information on the silver claim, or killed her if she didn't know. Adelita drove them back but slept with her eyes open, one hand on her weapon. He muttered in his sleep and Adelita watched him darkly.

Late that night, the men came for Pat, Adelita watched but didn't speak out. They cut her loose, dragging her to the edge of the campfire light before Pat called out, waking the dark man. He saw the men and behind him on the forest wall his shadow stretched like a hellscape devil. He palmed leather and the air filled with the smell of gunpowder, blood, and loose guts.

He killed six men all around Pat, dropping them in a neat circle. Then he collapsed back to the ground. Pat and Adelita watched each other over the fire. After a long time, Adelita stood and cut their bonds.

"Listen, Pat, you know this wasn't my idea. Take the horses if you want, just go."

"I don't think so, Adelita. Not after all this, I think you know that. I owe you."

"Listen, I'm carrying a child, Pat. I was fixin' to leave when we hit town. I'm planning a return to my mother's people. I was going to do that for him myself, so he didn't come after me. You saved me the trouble." She stood and stretched, showing no signs of fear.

Adelita looked regretfully at the dark man, deep in his fevered sleep, picked up her saddlebags, and mounted with a smooth motion. Soundlessly, she and the hawk slipped into the night. Pat rubbed her wrist where the rope had left her skin bubbled and red. She went over to the dark man and shook him awake, giving him a grim smile despite her aching cheek. She pulled a large knife from one of the men's bodies.

The dark man looked around wildly, eyes unable to focus. He saw Adelita gone and the dead men scattered around the fire. He saw Pat and Leah with frayed bonds by their feet. Then he started to scream. Pat moved toward him carefully, a woman approaching to kill a viper. He was weak now with wound-sickness, but she didn't want to take any chances.

After it was done, the dark man dead, they moved away from the camp. Leaving the bodies for scavengers, they took the horses and camped near a fresh-water spring. As they washed away the blood, they spoke of what they would do now, woman to woman and mother to daughter both.

Pat told Leah the papers to the silver mine were hidden in the city. She warned Leah she was a wanted woman, they couldn't have any sort of normal life. She'd done bad things, long ago, in the deserts of Mexico, the dark man at her side. As dawn broke hot and sharp over the trees, they had spoken enough of the past, now was a time for their future. Side by side, they rode together toward the rising sun.

———

—*Blanche Deschain writes books about the women that live inside her barbarous mind. Strong, strapping women, fox-clever females, hero-women that step in, when the world has become too wild. Her passion for the west was ignited when she moved to Utah to live with her grandmother, an avid genealogist and story-teller. This wise-woman imparted a love and a passion for giving life to the stories we tell ourselves.*

Blanche has a short story in the winter anthology Greed, Gold and Gunsmoke. *She currently resides on Vancouver Island with her husband and daughter.*

COFFEYVILLE

ROB COOKE

IT WAS 1932 in Muskogee. The Depression hit us Okies extra hard as many of our neighbors sold off almost everything they owned to trade it for a vehicle that might make it to California for serious fruit picking. I made the decision to stay put. Too many of my kinfolk were buried on the land, including my wife and son-in-law. It left me and my daughter to raise her kids and make them strong to persevere in the brutal Oklahoma winds.

I was whittling them some arrows from a fallen oak with my Bowie knife when my granddaughters snuck up on me catching me by surprise. "PawPaw, we're learning about the famous outlaws in school, and we're learning about the Dalton gang."

My other granddaughter interrupted her. "Ma once told us you rode with them. Is that true?"

My grandkids had heard the story several times before, but I enjoyed telling it.

I left home in 1890. I was only twelve years old and got a job as a ranch hand west of Tulsa. All I wanted was to be a cowboy, and I landed a job on Jim Riley's ranch. I never really met the other men on the ranch who were much older than me, plus they disappeared into the wind. They knew of my existence, and I knew most of their names, but that was our relationship.

I was curious about the men named Bob, Emmett, and a couple of guys named Bill. They rode off for weeks at a time and always returned with money. I had the urge to follow the group but chickened out, especially watching the law stop by from time to time when they rode off.

"PawPaw, no need to tell us the beginning. We want to know about Coffeyville. Ma says you went with them." They were correct. It seemed every time I told the story it got shorter and shorter. They did not care about the mundane life of riding and roping. Thinking back on it, following those Dalton boys to Southeast Kansas was something a young boy dreamt about.

"Well, youngins, I started riding with them.

"It was a three-day ride if we pushed it. I ain't ever rode that far, and I couldn't keep up, but they were always in my eyesight through my field glasses. I knew their plan—two banks in one day. I was a few hours behind them when everyone bunked for the night outside Coffeyville.

"I wanted to help and be part of the infamous Daltons, so I made sure I was up before sunrise to catch up with the men. My horse galloped down the path into the valley where the town sat.

"Bob Dalton shouted at me to turn around. His partner, his brother, turned, pointed his rifle at me, and cocked it. Bob had his Colt .45 aimed at my brain, and I knew he'd shoot. I didn't want to return to the bluffs surrounding Coffeyville, but it was either returning or being filled with bullet holes. I spun my pony around and retreated to the hills. I found a safe spot where I could witness the bank robberies and that's what I did. I laid on my belly and pressed the field glasses to my eyes. I had a perfect view of the gang, the banks, and the townies surrounding them.

"Something went wrong. Townspeople were ready and opened fire. Shots rang all over as war broke out between the gang I wanted to be a part of and the residents of the town. I witnessed my boys dropping a few of the Coffeyville citizens, but my Daltons were outnumbered. The boys gave up their lives as they fell dead.

"The phrase, 'curiosity killed the cat,' came to mind as I snuck closer to catch a grasp of what just happened. I was in shouting range as the bullets subsided. Emmett Dalton was still alive, and I swear to this day, he stared in the direction I hid. I heard, "The kid. He set us up." He pumped his rifle, continuing to glare in my direction. He began riding straight toward me, and I raised my horse, straddled it, and rode off like a boy possessed by the devil. I rode harder and faster than ever, only breaking to give the steed some water and food. I refreshed myself too. I rode for five straight days and ended up in Creek territory. I squatted on this land and made friends with the indians here including your MawMaw.

"Mawmaw was an indian?" The youngest asked.

"Of course she was. You knew that. I told you that over and over."

My oldest granddaughter put in her two cents. "Yeah, Pawpaw, but the rest of your story changes every time you tell us."

<hr>

—*Rob Cooke is from Omaha, Nebraska, single with three grown children. Cooke has published seven novels including* Moonshiner's Legacy, The Lost Song of Miriam Landry, *and* The Emancipation of Kat Turner.

His short stories have been included in various anthologies, and he spent way too many years in customer service where he develops his characters. Cooke is divorced with three grown children. Music is his first love, where he dabbles with guitar and his trusty banjo.

Outcasts by Herman W. Hansen

THE RETURN OF WYATT, BILLY, AND DOC

PHILIP ATLAS CLAUSEN

"YOU SURE ABOUT this place, Billy?" Wyatt was not easily perplexed, but Billy and Doc were trying not to laugh. Plywood was sandwiched over broken windows. There was an old flying red horse sign, rusted and punched with bullet holes.

"Not this place. That place." Billy pointed to the next place.

Something called Red's Bar & Grill, its sign glowering red neon flames like a dying star. The bar appeared drowsy, like maybe it was only semi-open or half closed.

It was an old-fashioned diner, a low-slung front lined with venetian-blind windows.

Parked out front like horses in a row were big motorcycles, choppers, chrome and black monsters. Four of them. Wyatt explained, "People ride these things instead of horses."

Doc stumbled on a curb. "Don't care what they ride. Do they have any whiskey in this horseless town." Wyatt explained it was called Los Angeles, and everything was new.

Billy said, "Some signs say it's called LA. La what?" Billy reached in his pocket for his tobacco pouch, but in this strange town he had no tobacco fixings. "Anybody got tobacco?"

Wyatt ran his hand over chrome handlebars of a goosenecked bike and whistled. "I'm going inside to see Red." He headed for the door. "Remember our deal. Everybody acts nice."

Inside, they fanned out into a loose semicircle, ready for action.

Loud music blared senseless words coming from thin air. A long bar glowered like a pagan altar bathed in blood pouring from red troughs of light above it. The grim light mingled with cigarette smoke to create a hellish appearance. The gunfighters exchanged glances. Nobody wanted to go back to that place again. It was why they had signed the agreement.

A barman stood behind the bar. Maybe a mixture of Mexican and white, and maybe not happy about it. Was this Red? His short, pointed beard, and black hair brushed severely back from a high forehead gave him a devilish look. He glared at them and folded his arms.

Wyatt knew better than to make small talk. He looked left and right. "You Red?"

A dozen stools fronting the bar were empty except for a lone man sitting at the very end. He was sipping beer, watching a baseball game on a TV mounted at the corner of the ceiling. His disgusted voice said, "Come on, get a hit, you bums."

The barman's name was Hack, embroidered in red on his black vest. He placed the last case of Budweiser in the cooler. The gunmen read the back of his vest, "Hells Angels. So. Cal."

He spread his hands across the bar. "We just closed. Maybe you can tell." When they didn't move, he added, "You look like circus people."

The first dude wore a pale blue suit and a brown handlebar mustache like a gambler in an old western movie and a white shirt ruffled in front. Maybe it was the circus remark that made him brush his coat open showing a walnut-handled pistol on his right hip. The second dude was a bleary looking drunk with a sawed-off shotgun. The third dude wore a shirt and jeans, sun-faded gray and brown leather vest, and an easy smile like walking in with a six-gun was normal.

He had a lopsided friendly smile. He said, "You got any tobacco?"

Hack said, "The studios are in Burbank—if that's what you're looking for."

Billy smiled. "You think you're an Angel of Hell? Boy, you don't know the hellfire you're playing with from a hole in the ground. The Red Angel would use you for a footstool."

Hack folded his arms. He wasn't worried about cartoon cowboys because he had plenty of backup on Friday nights. They were called Satan's Pride, and they were having a little powder party in the back booth farthest from the door.

Wyatt said, "We're told to come here to parley with the Pride Group. Ever hear of them?"

Hack yelled, "Nick!"

Nobody came. And the bartender glanced down the diner where there were empty booths except for the one behind the baseball fan. Two men sat across from each other in the last booth. The man with his back to them had shoulders a yard wide, and he was sipping beer and seemingly absorbed in watching the other man's face—a movie star handsome face—marred by a mouth twisted in agony or pleasure. The handsome man's arms were outstretched on the back of the booth, and he had white powder under his nose and his head lolled back and forth.

A woman surfaced from beneath the table, stood and stretched, and went under again. She was milk white, her green eyes dazed and shiny. The handsome face nosedived onto the table, then flopped back again, gasping noisily, more white powder on his face.

Loud music blared. It was The Animals, singing, "We Gotta Get Out of This Place."

Billy smiled at Hack. "Lousy bar, lousy music, lousy barkeep." He folded his arms.

Doc said, "Pour whiskey if you got it, and we'll sit down for a nice talk." The barman yelled, "Cops are here!"

That did it. The party in the back booth halted. Handsome sat up. Big shoulders half rose, and his hairy face turned around. He was as caveman ugly as the other was handsome, and he wore the glaring expression of a man waiting for something but has been interrupted.

On his back was *SATAN'S* in black letters on a denim vest, and they couldn't see below that. The baseball fan got up, unplugged the jukebox, killing the song, and came down the line carrying a baseball bat like maybe he'd been a real slugger a hundred cases of beer ago.

"Dammit, Hack, it's one-one bottom of the eleventh and you gotta say something like that." He strutted toward the stupidly smiling boy, and his bat began a home run swing for his head.

Billy drew iron and lightning-flash-thunder blew the bat into a shower of splinters. Baseball man stood with a shattered stub, shook his head, and laid the remains on the bar. He kept shaking his head. "You should not have done that. That was Ted Williams' home run bat. Never gonna be another bat like that. I'm going to kill you for that."

Billy stopped his smile, and his eyes narrowed. "I'm sorry for your loss."

Now the caveman lumbered forward carrying the largest revolver any of them had ever seen and pointed it at Billy.

Wyatt drew his Colt but didn't shoot, hoping his restraint would count for something. Doc swung the shotgun, letting the double-barrels track the Caveman past the stools.

Wyatt said, "Deep breaths, Doc. Nice and slow. Nobody gets hurt.."

Doc said, "I don't like unfriendly people. Never have. I only asked for a drink."

The woman rose up from the table and handsome came bristling toward them with crazy glassy eyes and a weapon Wyatt knew was called a machine gun that could spray bullets like a firehose. The bar went quiet. The footsteps of the men made no sound, and Wyatt figured the floor was adobe. Billy's pistol made a well-oiled metallic click. His smile had turned into a snarl.

"Don't point your ugly contraption at me or I'll blow you directly to Hell."

Wyatt holstered his gun and spoke loud enough for all, "We all need to show restraint. Can we please talk to Red? Which one of you is Red?"

Hack said, "You cowboys are outgunned, and I don't feel like cleaning up a mess. This concrete soaks up blood."

Handsome man had roostered-up hair and eyes mottled chips of red and blue flame and a voice full of accusation. "You boys undercover? I don't think anybody here believes it."

He swung the machine gun in a killer arc.

Caveman spoke in a voice so nasally crushed it sounded like he was wearing a clothespin. "What kind are yuh come round here asking such questions?" The bad thing was, he talked a lot despite his difficulty. Wyatt made rapid translations as he continued. It amounted to, "Would I come to your place asking questions? We're closed and you're still inside. You want information at midnight. Who sent you, huh?"

The man was solid beef oozing with a raw-meat smell of a butcher shop. Bone-crushingly ugly. Deep eye sockets gave the impression his skull was an inch thick. He had a fight-flattened nose. Strawberry faced, rusty red hair combed scraggly back down his neck, and big freckles like pennies, like the kind that get your attention as a kid. Was this Red?

Wyatt said, "Are you Red?"

The woman now made her pretty way down the line, making sure all blinds were closed. They heard the klatsch of something locking. It was the woman fastening the glass door. She was really tall with a mask-like face of heavy makeup. Eyes of wet jade. Flaming hair. Was this Red? She was surprisingly old and looked at them with a young woman's eyes, appraising them.

Wyatt on the left. Doc in the middle. Billy on the right.

She said, "I want them, all of them." What was that supposed to mean?

Wyatt said, "We come in pea—"

Handsome said, "She owns the bar. Everything in it including you circus knuckleheads. You clowns drop your guns and face the bar, or we're gonna rat pack you."

Caveman cocked his gun. Handsome racked a lever on his machine gun.

Billy holstered his Colt, assumed the gunfighter's stance, and smiled. "Screw you."

That did it.

The machine gun roared flame stitching the gunmen's chest high, punctuated by three cannon blasts of the caveman's revolver.

The Satans stopped to admire their work. The red room filled with silence.

The targets stood there talking.

"Gosh darn it, Billy."

"That could not be helped. I won't take no blame. I only wanted the tobacco."

"I didn't come here to get insulted. All I wanted was a drink."

Handsome said, "These knuckleheads are wearing body armor. Blow their heads off." They cocked and racked their weapons and aimed head high.

Doc fired both barrels blowing off Caveman's head above the eyebrows like an exploding watermelon. Handsome startled backward, and the machine gun sprayed the ceiling.

Billy plowed a neat circle of black holes around his heart.

Satans fell like puppets loosed from their master's strings.

The woman screamed, and the barman threw up his hands.

Wyatt said, "Good God, dammit now you've—"

A thunderclap voice boomed over them, "Cut!"

Red's Diner dissolved into nothing more than an overheated oil painting.

Back again. They were back again in the white room. They stood before the shining figure that resembled a golden statue nine feet tall with large eyes that radiated light, not of anger, but of disappointment as of a parent for a child.

The shining head bathed them in white light.

Behind the Gold Angel a wide portal opened on a field of yellow flowers blowing in gentle breezes like waves smelling faintly of honey. In the middle of this yellow sea stood an amphitheater of low walls that looked like a giant rose blossomed with tiers of white petals. The petals formed seats. Shining men and women sat shimmering in robes like living rainbows. All of them focused on an altar at the heart of the rose where a man and woman in plain white robes answered questions from the shimmering ones whose approval rose as a haze of pink light.

The portal closed abruptly. The Gold Angel pushed over a huge slab of stone.

"Not for you."

The gunmen tried to shuffle their hands into their pockets, but their gray robes had no pockets and no guns.

"You did destruction when living as men. You responded to violence with more violence. You will not get to do that again." The words hung in the air like notes struck from a bell.

They gray men hung their heads. Their sorrow radiated from them like a soft gray mist. The Gold Angel observed their sorrow and felt pity.

"Your world believes you are hard and brave. But just the opposite is true. You are soft and lazy. Smashing people like a child smashes a toy. You drink whiskey to numb yourselves. Then others write stories about you, so you swagger around drunk."

"We are guilty, Your Honor. We're sorry."

"You failed. Red's Diner was only a true test. We asked you to do something very hard. To respond to hatred with patience. To be kind to unkind people. Can you do that next time? Each of you must respond."

"Yes."

"No."

"No."

"I will share some news for you, my children. You're not going back as harmless ghosts. You're going back as living bodies and this time not strong bodies. You'll be weak and scared. Too shaky to hold a gun. You will learn humility and humanity. You will ask for kindness and learn kindness. You will learn true bravery in forms of weakness. Any questions?"

"How are we supposed to live without whiskey, women, and guns?"

"Or tobacco?"

"That is yours to learn. The first step is learning about the tee-ter-totter."

"That sounds like fun."

"It's not. Evil must be balanced by goodness. All of it. Go find balance. Go in love."

They trudged down a long pink stairway that seemed soft and spongy. They departed grumbling about the injustice of it all. They were joined by others looking as confused as they were.

A short time later they could no longer understand one another. They mumbled and tumbled into separate rooms. Rosy rooms, soft as a woman's stomach. And there they fell asleep.

The rooms were gently rising and falling chambers.

A short time later they were crying and kicking, and they had returned to the world of ignorance and stupidity where they must learn knowledge and wisdom. Where they would learn the teeter-totter and how perfectly balanced it was and how they must balance and be kind.

Three babies began crying out loud.

———

—*Philip Clausen is a blue-collar worker/writer retired to Tucson following a lifetime interest in the Old West, the Gold Rush and the Civil War and now is working full time writing fiction under those magnificent brands. He has a B.A. Degree in Journalism from San Jose State. His free time he spends traveling the beloved great American West. His fiction infuses trail experience, research and an undercurrent of mysticism. He is a lifelong Rosicrucian (AMORC). He is working on a four-volume epic adventure of the California Gold Rush.*

GOOD RIDDANCE

M. F. MCDONNELL

J. P. HEWITT AND Frank Gilles had not seen each other since parting company on the banks of the Laramie River in the spring of 1875. Neither man had found his fortune during the intervening years. Both earned just enough from crouching at the edge of icy streams to get by. It was a hard, solitary life that each man enjoyed.

By the autumn of 1879, however, both men had lost the desire to spend lonely winters scrabbling to stay alive. Hewitt was headed to a widowed sister's place in Minneapolis. Gilles was bound for New York City to visit his mother. After a fortuitous reunion in the grasslands of eastern Wyoming Territory in September, they decided to travel together for a time.

"You know," Hewitt said as he warmed his hands over a small campfire, "we should stop at Deadwood. It's not far out of our way, and it's something I'd like to see just once."

"There may be a parlor or two I'd like to call on," said Gilles. "If the price is right."

"I wouldn't mind doing the same."

Riding into Deadwood two days later, they heard it before they saw it. Drunken laughter, tinkling pianos, shouts, and the occasional gunshot greeted them as they crested a ridge just to the west of the town. It was not yet noon.

"You're certain we ought to do this?" asked Gilles.

Hewitt didn't answer immediately as he listened to the commotion coming from the town.

"Let's have a look, and if it's not to our liking, we'll move on."

"That's fair," said Gilles. "We can't stay long, anyway. Winter will be coming soon enough."

Deadwood had sprung up a few years earlier after gold had been found in the Black Hills. That the land was stolen from the Lakota Sioux had not mattered to those who founded the town. In no time, word of its debaucheries had spread across the northern plains, making the place a mecca for miners, gamblers, prostitutes, outlaws, and the various sorts of reprobates that such towns attract. Three years after its founding, there was no school, no church, no real law, hardly a woman who was not selling herself, and thousands of men desperate to find wealth by any means.

Gilles and Hewitt rode down the main street, a muddy lane bordered with every manner of business, legitimate and otherwise. Wagons, horses, and men crowded the street.

They tied their horses near the Gem Variety Theater. Despite the name, the place was a saloon and bordello. From the boardwalk, they noted that many of the businesses were fronted with a wooden facade that hid crude tents and shacks. The two-story Gem seemed to be one of only a handful of buildings made entirely of clapboard.

Women in various stages of undress lounged on chairs on the boardwalk in front of the place, enjoying the sun and fresh air.

"What do we call them? Ladies of the Morning?" joked Gilles.

"I don't know about you, but they are about the hardest looking lot of women I have ever seen. I may think twice before I take my leisure with any of them. I don't need a souvenir to take to my sister's," said Hewitt.

"You are correct, my friend. They are a scruffy looking bunch."

"Are you talking about my ladies?" asked a tough looking man leaning in the doorway of the Gem. Appearances aside, he spoke in a friendly tone of voice.

"I trust not." He pushed himself away from the door frame. "These are the finest collection of courtesans in the territory. Good sirs, they have come to Deadwood from New York, Philadelphia, Chicago, and elsewhere to lend some class to this town. You will not be disappointed with any of our ladies."

"I think we're good for now," said Gilles. "Perhaps later we'll pay a visit."

The women showed no interest in the conversation.

"You had better not be saying anything against these fine women." The friendliness was gone. He tipped his bowler hat back on his head. "If you do, you'll be answering to Mister Swearengen, the owner of this establishment. He does not take kindly to the likes of you straggling into town and acting so high and mighty."

"No offense intended," said Gilles. "We've not been to Deadwood before, so we wish to look around before taking our leisure. What is your name, sir?"

"Sir! Listen to the fancy words coming from sassy pants." The man stared at Gilles for a moment. "The name is Coughlan. And who might you be?"

"Gilles, and my partner here is Hewitt."

"Gilles. Where are you from, Gilles?"

"I grew up in New York, but me ma and da were from County Mayo."

"Glad to make your acquaintance, Gilles. It's always a joy to meet someone with a lilt in his voice. But unless you and Mister Hewitt want to meet some of the ladies, I suggest you move on. Be forewarned, though, it's only afflicted gals you'll find elsewhere in town. The Gem has the cleanest and finest of all."

"Thanks for the advice. Proud to have met you, Mister Coughlan."

Loud voices from across the street preceded a wild shot that struck one of the women sitting outside the Gem, not ten feet from Hewitt and Gilles. The girl fell from her chair, collapsing in a heap of bloodied crinoline. The other girls crowded around her.

"She's dead, Billy," one of them said to Coughlan. "She's shot in the heart."

Coughlan stalked across the street toward a drunken man who held a pistol in his hand. As Coughlan neared, the man holstered the pistol and sputtered an apology.

Coughlan stepped onto the boardwalk, grabbed the man's lapels, and threw him into the street. Trying to pick himself up out of the dirt and filth he was kicked in the stomach by Coughlan. It was a vicious kick that knocked the wind out of him. Helpless now, he was beaten by Coughlan until he was unconscious. Coughlan finished by kicking the man in the face. No one made any attempt to stop the assault, nor did anyone come to the man's aid after Coughlan had returned to the Gem.

Coughlan breathed heavily after his exertions. His face was a study in violent hatred.

"Go on, then," he barked at the women.

Some of them in tears, some glaring at Coughlan, they went back inside the Gem, leaving their friend lying on the boardwalk, her blood soaking into the wooden planks.

Gilles and Hewitt walked away. Hewitt looked back to see a woman looking directly at him from the second-floor porch at the Gem.

"Well, I'll be damned," he muttered.

"If we stay any longer in this town we very well may be," said Gilles.

"I do swear. That young lady looking at us from the balcony is my sister, Charlene," said Hewitt.

"What?" exclaimed Gilles. "Surely you're mistaken."

"I am not, Frank. I haven't seen her in years, but I couldn't forget that red hair and the birthmark beside her eye."

Gilles had no idea how to respond. For a man to find his kin working as a prostitute was a shocking thing.

The two men found a place to take a meal. Hewitt in disbelief, barely spoke. He poked at his food but ate little. As Gilles finished wiping his plate, he asked, "What do you want to do, Jimmy? Are you certain it's her?"

"I am. And I aim to take her away from here. This is no place for any sister of mine. Charlene was always strong-willed and ran off when she was young. It's time she went home. I'll take her to Minneapolis."

"I don't know that Coughlan will let her go," said Gilles. "Many of these places treat their girls like they were in servitude. Or she may not want to leave."

"I'll find a way. I surely will." He paused. "Frank, I'm going to need your help."

Gilles had misgivings about getting involved. After watching Coughlan beat a man almost to death while no one made any attempt to stop it, he was certain they would get no support from anyone in Deadwood.

"You'll have whatever help you need, my friend," said Gilles, despite his concerns. "Let's figure out a plan."

"GOOD EVENING, MISTER Coughlan," said Gilles.

"You've come back, have you?"

"We have," answered Hewitt. He glanced at the boardwalk. The only effort made to clean up after the killing was to remove the girl's body and throw a bucket of water down to wash away the worst of the blood. The beaten man had been taken away.

"There was a young lady this morning, red hair and a birthmark on her temple," said Hewitt. "I found her rather fetching and would like to meet her."

Coughlan bared his teeth in what he likely thought was a smile. It made him look like a grinning cadaver.

"Let me see what I can do for you, Mister Dandy."

"The name is Hewitt."

"Oh, excuse me, Mister Dandy Hewitt. I didn't mean to offend."

They followed Coughlan to the back of the bar room where several of the girls sat talking among themselves.

"Lena," Coughlan called out.

The red-headed woman turned. Upon seeing Hewitt, she looked very frightened.

"Customer for you, Lena," said Coughlan, oblivious of the way she looked at Hewitt. "If the rest of you ladies would care to try, you might attract some customers of your own. That is what you're here for."

A woman with a long scar on the left side of her face stood and confronted Coughlan.

"Jenny was murdered while she was sitting there doing nothing to anyone. She was our friend and now you expect us to entertain so-called gentlemen?" She gave a disgusted look to Hewitt and Gilles. "You can guess again, Billy Coughlan. We're taking a break."

Coughlan stepped forward, grabbing the woman roughly by the arm.

"Now you listen here, missy. I'll scar the other side of your face if you don't watch your mouth. Remember what happened the last time you got up on your high horse."

The woman looked defiantly at Coughlan. "Get your mitts off me, you Irish buffoon," she snapped.

The two glared at each other before he released her arm, pushing her away.

"I'll deal with you later," he growled.

"You can try," she snarled back at him.

"Well," Coughlan turned to Hewitt. "What are you waiting for?"

Hewitt followed the woman named Lena upstairs and into a cramped room. A small window looked out onto the roof of the building next door.

"Oh, Jimmy. I knew it was you," she cried as soon as she shut the door. She threw herself into his arms. He embraced her, stroking her red hair.

"I recognized you right off, Charlene. There's no mistaking my baby sister."

She pulled away from him and turned her back.

"They call me Lena, now. I'm not anyone's baby any longer. Any innocence disappeared years ago."

She whirled around to face him but kept her eyes downcast.

"I'm so ashamed. So ashamed."

"Now, don't you be ashamed of anything. You've done what we

Hewitt's have always done. You did what it took to survive. That's what Ma and Pa did when they sailed across the Atlantic. It's what Ma did after he died, taking in laundry and sewing until the day she passed. It's what I did to get through the war."

Charlene looked up at her older brother, somehow afraid, sad, and relieved at the same time.

"I hadn't heard about Ma." She wiped her eyes. "Oh, James, I've so missed you and Katie. I didn't know where either of you were. I barely know where I am or how I got here."

"We're taking you away, Charlene. Katie lives in Minneapolis and that's where I'm going. You're coming with us. Tonight."

"Who's that man you're with? He looks like he crawled out of a pigsty and fell into a backhouse."

"Smells like it too," Hewitt said with a grin. "But he's a solid man and a good friend. He'll do whatever needs doing to get you out of this place."

"I owe them money. Travel from the east, room, and board. This dress. They have me and the other girls trapped here. If I run off, they'll come after us. That Coughlan is a mean one."

"You let Frank and me tend to that. I need you to gather your things and get ready to head out. Can you do that? Will you trust me?"

She gazed up at him with damp eyes. "Of course I can. I will."

He glanced around the small room with the unmade bed. A small armoire stood in a corner. On top of a small dresser sat a washbowl and an oil lamp. A dirty towel hung over the back of an old kitchen chair. There was no other furniture in the room. A calendar hung on the wall indicating it was September 26, 1879.

"What do you need me to do?" she asked.

"Pack your things. Do you have a valise?"

"I've not much. It will all fit in my carpetbag."

"Good. You be in this room at ten o'clock tonight. I'll come to the window for you."

"The window? But how....?"

"You let me and Frank worry about that. You just make sure you're here."

THE TWO MEN carefully leaned the ladder against the side of the Gem. The narrow alley did not give much room. Hewitt told Gilles to hold the ladder tight. He climbed silently and peeked over the edge of the windowsill.

He was shocked to find his sister being rutted on by a rough looking man, her skirts up around her waist. She stared at the ceiling while the bed bounced. Glancing at the open window she saw the top of Hewitt's hat and began to cry.

"What are you crying for, girly? Ain't I pleasing you?" panted the man.

"Of course," she cooed. "These are tears of joy. You're just wonderful, lover."

In that moment, she hated herself and everything about Deadwood.

Hearing the words, Hewitt was tempted to climb into the room and heave the man through the window. He held his temper and tried his best to ignore the sounds coming from above.

When it stopped, he peeked into the room to see the man leaving while buttoning his trousers. Charlene, pushing her skirts down, turned to find her brother motioning at her to come to him.

"Oh, Jimmy, I'm mortified. I'm sorry you had to see that. I planned to be in the room at the right time. Coughlan is watching us carefully after this morning, so we can't wander off for too long."

"It's no matter, Charlene. Where's your bag?"

She reached under the bed and handed him a worn carpetbag. It was surprisingly heavy, but Hewitt said nothing.

Charlene crawled through the open window, the only sound the soft swish of her skirts. They climbed down the ladder and made their way to the rear of the saloon where the horses waited. The two men had pitched in together to purchase another horse and saddle from the livery.

Charlene allowed Gilles to help her into the saddle while Hewitt checked to make sure no one was peering out the window looking for her. He mounted his horse. Charlene immediately dismounted and strode to where a lit oil lamp sat on the back stoop. A can of oil sat near it. She poured the oil onto the wall and steps.

"Charlene, what are you—" Hewitt asked.

"Are you ready to ride?" she asked.

Stepping off the small porch she heaved the lamp with all her might at the back wall of the saloon. The wall burst into flames that quickly spread. She ran to her horse. With an agility that surprised both men, she jumped into the saddle with one smooth movement. The three fugitives rode quickly into the dark. Shouts of alarm sounded behind them.

They rode hard for half an hour before stopping in a treeline at the foot of a steep slope. Both men were surprised at how well the girl handled the horse.

Charlene pulled the carpetbag off the pommel of her horse and stepped away from the men. They heard a rustle of clothing in the darkness. She reappeared wearing men's attire, with her hair tucked under a flat cap.

"Courtesy of a bad customer from some time back. Coughlan chased him off dressed in his long johns. I kept his clothes, boots and all. Even then I was planning to somehow escape."

The three of them looked west to see the sky filled with flickering orange and crimson that swayed and wavered like the aurora borealis. As they watched the colors dance there was a sudden bright burst. Sparks leapt and swirled into the night sky.

"That must be the Gem collapsing," said Gilles. "I think you burned down the whole town, young miss."

"Good riddance to Sodom and Gomorrah, both," she said, looking up wistfully at the flaming sky. A small smile graced her face.

They remounted and rode on.

A month later Charlene was playing jacks with her nieces on the parlor floor of her sister's house. Hewitt sat in a comfortable chair next to her.

Their sister Katie chatted amiably with a bathed and shorn Gilles, who she insisted on calling Francis. Hewitt had only ever seen the mountain man side of Gilles. He was surprised how well he cleaned up.

Hewitt and Charlene exchanged smiles.

They were home.

—*M. F. McDonnell is an emerging Canadian author from Waterford, Ontario. A devoted reader, he has an extensive library of history books and has a life-long interest in the American Civil War and WW2. He has visited battlefield sites throughout North America and Europe. An avid hiker, he has trekked trails in the Rocky Mountains from Alberta to New Mexico, throughout the Bruce Trail system in southern Ontario and in Algonquin Park. His non-fiction work has appeared in the* Hamilton Spectator *newspaper. New to writing fiction, a short story "Thirst," was published in* Under the Hot Prairie Sun *in April, and "Heroes of a Sort," in May at close2thebone.co.uk. In addition to writing further short stories, he is currently completing work on a novel.*

THE GRAVEDIGGER OF DEADWOOD

GEORGE COTTONWOOD

THE ROOM WAS packed with working men with the mingled smells of sweat, tobacco, wet wool, and desperation lying thick in the air. Saloon girls wearing little more than a bodice and violet sachets prowled around the room with powdered faces, looking for buyers. A man who looked like he had his last bath two years ago sat at an out-of-tune stand-up piano banging out "Camptown Races" with clumsy fingers. It was a busy night for the prospecting town. Here men drank, cussed, and gambled with their lives and their wallets. Everyone who had money to spend was in the Nuttal & Mann's Saloon.

"Life is cheap in Deadwood. We're all just another grave waiting to be dug," said a man at a poker table. Five men sat playing five-card draw. Each looked unique from the other, one fat and one thin, one in clothes without any holes in them, another whose boots were about to fall off, and the speaker in all black. They were a mixture of gamblers, businessmen, and prospectors. But all had one thing in common—they were dead set to make a fortune in Deadwood.

The man who spoke was the local gravedigger, and he wasn't prone to wait for an invitation to talk. His name was Mortimer Du Bois, but everyone called him Mory because he always said the Latin phrase *"memento mori"* at a grave site. He didn't know what it meant, just knew it was a motto about death he heard from somewhere and mottos speak for themselves.

He hadn't asked the other players their names. He didn't care. They were all just potential business. In his head, Mory named the fat one "Lard", the skinny one "Just Bones", the one with nice clothes "Money", and the threadbare man was called, "Dirt."

"What's the bet?" Dirt asked. He had an eager expression on his face, still anticipating a turn of luck in the cards.

"Four bits to call," Mory replied.

"I can do that," he said optimistically, reaching behind his dwindling pile and putting the required amount of coins into the pot. Each player revealed their hands and the results were that Dirt had to postpone buying his new boots.

In the next round, Mory was the dealer. He shuffled the cards, asked Money to his right to cut them, and then dealt five cards to every man at the table. He covered his cards with his hand and turned up the corners to peek at them. Ace high and a bunch of nothing. He sucked his teeth in thought. A round of modest bets followed.

"I'll take two," Just Bones said. He coughed. A draft in the fireplace trapped smoke with the cold air outside and mixed with the aroma of the saloon patrons. He was dealt the two cards and then was watched for a sign of good or poor fortune. A twitch of the nose, fiddling with his money, anything the other players could use to divine his hand. Just Bones was probably a prospector, Mory thought. His hands were chapped and calloused— the hands of a man who lived in cold mountain air and swung a mattock.

A nearby poker table erupted in laughter. Coins clanging as a winner pulled his haul toward him. The piano struck a wrong note, but the man kept playing, fingers pounding with drunken determination. Mory took a drink from a dirty glass and then wiped his hand on his trousers. The whiskey glass had left behind a sticky residue.

Lard asked for a single card, which made the others nervous. "How does one become a gravedigger?" he asked aloud while studying his hand. Lard was a businessman traveling from Philadelphia to oversee holdings out west. He was well-dressed and genial, but also calculating. He always knew when to fold and when to hold, and as a result, his pile of paper and coin was the largest of the five.

Mory shrugged. "The town needed someone to bury the dead. I was tired of digging for gold and not finding any. This way, I get paid whether someone wins or loses." He tossed a few coins into the pot. "People die easy in Deadwood. Steady business."

"Buried anyone famous?" Money asked. It was hard to hear him through the din of clinking coins, raucous laughter, and everyone talking at once.

"A few," Mory said. "I done buried Wild Bill Hickock hisself but didn't get Jack McCall. He was buried over in Yanktown. It's too bad, I'd have liked the set."

"Hickock died in this very saloon, that right?" Lard asked.

"He shore did," Mory said while they put in their bets. He took a look around the room, examining the walls and making estimations in his head. "Reckon it was this very table, matter of fact." He looked down at the floor and led his gaze up to the batwing doors. He turned back around and smiled. "McCall came right up and shot old Wild Bill in the back of the head with his .45. Fell right here."

Dirt asked for two cards. He pushed a pair face down from his hand toward Mory's discard pile. The gravedigger stripped two cards from the top of the deck and passed them to the poor man. "You like the work?" Lard asked.

"No less than other work, I suppose. It's real peaceful. Way I see it, is I help usher those poor souls along." He looked down at his own cards again. He had the ace of clubs, two of diamonds, seven of spades, jack of hearts, and eight of clubs. "Dealer takes two," he announced and added the seven and two to the discard pile before drawing two more face down. He slipped the corners of the cards up and looked. He froze. He saw the ace of spades and the eight of diamonds. It was a good hand. He cleared his throat and tried not to look excited.

A chair scratched on the floor behind them, and Mory saw a man get up and head to the bar with wobbly legs. As he passed, the man stopped and looked at Mory with bleary eyes and frowned. Mory looked up at him and smiled, and the man continued to the bar. He ordered a drink and drank it with a dark expression.

They made another round of bets. Dirt hesitated before folding, fingers shaking as he slid the cards across the table. He slumped in his chair, distraught, and looked at the others' winnings, licking his lips like a dog. He pressed them into a thin line, and for a moment, Mory thought he saw the man glance at his boots—not the cards. "New boots can wait," Dirt mumbled, his voice like gravel.

The others increased their bets by a few bits. Mory hesitated, then raised by several dollars, substantially more than the others. They looked at him, trying hard to be clairvoyant. Was he bluffing? Or did he have something?

All bets were settled, and it was time for the reveal. "All right, show 'em," Just Bones said. One after another the four remaining hands were flipped over. A pair, a king high, another pair, and then Mory's aces and eights.

The players looked at the cards and then looked up at Mory. He had an odd smile on his lips, almost a wince. Money asked, "Ain't that the hand Hickock had when he was shot?"

"Was it?" Mory asked, pretending not to know. He did though. He was obsessed with Wild Bill Hickock and knew everything there was about the circumstances of his death. He was always willing to bring it up in conversation.

"That there is the 'Dead Man's Hand,'" Lard confirmed. "Supposed to be a bad omen."

Mory shrugged and then gathered the paper and coin money in front of him, sorting. As Mory gathered his winnings, his fingers brushed against the aces and eights. He slid them into the pile, careful not to meet Lard's gaze. The 'Dead Man's Hand.' Hickok died here, at this table. Mory snorted to himself. Superstition was for fools.

Yet, he didn't look at the others as the deck passed to his left, and he busied himself with his winnings while new hands were dealt.

"That don't trouble you none?" Lard asked again.

"Why ought it trouble me?" the gravedigger asked. He forced a smile. "It's just a poker hand." He was growing less talkative now.

The fat man shrugged. "Just a mighty odd coincidence, being in the same chair, with the same hand at the same saloon. Some people might see that as a sign to not push their luck. Fate isn't partial," he said sagely.

"Not me," Mory said. He grew irritated. He wasn't going to let the fat man scare him out of a good game of cards. But he thought of little else afterward.

They played a few more hands. Lard and Money won more hands than the others. Not long after, Dirt had run out of money and left the game. It was late, but a new player took his seat and they played for another hour. After losing several hands in a row, Mory felt like his luck had indeed run out, so he too left the game and went to the bar. He flexed his fingers, shaking off a sensation like dirt clinging to his hands after digging a grave. Just a hand of cards. Luck, not fate. The bartender poured a brown liquid into a dirty glass and put it before him. As he took a swig of whiskey, his eyes flicked to the batwing doors. He could still hear Lard's voice, "Some people might see that as a sign" lingering in the air like smoke.

A saloon girl slid in next to Mory, her heavy makeup cracking like dried paint. They exchanged grins, and she pulled him upstairs. The room was small, and their time brief. When he returned to the bar, buttoning his jacket, he ordered one last whiskey and downed it in a single gulp.

"Easy come, easy go," he said to the bartender with a wink before heading toward the door. He waved at the remaining players at the poker table. "You fellers stay safe out there. Hopefully, I won't be seeing you at work one day," Mory said. He stepped outside.

The night was cold, and the air was clear. He breathed in deeply as he adjusted his jacket. The air had a clean, crisp smell, like snow and spruce. Mory popped his jacket collar to block the biting air from his neck and pulled a dirty hat down over his ears. He breathed into his hands and watched the remaining residents still out for the night walking to their respective homes.

A crunch of gravel made him turn. No one was there. He shook his head and stepped into the street, boots clicking softly on the dirt-packed road. As he walked, another crunch sounded behind him. This time, he stopped. He turned again and squinted into the darkness. His breath fogged the air. A shadow moved in the alley, staggering toward him. A man materialized out of the night, holding something in his hand. It was a pistol. He raised and leveled it at Mory, eyes glassy and unfocused. He swayed, and for a moment, Mory thought he might collapse. But the pistol stayed steady.

"Joe Blackwell?" the man slurred.

Mory's brow furrowed. He took a step back, his heart thumping against his ribs. "Ain't no Joe here, friend."

The man blinked and squinted at Mory. Then Mory recognized him—the man who had given him that funny look inside, just after he got the dead man's hand.

The man with the gun blinked again and then curled his lips into a drunken sneer. "You shot my brother. Time to settle."

Mory opened his mouth to protest, but his tongue stuck to the roof of his mouth. He took another step back, hands raised in the air. He struggled to breathe like a man being buried alive.

The man cocked the hammer, the revolver's cylinder rotating into place.

"Wait...." Mory pleaded, voice cracking.

The man squeezed the trigger. The hammer came down and the gunshot shattered the night before the words were finished.

No one came running. Everyone in the street watched with little interest as the ragged-looking man stumbled off into the night.

A few men emerged from the saloon, including Lard, who glanced at the body and shuffled past without a word. The wind swept through the empty street, kicking up dust and dirt that settled over Mory's face. His open eyes stared at the night sky, unblinking, as if waiting for the stars to blink back.

The bartender leaned against the batwing doors, lit a cigar, and puffed lazily. "Deadwood eats its own," he said, flicking ash into the dirt.

Lard nudged the man next to him. "Looks like we'll be needing another gravedigger."

Blood trickled from the .36 caliber hole in Mory's head, staining the ground. The killer had vanished into the night, never to be found. In the distance, someone struck up a lively tune on a fiddle, mixing with the bad piano playing, drowning out the sound of one more grave waiting to be dug.

—*George Cottonwood is a storyteller with a passion for grit, action, and the untamed frontier. He specializes in western pulp and "men's adventure fiction," crafting tales where rugged heroes face high-stakes challenges under wide-open skies. An avid outdoorsman, he enjoys hunting, camping, and fishing with his wife and young son, soaking in the spirit of the frontier, or digging into history to uncover the truths behind the legends. Every story he writes is his way of paying homage to the rugged individualism and timeless values of the American West and as a way of connecting to the past. In his day job he works as a communications specialist for a faith-based child foster care agency in South Texas.*

In Without Knocking by Charles Marion Russell

DEADWOOD VENGEANCE

LEE CLINTON

FOR MY SINS, I was sent to Wichita. Washington said it was for my own good. Others argued that I'd brought it on myself by accusing a judge of corruption.

Judge Edward Taylor of West Virginia, was exchanging favorable rulings for financial bonds. So, I named him in a report. Was that wise? Maybe not, but it was my job.

His influential friends included Senator Samuel C. Larson, who demanded my dismissal. On what grounds, I was never told.

Anyway, it half worked.

The Department of Justice shipped me out to a town full of cattle and cowboys, both of which were known to be mean and prone to stampede. I should have resigned, but upholding the law was all I'd known since hanging up my uniform twelve years prior in '65. So, instead of investigating corruption in the judiciary, I got good at identifying brands, delivering government proclamations on stock trading violations, and throwing two-bit rustlers before the courts.

Matt, the district marshal who I reported to, was sympathetic to my situation and sometimes threw me a bone. On this occasion, it came when he said, "Jon, I need you to go to Fort Collins and pick up a witness. You just have to get him to Kansas City. They will then take him back to St. Louis where he is going to testify before a grand jury."

"Why us and not Denver?" I had to ask, after all it was in their backyard. We were some 500 miles away.

"It's political, but don't know how exactly. Your name came up and Washington endorsed it."

I cocked my head in mockery.

"You are still well regarded in Washington, Jon."

Nice compliment, but... "Fine," I said and asked for the paperwork.

The name of the witness was Louis Bosier, a French-Canadian cotton trader working out of Louisiana before moving north to St. Louis where he had made payments using counterfeit bonds. A five dollar 'baby' bond, so called for the embossed image of a baby in a bonnet upon the surface. One was included with the papers. It looked genuine and would have fooled me. A warrant had been issued for Bosier's arrest, but he had disappeared, until he tried cashing one of his forged bonds to purchase a railroad ticket to the Canadian border at Fort Collins. The astute railroad agent handed him over to the local sheriff, where Bosier decided to come clean and cut a deal. The marshal in Denver being notified, he contacted Washington. They wanted to put him before a grand jury as a witness for the prosecution. The person being prosecuted was not detailed, just that the department now needed an escort from Fort Collins to Kansas City, and somehow, I'd been selected to be the babysitter. A physical description of Bosier was provided in height and weight, which were almost the same as mine, as was the birth year of 1837, but that was about all. I returned the papers and commented to Matt that it was a simple job.

Or so I thought.

I planned the trip using a bunch of railroad maps and timetables and drew down funds to get me to Fort Collins, then both of us back to Kansas City, before returning to Wichita. The timetables suggested it could be done in a week to ten days, if all went to plan. That evening I packed a bag and cleaned my pistol, an 1873 model Colt. The barrel was just four-and-three-quarter inches in length, a special order from the distributor in Cincinnati, so I could draw it fast if needed.

The train got away on time at six the next morning, and I rode with the signalman in the caboose to arrive in Abilene by four that afternoon. By eight, I connected on a mixed passenger-freight coming out of Topeka heading for Denver. We got held up in Hays for a little while the following morning then overnighted in Burlington, but by early Thursday morning, I was in Denver. I went straight to the district marshal's office to let him know I was passing through his patch and would be back in a day or two.

On arrival at Fort Collins, I knew something was up as soon as I handed over the custody papers. The sheriff gave a sheepish look before saying, "Ah, we don't have your man anymore."

I waited for an explanation, but it wasn't forthcoming, so I had to ask, "Why's that?"

"He absconded."

I again had to ask. "From a cell?"

"Well, my deputy let him out for a little fresh air."

The deputy chimed in, "It's not like he is dangerous, and I guessed he wouldn't go anywhere as we had his money in our safe. One hundred dollars of it."

"Eighty-five actually," said the sheriff.

"Cash?" I asked.

"As good as," said the deputy, "bonds."

I was dealing with idiots. "You got any idea where he went?"

"Yes, he was seen getting on a stage for Deadwood."

"Deadwood." I knew the place by reputation only, everyone did, the newspapers couldn't get enough of the gold strike or Hickok's murder the year before. But hell, it had to be at least 300 miles north. "Does the railroad go that way?" I asked.

"Nope, but the stage runs every day. Getting a seat though might be difficult—"

I cut the deputy short. "Get me on the next departure. This is Department of Justice business, and they are expecting a warm body to testify before a grand jury. I don't care who you have to throw off. Just get it done."

He and the sheriff got the message.

I ARRIVED IN Deadwood five days later to step into a world of congestion and confusion. Even the Main Street had been dug up in the search for gold. It was a town out of control, with no rules, and no one seemed to care. All had come to find their fortune, be they miner, merchant, gambler, or shyster.

I found the current sheriff unbadged and unprepared. He'd taken the job after a leg injury, falling from his horse. I suspected, while drunk. He had no idea who Louis Bosier was or where he might be, so that made two of us. He did, however, walk me to the Sahler Hotel and introduced me to the owner, a woman named Mollie. Without that introduction, I would have had to sleep in the cells as Deadwood was full, with no accommodation available. He also told me that I could get a decent meal at Delmonico's restaurant.

Over a beef steak and beer, at an exorbitant price, I considered how I was going to find this rooster. I knew I had to be careful asking around, as word could get back to Bosier. The other concern was the sheer size of the itinerant population. I had expected a town of a few hundred, but this place was teeming with thousands. It was a haystack and Bosier was the needle.

All I could come up with was just walking the streets, while depending on elimination and a lot of luck by sizing up those who fit the description and spoke with a French accent. It was a long shot at best, but what other choice did I have?

WHAT IS IT in life that allows the unexpected to knock the wind out of you? Is it fate, bad luck, or a curse? I couldn't believe it when our eyes met. There was no time to look away, not that I wanted to. With her, I was like a moth to a flame. Yet the words came tumbling out, "What the hell are you doing here?"

Her response was relaxed, confident, and a little sultry. She had my measure—she always did. "Language, Jon. I guess I'm doing the same as you, making a living."

I took in a deep breath to gather my composure. "You were doing that in Charleston in grand style."

"Yes, but one year of work here is worth ten any place else. Here there is gold and the chance to get rich quick without having to dig a hole in the ground." She twirled the parasol on her shoulder. "So, you're no longer at Wichita?"

We had history. She knew of my circumstances and had even written to me after I'd been moved out of West Virginia. I didn't write back. It was never going to work. I was the one who was serious. She just enjoyed my company from time to time.

"Me and my girls need to be kept safe while we are here. We could do with some looking after by a lawman with a reputation like yours. I pay well, very well. The only men who can afford to come into my establishment have either struck it rich or robbed a bank."

Damn it, those blue eyes that I remembered so well were fixed on mine. It had been two years since I had seen her, and her beauty had not diminished an ounce. And all those feelings of desire came flooding back. I did my best to retain self-control. "I'm still in Wichita and won't be here long. I just need to pick up a witness and escort him to Kansas City."

"Anyone I know?"

I hoped like hell she did. "A French Canadian called Louis Bosier."

Her unfamiliarity came as a shrug. "You know where to find him?"

I had to come clean. "No."

"Could be difficult in a place like Deadwood. You have a picture? I might be able to recognize him for you."

"I don't."

"Description then."

"My height, weight, and age."

She smiled. "Sounds like my kind of man." It was fine flirting. "I have an appointment at the bank but come over this evening. I'm on Lee Street in a boarding house for women, just up from Welch's Hotel."

I hesitated.

"Come on, Jon, we can sit in the parlor and become reacquainted. I don't bite... much."

I nodded and tilted my hat back with a finger.

She twirled the parasol on her shoulder again. "Make it around nine. We'll have the parlor to ourselves."

I'D BEEN THROWN, and it must have been written all over my face. Rose was the last person I expected to see in Deadwood. This was a rough place while she was all class and refinement. It had always been that way. She had come from a well-to-do family and was married off at eighteen as a contrivance of joining together two inheritances. It was a big mistake. Her husband gambled away their combined fortune, borrowed money, defaulted, and finally committed suicide by jumping off the Wheeling Suspension Bridge into the Ohio River. Remarrying back into wealth was an option as she moved in those circles, with the beauty, poise, and wit to seduce any man who took her fancy. But she wasn't falling for the same trick twice. Instead, she set out to become financially independent and her own woman. Using her charm alone, she developed relationships with older, wealthy men to raise sufficient capital to buy a large house on Lewis Street. Its declared purpose was to assist young women to become ladies. In reality, Rose was about to become one of the most successful madams in West Virginia.

I met Rose during the census of 1870. My documentation identified the address as a ladies' school for deportment and manners, but I had heard the street talk. On entering, I found the furnishings to be lavish and the young women crisply dressed and exceedingly agreeable. As for the proprietor, Rose Neilson, who had returned to her maiden name, well, she was the epitome of proficiency and provided all that was needed on the census form.

This encounter opened my eyes to another side of life and with it, I saw a fierce protection of her girls and also her generosity which extended to some prominent charities. This gave her immunity from those who would normally seek to close such a place. I also guessed that she was paying inducements, but as it was associated to prostitution, which didn't come under federal law, I had neither jurisdiction nor interest in pursuing such matters. As for the morality? I had dallied as a young soldier in such places when seeking comfort, so I wasn't about to start throwing stones.

Somehow, we clicked, and to this day I don't know why. But whatever it was, I somehow got it into my damn fool head that maybe we could get hitched. Crazy. It was never going to happen. Our stations in life were too far apart. Still, when we were together on our own, it was as if it was meant to be. And once you have sipped nectar from the well, there's no going back to the old waterhole. It certainly was that way for me. It was Rose or nobody else.

I tidied myself up, even polished my boots, forcing me to walk like a ballerina to keep the mud at bay on my way down to Lee Street.

She saw me into the parlor. "You know, I wasn't sure you would come."

I paused to settle myself, then said, "Why is that?"

"You didn't reply to my letters."

In truth, I didn't know how, but all I said was, "I thought it best."

"For you or me?"

"For us both."

"I'm not sure about that."

I didn't know what to say, and the silence was embarrassing.

"So, tell me about this Frenchman you are looking for."

"French Canadian."

"There are a few of those here, along with some Frenchies from down south. What's he been involved in to get your interest?"

"Trading bonds."

"Is that a problem?"

"His bonds are counterfeit."

Rose's head tilted. "Which ones in particular?"

"Five-dollar baby bonds. They have the image–"

She cut me short. "Just wait a minute."

"Sure, I'm not going anywhere."

When Rose returned, she handed me a $5 bond with the engraved image of a baby in a bonnet. "Like this?"

"Yep, just like that."

Rose examined it closely. "You sure this is counterfeit?"

"Well, so I'm told, but it's no good asking me. I can't tell the difference."

"Nor me," said Rose.

"How many have you got?" I asked.

"Just this one, it turned up early this evening. I'll talk to the bank tomorrow."

"Could you just hold off on that for me. I don't want to spook Bosier, or he'll abscond again. Who did he pass the bond to?"

"One of my girls. Don't know which one. I saw it in the cash tin. But I will find out."

I nodded with relief. "Thank you. I thought I was going to go home empty handed," I said.

Rose looked at me for a second or two. "Really, Jon DeWitt, I wasn't going to let that happen."

THE FOLLOWING DAY I received a message via Mollie that I was wanted at the Wild Roses, quick. It took me a moment or two to figure out that this was Rose's establishment. I found her in a crowded office just off the vestibule. Four of her girls were quickly shooed out to make room for me to enter.

"I know where you can find your man?" she said.

"I'll go and pick him up now. Where will I find him?"

Rose held her hand up to signal to me to wait. "He will be at Hickock's grave up on Mount Moriah at noon."

"How do you know that?"

"Your man came around again late last night, and he asked for Lilly. I don't like men getting attached to just one girl, but he had paid up front with another one of those bonds. I got her to ask where he was staying, but he wouldn't say, so against my better judgement I told her to see if he would like to take her on a picnic at noon tomorrow. And the only place I could think of that was out of the way was up on Mount Moriah."

"At Bill Hickock's grave?"

She nodded. "Lilly is going to show him where it is."

"You're in the wrong profession. You should be working for Pinkerton."

"He couldn't afford me."

True, I thought.

WE LEFT AT half past the hour to give us plenty of time to get into position. Rose strode out in front with the hem of her white cotton dress catching the breeze to lift and show the slender curve of her leg just above her boots. On arrival at Hickock's gravesite, I told Rose that she could go, but she wouldn't have it. She wanted to make sure that Lilly was safe, saying that some of the other girls had told her that the Frenchman was a hothead. I tried to reassure her that all would be fine as I was about to take him into custody. Together we moved off a little way to be on the high side of the hill so that we could see the trail coming up to the cemetery. It was then that Rose took me by surprise. From her belt hung a pocket bag that she now opened and withdrew a double barrel derringer.

"What are you doing?' I asked.

"I need to protect Lilly."

"From what?"

"Harm."

"What harm?"

"Men's harm. He could be dangerous."

"Rose, he's a counterfeiter."

"He's nasty."

I thought this conversation was bizarre, but before I could ask her to put that darn fool thing away, I saw two figures through the pines. "Is that them?" I asked.

Rose strained to look. "I think so."

As they drew close, I said, "Stay here, I'll go down and talk to him."

"What if he tries to harm you, or worse, Lilly."

Rose was waving the small pistol around and acting as if she was Calamity Jane. I had never seen her this agitated before. Or was she just being overprotective?

I stepped out from the cover of the pines as they both looked up, and to my amazement, I saw a gun being pulled. I lifted my hands high to show that I was no threat. "Louis Bosier...." I started to say, and that's when it all went to Hades.

Two shots were fired, one from behind me, and one from Bosier to my front. Both cracked over my head as I ducked and drew my pistol. "Don't be a damned fool, Bosier, I'm here to...." His next shot hit me high on the inside of my right leg and dropped me to the ground. Instinctively, I returned fire, hitting him in the chest.

Lilly froze, hands to her face and screamed in alarm.

As the blue haze of the gun smoke cleared, I called, "Quiet, Lilly. The shooting's over."

Her screams became sobs, and she began to shake uncontrollably.

I stood up and hobbled over to Bosier, who lay with red froth appearing at the corners of his mouth as he gasped for breath. My shot had passed through a lung.

As I leant over him, he murmured, "I know who sent you to kill me. It was Taylor, wasn't it."

"Taylor? I was sent by the Department of Justice, I'm...."

Before I could identify myself or explain further, he said, "So this is justice from Judge Taylor."

The fog lifted. That name was indelibly printed upon my brain. He was the judge who had done his best, along with Senator Larson, to have me removed from the department and out of marshaling. But what did Taylor have to do with this? "You've got it wrong. I wasn't sent by Taylor, I'm a US Deputy Marshal here to protect you and escort you as a witness. What does Judge Taylor have to do with you?"

His speech was labored. "It was their idea."

"What idea?"

Bosier lips had turned blue, and he was starting to shiver.

"What idea?" I repeated.

His eyes were starting to glaze.

I grabbed him by the coat collars, lifting as I shook to get a response. "What idea?"

He mumbled and I couldn't hear the words, so I shook again while putting my ear close to his lips. "Tell me, what was their idea?"

"The counterfeit bonds. It was the judge and the senator's idea," he whispered as I felt his body go limp.

I released my grip and pressed my hand to my leg to feel the sticky warmth of the blood. "Get Rose," I said to Lilly, "she's up just a way."

Lilly was in a state of shock but made her way up the hill, stumbling. Then she began screaming again. I turned to see why. Upon the ground lay Rose.

"Oh God no," I heard myself say, "not Rose. God no, not Rose." I struggled to my feet and staggered toward her to see the blood upon the bodice of her summer dress. Her face pale with eyes open but unseeing. In death she looked like an angel. One that had just fallen from heaven while the soft breeze flicked at the hem of her white cotton skirt.

WHEN CONVALESCING IN Denver, I met an old timer, a muleskinner, tough as boot leather, but with not long to live. His lungs had all but given up on him. He told me that I looked like the stuffing had been knocked out of me.

I said I was okay and that, with a stick, I could walk all right.

He said, "I wasn't talking about your leg, I was talking about your head. I've been watching you. You just sit there staring into space. You do it for hours on end. Got me thinking if you are ever going to get back on that horse."

"What horse?"

"The one that threw you over a cliff."

He passed a week later and that conversation of his did me a service as I had been contemplating some dark thoughts.

When I got back to Wichita, Matt saw the change in me. Others seemed to see it too. If I got into a grievance, the cowpokes backed off quickly. It was then I noticed my face in the shaving mirror. My eyes were lifeless, cold, and distant.

Washington kept pressing for my report, and I kept stalling. Finally, Matt had to intervene. "Is there anything I can do to get you started?"

"Why?" I said as I cleaned my pistol. "What's the use, who's going to read any report I write, or worse, who's going to do anything about it? The grand jury was dropped once Louis Bosier was declared dead."

"True, but the matter of the counterfeit bonds hasn't gone away."

I didn't know what he meant and had to ask, "How come?"

"Politics as usual. The St. Louis Dispatch reported on the dismissal of the grand jury, saying that where there's smoke there's also fire, along with too many unanswered questions about the source of the counterfeit bonds. The story then spread to Washington and the attention of the senate judiciary committee. Then it got the Treasury involved and now our department is calling for all information held or pending on the subject of the counterfeit bonds. And that includes your report."

I had just put the cylinder back into the frame of my pistol but now sat bolt upright.

"Seems I've got your attention," said Matt. "You going to write that report now?"

"I'm going to do more than that. I'm going to deliver it personally and give evidence before the committee."

Matt looked more than a little surprised.

"And if they have trouble in getting a conviction, I'll fix that too," I said, as I spun the well-oiled cylinders of my '73 Colt.

—*The author is an Australian writer of Western novels published under the pen name of Lee Clinton, as part of the Black Horse Western (BHW) series. Unfortunately, that line of books has now been discontinued by the publisher. However, titles such as* Reaper, Reins of Satan, No Coward, *and* Divine Wind *remain available worldwide in digital form via Amazon. In the meantime, he has now turned his hand to short stories as he continues his love of the American Western.*

Night at the Trading Post by Frank Tenney Johnson

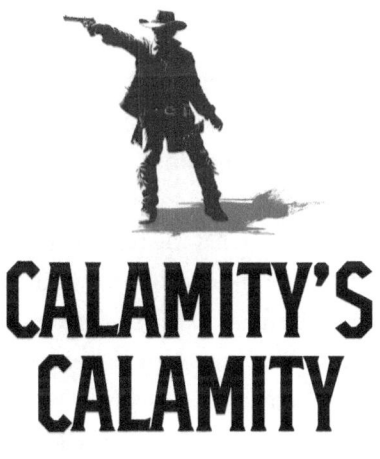

CALAMITY'S CALAMITY

LAURA RODLEY

THE NURSES SHOOK their heads.

"She keeps calling out 'Jim, Jim,' in her sleep. The fever has made her delirious," said one nurse wiping her hands on her apron. "I'll cut more ice from the ice block, set some under her underarms, and try to bring her fever down."

"What does she expect, swimming the Platte River in the spring with ice melt floating alongside and riding soaking wet for ninety miles. She's a fool."

"Now, Erma, the soldiers that brought her here were quite clear, she swam the river and rode delivering army dispatches. Heroic work. We have the army uniform we peeled off her as proof."

"Men's work. No wonder she's ill."

"She arrived here, Fort Fetterman, in General Crook's ambulance, I'll have you recall. The army's paying the bills, so mind your tongue, don't let Matron hear you. If Matron hadn't caught pneumonia too like this poor soul, she'd be washing your mouth out with soap."

"Tsk," the second nurse patted the back of her bun, tapping in hairpins around her cap more firmly.

"Tsk yerself," said the first nurse. She studied the red line in the thermometer. "That can't be right," shook the thermometer, placed it inside the underarm of her patient, waited five minutes, and withdrew it. "Still one hundred and five degrees Fahrenheit. Martha dear, if you can hear us, hang on. Please hang on. The army wouldn't forgive us if we couldn't nurse you back to health."

"Not our fault what turn illness takes, it's God's. You might as well call her Calamity Jane, that's what the soldiers called her."

"It's our skill that determines what turn illness takes, as well as God's. But you're right, Erma, she might respond better to Calamity. Go get me ice, be quick. We have other patients to attend."

The nurse squeezed water from a cloth over a white enamel bowl sitting on the side table. "Now, Calamity, I called you Martha because that's on your records. Martha Jane Canary. What a lovely name. I wonder if you can sing. If I had that name, I would try to learn. But the soldiers said you could ride like an Indian brave, so if you can't sing, you have that. You're four days fevered now, dear, and more days before you were brought here—fever must break soon or we'll lose you. Can't have that."

She hummed as she sponged Calamity Jane's face and hands. "I'll wait for Erma to help me give you a proper bed bath. You're limp as a wet rag, too heavy for me to move."

"Here's the ice you wanted, Justina."

"Thank you, Erma. Help me change this nightgown, wash her, and then set the ice. Lucky we don't have many patients right now. I heard there's smallpox coming. We would have to isolate her."

Half an hour later, the pair left to attend to other patients in the infirmary. "I can't leave the ice or she'll get frostbite in her underarms."

"Frostbite in her underarms, whatever next," Erma giggled.

Justina repressed her giggles, but giggled just the same.

It was a long night. Morning found Justina sponging Calamity Jane's face yet again with the washcloth, the heat of her face warming the cloth further as sunlight streamed through the window onto the narrow bed in stripes through thin curtains. "You passed the witching hour, three a.m. Perhaps you'll be all right. Don't give up, Calamity. I'm not."

"Justina, shift's over," Erma's starched uniform rustled as she reached Justina.

"I'm waiting this out, her fever has to break before I'll leave. Without Matron, we're short-staffed. Matron's used the last of the calomel or we could have given Calamity that. Doc has to sign an order for many supplies when he returns."

"Suit yerself." Erma said. "You're on again tonight, don't forget."

"I won't."

"Pity we can't forge his name and sign the reorder ourselves. Or Matron's," Erma giggled.

"Erma, hush. Don't let anybody else hear you say that. Calamity, another temperature check." Still high. "Let's try more ice. Under your neck as well this time. You're lucky Doc is away on his honeymoon and Matron's also ill, or you'd be in for bloodletting, even if we don't have the calomel Erma's talking about. We nurses are not trained in bloodletting. Or applying leeches, but ours died in the solution that Doc kept them in."

Ten minutes into the ice application, Calamity Jane's teeth started chattering. "Too much then. Let's remove the ice," Justina made the adjustments and sat in the chair beside her.

"Shivering is a good sign. One hundred and two, fever's started to come down, might break soon. Well done, Calamity. We'll set you right." Justina dropped a few drops of willow bark tea on her tongue as Calamity Jane was still unconscious.

Two days later, Erma came on shift and found Calamity Jane sitting up in bed. "Look at you, Calamity. On the mend. Who's Jim? Yer fella? Must be handsome, you kept saying his name over and over."

Calamity Jane turned her head and squinted her hazel eyes to study Erma. "He's sure tall, dark and handsome, big-boned, but slim. He's my horse. I wanna know what's happened to him. If the army is taking care of him. Or did he come in tethered to the ambulance?"

"Goodness. I'll see what I can find out. Ready for some tea?"

"Rather have whiskey and a cigarette."

"With your lungs, you shouldn't be smoking. You have pneumonia, you know. The only whiskey we have here is for anesthetic purposes only—and the doctors."

"I know all about pneumonia, my mother died of it on the wagon trail. I nursed her on the wagon, but she died anyway. Maybe I didn't do a good enough job," Calamity Jane turned her head, looked out the window, and coughed.

"Did you have ice to bring the fever down? Clean water at yer disposal?"

"No. Just five other children and our father. He took off and died too."

"Being on the move wears a body down. You should know. You were skin and bones, still skin and bones, swimming the river, then riding ninety miles delivering dispatches. Did you really do that?"

"That's nuthin. I don't want any tea, I want to know about Jim, my horse."

"I'll see what I can do."

A couple hours later, Erma reported. "Your Jim is in the stable, eating. Doing fine. Seems he might have been on the same rations as you, as he's mighty thin."

"Your opinion is not welcome, thanks very much."

"It's a hardscrabble life for us women as it is, and a tiny mite like you, riding for the army. You're not even as tall as me and I'm five-foot-one in my stockings."

"My Winchester makes me six-foot tall. You're wearing me out, all this talking. I'd say yes to the tea someone offered just to have you go away."

"Well, of all the things. Best not talk to Justina like that."

"Who's Justina?"

"Just the redheaded nurse who sat with you during her off shift heading your fever out the door."

"I don't remember her."

"Not surprising, you were too high-fevered, unconscious, or delirious. Just Jim on your mind."

"Listen, get me my clothes, and I'll be on my way."

"No, you have to wait till we say so. Till the Doc returns or Matron's back, whichever is first."

"Don't think I can wait till then," Calamity Jane started rising from the bed, but fell back down against the bedclothes. "I think I'll take a rest first."

"Told you you weren't ready. I'll bring you sassafras tea. It helps with fever, pneumonia, and fatigue."

"Aren't you gone yet?" Calamity Jane whispered. "You're getting on my nerves."

"It's good for that too."

Eight days later, Calamity Jane was saddled on Jim headed for Fort Laramie. The doctor had returned from his honeymoon and declared anyone having a tongue like hers would snap the head off a rattlesnake and that she was ready to go.

He warned her anyone who had been as sick as she was in danger of relapse. And to take it easy, though he knew she wouldn't. "You're lucky the army is footing your bill or we would have got rid of you earlier for bugging all my nurses, being so eager to leave."

Justina handed her a bottle of tonic infused with elderberry and warned, "Seriously, Calamity, you should be resting for another month, not going off already. You're lucky it's just turned June, hopefully good weather." She smiled, "Send us a letter of your adventures," and in a lower voice, whispered "You're lucky you're leaving now, Doc has a new supply of leeches."

"Those bloodsuckers!"

"Don't talk to my nurses in that manner, that's exactly what I'm talking about. A woman traipsing around in men's clothing and throwing herself into rivers. You have only yourself to blame if you become ill. Away with you. I'll send a dispatch to Fort Laramie alerting General Crook that you are recovered and leaving on your own accord."

"Delivering dispatches is my job. I'll take that along with me then."

"No, you won't. I don't hold with women doing men's work though you are all killing yourselves alongside each other in this miserable backwater."

"Well, suit yourself. But someone will have to inform General Crook... officially."

"I'll send it when the next soldiers drop someone else off ill, arm or finger cut off, bullets shot through their thighs. I don't trust you, can't even bring myself to admire you for your exploits."

"You don't say," Calamity Jane shoved her Stetson over her dark hair. "Thought a body would surely be in better humor after their honeymoon."

"Out." Doc pointed to the door.

Her horse, Jim, was glad to be back under saddle, stepping carefully when Calamity Jane fell asleep astride. She didn't wait for soldier escorts to return to the fort. As a scout, she figured she knew her way around danger. She wore buckskins she had packed to blend in. Unshod, Jim moved quietly, no metal shoes clicking against rocks.

She took good care of Jim, finding him water and forage, then sleep claimed her. Sections of days passed where Jim grazed as Calamity Jane slept, sometimes on the ground. Her weak leg muscles trembled, found it hard to stay mounted, and never experienced such prolonged weakness. Nurses had packed her some food. With little appetite, it lasted. Too tired to make a fire and boil water from streams, she didn't drink any. Weeks into her hundred-mile journey as the crow flies, which should have taken ten days, she saw clouds of dust kicked up ahead. Late for buffalo to be migrating, she thought. Jim pricked his ears forward but was unperturbed and the ground wasn't rumbling beneath his hooves. Then he nickered. Maybe wild horses. I'm ready for that, she thought, reining him in at a crest in the hill. The dust cloud thickened. Within it she could see smaller clouds, the canvas brims of wagons. What luck. Maybe they could feed her. She'd been too tired to shoot a deer for dinner, drunk the bottle of tonic, and eaten the packed food.

She nudged him toward the wagon train.

With her dark hair, fringed buckskins, carrying her rifle, and riding her horse as skillfully as a Sioux brave riding a plains pony, she had to be careful. Her Stetson didn't differentiate, didn't declare her belonging to a Lakota Sioux or other plains tribe or on the side of the soldiers, or not, which side she represented. Any side could shoot her.

As she rode nearer, and was sighted, two men rode up, sending up more clouds of dust, even though it was too early for it to be this dry.

They held rifles in the crooks of their arms, ready to fire. They had long flowing hair and could also have been mistaken for plains tribesmen, except they were both blond with handlebar mustaches. The taller one wearing a flat pancake hat had a straw colored mustache. Choosing to keep a low profile, he didn't call out using his bugle. Instead, he called out, "Who are you? Where you headed?"

Urging Jim closer, Calamity Jane called out, "Anybody for a game of cards? Got anything for a hungry rider first?"

"What are you doing riding all alone?" the other rider asked.

"I'm a scout, returning to Fort Laramie. Calamity Jane."

"We've heard of you," said the rider with piercing blue gray eyes looking down at her .

"No idea who you are. Introduce yerselves."

"Wild Bill Hickok, ma'am. This here's Charlie Utter, wagon train leaders." He reached into his saddle's side pocket, pulled out a little packet filled with something dark and threw it over. "This here's beef jerky, will hold you till we make camp. Good catch. Beware, it's mighty salty, will make you thirsty. I see you're well equipped. How good are you on that rifle and pistols?"

"I'd give you a demonstration, but I don't wanna spook those horses and mules driving the wagons. They look sore tuckered."

"True enough. No demonstration then. Your reputation speaks for your shooting skills. Care to ride with us? We're on our way to Deadwood, South Dakota, from Cheyenne, could use someone who knows their way around here and takes care of their beasts, someone who can shoot. We'll pay," he said as he noticed her looking in the direction of Ford Laramie.

"You're more than halfway there already, you know. You're on," said Calamity Jane, pulling her Stetson down. The trio spun their horses around and trotted toward the wagon train.

Wild Bill and Charlie had started out guiding a group of prospectors and gamblers from Cheyenne riding horses and leading mules, ready to make their dreams come true by digging for gold in the Black Hills. At Fort Laramie, soldiers advised them to wait for at least one hundred people to go—safety in numbers—plus advised being heavily armed against Indian attacks. The resulting thirty wagons were driven by two-horse, four-horse, and six-mule teams and included an assorted bakers' dozen of "fallen angels."

The night Calamity Jane joined their party, it stormed, thunder and lightning. The mules and horses in two makeshift rope corrals whinnied with their backs to the wind. They pushed hard against the ropes. The men guarding them rode the perimeter, hedged in on the side by trees as they had reached the edges of the Black Hills where ponderosa, lodgepole, limber pines, and spruce lined the slopes, growing more stunted the higher the altitude where they had taken root.

In the morning, the air was clear, and the travelers drew in long breaths of its pine scent.

With the rain came mud. They had started to ascend the hills when a two-horse team halfway through a heavily flowing stream got stuck. Passengers clambered out to lighten the load as the driver snapped his blacksnake whip against the horses' flanks. They only got mired in further.

Calamity Jane rode up and snapped, "Give me that whip," reaching out her hand. Protesting, the driver noticed Charlie as he reined up beside her. The driver reluctantly handed over his blacksnake whip, aiming tobacco juice near her horse's hooves.

"Geeyup, yup, yup," Calamity Jane yelled as she snapped the blacksnake whip around the heads of the horses, "Yup, yup." The snapping whip whooshed in the air like stinging bees and crackled like fire as the horses struggled to get away from its noise, their hooves treading up more mud. "Hup, hup, heeyah," she yelled, accompanied by hearty curses. The whip never touched them.

Other passengers from the wagon halfheartedly yupped as well.

The driver shot his pistol into the air. Calamity Jane twirled round, snapped the blacksnake whip near his left ear. "You crazy, you want to get the Sioux attacking us, thinking we're launching an attack? We're on their land. No pistols. Wait till you get to town, you can shoot off your gun as often as you like with every other crazy loon."

Charlie rode to the opposite side, encouraging the team, giving them a direction to follow. They bucked up their hindquarters and heaved, half swimming, began lunging forward.

Wild Bill rode up. "We'll have to cross further up the stream."

"Row of bogs you can't see further up to our left. Further down should be shallower. I'll go see," offered Calamity Jane.

Charlie rode with her.

Wild Bill rode down the line of waiting wagons, warning, "Everybody stay in your wagons, be ready to move when they return." Those riding horses had already gone across.

Toward the last wagon, he heard moaning, muffled screaming. "What's going on in there?"

The driver cocked his head. "One of them 'ladeez' is having a baby. If I'd known, I'd never brung 'er, no matter how much she paid."

"Couldn't you see she was pregnant?"

"They bind their bellies so they can still do business, so no one knows."

A woman with long curly black hair, ivory white skin, and dark eyes lined with kohl opened the wagon's back canvas flap. "Storms bring the babies on, girls start dropping the babies, like cows."

"You don't say."

"I do say. Baby's fine. But the girl's had a hard time of it. The shaking wagon hasn't helped much."

"We'll have to bury the afterbirth, don't want wolves following us."

"You know an awful lot about it, Wild Bill," the woman crooned.

"Ma'am." He tilted his hat forward and rode back up the line.

"She was right. We've found a shallower place further down. Once they start churning up mud, won't be shallow for long. We can't stay here, half this side, half across," said Charlie.

"I'll ride across, tell the others to wait. Too dangerous to be separated."

Late morning they were all finally across the stream when a deep fog enveloped them, mists rising from the streams hemmed in by the hills. Visibility was limited to one wagon ahead, if that.

"We'll have to wait it out." Wild Bill decided. "Not a good place to make camp, but we have no choice. Remember to boil the water before you drink it."

He rode back to check on the new mother and baby. When he called out softly, the dark-haired woman opened the wagon's back canvas flap, the baby at her breast. "It was too much shaking for her. She started bleeding, and it didn't stop, I couldn't stop it. I only have medicines—herbs, like tansy—to start bleeding, not stop it. We were in the middle of crossing the stream, everybody yelling, no one heard me yelling for help. I couldn't hold the baby and jump out too. I might have dropped her."

Wild Bill took his hat off and held it against his heart. "I'm sure sorry, ma'am. What was her name?"

"Amy. Amy Wilder."

"Excuse me for asking, but how do you happen to be able to nurse the baby? I don't see another infant."

"I gave my own baby to my mother before this trip. She was too little to travel, two months old. I'm sending for them when I make enough money. I was almost, um... dried up too. I would never ask one of the other women to wet nurse this baby."

Wild Bill looked at the blanket-covered woman inside, only her very young-looking face exposed. This "fallen angel's" journey was over. "We will bury her—Amy—when the fog lifts. Can't be making holes when we can't see."

"You're a gentleman, sir. Don't worry about the baby, I'll take good care of her. I'm giving her her mother's name. Amy Wilder. Meybe she should have my surname. Amy Deacons. That's better."

"It is, ma'am. For the best."

"Haven't done this long. My husband was a prospector, good man, Arnold Deacons, drowned prospecting. We lost all our money staking our claim, gave money to a friend, said he'd file it for us, then he ran off."

"Ma'am, you owe me no explanation. Take care of that little girl."

One man wandered off as they waited out the fog. After the fog lifted, tendrils of mist swirling away like ghosts, they came upon him as they ascended the hill, his chest crushed by a fallen pine, little grooves where his fingers had churned up dirt and tiny stones desperately trying to dislodge himself. As the mountainous ground held little dirt, they piled stones atop of him. Six feet away they laid down Amy Wilder's body, covered her with stones, said a short prayer for them both and continued on. Death doesn't differentiate.

Charlie was glad the ground proved impossible to dig, because if someone started digging and hit gold they'd never get to Deadwood as arranged. Though they might get rich...

Two more streams followed the first, with more blacksnakes whipping through the air, more cursing as Calamity Jane shouted them on, and got them across. Left to their drivers, the teams might have been badly injured from beatings, unfit for travel. She saved the outfit a bundle in horseflesh. The snake-whip's owner was reluctant to ask for his whip back. Soon the streams they crossed became more shallow.

Calamity Jane and Wild Bill noted a Sioux party watching from the treeline. "If we keep going, we should be fine," Wild Bill said, hand on his pistol.

"Avoiding battle's better for all of us. They named me 'Woman Who Swims Like Otter,' for swimming in rivers," said Calamity Jane.

"I'll drink to that." Charlie sashayed up on his horse. "Three more days. No fodder here, hay's running out. We'll have to push them. Don't like the look of those clouds." He nodded toward the west.

"Agreed." Wild Bill spun his horse around to hurry the others, kept quiet about the sighted Sioux to avoid panic. They already had enough nightmares.

"Sure ready for a whiskey. My mouth's dry as a rattlesnake's skin," said Calamity Jane.

Mid-June, the wagon train unloaded its passengers in Deadwood to find somewhere to stay at a boarding house or wait for relatives to retrieve them. The town was too young yet to have its own hotel.

Wild Bill, Calamity Jane, Charlie, his brother Steve, and trader Dick Seymour rode five abreast in the middle of the dirt road in the bustling brand new town. Their metal spurs clinked as they climbed up the wooden steps of the Nuttal and Mann's Saloon.

Standing six-foot-three in his custom-made boots, Wild Bill picked a table facing the room with his back to the wall. He drew off his thick kid gloves. The red sash around his waist gleamed as he undid the buttons on his long blue wool coat, shoved its tails behind him, his pistols butt-forward tucked in his belt, gold brocade vest and white linen shirt shining, his black ribbon tie slightly askew.

They played poker, slugged back whiskey, and joked.

Impressed with their tales of Calamity Jane's blacksnake whipping the wagons across streams, Dick Seymour offered her a job with his and Charlie's newly founded Pioneer Pony Express, delivering mail from Deadwood to Fort Laramie and back, plus mining camps. She studied her card hand.

Before she could answer, Wild Bill said, "Bet you can get the mail there faster than his riders. They aim to do it in just over two days."

She set her cards face-down and slapped Wild Bill's back making him choke on his whiskey.

"I bet I can. Sign me up. But I need four days before I start, cause my horse, Jim, needs a rest, and I don't wanna ride no other horse but him."

"Deal." Dick Seymour stretched his hand across the table, which she shook, her hand tiny in his.

"Hey, I was just fooling, you'd be a target all alone," protested Wild Bill.

"Here, Wild Bill, let me buy you another whiskey, make up for the one you spilt. Don't you worry about me. I'm invisible when I want to be."

***

—*Pushcart Prize winner Laura Rodley's latest books are* Turn Left at Normal *by Big Table Press,* Counter Point *by Prolific Press,* Ribbons and Moths Poems for Children *by Kelsay Books. She has loved horses all her life.*

THE HAUNTING OF JACK MCCALL

J. BENJAMIN SANDERS, JR.

JACK MCCALL—SOMETIMES called Broken Nose Jack—had to be the most hated man in the Dakota Territories. He sat on the edge of his bunk while his breakfast rested on a small table nearby. A bloody rare steak, hard-fried eggs, and fried-up potatoes, all to be washed down with strong black coffee from a tin cup. He didn't feel much like eating though. Waiting to be hung can do that to a man, put him off his feed.

"Looks mighty good, a lot better than my last meal. You know I stopped off at the Chinaman's on my way to the Nuttal and Mann's. Most folks in Deadwood might not have cared for Charlie very much, but he always treated me decent enough." James Butler Hickok lounged in the bunk across from Jack. "Damned good cook, too, as long as you knew what you were getting." Jack spit on the floor. "When are you going to leave me alone, damn your hide, and go to hell where you belong?"

"What's the matter, Jack? You're going down in history as the man who shot Wild Bill Hickok, ain't you? Isn't that what you always wanted? To be famous?" Hickok ran his fingers across his thick mustache, then gave the ends a twirl.

"I should have shot you somewhere other than the Number 10 in front of all those people. Then I wouldn't be in this fix."

"You're in this fix because you had to get yourself drunk to get your nerve up enough to back shoot me. I never thought anyone would get the drop on old Wild Bill like that, especially someone like Broken Nose Jack. That's hubris for you. It can whittle a man down to size every time."

Hickok stood and walked across to the window, wrapping his hands around the rusty iron bars while he looked out. "You know if you turn your head just right you can see the scaffold from here. They tested the drop yesterday. You should have seen how that sandbag bounced when the rope jerked up hard. I swear it made my neck ache to watch it. You should get a gander at the crowds gathered out there, Jack. I imagine folk came from all across the territory to watch the man that killed Wild Bill Hickok swing. It's going to be like a county fair out there today. Yes sir, a county fair."

Jack said nothing. He just scowled across the cell at Hickok, who looked exactly as he did the day that Jack killed him, but noticed something was off. "Your hat."

"What about my hat?" Bill turned around so he could look at the condemned man.

"You weren't wearing it when I shot you."

"And?"

"You're wearing it now."

"It's my hat, so why wouldn't I wear it?" He pulled it off and flicked the dust off the brim, then turned it as he admired the cut and style before he combed his long hair with his fingers, and flipped it back on. "Somebody was kind enough to pass it to the undertaker so I could be buried with it, to accompany me into the hereafter."

"If you say so." Jack slumped back with a sullen stare. His arms crossed as he watched the ghost of the man he murdered. Taunting him nearly every day since the end of his trial.

"It ain't fair, you know," Jack said.

"What ain't fair."

"Me swinging for killing you after all the men you killed."

"I killed my men fair and square."

"Tell that to Mike Williams, the deputy you shot."

The specter turned away. His face was as red as a sundown. "Now that was a pure-dee accident. I've suffered a lot over that killing, and it worried me down to my soul. I even thought of giving up the badge over that little incident because it ate at me so much."

"Incident, my ass, it was murder pure and simple. Everybody said so."

"I admit some folks saw it that way, but more didn't. It's been my cross to bear ever since."

"That's mighty Christian of you," Jack mocked him.

"Well, I guess it is, ain't it." His thick lip brush hid the smile that formed there.

"You're mighty proud of that mustache, ain't you?"

"Why I suppose I am. Want to know a secret? I mean it ain't like you'll get the chance to spread it, and even if you did, nobody would believe you. They would chalk it up to malicious gossip on your part. Like you were after some petty revenge to dirty up my good name before you hang."

"Good name, shit. What's your secret?"

"I grew this mustache for a reason. See, when I was just a boy growing up in Illinois, I had this little imperfection that all the other kids would tease me about. My upper lip stuck out something awful. Because of that, they called me Duck Bill. I quickly grew to hate that name, and it led to more than my share of rolling in the dirt, eye gouging, and bloody brawling. As soon as I got big enough, I grew this brush to cover it up. No need to say that nobody teases me like that anymore." Bill stared at Jack to gauge his reaction.

"Is that supposed to make me feel sorry for you? Well, it don't."

"Even going to your death, you still have to act the jackass, don't you, Jack?" Bill sighed, stood, then went back to the window.

"If you don't like the company, you can always leave."

"Oh, I'll be departing quick enough. Just as soon as this is all done and dusted." Both man and ghost turned when they heard a key rattle in the lock to the main door, just before it swung back to expose Marshal Burdick stepping through, followed by his deputies, C. P. Edmunds and Stanley.

The marshal stopped before the cell, pulled a folded paper out of his pocket, and waved it. "John McCall, it's my duty as U.S. Marshal in the Dakota Territories to read you this here death warrant before you are delivered to the place of your execution."

So saying, he unfolded the paper to recite the warrant, but it was nothing that Broken Nose Jack hadn't heard before so he only listened with half an ear. When he finished, the marshal refolded the paper and stuffed it into his pocket. "The Reverend Father Daxacher will soon be here to prepare you for the next step." His duty done, the marshal turned to lead his deputies out, pausing long enough to lock the outer door.

"Why I don't believe that prettier words were ever spoken, beyond what's said at the pulpit. You will be taken out to the appointed place of your execution where you'll be hanged by the neck until you are dead," Hickok said from across the cell with a laugh.

"Shut up, Bill, you seem to be enjoying this entirely too much."

"True, but it's not every man that receives the dispensation of seeing his killer strung up. I have to say, there is a certain satisfaction to me being included in this here historic event."

"I know what you mean," Jack said with a malicious leer. "I felt that way when that bullet entered the back of your skull and scrambled your brain."

"Now, Jack, you're just being spiteful. Ain't no need for that kind of behavior, considering this is all your own doing." Bill pulled a slim cheroot from his inner pocket, wet the tip, and bit off the end before he scratched the Lucifer across the sole of his boot until it flared. He cupped his hands around the flame and puffed till he had a red glow, drew deep, and then expelled a cloud of blue smoke in the air. "Even death can't take away the pleasure of a good smoke."

The lock rattled again. The outer door swung back to admit the local Catholic priest, Father Daxacher. A tall, thin man with sparse gray hair wearing wire-rimmed spectacles that rested atop a spectacular nose. "Good day to you, Mister McCall."

"Padre."

"I know this is a day that few men can truly prepare themselves for, but I'm here to help you make that transition and wash away your sins in the eyes of the Lord. Unless you find yourself amenable to take such a step on your own. Are you prepared to face your maker, Mister McCall? To ask forgiveness from the Almighty who resides in heaven above?"

Hickok laughed as he mocked the condemned man. "Well now, I figure the Lord's gonna need a mighty big tub to wash away all your sins, Jack. It will take a heap of soap and a lot of hard scrubbing to remove all those stains from your dark soul."

"I am prepared to make my final confession." Jack ignored the jibes from the dead Hickok, dropped to his knees, bowed his head, and folded his hands beneath his chin. "Forgive me, Father, for I have sinned."

"No shit, Jack, I would say murdering an iconic Western hero could be called a sin," Bill taunted with a grin as he leaned back against the wall, then kicked his legs out so he could cross his ankles. He took another deep draw from his cheroot, exhaling a cloud that rose toward the ceiling through pursed lips.

Jack continued to recite his litany of sins, which bored Hickok to no end. So, he stood and ambled over to the window where he spent the next few minutes watching the crowd that milled about in the streets. Husbands and wives with their children treated it like a Fourth of July celebration. Several drummers walked among the crowd hawking their penny wares. Treats and doodads for the young 'uns, ribbons and fans for the ladies. Libations of various sorts for the men. Somewhere an unseen band struck up a rousing rendition of the latest San Francisco saloon song. Although they did their best to do it justice, to Wild Bill's mind, it might as well have been a couple of tomcats tied up in a tow sack fighting to get free.

The main door opened for the last time that morning, and Bill turned to watch as the marshal, followed by his two deputies, both toting a Greener, made their way to the cell just as the priest completed his religious hoodoo for the soon-to-be dead. Bill never had much truck with Catholics, not that he bore them any hostility. Their ritual fol-de-rol didn't much matter to him one way or another.

"It's time, McCall," Marshal Burdick intoned with all the solemnity of a reluctant executioner. He unlocked the cell. Deputy Stanley stepped behind Jack, then placed a set of manacles around his wrist and ankles. Then with the marshal leading the way, and the two deputies flanking Jack, they headed for the door, which left Father Daxacher to trail behind. With a grin, Hickok ambled along behind.

Out in the street, the deputies helped Jack to climb into the wagon then took a seat on either side of him. The priest headed for his surrey, so Bill climbed up to sit alongside the marshal, who drove the rig. Burdick snapped the reins causing the wagon to start with a jerk. He took his time to guide it to where the scaffold waited. The crowd parted willingly and pointed excitedly toward the man who had killed Wild Bill Hickok. Some offered impolite deprecations, while others gave out with subdued cheers. Hard to tell if the cheers were for what Jack did, or for what was about to be done to him.

Bill turned in his seat to look back at Jack. "Look at all the people that came out to see you swing. Yes, sir, fame can be a mighty invigorating thing. Why, these folks will be talking about this day till they meet their maker themselves. Bragging about how they saw the man who killed Wild Bill hanged. You ought to be mighty proud of the mark you made in your life. Yes, sir, mighty proud."

Jack glared thin-lipped but said nothing. "What's the matter, Jack? Afraid they'll think you've gone crazy if you speak to me?" Bill laughed while he slapped his knee. "Wouldn't that be a hoot if they claimed that Broken-Nosed Jack McCall was crazy when he killed me? Then all that admiration for you would melt away and turn into pity. Yes, he killed old Wild Bill, but he was teched in the head."

"I won't give you the satisfaction." Jack snarled.

"Are you talking to me, McCall?" P. C. Edmunds asked, tightening his grip on his shotgun.

"Just making my peace, Deputy, nothing more."

The wagon pulled up before the scaffold. Everyone climbed down and then scaled the steps single file up to the platform with the marshal leading the way. He guided Jack over to the trap door and made sure he stood in the center. "You got any final words you want to say?"

"I done said my piece to the preacher." Jack shook his head. P.C. slipped the hood over his head from behind. Stanley removed the manacles and replaced them with a short length of rope. Burdick slipped the noose over his head to tighten the knot until it rested just below the left ear, then he stepped back. "Are you ready, son?"

"Marshal, would you mind snugging that knot up a bit more?"

Burdick stepped up, tightening the knot so that no slack remained. The crowd went silent while the unseen band struck up "Rock of Ages." The marshal pulled out his watch and flipped it open to check the time. Seconds later, he gave a nod. The trap door released, and Jack fell from sight. The rope jerked tight, and it was all over.

Bill sighed wearily as he moved down the steps and around the side of the scaffold to wait. A moment later, a figure stumbled from beneath the scaffold. Bill stepped up and drew his skinning knife to slice through the rope that bound Jack's hands. Free, the man fumbled at the hood that covered his head. He ripped it off and looked around in confusion, then up to where he had been standing only a moment before. He stared at the taut rope that swayed back and forth in tight circles. It creaked rustily where it rubbed against the raw wood of the cross member. Then Jack reached up to massage his neck. "So, it's over then?"

Wild Bill took the arm of the dead man and tugged him along. "It's over now. Come on, Jack, now that you're dead, I figure it's my solemn duty to escort you to hell myself."

———✦———

—J. Benjamin Sanders Jr is a freelance writer in Richardson, Texas and a Marine Corps Vet. He lives with his wife, Rosemary, a pair of loving Airedales called Fiona and Angus Og, as well as a rescued feral cat he calls Loki. He's a longtime member of the Dallas Fort Worth Writing Workshop rubbing elbows with several noted authors. An eclectic reader with a special life-long love of pulp fiction and thirties noir. His Texas Noir novel, Mexicanos Hustle *was released July of 2024 by Fawkes Press.*

On the Trail by W.H.D. Koerner

THE LAST OF THE O'MALLEYS

JOHN MORT

MARIE WAS BORN to a French boatman, Joseph, and a French-Kaskaskian woman, Marguerite, up the Missouri River forty miles from St. Louis, in 1843. Joseph was not often home during the summers but found time to ferment his wine-grapes, lamenting all the while that the grapes in America were without subtlety. In late fall, as barge traffic waned, the boatman cut great piles of firewood from logs the river deposited, and he butchered two hogs, a grisly undertaking that involved all the family. They ate like pigs for several days afterward but most of the meat, the bacon and hams and shoulders, went into the smokehouse.

Through the winter, the boatman sat by the fire, carving little toys from the bleached driftwood, his blurred blue eyes full of memories and myths. Occasionally, he delivered a powerful speech as if he were transmitting the words of God. He talked about the treacherous river, the great clouds of birds, and the remnants of houses washed away by floods. But there was nothing personal in his speeches, nothing about the family. Mostly, he sat by the fire with a blanket over his knees, drank his wine, and slept. To Marie, he seemed as inscrutable as a turtle.

Marguerite kept a large vegetable garden and employed Marie to weed carrots, pick green beans, and shoo the birds from the tomatoes and peppers drying in the sun. Marie's two feral brothers trapped cottontails and brought in quantities of fish from the massive, teeming river. Marguerite smoked the fish with the pork. She raised tobacco for her cob pipe, also curing it in the smokehouse, so the sausages and fish tasted a little of tobacco.

The midwife couldn't stop the bleeding for the French-Kaskaskian woman's fourth baby. Big, frightening men buried her on a little hill above her garden and Marie understood none of it, nor what happened to her baby sister. She soon lost track of her brothers as well because that same summer, the French boatman died in a Westport tavern, just sitting there with his eyes full of questions. Marie was sent to a Catholic orphanage in a St. Louis enclave called Kerry Patch. The poor Irish lived in Kerry Patch in mudflats along the malarial River des Peres. The Irish knew not much more about the world than they could no longer grow potatoes.

A priest might have called Marie's fate divine intervention because, Marie proved a favorite of the nuns. She was dutiful, hard-working, and observant of the faith. She graduated first in her class from the eighth grade, but because she was penniless, and almost without identity, could go no farther.

That eighth grade credential proved sufficient to teach at a church school in Kerry Patch, and she was able to rent a tiny apartment above the Robert Avenue Haberdashery. In Ireland, a haberdashery meant fine suits and other nice things, but in Kerry Patch it also meant handling working men's clothing, some of it donated by rich German families. They lived high on their hills on the other side of the River des Peres.

Marie was not homely, but marriage to a grimy dock worker had no appeal. Likely, such a fellow would be impressed into the Union Army anyhow, or he'd light out for the frontier. Professional men, shopping for suit coats, gave Marie a hard stare, but the nuns had warned about such men and how a poor girl could be ruined.

Peter O'Malley—a slight fellow with balding hair, but dapper in his way, with a trim moustache—clerked at the haberdashery. True, he sometimes wore a suit coat, but he'd graduated from high school in Killarney and could talk about books. He'd read some Shakespeare and, with deadpan seriousness, read sonnets to Marie. He'd read Swift and Goldsmith and often quoted from Pilgrim's Progress, but mostly he talked about the Bible and the great work of the Church. When he was a child, he 'd wanted to become a priest and wear those fine clothes, which sometimes he called raiments.

Peter was not quite a dandy. He was too poor for fine clothing, and also, his humility got in the way. He was not quite a zealot, either. He was a gentle man who was kind to Marie, and so they were married.

When Father Hogan approached Peter with an offer to go into the Missouri wilderness as a deacon, empowered to conduct marriages and baptize infants, Peter discussed it with Marie. They'd be helping the poor Irish in work blessed by the Church. She was born in the Missouri wilderness and it didn't frighten her, but still, it would be a hard life. "What if I am with child?" she asked.

Peter looked troubled. "That's a hardship all pioneers must face. But as for a physician's care, we don't have that here, Marie."

True enough. Women attended to birthings—few French or German doctors visited Kerry Patch.

Marie remembered sitting on her buttocks, weeding her mother's endless row of carrots. "We are not farmers, Peter."

"No, my dear. We'll run a small store, and you will teach the children."

"Will we be paid?"

"Father Hogan will help as he can, but we must depend on the good Catholics there."

It might be years before those good Catholics made money. Looking into Father Hogan's eyes, all you saw were stars. Father knew something about farming but thought of it as ennobling rather than brutally hard. Hard work was itself a virtue, and that wilderness down south was far removed from Kerry Patch's temptations of gambling and drunkenness and whoring. Maybe Father thought, with every strike of the hoe, you'd breathe a prayer of thanksgiving.

The deciding factor for Marie, and perhaps for Peter though he didn't say so, was the cursed war. In New York City, they pulled Irish off the boats and stuffed them into blue uniforms. Union recruiters lurked about, too, along the River des Peres. Peter had dodged several when they came into the haberdashery. But that awful war couldn't last much longer, and they'd be safe from Union predators in the remote Ozarks.

PETER DELIVERED SERMONS, drawing as many as twenty nostalgic Catholics, some walking through the woods from other settlements. Most were neighbors from the scattered cabins in their town with no name.

Mothers, even with their restive children underfoot, often fell asleep. It was hot in the church and they were bone-weary. Also, the good deacon was boring. His homilies were rather good, but he delivered them in a pious, droning tone. The women liked him, even so. They called him "Father Peter" and he didn't discourage them.

The nearest railhead, Pilot Knob, was one hundred miles away. But the road was passable from Pilot Knob to Van Buren or from Pilot Knob to Doniphan. Doniphan, there and back, took a day on horseback. To Van Buren and back took two days if the weather cooperated. Sometimes, Marie accompanied Peter, riding one of their two mules to Van Buren and staying overnight in the slovenly place that passed for a hotel. The restaurant was better, serving fish from the Current River. She slept almost until ten, reclaiming her tired muscles, while Peter paid his bill with the freighter and loaded the mules.

Once home again, Peter sold work clothing, boots, hoes and shovels, salt and other seasonings, and canned fruit. He sold sugar and molasses for the home brew some of the men made. Often, Peter worked trades for potatoes and venison, even accepting whiskey because, in Ripley County, it was the nearest thing to cash. It took two trips to pack in a Swedish stove and stovepipe but even at fifteen dollars, it proved too costly for any settler. Peter installed it near the church altar and the good Catholics would have nominated him for sainthood if they'd had the power.

Every year was a little better, even at the school. She had thirteen students, ages five to thirteen, who met in the church. With a donation from the Doniphan faithful, she had McGuffey readers, two dictionaries, and some illustrated Bible stories on newsprint.

And she had eleven chickens, which scratched their way from the cabin to the church and all over Marie's garden. There were foxes and raccoons in the woods, but the chickens knew to come in at night. She remembered steadying fifteen chicks atop the mule, hungry, helpless little things gulping at air too cold for them. She kept them near the stove for three weeks and only four died. As the summer wore on, the survivors laid brown eggs, enough they could sell a few in the store. Marie loved her chickens but didn't name them. She remembered her father saying you shouldn't name what would become food.

And then, the barbarians came.

RAIDERS, RUFFIANS, BUSHWHACKERS—whatever you called them, they were all barbarians in Marie's estimation. They came in cold September just before dawn, and the birds in the woods fell silent. Ten of them in faded blue, their rifles and shotguns stabbing the crisp air, took away four men, all farmers with families except for Peter and Bobby Collins. Bobby Collins had taken to drink last winter when his wife died. Sympathy had begun to dry up for a man who did no work.

The raiders took away old Merle, tireless with the plow, and young Jim Walsh, father of three girls, a magician with his double-bit axe. You could hear him in the evenings filing it, a mournful counterpoint to the whippoorwills and owls.

Marie's chickens flew up to the church's rafters except for one fat hen, which roosted in the dead corn until a ruffian wrung her neck. Most of the pigs escaped into the woods. But the barbarians took three plow horses and three milk cows, and raided the vegetable gardens, leaving the okra which wasn't good for much but thickening soup. They took most of the tobacco, curing in an open air shed, and made a mess of the remains. Somehow they missed the smokehouse even though a low fire burned.

Peter stood before the church, holding high his Bible. "We don't care about your war!" he shouted. "You are taking our food for the winter!"

A short man with wide shoulders and a thick chest stared down from his mare as if trying to identify Peter's species. He motioned to the bald man nearest him, who dismounted and grabbed Peter's arm. Peter tore away fiercely, and the bald man laughed. "He's pretty scrawny, Tim."

"They're all scrawny. He'll do."

Another fellow appeared, and along with the bald man, they prodded Peter until he climbed up on saddleless Benjy, Marie's favorite mule. Peter had staked the other, Thomasina, down by the spring where grass still grew.

Peter had a hard time hanging on without a saddle and just a rope for bridle. As the file moved out, Marie half-walked, half-ran alongside him, and he stretched low for her hand. His eyes were full of fear mixed with worry for her and the good Catholics he left with so many troubles. He tried his best. He squeezed Marie's hand and said, "The war is almost over, they say."

"I will wait for you, Husband."

He nodded and now the mule outpaced her and she stumbled. The man with wide shoulders drew near on his big gelding, and she almost screamed. "He is a man of God!"

"Dear lady," the man said, touching the bill of his hat. "I'm sure we are all godly men."

THE SETTLERS BEGAN leaving, sometimes without announcing it, gone in the deep of night and taking along a ham or peck of potatoes. Soon, only five families remained, but if they were careful, with cottontails and squirrels and fish from the creek, and if someone killed a deer or pig gone wild, they had enough for the winter. Marie had nothing left to sell from the store unless you counted an egg or two and ten plugs of tobacco. People gave her a pail of sprouted potatoes or wizened turnips for one plug, which they sliced and chewed to suppress their appetites. Marie tried it, knowing Peter would be appalled—maybe she spat out the vile stuff for his sake. She thought of her mother, sitting in front of the cabin with her pipe, the two rangy hounds at her feet.

Barbarians, different men than those in faded blue, came again in spring. These men looked starved and wild as did their horses, stumbling through a late snow as if taking their last steps. The men's coats were torn and several had improvised their shoes from canvas. The men were angry and didn't talk except to bark out orders, such as "Get out!" and "Over there!" They took Thomasina, fatter than any of the humans. She turned her head toward Marie, her big eyes alarmed. Methodically, the men set fire to every cabin, though in the end several remained intact. Marie's neighbors stumbled into the church with blankets and morsels of food.

Maybe it was a sign from God when the next day dawned brightly and the snow melted. With no group meeting, little talk among them, settlers trudged into the woods toward Doniphan. They had no horses to bear their belongings, but they hadn't many belongings, and at least no one was sick. Everett Ryan bore away Jim Walsh's prized double-bit axe, which Walsh's pretty wife had awarded him when he split some gnarly stumps Jim hadn't conquered. Everett and Colleen had been spending a lot of time together, to the chagrin of Ruth, Jim's wife of thirteen years.

The last to leave were the Stones, not until late July. The man, Ronald, waited so long because he had potatoes to dig and sell. He loaded two bushels—leaving a third for Marie—onto an ornery mule he captured in the woods. The potatoes wouldn't bring much, but Ronald had some whiskey to sell too.

"You need to come with us, Marie O'Malley," Bertha Stone said.

"Peter will not know where I am."

"When was your last letter, dear?"

"March, from Georgia." Peter was a prisoner of war. "He has lost some weight but he said they were receiving regular rations."

"The war is over now," Bertha said.

"Yes," Marie said, staring into the woods. "So they say."

FOR A WEEK and more, Marie enjoyed the solitude. She sang hymns. She found the harmonica she'd had since a child and played bits of French folk songs, the melodies bouncing off the tall pines and echoing in her soul. She read from Ivanhoe. She made nests inside the church for her chickens, faithful layers all, each a silly, irritable friend, the ten of them reliably producing eight eggs a day. She let them out in the mornings to forage, and they found grasshoppers and worms in the trampled gardens.

She walked over those gardens herself, digging small onions, some turnips and little carrots which were better than nothing, and lots of tomatoes poking up through the weeds, the surplus of which she dried in the sun as her mother taught her.

One morning, she shut her chickens inside the church and went down to the spring. It had never run dry, but now in late summer, its torrent had become a trickle, revealing a cave where the settlers kept eggs and butter back when they had chickens and cows. The years were lean but still those were good times when they sat below the cave on stumps padded with corn shucks and worn-out blankets. The air felt deliciously cool. Night sounds of whippoorwills and fluttering owls made a person feel hopeful or sad, depending on how the harvest looked or how much you grieved for your dead.

Saturday nights, they built a fire near the creek and fried catfish or roasted a turkey. They had wine, too, made from blackberries or wild grapes or choke cherries. A traveler on the ridgeline trail might have heard a wistful Irish tune through the pines and paused for a moment to think.

Marie thought she could survive until winter if loneliness didn't kill her. More and more, she drifted off in reverie, then simply blankness, where minutes passed and she was a child again by the wide river, placid and shining with cranes flying low. She found herself snipping and weaving river canes and realized she was making a fish trap, and that she knew how to because of her mother.

The first pool had been fished out, but she went downstream a quarter-mile and secured the trap in a deep, cloudy pool. Next day, she'd caught ten perch and six catfish. The catfish were almost too big to handle, but she carried them to the church, cleaned three and put them on to fry with lard she'd retrieved from one of the cabins. She carried the rest to the smokehouse where she built a hickory fire. In five days, she caught one hundred more fish and put them to smoke, and she thought, the Lord will provide. But it would be a diet of smoked fish, boiled eggs, and onions, nothing more.

The nights were the worst. She lay in the center of the church, sealed away from the darkness, with animal sounds muted and the stub of a candle burning low. The chickens moaned and cackled, maybe devils, maybe angels. She slept fitfully, calling out for Peter, and then heavily, oblivious to raccoons and bobcats and sundry other thieves in the night. The church floated away into a lighted place and if she stepped out the door, she'd tumble into space.

One morning, she awoke suddenly and sat up shivering in the cold, alien church. "Bread!" she shouted, because she'd dreamed of it. "I want bread!" she shouted again, because no one could hear and think her crazed. She laughed at herself. She laughed again because she still could.

HE LOOKED LIKE Peter. Walking from down the field, he was no taller, and like Peter he turned his head at every sound in the woods and watched the crows fly. Marie fought back tears.

He wasn't Peter. He was as neat as a tramp could be but his face showed long scratch marks and his nose had been broken. His trousers were in tatters, but she wondered where he'd found his sturdy boots.

"Good morning, Madam," he said, almost bowing. "What a warm day our Lord has given us!"

The sound of a human voice jolted her senses, but Marie tried to reason past her shock and ascertain if she could trust this man. She glanced to the corner where, only five feet away, the rifle leaned. She had fired it several times but had no confidence in her aim. Also, though she could make patches out of almost anything, she had little powder and lead. "Yes," she said, staring up at the cold sun. "God is good to us."

"All alone here, Madam?"

"Oh, no. My husband is just over the ridge cutting firewood." She reached to grab the rifle and pointed it toward the vague north.

The little man stepped back. "Looks as though this cursed war has not been kind to your small camp."

"No."

"The war is over, dear lady." He sighed. "I am on my way home at last."

"And where is that, sir?"

"Ottumwa. That is in the state of Io-way. I am only a poor, wayfaring stranger, a child of God like yourself, and I wonder if I might prevail upon you to give up one of your chickens?"

Probably the only way to rid herself of the little man, and she was reasonably sure the little brown one had stopped laying. "My—our—chickens are needful to us. Have you anything to trade?"

The little man reached within what looked to be five layers of coat and sweaters and shirts to produce a small paper package. "Only this."

Flour! Enough only for some stove top biscuits, but they'd go so well with smoked catfish. Manna from Heaven.

SHE DIDN'T KNOW the day but judged she must have entered November. She had plenty of firewood and the chickens could forage for themselves but she had to face reality—Peter was dead. She was beyond grieving. She'd waited as she'd promised, when probably she should have left with the others.

She had to make a life on her own but at least she didn't have a child to feed. From the ruined store, she'd taken almost ten dollars in coins.

Somehow, she'd reach Pilot Knob and catch the train to St. Louis. Perhaps she could teach school again, yet whatever happened, the church would help. She had been a dutiful wife, but she wouldn't mind so much becoming a nun. What man would want her other than godly Peter?

She resolved to make a pack for herself of dried fish and boiled eggs and strike out for Doniphan. But the morning turned cold and rainy, and she waited another day. That evening, only four chickens returned to the church. The little beggarman, whom she'd thought God sent, was the Devil.

She shut in her remaining chickens. They settled irritably near the stove and slept.

"Ladies, lay some eggs!" she commanded in a voice she didn't recognize. No, no, she told herself. I am not crazy.

She sat in the doorway, staring into the rain. She had no idea what time it was when the figure of a man appeared out of the weeds by the smokehouse. She didn't hesitate. She brought the old rifle up against the door frame and fired. Nothing changed. The figure remained because it was nothing but a sapling pine. Laboriously, she reloaded the rifle and kept vigil in the doorway until she fell asleep.

At dawn, she ran out to the smokehouse and three-quarters of her fish were gone. Why didn't the Devil take it all? Because the Devil was the Devil and delighted in torturing God's children.

"Well, Devil, I don't care! I'm on my way out of here when the rain stops. You can't hold me here in Hell, Devil!"

Maybe the Devil wasn't the Devil. God had provided what she needed for her journey to Doniphan. God was telling her it was time to leave, that her good and faithful husband was with Him. "Lord, thank you for showing me the way," she said in a reverent, hoarse whisper that seemed to issue from a stranger.

She stood guard one more night. She built a strong fire to boil two more eggs and sat in the doorway with a blanket around her, the long rifle across her lap. The rain had stopped and the moon shone bright and cold. In a few hours, she'd be on her way.

She woke in confusion as to where she was. She had dreamed of

Kerry Patch and the poor children she taught. Then she ached all over, dreading the long walk ahead. She yawned and in the moonlight made out that shadow again, just the pine tree, but then the tree moved and an arm reached toward Heaven.

She could aim at the little man and be nearly certain to miss. But suppose she hit him? She had already packed enough food for her journey. Even the thought of killing the thief was wrong, so instead she pointed the rifle toward the smokehouse. The little devil should be punished for terrorizing a defenseless woman! She'd fill him with the fear of God! The roar of the rifle kept on roaring in her ears, and she coughed from the smoke.

The figure by the smokehouse staggered out of the weeds, took two steps, and crumpled. She couldn't have hit him. Had she?

His voice was so weak she might be imagining it: "Marie. Marie."

She ran to the smokehouse and knelt by his side. "Oh," she said. "Peter, dear Peter, have I—?"

"No." His voice was a whisper, "But a fine greeting for your husband, Marie."

A witticism? From Peter? She lifted him to his feet with strength she didn't know she had, but he didn't weigh much. She walked him into the church and placed every worn-out blanket over him and built up the fire again. She tore away his worn boots and muddy socks and caressed his bony, dirty feet. He snored.

"Yes, yes, sleep," she said. "Just sleep. In the morning, I will make some chicken soup."

———————— ✦ ————————

—John Mort's most recent novel, Oklahoma Odyssey *from Bison Books, won a Will Rogers Silver Medallion in 2023. His collection of Ozarks stories,* Down Along the Piney, *won a Richard Sullivan Award and was published in 2018 by Notre Dame. His short story, "The Hog Whisperer," won a Western Writers' Spur in 2014. John is working on a new novel set in southwestern Missouri. He lives in Oklahoma.*

THE LEGEND OF JEZZEBELLE JAMES

JOHN E. RAHNE

IT WAS DECEMBER 5th, 1933. The former Ragtime Tavern which became the Easy-over Speakeasy now known as the Bootleggers Inn, was more abuzz than a honey hive of bees celebrating the summer solstice. Prohibition had ended that day and the city was bubbling with booze, debauchery, and impending hangovers. It was New Year's Eve, Mardi Gras, Independence Day, and Christmas Eve come early rolled into one big pagan festival.

The Bootleggers was jammed with celebrants, and the suds and scotch were flowing like water from a gushing countryside spring. Amid the merriment was heard the barely audible strains of "Happy Days Are Here Again".

"Three cheers for FDR," shouted one inebriant.

"Let's hear it for some real bathtub gin," said another, a mixture of spittle and Pabst or Schlitz dribbling down his chin.

An old man sauntered through the crowd, his wobbling legs aided with a cane, his head held proudly. An aged mucky slouch hat sat askance above his bushy eyebrows. Worn out boots from another time shod his feet. A scraggly gray beard matched what remained of his unkempt hair.

Magnanimously, a gentleman offered his stool as the man rested his elbows on the bar.

"Whiskey," the old man ordered as he slammed a .45, courtesy of Colonel Samuel Colt, on the bar.

"What the hell is this?" barked a harried bartender.

"What in Sam Hill does it look like? That's how we did it back in my day."

"Old timer, your day appears to be long gone. Welcome to the twentieth century." Patrons near the bar laughed. "That'll be twenty-five cents."

The elder shook his head. "Twenty-five cents. Everything's goin' up these days. Here's your two bits."

"You're right, old man. Everything is going up these days... except employment."

"Hey, pal," a drunkard called. "You ain't from the big city, are ya?"

"No siree, you bet. From South Dakota way."

"I don't mind asking how old you are?"

"You should mind, but I'm proud to be eighty-three."

The gentleman who had offered his seat squeezed the old man's shoulder. "You were around during the Wild West. I'll bet you could tell some tales."

The old timer sighed and spoke loudly to himself. "The old Wild West." His eyes glistened as they traveled back to a misty time still clear to him. "It was as wild and untamed and as free as a blazing black stallion prancing as proudly as he could atop a butte. It was bawdy and brave and as wide open as the oceans. A man could make something of himself or just as easily come to no good. I knew plenty of characters back then. From both sides of the fence. Tales, you say, why I could tell you a wagon full. Come to think, I could tell you one I'd bet a coupla 'yellow boys' none of you ever heard."

"Yellow boys, what's that?" the gentleman interrupted.

"Cash money. Goldbacks they called 'em back then. Don't print 'em no more."

The old man continued. "It's a tale of bad doin's, backstabbin' and a bit of revenge. I reckon it's time, too, before they cart my pine box up to boot hill."

"We'd like to hear it," said the gentleman to much acclaim. "Spike, get the man another whiskey, on me."

The old cowboy gulped his gift and unraveled his tale.

"Any of you all ever heard of Jezzebelle... Jezzebelle James?" No one nodded. "I didn't think so. You all know about Jesse James, yes you do. Jesse James, murderer, thief, and cutthroat, shot in the back by that coward, Bob Ford."

"Jesse was born in '47. It so happens that his mama's sister was carryin' too. They were quite close. Not much after Jesse came a'kickin' and a'screamin' into the world she birthed the most beautiful baby girl. Named her Jezzi. That's right, Jesse and Jezzi. Cousins."

"Well, a coupla years later Jezzi's mama died of the fever, and before he knew it, Jesse had hisself a 'sister'. Those two were as close as two siblings who weren't could be. Jesse, he was a rascal, that one. Now Jezzi, she was the sweetest little thing eyes ever beheld but she had that mischievous gleam in her eyes. She was the match that lit Jesse's fire."

"When those two were about seven or eight Jesse stole his grandpa's cigars, and they took to hidin' behind the old outhouse. Sure enough, just as Jess was about to take his first puff, grandpa heard the call of nature. The two stood still as a winter night until Jezzi tugged on her cousin's shirt and whispered into his ear. The next thing you know the back of that old outhouse was a cracklin' like a firecracker and just as grandpa was about to take... there's ladies in the house."

The swelling audience laughed.

"It wasn't but a few years later when the two crept into an out building grandpa forgot to lock. That's when they found the jugs of corn liquor. It only took a few swigs for Jezzi to get her stomach a'jumpin'. Jesse, ever the boy, had to prove he was tougher and all, kept on a'sippin' until he got tipsy and joined his cousin in a rousing goodbye to their breakfast."

"Neither one of 'em was much for schoolin'. Jesse was a'failin' from the beginning and there wasn't but one time when he wasn't nabbed for cheating. Jezzi, on the other hand, was sure to get good grades. She'd wave those peppermint sticks her auntie gave her as a reward right in Jesse's face. He could only hope she'd give him a lick. Not bad for a little girl who never studied her books. Hmmm!"

"By their mid-teens, the two had developed talents that would serve them well. Jesse knew how to handle a six-shooter just about better than anyone, and Jezzi had a singing voice that could make a cactus cry. Jesse was as tough and crude as a rusty nail, and Jezzi had blossomed into a beautiful yellow rose, her flowing golden hair framed the softest of cheeks and the sweetest of smiles. And those blue eyes, why they were as bright and glittering as sapphires."

"After that damned war the two left Kansas and made their way west lookin' for adventure. They found it, too, and most of it was just plain no good."

The revelry was interrupted by sirens and distant gunfire. Were people celebrating or did a gang war erupt? Were the cops on the go or the fire department?

The storyteller rubbed his brow.

"It was over a campfire when the two decided to make some easy money. And it was Jezzi's idea. That's how 'Jezzebelle James, the Wildest Woman in the Whole Wild West' was born.'

"She would ride a stage into town lookin' for a job. Jezzi would pick a suitable saloon, sing a few songs, show a bit of leg, and give the owner a wink that would make a mountain melt.

"The next thing you know she'd be a singin' and dancin' up a storm and driving the boys plum crazy. Hell, the whole town'd be there." The old timer laughed. "Even the sheriff and his deputy.

"She knew how to tease those boys. They'd be drinkin' up a hailstorm and couldn't take their eyes off her. And she'd always sing a song that went something like this—"

The old gent warbled the tune with a raspy voice that age and too many doubles had graveled.

"'Oh, you naughty boys, you saw my garter slip. Howdya like to come with me and take a l'il trip... up to my place so you can pull it up nice and tight. I'm a thankful li'l girl, you know, and I'll make you feel just right.'

"Then she'd kick up her leg and give 'em that look, and the boys would lose their minds."

The crowd hooted. "Hey, old timer, show us how she did it. We wanna lose our minds too," yelled an inebriant much to the delight of the revelers.

The old man went on.

"You see, that was the thing. While Jezzi was raisin' hell, Jesse would ride into town and give it a looksee. Next thing you know, just about every business had lost that day's proceedings.

"A day or so later Jezzi would say goodbye 'cause she was lookin' for greener pastures, you see.

"And I can tell you after they'd looted a town or ten or so, her pastures got mighty green... if you know what I mean.

"The two would divide the contributions and share a bottle, all of it courtesy of the town denizens.

"Those two had raised quite a fuss by then. Jezzi had just driven the whole town of Bon Homme crazy. It was in South Dakota." The grizzled cowboy paused. "Bon Homme. Held the dreams of every pioneer movin' west. Wild and proud. Place where anything could happen... and did. Boys, that's where I was birthed." Pensively, he stared at his boots. "The railroads never came. All that lives there now is the ghosts.

He rambled....

"Anyway, when Jezzi went to meet Jesse at some rock outcrop off the beaten path that scoundrel was no wheres to be seen. He'd run off with all the profits leaving Jezzi high and dry.

"Now, this didn't sit none too well with the lady and she set about to findin' him... on a horse. A stolen horse. Whooo... wip," the old man bellowed, "I'll tell ya but that ol' gal had plenny of spunk.

"That's when the good Lady Luck took a shine to Miss Jezzi. She pert near stumbled onto Jesse's encampment. And there he was taking a bath in a nearby pond. Jezzi, she got that smile that Ol' Scratch woulda loved. Scribbled a note and left it pinned to a saddle. Then she made off

with the saddlebag stuffed with cash. And she took something else...
all of Jesse's clothes.

"Left him high and dry. 'Cept for his boots. Man's gotta have his
boots, you know.

"You could use a new pair yourself," barked a wag while quaffing
his fourth brew.

"Wouldn't ya know it but that's when the trouble started brewin'.
Jezzi rode back to town to return the horse. So happens that Sheriff
Malcolm Blackburn was on the lookout for a horse thief and intervened.
He found the stolen loot in Jezzi's saddlebag and into the hoosegow
she went. And wouldn't you know but a fella had been arrested earlier
that day for public indecency?

"Two cousins in the same jail. Eweeee-wheee but did the cussin' fly.
They called each other names that woulda made a goldminer's mule cry.

"Jesse was released soon after. He never forgot his cousin 'cause
she refused to turn on him. He drifted and formed his own gang with
his brother, Frank. Murder would become Jesse's trademark, and he
got what he gave.

"The law wasn't so kind to Jezzi. She was sentenced to five years
in the Dakota Women's Correctional Institute. She was paroled for
good behavior after serving three years and vowed to the warden that
she'd become a nun.

"Knowin' her days of crime had ended, Jezzi took a try in Deadwood,
out Dakota way.

"Ever hear of the Dead Man's Hand?"

"That'd be Wild Bill Hickok," interrupted the gentleman.

"Sure was. Deadwood's where it happened. Instead of cashin' in his
chips, Wild Bill cashed in his life.

"Anyways, Jezzi practically begged for a job at The Saddlesore
Saloon, it was. The saloon keeper took one look and swore he'd marry
that darling. It was a marriage made by the Pearly Gates. Those two,
oh my, but were they in love. And the saloon's profits got healthier.
For three years, life couldn't have been a-better for both of them
love birds."

The old man cleared his parched throat and stared into a day long gone.

"It was a hot and dusty August day, a day when the dirt was flyin' everywhere and the flies was bitin' everybody crazy. That's when the rotgut drummer stopped by. Drummer, that's what we called 'em back then. Today the highfalutin call 'em a salesman. And rotgut is what it was."

"How was the liquor, good as it is now?" the crowd wanted to know.

"Good as? That rotgut woulda killed the whole United States Cavalry.

"A sweet talker, that's what that drummer was.

"The cowboy stared glumly at his empty shot glass.

"Next thing you know she ran off with him, never to be seen again."

The gentleman intervened. "Get this man another shot. His throat is getting mighty dry."

The old man coughed. "Thank ya kindly. My granddaddy told me to never refuse a free drink.

"So there you have it. That was the last heard of Jezzebelle James."

The bartender poured a draft. Before he could ask....

"Now you all must be wonderin' how I know so much about this story." The old man arose from his stool, harrumphed, bowed, and then proclaimed loudly, "Ladies and gentlemen, say hello to Mister Jezzebelle James."

The crowd roared.

"I owned the Saddlesore Saloon. One look at that gal made my eyes feel as sweet as honey. And that singin' voice, as soft as velvet with just the right dash of pizzazz. Made a man shiver. Took about three weeks to propose. We did the 'I do's' at the saloon. Seemed like the whole town was there. Even the minister overdid his share. My first wife died in a stagecoach accident. I thought Jezzi was my forever. I reckon it just wasn't meant to be."

The crowd grew reverentially silent.

"Ya know, I often wonder whatever happened to Jezzi. Did she find Jess and team up again? History doesn't say so. Maybe she made it to Frisco and the Barbary Coast. That was always her dream. Could be she just settled down and raised a family and became a credit to her place...

You know, I like to think she became true to her word and entered the convent. Sister Jezzebelle, yep, that's what she did."

The old timer gulped the last of his whiskey and smiled.

"Naaaahhh!"

———◦◦◦———

—John E. Rahne is a Wild West enthusiast who has had several stories published covering various topics. Retired, with a degree in Political Science, he was employed by a Fortune 500 corporation in the Research Division. He counts among his favorite novels The Outcasts of Poker Flat *and* The Octopus: A Story of California. The Virginian, Cheyenne *and* Laramie *are among his favorite western TV programs. He has viewed the John Wayne movie* El Dorado *too many times to count.*

DEADMAN'S GOLD

JAMES A. TWEEDIE

"SMOKEY" O'HALLORAN KNEW better than to wake up in the morning and put his boot on without first checking to see if a snake had curled up inside during the night.

"Darnation!" he swore as he felt the fangs of a small foot-long rattler sink into the bottom of his left foot.

Although the curse echoed back from the adjacent ridge, it is doubtful that anyone but God heard him say it unless a stray Lakota happened to have been nearby.

It was late August of 1873, and Smokey had been searching for gold high in the Black Hills of the Western Dakotas.

According to the 1868 Treaty of Fort Laramie, the whole of the Black Hills belonged to the Lakota. But after the Pike's Peak Gold Rush during the 1850s and the rush for gold in Western Montana Territory in the 1860s, men like Smokey had scattered across the American West hoping to strike a new lode as big or bigger than anything that had come before—including the '49er rush in California which, to date, had been the biggest of them all.

Since the signing of the 1868 treaty, both the Lakota, federal troops, prospectors, and settlers had taken liberties with the treaty's boundaries.

Even so, although the Lakota did not take kindly to trespassing prospectors and settlers making claims on their land, they didn't generally go out of their way to track them down except in Wyoming where Red Cloud fought to regain control of land the earlier 1851 treaty had given to the Crow.

Stray folks like Smokey didn't bother the Lakota too much. After all, the Lakota had been dealing with trappers and such since Lewis and Clark had followed the Missouri River through their territory back in 1804-05.

In any case, the way to treat a snakebite back in those days was to apply a tourniquet above the bite to contain the venom and then cut open the area of the bite and attempt to suck out as much of the venom as possible. Maybe this helped and maybe it didn't, but no one does it this way today and for good reasons that I won't go into.

Unfortunately for Smokey, even if he cut into the bite there was no way for him to suck out the venom although it's doubtful it would have made much of a difference. In any case, he felt the effects of the venom almost immediately. He was alone and there was no place to go for help. Knowing this, he decided to stay where he was and see what would come of it.

The history books tell us that Black Hills gold was discovered by an expedition led by Lt. Col. George A. Custer in 1874, one year after Smokey got bit and forty miles south of where he now sat with one boot on and one boot off. Next to Smokey was a dead rattlesnake and the smoldering remains of the small open fire whose warmth had attracted the snake to Smokey's campsite the previous night.

The venom quickly began attacking and destroying his body. There was dizziness and headache and pain, especially where his foot began to swell, and as the hours passed, the swelling turned black as the surrounding flesh began to die.

Smokey's camp was located on a high ridge above, and between, two streams that would soon take on the names Deadwood and Whitewood. As he sat, he breathed in the smell of the warming pine-scented air of the late-summer morning. Dimly in the distance, he could hear the distinctive splash of flowing water accompanied by the sound of wind whispering through the needles of surrounding trees.

He savored memories of his childhood and home in Fort Wayne, Indiana, back when he had been known by his birth name, Todd. He thought of his father, who had died young, and his mother, who had still been living when he last left home. There was also his sister, Verna, now married to a banker, and his older brother, Colin, who, like Smokey, had fought in the war and survived it.

Colin and Smokey had signed on with the 44th Indiana Infantry Regiment as soon as their Fort Wayne druggist, Hugh B. Reed, had organized it in October of 1861. Reed commanded the regiment as Colonel while Colin and Smokey served in Company "C" under their friend and neighbor, First Sergeant Caleb Carman.

In less than a month, the regiment was mustered in and over the next four years suffered four hundred casualties from battle and disease as they engaged Confederate troops at Shiloh, Perrysville, Stones River, Chickamauga, and Missionary Ridge at Chattanooga.

"What are you going to do when our hitch is up?" Colin asked Smokey shortly before they were mustered out in September of 1865.

"Don't know for sure," Smokey answered. "You're the oldest, so I suppose you'll get the farm and take care of Ma."

"It's big enough for the both of us," Colin offered. "The creek cuts it almost in half. How about I take the west side with the house and barn, and you take the east half and we work it together and share what it costs to make a living out of it?"

Now, eight years later, as the pain in his leg crept up to his knee, Smokey remembered the grasp of his brother's hand as they shook on the offer.

When the war was over, Colin helped build what Smokey dreamed would become a home for his wife and family.

As he shivered in the heat of a Dakota afternoon, he recalled the face, the voice, the warm embrace, and kiss of his childhood sweetheart, Louisa Beth.

Smokey and Louisa Beth had grown up together on neighboring

farms, their parents being two of the earliest Irish immigrant families to settle in Fort Wayne. Although neither of the children had ever spoken of it, both families assumed that young Todd and Louisa Beth would one day marry and that Colin would wed Louisa Beth's older sister, Margaret.

Soon after his new house was completed, the then twenty-four-year-old Todd O'Halloran, asked Louisa Beth's parents for permission to marry their youngest daughter.

Five days later, after church on Sunday, May 12, 1867, he walked Louisa Beth to the front porch of his new house, and, at 3:30 in the afternoon, took her hand in his, knelt on one knee, and gave a small speech he had carefully and prayerfully written out and memorized for the occasion.

"Louisa Beth," he began, "I have come to love you with a love that I swear shall never be broken except by death. Having received the blessing of both my mother and your parents, I now ask if you will be my wife. While I was away at war, there was not a day that I did not dream of the moment when I would ask you this question. Now that the war is over, I have built this house to be a home for you and the children we shall, by the grace of God, bring up together in this place. And so, I ask with all my heart and soul, Louisa Beth, will you marry me?"

To his relief, she answered with a smile and a "Yes" that lit up his world more brightly than the sun.

Adding to his delight, she then pulled him to his feet and wrapped her arms around him in an embrace, accompanied by a kiss that thrilled his body with anticipation of the joy they would share on the night of their wedding.

For Smokey, sitting painfully on a fallen tree in the Black Hills, the happy diversion provided by these sweet memories vanished in an instant as he recalled how the love of his life fell ill and died of typhoid fever two weeks before they were to be married.

Louisa Beth's death left him devastated and depressed, and two weeks after her funeral, Todd formally gave his house and property to his brother and left Fort Wayne to work through his grief in what he imagined to be the endless expanse of the Western wilderness.

While attempting to homestead on the Nebraska prairie, he acquired the name "Smokey" after his sod house burned to the ground for the second time. After five years, his right to the land was forfeited when it was determined he had not sufficiently improved it.

Homeless once again, he wandered up the Platte into Wyoming where he heard tales of the gold that had brought so many people to Colorado, Montana, and Wyoming in the 1850s and 60s.

Hearing rumors that Lakota warrior, Crazy Horse, was distracted by personal conflicts in Montana and that Sitting Bull was fighting surveyors laying a route for the Northern Pacific Railroad, Smokey decided to take the risk of looking for gold on Indian land where he had no right to be. A decision that led to his being snakebit on a high, lonely ridge in the forbidden, unsettled wilderness of the Black Hills.

That evening, and with great difficulty, Smokey crawled across his campsite, got his fire going again and lay as close to it as he could so as to fight off the cold chills that caused his body to writhe and tremble uncontrollably.

Lighting the fire turned out to be the last thing that Smokey did in this life, for as he slept, he passed away from this world and was reunited with Louisa Beth in death.

Over the next three years, as his bones were picked clean and scattered by wolves, bears, coyotes, and high-circling buzzards, prospectors swarmed north through the Hills and found traces of gold in nearly every creek they panned.

By late spring of 1876, claims had been made along nearly the entire length of both Deadwood and Whitewood creeks where placer gold was found in abundance. Soon the towns of Deadwood and Lead sprang up to accommodate and supply the thousands of men who came to claim their slice of the gold-nugget pie.

Four miners, Fred and Moses Manuel, joined by Hank Harney and Alex Engh, left the placer works behind and began searching for the mother lode itself.

On April 9, 1876, on a high rise between the headwaters of Deadwood and Whitewood Creeks, they found the remains of a man scattered around what had once been a stone-lined campfire. Out of respect, they gathered the bones and buried them in a shallow, unmarked grave. Among the few personal items they found was a large, weather-worn leather pouch filled with enough raw, unprocessed gold ore for a man to live like a king for the rest of his life.

The men spread out and quickly found the source, not only of Smokey's gold, but the source of the gold that had been washed down from the hills.

They called their new claim "Homestake," and it wasn't long before the entire ridge and surrounding area had been leveled and, in the years that followed, reduced to a vast hole in the ground with shafts dug to a depth of over 8,000 feet.

By the time the mine closed in the year 2002, nearly 44,000,000 ounces of gold had been extracted which, at the price of gold in 2021, would have been worth over $77 billion.

There is, of course, no historical record of Smokey O'Halloran for he is a fiction.

Even so, his character represents thousands of other mountain men, prospectors, and early settlers who lived, died, and disappeared from mind and memory as if they had never been.

In Smokey's case, his bones, which were prayerfully laid to rest by those who found them, were subsequently unceremoniously exhumed and tossed aside in the frenzied attempt to extract as much gold as quickly as possible from a lode which, had it not been for a small snake hidden in his boot, might well have made a man like Smokey O'Halloran one of the wealthiest and most famous figures to come out of the Old West.

—James A. Tweedie has lived in California, Utah, Scotland, Australia, Hawaii, and presently in Long Beach, Washington. He has published six novels, four collections of poetry, and one collection of short stories with Dunecrest Press. His award-winning stories and poetry have appeared in regional, national,

and international print and online anthologies. He is a regular contributor to Frontier Tales and Saddlebag Dispatches.

He recalls moving from San Francisco to Logan, Utah, in 1979 and being both baffled and amused when he was asked, "What made you decide to move out West from California?"

In that moment, he learned that "the West" was not just a direction, but a cultural space infused with traditions and tales embracing a heritage of mountain men, pioneers, Native Peoples, cowboys, homesteaders, prospectors, ranchers, railroads, and a host of conflicts that stretched and expanded the United States into the country it is today.

His favorite corner of the West is the Sierra Nevada, where he has hiked and fly fished since he was old enough to walk.

Hard Winter by W.H.D. Koerner

MY LUCKY DAY

DERRYL YORK

THE SPADE SOUNDED gritty as it sliced through the sandy, dry loam, and the wind blew away the finer grit as she pulled the shovel out of the ground. A second grave and now she was alone. No husband and no baby. Who knows what kills people out on this godforsaken prairie. Living in a sod house, trying to make a crop of some kind, somehow. Impossible in a dry year. She added a few rocks to the top of the small grave and stood up. Her husband, Robert Murphy, had caught a cold and after a few days just couldn't breathe. His last breath was during the night three weeks ago. The baby was fine but had a runny nose a week later. One morning, he too was cold and blue. And she was alone.

She turned from the graves, looked around at the horizon, then at the sod house and canvas flapping door. You couldn't have much less, she thought. Barely enough food for a week, a skinny cow that gave a little milk, and a well that you could dry up if you pulled too much water. She wondered what her options were.

She walked to the house without a tear or a feeling of sadness. Numbness is what she felt, numbness without any feelings at all. Completely exhausted. She pulled away the canvas drape and stooped inside. She poured some water into a pan, threw in some coffee, and set it on the warm coals. She stoked the fire and added some kindling and a log. A cup of coffee and a long morning conference with herself awaited.

As the pan warmed, she noticed the picture of Robert on a shelf. He was a fine-looking man, but without a doubt, life had beat him down. She picked up his small derringer that lay by the picture, a two-shooter, if it would fire at all. Certainly, could do no good with it in this empty, wild world. She turned to see the pan boiling and tucked the gun in her apron pocket. Need to keep the dust away as much as possible. She poured coffee, added some milk, and thought sugar would be nice if there was any.

Sitting outside on a small boulder, she noticed a dust devil out toward the mountains to the east. They come and go, like ghosts in the night. It was a fine morning with no clouds and a gentle breeze. The sun was not yet too high, and the temperature was tolerable. You could close your eyes and be in a fine, fancy hotel back east. It was hard to remember those days. She was never a pretty woman, but out here it didn't take much to attract men. Her husband was one man she liked, and they had agreed to try to make a go of it on this wild prairie. It just hadn't worked out.

She rested again and thought, I'll have to do something soon. Maybe head to San Antone. There might be some possibilities. Maybe catch a wagon train, but the odds were long. She looked up and noticed the dust devil was still swirling, but it looked more like a dust cloud now than a typical dust devil.

It looked like maybe some riders. Maybe a chance to get out of here. She went inside, picked up her hat, and walked out the door. She waited and watched as two riders approached, slowly and methodically, they came toward the dugout. Eventually, they pulled up.

"We noticed the smoke from back out," the skinny one said. He had a hard, worn-out look, but couldn't have been over thirty. The second rider was older, more weathered and tanned. "We figured there might be some folks in the area, and we might get some water," he wheezed. He seemed out of breath as if he'd been running.

She looked at them both, squinted, and pointed to the well. "Not much water here, but probably get enough for the horses." They dismounted, and the older one said, "Your man around?"

"Yes." And she pointed to the two graves. "Till three weeks ago."

The riders dismounted and the younger one led the horses to a wooden trough. Then headed toward the well to fetch the water. "I'm Josiah, Josh for short. We've been working on a ranch in Oklahoma Territory but thought we might do a bit better down in Texas."

"Lovie," she replied.

"You got any grub?"

"Just biscuits, coffee, and some beans. It's not much, but I can fix some up."

"Well, we got a little bacon. Let me git that for ya' and we can share?"

She nodded and headed for the door.

Inside, she stoked the fire not thinking about the men or the food, just the deep tiredness she felt. She got out a pot, poured in some water, and threw in the beans. She mixed the flour and water, rolled out some biscuits, and placed them in the skillet. Josh pulled back the canvas door cover and stepped in, placing the bacon on the table. They looked at each other and said nothing. She put a cup on the table and poured in some coffee then turned back to the stove.

After some time, the biscuits were done so she dumped them out and started cutting slabs of bacon. As she lay them in the skillet, the grease popped, and the smell of biscuits, bacon, and coffee filled the hut. It made her think of mornings past when she and her husband sat at the table and enjoyed the quietness together.

Josh stepped outside with his coffee cup and began to talk to the other man. She could not hear what they were saying, but they seemed pleasant enough. In a few moments, the food was ready, and she called out to them. They entered, sat, and began to fill their plate with beans, bacon, and biscuits.

"Sure beats livin' on the road," said the younger one. They ate in silence.

After the meal, she got up, gathered the utensils together, and walked outside laying them in a nearby wash tub. She went back into the hut and started straightening the stove and table. No one said anything, but the younger man, still sitting at the table, said, "I ain't seen a woman in six weeks." In seconds, he had his hands around her, holding onto her breasts.

She stiffened. "There are some things I just don't do."

He grabbed her by the shoulders, spun her around, and grabbed her blouse collar up high around the neck. "You don't have to do nuthin'," he said and pulled her toward the bed.

She was still numb and didn't resist. He threw her on the bed and proceeded to have his way.

He smelled of tobacco, sweat, horses, bacon, and beans. His beard was coarse. She lay still and never looked at him. Slowly, he pushed himself up off the bed and looked at her. "Well, you might say it's my lucky...."

There was a pop and blood gushed from his left eye. He was stunned, staggered back against the wall, caught himself, and tried to figure out what had happened. Finally, he noticed a wisp of smoke rising from her skirt. "You shot me?"

"You weren't no good," she said in a monotone—almost a whisper.

He stood there holding his eye. His other eye seemed to wander, to lose focus, and he collapsed on the bed between her outspread legs.

"Owen? You 'bout through? You better not hurt that woman."

She heard the yelling, reached over and pulled the man's pistol out of the holster and put it under her raised shirt.

The older man stepped in the dark entryway and could see nothing. His eyes could not adjust from the bright sunlight to the dark. In a moment, he stepped to the curtain and pulled it back. He was not sure what he was looking at. His partner was face down on the bed, moaning. His pants were down, and his butt was shining. The woman was lying still on the bed half naked. He stepped in and said, "Owen, what are you doing?" The hem of the skirt began to rise like a small curtain, then a deafening roar. A blow threw him back against the wall, and the breath was knocked out of him. He tried to get his breath, but there was blood all over his shirt. He looked at the woman, then at Owen, down at his chest, and back at the woman. Sliding down the wall, he tried to understand what he was seeing and toppled to one side.

The younger man continued to moan.

Finally, Lovie swung her leg over the body and moved to the side of the bed and sat, head in her hands. She just felt release. After some time, she stood up, walked back to the stove, poured more coffee, and went outside and sat down on the bench. It was barely noon, but there was a smidgen of shade on the bench. She just sat, not thinking, not feeling, just sitting.

She woke up in the late afternoon, walked over to the horses, pulled off the saddles, and led them to the corral. She filled the trough with a little water. She walked back to the pile of saddles, removed one bed roll, and laid it out by the front door. The sun was setting, and it was cooling off. She dozed again before waking up and seeing the starry sky in all its brightness.

The sun's warmth woke her up. She was exhausted, numb, and stiff from the hard ground. But it would be a busy day. First things first. She got a shovel and moved to where her family's graves were. She had no feelings about where folks were going to be buried. She went inside the house, tied a rope around the older man, and then proceeded to drag him out to the grave area. She did the same with the younger one not bothering to redress him. At the gravesite, she stripped both men of everything and started to dig. No sense in a deep grave as she would not be around to see to it.

She proceeded to gather all the men's clothes and wash them as best she could. The bullet holes and blood would not all come out. Looking through the possessions she found a little food, thirteen silver dollars, and seventy-five dollars in Confederate script. After changing clothes herself, she packed all the remaining clothes in two cloth sacks along with one of the pistols. She looped the second holster and pistol over her shoulder around her chest and wore it like a bandolier. She was not a good shot, but maybe she would not have to use it.

Finally, she led the horses from the corral, saddled them, slung the bed rolls and sacks on one, and mounted the other. She took one of the coins she had found and looked at it. "Heads it's San Antone, tails it's St. Louis. Maybe it's my lucky day."

—*Derryl York is a writer who lives in Houston, Texas. He holds a degree in Chemical Engineering from the University of Maryland and spent a long and illustrious career in the international oil business. After retirement he was a high school science teacher, a Habitat for Humanity volunteer, and a "go to" guy for his granddaughters. He has published a few technical articles, but never any non-fiction. He's a golfer, hiker, and swimmer in his off time.*

CANVAS SKY

BENJAMIN THOMAS

1848

THAT DAMNED FLY.

Bouncing off the stretched canvas again and again. Trapped, or so it thinks. Angry buzzing. Not smart enough to try a different route of escape. Just bounce, bounce, bounce, stop and rest for a spell then bounce again. And all the time, buzzing. Annoying as all get out. Although now that he thought about it, James could admit that it did provide something to stare at. Something besides the dirty gray canvas that formed the roof of the wagon. Just frustrating that the fly refused to try any other direction.

Mayhap, a metaphor for his own life. Always headed in the same direction no matter how many times he failed.

And now he was dying.

Stubborn damned fly couldn't leave a man in peace. He continued to stare at it. Nothing much else to do. Lying helpless, flat on his back, didn't leave him many options for entertainment. Anything to take his mind off the earthy stink of the wagon's canvas cover and the monotony of the never-ending trail. He heard a groan and realized it had come from deep within his own chest as the wagon rolled over a particularly large stone or a clump of grass or maybe it was a wide rut or something. Made no matter. When a man lay gut-shot and feverish, any jolt in the wagon was bound to irritate.

After another ten minutes or so of incessant jolts and lurches, he heard the shout of the wagon master calling for a halt. Thank God. A respite from the jostling, no matter how short the break, was welcome indeed. He wondered though, why the halt? Too early to stop for the day, unless he had passed out and it was now later than he'd thought. Hard to tell where the sun lay when they kept creeping in and out of the steep mountain passes of the Sangre de Christos. Must be an obstacle of some kind. No way they'd stop any sooner than necessary. Not after yesterday's massacre in Manco Burro Pass.

Yesterday? Or was it the day before?

Sounds of horses nickering and snorting mixed with orders shouted from the wagon master, Lucien Maxwell. His voice was calm, reassuring as it had been even back in the Pass, a fact that had probably saved some of their lives. Several minutes later, James heard the canvas flaps part at the rear of the wagon, a welcome puff of cool air caressing his scarred cheeks. He tried to look down the length of his body to take a gander at his visitor, but he couldn't bend his neck. That was new.

Soft, whispering footsteps neared him. Not boots. Moccasins. Indian George, then.

"Checking on you." A man of few words was Indian George. Formerly the devoted servant of Charles Bent until the former New Mexico Territorial Governor's death in 1847, the Cherokee had transferred his allegiance to fur trapper and guide, Lucien Maxwell.

"I'm just dandy," James said. "Be up and at 'em shortly." A grunt was the only reply. The Cherokee moved up closer so James could see him clearly. The ruddy, lined face was blank, but the eyes were deep pools of oily blackness. Clearly, he would not reply further so James asked, "How's Maxwell doing anyhow? He caught an arrowhead or two, I know. Heard how you packed him on your back and carted him all the way out of the Pass. That's a good many miles."

The attempt at flattery seemed to have fallen on deaf ears. Indian George just gazed at him for a minute or two, those dark eyes looking deep into him. Delving into his future probably. Finally, he said, "He will be good. He is not good now. You, also, are not good now."

"Sounds like you think I won't be good later, either."

Another grunt, and then, just as swiftly as he had appeared, Indian George backed out of the wagon leaving James alone with his thoughts once again.

AN ETERNITY PASSED but was probably more like half an hour. The canvas flaps parted once more. Had the Indian come back? Scuffling sounds came to his ears with that eerie sort of echo that always happened inside the wagon when it was covered. His visitor, evidently, was crawling over some supplies in the wagon. A bang and a whispered curse were the next things he heard and then a face entered his range of vision. It was a pretty young woman's face this time, light brown hair tucked behind one ear, and a smile as big as Georgia. A crooked tooth at the top left just added to her charms.

Luisa.

"Hi, darlin'," she said. Her voice was sweet as molasses and completely unconcerned. Seemed like he hadn't seen her in a coon's age. He tried returning her smile but realized it was more like a grimace.

"Hi, yerself."

"How're you? Getting to lollygag back here in comfort instead of putting more miles on that old nag of yours." The gentle tones of her accent reminded him of his Mississippi home.

He knew what she was doing, of course. Taking his mind off things. Teasing him, like usual. He let his eyes roam across her features—sharp cheekbones, dimpled chin, light freckles across her little pointy nose. The crooked tooth. And those eyes. He could fall in and drown in those emerald-green eyes.

She was waiting for his answer, so he tossed out a throwaway line about enjoying the view from under the canvas sky. But he couldn't just carry on like all was right with the world. He let his smile drop and then murmured, "I ain't gonna make it, honey. Not with this kind of belly shot."

"Oh, pshaw." She moved his blanket aside and tugged at the cloth that wrapped around his thick torso as if examining his wound. He heard a soft crackle and realized it was dried blood on the cloth splitting as she moved it. "Well, this don't look so bad," she said. He could tell she was lying.

A few more minutes passed while she took her look-see and then wrapped him up again. Then her face came back into view as she said, "You've been in worse shape before. Remember back when we met? Now that right there was some serious wounds."

"Yep. It was May, wasn't it? About seven years ago? On the Trace."

"Natchez, yes. But it was eight years ago. And it was May the 8th, 1840, to be exact. The day after the big tornado."

"The Great Natchez Tornado. That's what they call it now." He smiled at the thought of such a moniker, but then he sobered at the remembrance. Over 300 folks were counted among the dead and another 200 injured.

"Worst tornado in our country's history. So far, anyway."

"Yes, well... what I remember most is the pretty young gal that nursed me back to health." He was pleased to see the blush rise in her cheeks.

"Some nurse. All I did was clean you up and slap bandages across all your holes."

"Not all of 'em." He started to laugh, but his belly cut that off in a hurry. She made as if to slap him, but her heart wasn't in it.

"You had so many sticks comin' out of you, I thought I was working on a porcupine. That wind turned tree branches into arrows."

"Good thing there weren't no fence posts. Would have been hard bandaging over that kinda hole."

She shook her head slowly, back and forth, remembering. His thoughts too returned to that hellish day in May. On the night before the monster slammed into town, lightning had ripped through heavy clouds dumping more than three inches of rain throughout the area. Vidalia was his home, just a small town on the river. It's only claim to fame was the Jim Bowie sandbar fight thirteen years earlier—already a legend. But then the twister came. Nobody prepared. Nobody expecting anything more than a thunderstorm.

"I remember you were among the first to see what was coming," she said. "Least ways that's what you boasted of later."

"It's true. I'd been on the river, working a flatboat when I realized it was more than just a thunderstorm. Most folks were eating, the dinner bells having rung earlier, and I'd hoped they would have had the sense to stay indoors."

It had come from the southwest, following the river and crashing over fields and forests. The noise came first, a murderous riot of massive trees being uprooted, huge timbers cracking and splitting. James remembered moving toward the nearby riverbank, but no sooner had he reached it than the roar of the beast came upon him. He had run for a hill, dived over it, and looked back. His eyes tried to take in the width of the thing, touching both sides of the shore as it did, but his brain couldn't register its massiveness. He had seen other men nearby screaming, but he couldn't hear them over the cacophony of the tornado. Something had whacked him over the head, bringing him blessed relief from the oncoming tempest and plunging him into darkness.

He had awoken in a bed, a single lamp illuminating the dark interior of a house. A soft sheet covered him and for a few minutes, that's all he could concentrate on. The caress of the sheet and the soft glow from the lamp. It wasn't his own house, that much he knew, but there was nobody else around so might as well lay there and enjoy it.

A face had appeared above him, a girl's face, pretty and framed by light brown hair and featuring a delicate dimpled chin. The lips were frowning in concern and the pretty green eyes reflected the same. He tried to speak to her but discovered he couldn't open his mouth. She had shushed him, ordering him to keep quiet. She went on to describe his injuries, including a broken arm, several cracked ribs, and assorted scrapes, cuts, and bruises. But the look in her eyes told him there was more. Something she hadn't the heart to tell him. Why couldn't he speak? Or even open his mouth? He remembered lowering his eyelids and staring at her hard, attempting to communicate to her that he wanted to know the rest. Finally, she relented.

It was a tree branch. A good sized one, maybe an inch thick. It had speared him through his jaw, entering from below, missing his lower teeth and then exiting through the cheek just above his mouth. His upper front teeth were gone, and his tongue frayed. She'd had hopes that he would eventually heal, if the infection didn't take him, but he would be scarred for life. And it would be weeks before he could take solid food.

As the weeks had passed, James had grown stronger. The feared infection never materialized, but the torn muscles in his face had meant having to learn how to talk all over again. He had gone through periods of deep depression, wondering if it mattered whether he lived or died. Through it all, she was there, nursing him through the pain and urging him past his reluctance to go on living. Her name was Luisa.

And they fell in love.

He looked at her now, sensing the similarities with the day they'd met. Him lying flat on his back with a dreadful injury and her leaning over him ready to nurse him back to health through prodding, urging, arguing, joking, and storytelling to distract him from the pain.

"Penny for your thoughts," Luisa said, her voice soft as a kitten's purr but still managing to penetrate his memories. "What's that you're smiling about?"

"Ahhh... you know." He let his smile grow a little wider. "How you could come to love a feller with a mug like I got. Truly a blessing."

"Your mug, as you call it, don't look half bad, you know. Once your beard grew in, nobody could see the scars on your jaw."

"They're still there though. Gotta large area that won't grow nothing, so I've got to comb it over and kinda blend it into the other parts." His smile turned to a smirk. "And no mustache at all. If I tried, I'd end up with half a lip full of hair and nary a whisker on the other half."

"Well, that would be... different." Another smile but it was more on her lips and not so much in her eyes. And that too melted away, turning to sorrow.

He reached out and cupped her chin with one calloused hand. "My little angel of mercy."

There was silence between them for a minute or two, and then Luisa took his big hand in her two little ones. "Tell me, sweetie. How do you keep yourself entertained while you're lollygagging back here in the wagon?"

"There's that lollygagging accusation again. I swear, I shoulda gotten gut shot days ago so's I could enjoy all the entertainment available to me back here under this stinky canvas. What with the bouncing and the creaking, I've just been riding along as peaceable as if I was swayin' in our porch swing back home." He realized his tone was beginning to show some irritation and he felt bad. She was just trying to keep his mind off his trouble. "Well, there was one funny thing that happened this morning." He chuckled, gently as he could to keep the pain in check.

"Oh?"

"Yeah, it was a bird situation. With Lee."

"A... bird situation?"

"Yeah, you know... a bird flew over and... dropped a load. Right on Lee's forehead. Big white splotch. You know how his hair's receded so far back and how he's kinda sensitive about it? Well, he'd just taken his hat off and was stooping down to look in the back of the wagon. Checking on me I suppose. Folks do that now and again. Anyway, there he was just peering in at me and... splat!"

Luisa laughed, rocking back and forth on her knees, eyes twinkling with delight. "A big target, was it? That forehead of his?" she said, almost snorting out her nose. It was infectious and James started to join in. But his insides shouted at him to stop, agony streaming up through his chest and into the back of his neck. Like a white-hot branding iron pressing into him. It left him breathless and light-headed.

Luisa, bless her heart, waited patiently, still gripping his hand with the both of hers. She made soft shushing noises as he struggled to find a point of equilibrium. More silence. But eventually, as if nothing had happened, she once again tried to take his mind off the pain. "Tell me about the time you first met Lee," she said. "When was it? And where? I don't believe I've ever heard tell of it."

"Oh, you remember, surely. Well... I guess maybe you wouldn't. Let's see, what can I tell you...." As he pondered how to start the story, a slight tickle in his throat threatened a coming cough. He fought it off, waging war against the very idea of an actual cough and the inevitable result.

Managing a deep swallow to clear his throat and satisfy the tickle, he said, "I guess everything changed there at Bent's Fort. We'd come all the way from St. Louis, you know, picking up the Santa Fe Trail there in Independence. Trying for that new start we'd always talked about after the tornado. You remember how it was. Tried farming here and store clerking there, working our way up the Mississippi until we finally landed in St. Louis. But I have to say, that didn't work out so well either, did it. So, then we heard about that treaty. You know, the one from the Mexican War. Guadalupe-Hidalgo or some such name they gave it. Anyways, the government wanted all that new land populated. Didn't want the Mexicans to ever lay claim to it again. So, we set out for the territories hoping for opportunities. Always headed in the same direction but never learning a thing from our mistakes."

Another pause. Gotta fight that tickle a little longer, he thought. At least until he could finish telling her the story.

"Anyway, the regular Cimarron cutoff route to Santa Fe was proving to be a problem for other wagon trains due to the Indian troubles, so Lucien decided we'd head to the Fort to get some ideas on different ways to get ourselves down to New Mexico. We picked up Lee there. Elliot Lee. He was always particular about making sure you knew his name was Elliot, but we all just call him Lee."

Luisa nodded, encouraging him to continue talking.

"We also picked up the young 'uns there at the Fort. Mary and James Tharp. Pretty young they are, about six and four, I think. Their pa was a trader but was killed by Comanche some time ago. We promised to take 'em to Fort Union where they had an uncle waiting for 'em."

"An admirable notion."

"Well, it's just a bit north of Las Vegas so it was pretty much on our route anyways. So, we set out from Bent's on the sixteenth of June. I remember that because it was the day after my birthday. And it was a gloomy, cloudy morn. Made me wish we'd waited a day longer. Lookin' back, I wish we had."

A strange something was bubbling up from his stomach. Sort of like syrup except it tasted like an old horseshoe. Swallowing again, he tried to ignore it. "Fourteen folks and our horses, wagons, and of course the two little Tharp children. We headed straight up the Santa Fe trail, looking toward Raton Pass. See, that's still the preferred route if you skip the Cimmaron cutoff. But when we got down to the Purgatory River, we saw some Apache signs. Mister Town... well he had told us of another way, just a little east of Raton, through the Manco Burro Pass. 'A perfectly easy route,' he called it. Better than the Raton route, anyway, as Colonel Kearny proved when he and his Army of the West came through in the summer of '46. Remember that? Uh... never mind. They left parts of wagons scattered all along the Raton passage. So, Lucien made the call, and Manco Burro was the way we went."

Luisa was staring at him, lips tight, and eyes like pools of rain ready to spill over.

James had to clear his throat again, but now the iron taste had turned to something more like vinegar. "At noon on the nineteenth, we reached the little valley up top at the pass. Lucien called a halt for the wagons so we could eat our lunch and let the horses graze a little ways away. Most of the grass in that area was dry as old hay but there was this one patch. Beautiful green grass it was. Young growth. Healthy looking, you know?

"Yes, I know just what you mean. Sweet grass, we used to call it back home."

"That's right." He smiled up at her and saw the edges of her face were a little blurry. The tears in his eyes, still unshed, made him blink rapidly for a second and then her face was back as it should be. "And then... then it was that we heard 'em. Jicarilla Apaches, they was. Thousands of 'em. Least ways it seemed like that."

"Oh, James. Don't tell me no more. Not if it strains you so."

"No. I need to tell it. So's you know what happened. Let me tell it. It's important somehow. Please."

She was still for a moment, looking solid as a statue, brows worried together. Then she nodded.

"At first, we just heard their yellin' and whoopin'. Then we saw they was trying to run off our horses. As they passed us by, we fired on 'em, but they was so far off that it weren't effective. Then after a few minutes they came back. Surrounded our little camp. Set fire to the grass. The dry grass anyways. But we kept our position. Held 'em off like King Arthur and his knights. Heh. Now there's an image for you. We needed to keep the wagons safe, the baggage, you see. Couldn't make it much further without the baggage. We fired at everything we could, but we were outnumbered. By a whole lot. We lasted a good long while though. Three or four hours, judging by the sun. By then five of us was wounded and old Joe was killed dead." He lifted an arm and shakily pointed at the canteen that lay nearby. "Some water please. My throat."

"Of course," Luisa said. She opened the canteen and trickled some water into his open mouth. It took some effort to swallow it, but he felt better.

"Anyhow, we couldn't hold out forever, so we tried to hightail it to the mountains. We couldn't take much with us, but Indian George had gotten a couple of horses hitched up to a wagon by then. This wagon here as a matter of fact. Not much in the way of supplies but we got some stashed in here as we lit out. Mister Town was behind us all when I heard him cry out. Shot in the leg and couldn't walk no further. Couldn't get himself up to where the wagon was neither, so he got left behind. A Spaniard was also shot through the kidneys and fell by the wayside. Feel bad that I don't know his name, now I think on it. Lee took one in the thigh but could still amble along. I had turned to help him and that's when I got mine. Smack in the middle of my belly. Didn't seem too bad at first. Lots of blood but I was able to get on for a while. That left eleven of us, counting the two children. Eight of us wounded. Lucien and Indian George stayed behind to draw their fire. Later I found out Lucien caught a couple of arrows, but Indian George carted him out on his back. Pretty amazing when you think about it." He paused a moment and then added, "But still, we managed to escape."

He had to stop again, his chest heaving up and down as he tried to keep enough breath to finish the story. He wasn't certain he'd make it, but he knew deep down inside it was important that he did.

"Night came on. We traveled along until we come to water. We all huddled together, trying to rest and maybe get some sleep. I don't remember doing it, but I blacked out. Woke up here in the wagon. Somebody had taken my shirt off and used it to wrap up my gut like it is now. Holding me together, mostly. Anyways, it was still night, and we were moving on through the mountains. Lucien was afraid to travel in the day, see, and wanted to make sure we was far away from the Jicarilla. That was night before last. I think. I've not been out of this damned wagon since."

Luisa had taken a bit of her shawl, dribbled some canteen water on it and was busy wiping down his forehead. The familiar worry lines between her brows were as deep as he'd ever seen. She seemed distracted somewhat, not certain his story was done. But then her eyes darted to his, softened, and she said, "And now you're headed to Fort Union, I suppose."

"Yep. Heard Lucien tell somebody he thought it was near ninety miles away still. Maybe we can get patched up there."

She wiped his brow some more, content to let the comfortable silence linger a while. He'd always enjoyed watching her and relished the opportunity to do it some more now. His thoughts traveled back through time, back once more to when they met after the tornado in Mississippi, their courting after he had recovered from his wounds, the wedding on the little pier jutting out into a calm bend in the river, the jokes their friends had played on them during the so-called honeymoon. All of it was crystal clear in his memory. But her face, as he looked at her now, was blurry. His own tears getting in the way.

No, he thought. It wasn't his tears. Something else. Just a little bit more time. Just a little bit longer to spend with her. Don't let it all fade away now.

The coolness of the damp cloth on his forehead soothed him, relaxed him.

Her voice whispered to him, soft as a light breeze among the trees, "Don't fret, my darling. We will be together again, very soon. And this time, we will never part."

He tried to see her, but all he could make out was that damned fly, bumping and buzzing up against the canvas.

LUCIEN MAXWELL HAD called for wagons ready almost fifteen minutes previously and was now growing frustrated that they hadn't yet departed. Breaktime was over. They should have been on the trail by now. There was only one wagon left after all. Where was that Indian George? He would get 'em moving.

He turned and to his chagrin, saw Indian George standing right behind him. His face was as impassive as always but there was something around his eyes. Something that told Lucien not all was well.

"What is it?" Lucien said. "What's happened?"

"James." Indian George shook his head sadly. "We've lost another one."

Lucien bowed his head. It had been inevitable with such a wound, but the man had lasted much longer than he'd expected, and he had held out some hope.

"Funny thing, though," said Indian George. "I overheard him talking. From the wagon. He was telling the story of our recent experiences with the Jicarilla."

"Telling it to... who?"

"His wife."

"His wife? Luisa?" The wagon master reached a hand to his jaw to scratch at his beard but stopped it halfway up. "But Luisa died three years ago. Cholera, I think it was."

Indian George nodded, his face just as stoic as always. But then a slight smile broke through. "Sometimes we need help to make the final journey. It is, perhaps, for the best. They are together now."

—Benjamin Thomas is a retired US Air Force Medical Service Corps officer and former National Organ Transplant program officer for Veteran's Affairs. He has authored numerous short stories in a variety of genres as well as a time travel novel and a historical whodunnit. Published works can be found in western anthologies published by Western Fictioneers and Saddlebag Dispatches, as well as in Wyrd Werewolf Wrangler and Onwards Adventure anthologies. Additionally, he is the author of the interconnected "Leland and Charlie" stories featuring a grandfather/granddaughter duo as they travel through Colorado in the 1850s collecting bounties by outconning the conmen. A native of New Mexico, Benjamin has always been a "westerner" at heart, currently enjoying life with his family in Colorado Springs at the foot of Pikes Peak.

Beef for the Fighters by Charles Marion Russell

LEAVING DEADWOOD BEHIND

BRUCE HARTMAN

IT STARTED ONE night after they'd brought the heifers into the barn. Of the three cowhands—all good friends—Jake was the youngest, just turned twenty. He was restless, impatient, and quick with his hands and his tongue, though not a boaster like Billy or a diplomat like Ned. With a mischievous grin, Billy reached into an empty stall and pulled out a whiskey bottle. He gulped down a mouthful, shared the bottle with Ned, and then offered it to Jake. "Care for a swig?"

"No," Jake said, waving it away.

"What's this?" Billy said. "You won't drink with us?"

"Thanks, but no."

If they'd been in a saloon, Billy probably would have stepped up close and asked Jake if he was too good to drink with him. That's the kind of cowboy Billy was. Quick to take offense and spoiling for a fight. The three of them worked together all day, and they had to get along. Jake and Ned had grown up together in Deadwood where they still lived with their families. Billy had come to the valley six months before and slept in the bunkhouse at the ranch. When he went to town, he usually got in a fight.

"I just don't feel like drinking right now," Jake said. That was all the explaining he thought he needed to do.

"No, I reckon the way you were brought up, whiskey must be like mother's milk to you."

"Something like that."

Jake saddled his horse and rode the three miles into Deadwood with Ned. The stars were just peeping out, cold and curious in a clear gray sky. The empty landscape suited his temperament. Though he'd never lived anywhere else, he often felt that he was not of this time and place.

"I don't know why you let him talk to you that way," Ned said. "He's got no business talking about the way you were brought up."

"He knows nothing about how I was brought up."

Jake's father, Delmore Haggard, was something of a local celebrity. He'd been a bank robber and gunfighter back in the early days, served ten years in a penitentiary and came out lame from a jailhouse brawl. Jake was five years old when his father went inside, fifteen when he came out. He and his father had never been close. Haggard's years in prison had left him hollowed out. Men came to Deadwood just to get a glimpse of him, imagining the fame they could earn by killing him in a gunfight. He seldom left their ramshackle house and avoided people's eyes when he went out.

On Saturday night, Billy rode into town with Jake and Ned to attend a dance sponsored by some church ladies who'd taken it on themselves to civilize the local miners and cowhands. It was a cloudy, moonless night with a damp wind sighing over the Black Hills. Billy brought his whiskey and shared it with Ned, and the two of them were drunk before they reached the dance. A small orchestra of banjos, guitars, and fiddles played polkas and waltzes and cowboy songs that everybody knew. Jake danced with a cute brunette named Isabel who worked in her father's eating house. All the men liked her, but Jake was the one she wanted to dance with.

"It's just like him to keep her all to himself," Billy complained to Ned.

"Why don't you go over there and cut in?" Ned suggested.

"Cut in? You can do that?"

"Sure you can. She has to dance with you if you cut in."

Billy stumbled across the room and cut in to the dance the same way he cut cattle from a herd, sidling in and pushing the dancers apart. "What the hell do you think you're doing?" Jake demanded.

"I'm cutting in," Billy said and then put his hand on Isabel's shoulder. "May I?"

Jake pushed them apart. "Go sit down. You're drunk."

"It's up to her whether to dance with me."

"No, it ain't. It's up to me, and I said go sit down."

Isabel laughed at both of them. "Don't take it so seriously," she told Jake after Billy retreated. "It was just Billy being Billy."

"Go dance with him if you want to."

"I don't need you to tell me who to dance with."

She marched back to her seat, but she never danced with Billy that night. The next time anybody looked for him he was gone.

Jake stayed angry all day Sunday, sulking around the house where he lived with his parents. In the afternoon, Ned came over and they walked through the rain to shoot rats at the town dump. "You shouldn't put up with that kind of disrespect from Billy," Ned said. "Your father wouldn't have let somebody insult him like that."

"How do you know what my father would have done?"

"He would have fought him. He would have stuck to the code of the west."

"The code of the west? Where'd you learn to talk like that?"

Ned blushed like a bride. He was an idealist. He believed in the authority of certain conventions that were so compelling they had the inevitability of fate. "I must have read about it somewhere."

"You've been reading too many dime novels."

Delmore Haggard never talked about his past. What Jake knew about it came through the stories and taunts he'd heard while growing up. Ned was right about his character—even people who disapproved of him acknowledged that in his prime he was a man of courage and honor with rare skill as a gunfighter. Nobody could outdraw him, and he never ran from a fight. In his secret heart, Jake had always admired him and craved his respect. And yet, living in the same house for the past five years, they had remained strangers.

Delmore Haggard would not share any part of himself with his son.

———————◆◆◆———————

AFTER THE DANCE, Billy rode out into the vast darkness of the mountains, cursing and fuming and dreaming of revenge. Even that all-consuming darkness could not contain his rage. Where did Jake Haggard get off insulting him like that? Calling him a drunk, telling him to sit down, forbidding him to dance with Isabel. Such public humiliation could not go unanswered. On Monday morning, he finished his ranch chores early and rode into town. It was a gray, drizzly day, the kind that makes a man feel restless and desperate. At the gunsmith's, he bought a Colt .45 like the old-time gunfighters used.

"You need to simmer down," Ned told Billy when Billy showed him the gun. "Jake's a good shot, but it's his father's reputation you need to worry about."

"What do you mean?"

"Delmore Haggard was a gunfighter nobody wanted to come up against. He was a crack shot, and he never ran from a fight."

Billy studied Ned's face for signs of mockery. "What are you saying exactly?"

"Just be careful," Ned told him. "You ain't the only one around here who might have something to prove."

Some nights, Jake rode into town early so he could eat at Isabel's father's eating house. It had a long counter and an unvarying regimen of stewed meat and vegetables for men coming off the trails or out of the mines. Isabel and her mother ran the kitchen and kept the place clean. Her father dished out the food and collected the money. He was a bitter, unfriendly man and he knew Jake was there to see his daughter.

"You're not welcome here," he said when Jake sat down at the counter.

"My money's as good as anybody else's."

He flinched from Jake's gaze and served him a bowl of mutton stew. Jake smiled at Isabel and waved to her on his way out. She was embarrassed by her father's behavior. There'd been some bad blood between their fathers a long time ago, but why should that make any difference to them? As the winter crept on, they started walking out together after work. Jake never apologized for the way he'd acted at the dance, and Isabel never asked him to. It was understood that he would always protect her whether she liked it or not.

WHEN JAKE WAS alone on the range, checking the fences or rounding up strays, his mind would wander far away from that gray landscape he knew so well, filled with pictures remembered from his dreams. Somewhere beyond his line of sight there was an ideal place he couldn't visualize or describe, a place of color and feeling. He felt foreign, unknowable, like a plant that sprouted up where it didn't belong. He felt no more at home in town, though he'd lived there all his life. It was shabby and run down, blackened by mining dust and soot behind its false front arcade. His father's shadow hovered over him, guiding the paths of strangers bent on glory or revenge. They looked at him differently when they found out who he was. He avoided their gaze, never gave them an excuse to challenge him. Like every young man, he felt the need to prove his worth, but he wanted to be a man on his own terms. Not Billy's, not his father's, not according to some mythical code like the one Ned claimed to believe in. How could he expect Isabel—or any woman—to respect him if he didn't follow his own path?

THE TENSION BETWEEN Jake and Billy mounted as the winter wore on. Billy twirling his six-gun, whistling as he twirled. Jake pretending not to notice, Billy pretending not to notice him pretending. The two of them circling each other like alley cats, eyes pinched, claws bared, hissing silently. Billy grinning, loving the power he thought he exercised over Jake. Jake frowning back, scorning that power. Both brandishing hammers, branding irons, and wire cutters routinely as they did their work. All this in silent pantomime, invisible to everyone but themselves. It tore at their hearts but brought them into a strange kind of intimacy.

They were both fearful, if fear is the right word for something that seems inevitable. Dread might be a better word. Dreading to stop and dreading to go on. What was it about? Neither could have told you. They would have told you they were friends. If one of them had been drowning, the other would have risked his life to save him.

The crisis came one bleary afternoon in front of the feed store, where they'd gone with the wagon to purchase supplies. Whatever Billy said, nobody could remember it later. The words made no difference. The moment had come. The only witness, other than Ned, was a one-legged war hero named Mulgrew—touched in the head, by all accounts—who spent his days perched on an apple crate in front of the feed store, offering conversation to all who passed.

"I'm warning you," Jake told Billy, "if you threaten me again or anybody in my family, I'm going to shove your words back down your throat."

He was no less astonished than Billy at what he had said. The two of them glared at each other like a dog discovering his reflection in a pond. Neither quite sure which was the dog and which was the reflection.

"The only way to settle this is with guns and bullets," Billy said, his voice wavering. "Sundown today, back of the creamery. Unless you're yellow—which is what I think you are."

Jake held his pose and said nothing.

Billy eyed him with a fine disdain and turned to Ned. "I'll bet any amount of money he won't show up." Then he stalked away and disappeared around a corner.

"You'd be a fool to fight that fella," Mulgrew said, his eyes cocked and crazed. "Unless you're brave enough to die doing it." He shot a glance at Jake. "You consider yourself brave?"

"He's brave," Ned answered for him. "Ain't you, Jake?"

"I never been brave, myself," Mulgrew said, eyes beaming the light of madness. "They put me in a uniform, and I did what I was told. What was brave about that? They would have shot me if I didn't. Then a cannonball hit me at Gettysburg—what was brave about that? I woke up the next day missing a leg. They poured so much whiskey down my gullet I passed out and they sawed my leg off—nothing brave about that. They call me a hero, but I can't think of a single brave thing I ever did."

Ned grabbed Jake and tugged him into the alley. "Don't listen to this fool. There's things a man's got to do. You've got to stand and fight. Or else...."

"Or else what?"

Ned seemed to grope for the right words, or words that sounded better than the right words. "People will say you're a coward, just like Billy did."

"What else would they say?"

"They'd say you're weak—that you're not a man."

He wandered for hours through the gray muddy town lost in bafflement and dire speculation. Every day of his life, every breath, every beat of his heart for twenty years had brought him to this moment. Courage meant nothing to him. Avoiding disgrace meant everything. The code of the west Ned had called it. He had no choice. How could he expect Isabel or any woman to respect him if he ran away from this fight?

At suppertime, he stopped at the house to tell his parents of his decision, hopeful that just this once his father would be proud of him. But his bafflement would not find so easy a release. Delmore Haggard sat across from him in the kitchen. "Being a coward won't break your mother's heart," he said, "but getting killed will. That's what we're talking about. Getting killed."

"Not necessarily."

"Listen to you! Not necessarily. That's school talk. I never went to school, but I can calculate you got no better than a fifty-fifty chance. Probably less if that boy's as good a shot as I heard he is."

"I thought... I thought you'd...."

"You thought I'd send you out to fight. I ain't ashamed of my life, but there's a lot that's changed in twenty years. They got something now they call civilization, and it has its own notion of courage. You don't have to fall into the same trap I did. You can ride out of here—hell, you can even take the train—and leave Deadwood behind. Go someplace where you won't have to watch your back every minute. Where nobody'll care if you're a coward."

That hit Jake like a slap in the face. "Then that's what you think I am?"

"Of course that's what you are. That's what everybody is who ain't a fool."

Delmore leaned across the table, and Jake saw the lethal glint in his eyes that more than a few men had glimpsed in their last moments. "I'll tell you another thing," he went on, quietly now, as if trying to steady himself. "The best way this turns out is you kill Billy. Maybe that'll give you a thrill, I don't know. But one thing's for sure—it'll be the beginning of your legend. Men'll come to Deadwood from all over wanting to kill you, and you'll have no choice but to fight them. Once it starts you can't get out of it. Do you want that? Do you think I wanted that?"

Jake stalked out of the kitchen, past his mother, who sat in the front room listening in stony silence, her hands trembling on her lap. She didn't look up when he walked past her and slammed the door behind him. The sun stood low in the sky.

NED HAD STOPPED at the eating house to warn Isabel about the impending gunfight. He leaned over the counter and whispered the words Jake and Billy had exchanged. "Don't let him do it," he said and slipped out before she could answer.

She huddled sobbing in her mother's arms. "I hope I can talk him out of it."

"Don't you dare," her mother said, pushing her away. "Don't you dare tell him not to fight. If he runs away, he'll blame you the rest of your life for making a coward out of him." She shot a glance at her husband, his face twisted by decades of bitterness and shame. "You'll think he forgot, but sooner or later, he'll throw it in your face. He'll never forget it, and he'll never let you forget it. He'll hate you for it."

Suddenly, Isabel understood the loathing and bitterness she'd been trapped in all her life. "Did Papa back down from a fight with Jake's father?"

Her mother nodded, avoiding her eyes.

Isabel wanted to run away with Jake, marry him, anything to save his life. "I don't know what to do."

"You have to stay out of it," her mother said. "You have to learn to let men be stupid on their own. They do a good job of being stupid on their own without our help."

CONFUSED, ANGRY AT his father, ambushed by unexpected shame, Jake ran to the eating house and pulled Isabel outside. He feared that she would scorn him for a coward if he ran away from the fight. He intended to tell her he'd decided to fight Billy, but secretly—which was the source of his shame—he hoped that she would talk him out of it. "What do you think I should do?" he asked her. "Should I leave or stay and fight?"

"It's up to you," she said weakly, her face a wooden mask. "You have to decide for yourself."

He felt his world slipping away. "How can you say that? Don't you care what happens to me?"

"You have to decide for yourself. I can't tell you what to do."

Shocked at her coldness, her indifference, he turned and fled back to the house. There was no reason to sacrifice his life to some ideal of courage and honor in a town where nobody gave a damn about him. His father was right. Everything had changed in the past twenty years. There was no right or wrong anymore, no code of the west if there ever was one. He could just move on, as men had been doing since time immemorial.

BILLY WAITED ALONE at the creamery as the sun dipped below the horizon. He told himself that he had won without firing a shot, but it gave him little satisfaction. As the sky darkened, he felt more and more frustrated and humiliated. He didn't know what he was supposed to do.

A rider approached in the dying light and he recognized Ned. "Jake didn't show," he told Ned.

"You knew he wouldn't. He blew you off like a speck of dust."

"Is that how you see it?"

"He's laughing at you, Billy. You got to go after him."

IT WAS ALMOST dark by the time Jake left the house. His father walked him to the door, past his silent mother, and tried to slip a .38 caliber revolver into his hand. "Take this."

"I don't need it. I'm leaving Deadwood."

"Try not to leave it in a pine box."

"He won't shoot an unarmed man. They'll hang him."

"No, they won't." Something like a smile played over Delmore Haggard's riddled face. "They'd like nothing better than to see you pay for my sins."

BILLY AND NED rode up to the eating house just as Isabel's father began to close its doors. Billy leaped off his horse and forced his way inside. His color was high, his eyes mad in the dying light.

"Where is he?"

Isabel glared back at him with silent disdain.

A train whistle screeched and died like a falling bomb, and the pounding and huffing of a slowing locomotive turned their attention to the station.

"He must be at the station waiting for the train," Ned said.

They raced to the station, Isabel running behind them in a tumult of pounding hooves and dust and steam and grinding brakes as the train sputtered to a halt.

Jake had bought his ticket and stood on the platform waiting for the arriving passengers to clear the doors. When he climbed on that train, he told himself, he'd be leaving all this behind. All this false pride and violence and stupidity, and a future fated to relive the past. If only he could leave the ache in his heart that would always remind him of Isabel. Farther west, that's where the train would take him. Isn't that where life is always better?

Appearing from nowhere, Billy ran across the platform and blocked him from boarding the train. "Where do you think you're going?" he demanded.

"I'm leaving Deadwood, Billy, and all the viciousness and stupidity that men like you have made it stand for."

Billy's eyes were burning. "You owe me a fight."

"I owe you a whipping if you call that a fight."

That sounded too much like a challenge, Jake realized. He wished he could claw those words back, but when two men confront each other, there's a law written in the blood that spells the path they must follow. Once on that path the way is set, and there can be no going back.

Without a thought Billy took the next step. "Say that again." He pulled his gun out of his jacket pocket.

"I'm unarmed." A taunt more infuriating than any insult. Jake glared at Ned with a touch of scorn. "Tell him what that means, Ned. You know all the rules."

Ned wanted to back off the path he'd sent them down, but he was stuck on it, subject to the same law he'd so often invoked without thinking about the consequences. "You can't shoot him," he told Billy.

"The hell I can't." He pressed the gun against Jake's breast. "And when I'm done with him I'll shoot you."

"Easy, Billy," Jake said.

"Don't easy Billy me. I ain't a horse."

At that moment, Isabel, who had arrived unnoticed on the platform, threw herself between Jake and Billy, pushing the gun away and scratching at Billy's face to stop him from firing. Billy lurched back, and she flew on top of him, and the two of them staggered a few steps of a strange savage dance, until with his free hand Billy tore her away and threw her down. She clung to his arm, and he beat her down with the barrel of the gun.

That brutality sent Jake into a fury. He leaped on Billy and struggled to wrestle the gun out of his hand. Billy yanked it loose and brought it around to fire, and Jake jumped on him again, both hands on his wrist, beating the gun down on his leg. Billy tried to butt him away, but Jake held his grip and when the gun finally went off Billy fell writhing on the platform, cursing and moaning, clutching his leg to try and stop the bleeding. "Damn you, you shot me!"

Jake kicked the gun away and reached down to lift Isabel up beside him. Sobbing, she clung to his wrist and let him pull her up. He folded his arms around her and drew her close. Ned knelt down to help Billy, stanching the blood with his shirt.

"I'm leaving Deadwood," Jake told Isabel, "if you'll come with me."

"I would've already been with you if you'd asked me."

"You don't mind if I'm a coward?"

"I know you're not. You just saved my life."

Jake ventured a smile. "I guess we'll take the next train then."

Ned had Billy sitting up, breathing hard, sweat and tears pouring down his face. Jake stooped down and wrapped his arms around Billy to help Ned stand him up.

"First, we better get this boy to a doctor."

—Bruce Hartman has been writing fiction for over fifty years. His current project is the "Lost West Trilogy" set in Colorado, Montana, and Oklahoma, focusing on the great cattle boom of the 1870s and 1880s, its catastrophic collapse in the Big Die-Up of 1886-87, and the impact of those events on the men and women who built their lives around the cattle business, as well as on the native people in the region. The first volume of the trilogy, Legend of Lost Basin, *was a 2025 Spur Award Finalist for Best Traditional Western Novel. The second entry,* The Divide, *was published in April 2025.*

Bruce traces his roots to the West and lived for many years in Colorado. Currently he divides his time between Colorado and Pennsylvania. He is a member of Western Fictioneers and an Associate Member of Western Writers of America.

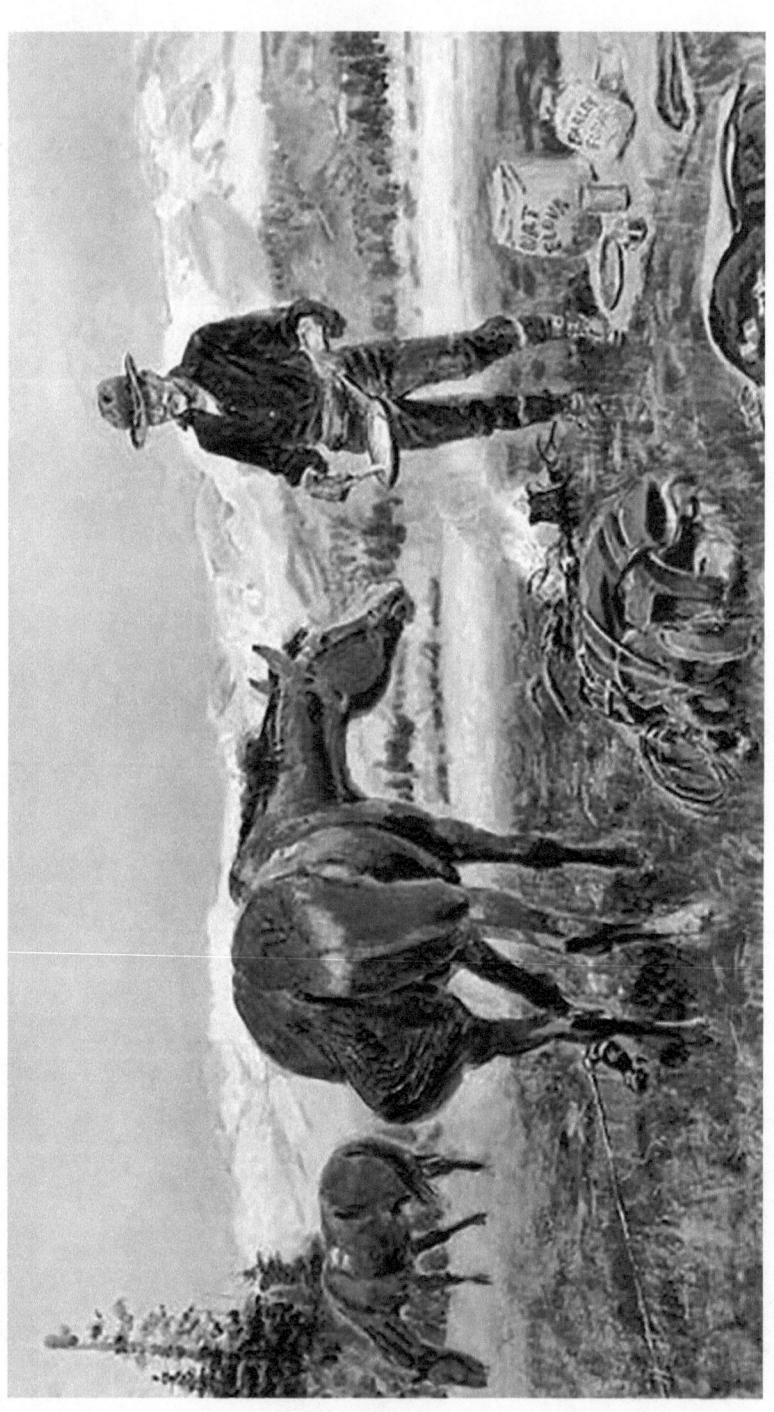

Partners by Charles Marion Russell

WILD BILL'S SKY BLUE RIBBON

BRIAN KEITH DAY

YOU MAY CALL me Timmons, but I call myself a low scoundrel. I have robbed the innocent and murdered my fellow man, but I do not condemn myself for these deeds. A harsh life and the army taught me these things. I brought about the murder of Wild Bill Hickok. This is my damnation.

I dropped into Deadwood on a hot summer's evening in August of 1876. A big crowd of men filled the Number Ten Saloon, some drinking at the bar, some seated at tables playing cards. I studied the crowd to get a feel for the people and situations between them in the tight confines of the saloon. My eyes settled upon a man whom I recognized from my days with the Jayhawkers. He was a bit older and time-worn, but then again, aren't we all. He wore his hair long now and a pair of spectacles perched on the bridge of his hawkish nose. His gaze drifted up from his cards at the table where he sat and a smile crossed his face in recognition, much to my relief, because I knew him for a man lightning fast with a sidearm and instantly decisive about death.

Hickok was his name, familiarly known as "Wild Bill." We had ridden together some with the Seventh and been occasional friends, which comes from watching each other's back in a tough scrape or two. Bill had been a stagecoach driver in his youth and had ended the career of more than one highwayman. If he had heard about the Rock River robbery that I had committed a few days before, he had made no connection to a man matching my description, or he would have drawn on me right there and then, regardless of our former association as comrades-in-arms.

Instead, he raised his hand slowly from his drink and motioned me over to an empty chair at his table, calling out, "Timmons, you old skinner! Come over and pull up a chair for a drink and a hand if you have got any brass. If your poke is empty, I'll stand you to a drink and a stake for a deal or two."

When a man as skilled with a pistol as Hickok calls you over for a sit down, you had better go to the table and be cordial or be ready to answer why not in a deadly hurry. I couldn't have asked for a better friend in a strange town than Hickok, even if he was wearing eyeglasses now-a-days.

The bodies of the dead from the Overland Stage had not been completely fruitless. Their pockets and purses had contained nearly six dollars all told. I poured myself a drink from the bottle on the table into an abandoned tin cup and sat down in the empty chair. The red eye was caustic. The devil only knows what was in it.

"Deal me a hand," I said as I lay my poke up on the table.

"Two bits to ante up," Hickok said. "Three card draw."

A couple of gravel panners and a man named Jack McCall shared the game. One of the particular pastimes that Wild Bill and I had shared during our Kansas days had been cards. He had always been fascinated with cards and the tricks a sharp could do to help his luck. He would spend hours in the barracks shuffling and turning over cards all by himself. Curiosity got the better of me watching him in the boredom of our off duty hours, and I sat down one evening at the table with him and asked what he was doing.

Well, that evening lesson led to many more. He showed me how to count cards and keep track of what had already been dealt. There is many a much cleverer hustler in the card parlors of any town than

Bill Hickok, but he could hold his own and usually come out ahead of the average man. He knew how to roll cards from one hand through a shuffle into the next so that it would benefit him, or perhaps a partner in the game. Toward the end of my card education, we would sometimes work as a team to get a little coin ahead at the expense of our barracks mates when payday wasn't arriving soon enough.

Bill was not good enough to be an out and out cheat and he knew it, so he only dealt to push the odds in his favor a little more often than not. He enjoyed the game and liked to come out a little ahead at the end of a long night's efforts, but he never tried to get rich off of the game. Even with his skill with a gun, he knew that being a flagrant cheat was a death sentence in a very short while.

Bill could read most men's expressions pretty well too. I suppose that was a skill he had used many times to alert him a split second before his gunning opponent would actually make up his mind to put a hole in Bill's hide. Reading a man's face was as valuable a talent as rolling over cards when it came to poker. Bill probably won more hands by knowing what a player was thinking than he ever did polishing up a deck.

We played cards and sipped the kerosene and rattler poison mixture for most of the night. Now and then, a couple of good cards would float into my hand a little too easily to call it chance, and I could stay in the game a little longer. Bill usually ended up winning the next pot after I pulled in a hand. The miners won often enough to keep them interested and not offended. As they drank more, they lost more, but did not seem to mind. Jack McCall drank too much and took the game much too seriously. He played so poorly and took so many risks on bad hands that a child would have cleaned out his poke in an hour or two. He began to speak poorly of Bill, the miners, and myself, making rumblings of cheating at our table. Ordinarily, Bill would have shot the man, but he held back for some reason. The two miners had actually been benefiting in the last few hands from Jack's reckless play, so they did not mind a little abuse as long as the money went to their side of the table. I had plans to spend some time in Deadwood and did not wish to start my first night there by killing a man.

When the deal came to me, I decided the best thing to do was empty Jack's purse in a hurry and get him out of the game completely before he had enough of the snake bite juice to get his nerve up and his pistol out. I had learned a trick or two with cards over the years that Wild Bill had not taught me. Broken Nose McCall got dealt a pretty good hand, but I got a better one. He bet everything left in front of him, and I meant to take it. Somehow, Bill had got a better hand than both of us. I thought Jack was going to explode as Bill pulled the heavy pot to him.

My hand was already sliding my six-gun loose from my holster when Bill said, "Think hard now, Jack, on what you are about to gamble. I do not want to kill you tonight. I just wanted to play a friendly game of cards. Now I'll tell you what I will do. I will let you take three dollars of this pot and leave this table alive. Three dollars will buy you a drink or two and a meal in the morning. Perhaps you will live to have better luck another night."

Broken Nose kicked his chair back from the table, and Bill's fist gripped the hilt of a Colt Navy while the other palm came down flat on the loot of the hand. McCall realized he was beat and probably already dead when his chair came up against the wall of the gambling house. He hung there, braced between the table legs and the wall, waiting to die, his ass a half foot off of the chair seat. Bill slid a half dozen coins loose from the pile beneath his left hand with his fingertips.

"Silver or lead, Jack. What'll it be?" Wild Bill demanded, devoid of passion.

Jack settled slowly down into his chair and raised his hands high away from his torso. "I ain't lost anything that I can't afford. Keep your handouts to yourself, Hickok!" He stood up slowly and slid along the wall to his left, then backed toward the door with Hickok's steady, ready gaze following him. "We will play again soon, Wild Bill, and you might not be so lucky,"

McCall found the nerve to growl after he had cleared half of the distance to the door and managed to place three or four other bystanders between himself and Wild Bill. Bill never uttered a sound. He just watched his target until it had left the building. He continued to gaze at the empty doorway for some minutes without moving until he was satisfied the smoldering man had decided discretion was the better part of valor. None of us other card players moved nor interrupted the silent drama in any way.

Finally satisfied that this particular hand of cards was over, Bill relaxed and calmly walked around the table to seat himself in McCall's vacated chair like some grand African lion settling down upon the corpse of a gazelle.

"I think I'll see if there is any luck left in this chair yet tonight," said Bill. "Broken Nose didn't seem to be wearin' it out much." He gathered up the scattered cards into a tidy stack and handed them to the miner on his left. "Deal them out, pardner," he said as he gathered in his winnings from the last big hand. Personally, I figured McCall had used up about all the luck that chair was ever going to give anybody for a long time. Bill should have shot him for the whining, spineless cur he was, without hesitation.

We played a few more hands. Hickok and I both lost most of them to the miners. My poke was down to a little better than double what I had sat down with, so I begged off tired and quit. Bill said I could bunk in his room if I liked, but I told him that I had been a long time on a lone ride and so many people still made me nervous.

"Oh, I wouldn't go sneaking around in the gulches in the dark anywhere around here if I were you, Timmons," Bill said in warning. "These tin pans are mighty touchy about who's skulking across their particular square of gravel, and every square inch is divvied up for miles. Even throwing out your roll a bit off of the main road is a bad idea. Someone will shoot you for a road agent—if the agents themselves don't cut your throat."

"I'll be all right. I'll find a couple of big rocks to crawl in between for some seclusion," I replied.

"Every stone is spoken for here, Timmons—especially the big ones. No one here is your friend, except maybe me." Bill persisted. "Out the front door of this place and up the street three buildings, on the other side, is a long, two story shack with a real shake roof. It is occupied with hired trollops mostly, but they have left me a little bunk room on the rear left corner. Me living there kind of keeps the clients settled down, although I really don't spend much time there."

Bill pulled a sky blue ribbon from inside of his vest pocket, next to his heart. Studying it for a moment as if he thought better of exposing it to such a vile place as the Number Ten, he held it out to me. "Take this with you and show it to the madam in charge of the stock of the place. She will know that I sent you. You can catch whatever rest you are able in this town there tonight. I'll catch up with you in the morning for my keepsake."

That faded little strip of satin cloth meant something to Hickok, and he wouldn't have offered it to just anybody, so I figured that I had better take it and his offer for the night at least. I could sort out my accommodations outside of Deadwood tomorrow. Wild Bill would kill a man—any man, friend or foe—on a moment's notice if he thought it was the thing to do. He would pull those ivory-handled Colts in the flicker of a mosquito's eyelash, but he had drawn that ribbon as if he had sliced it from his own rib. Bill was one-of-a-kind, a force of nature. I don't piss in a lightning storm, and I'll eat honey when I am offered it. Every man's got to respect a force of nature in this wild country, or he doesn't last here long.

The haggard, old bitch standing by the door of the building matching Hickok's description eyeballed me and my blue ribbon incredulously for a moment, grabbed me by the arm, and levered me toward the back room allotted to Bill. "Back there!" she grunted. "One night only. Tomorrow night you pay for a bed by the jump just like any other customer. This ain't no boarding house."

"I'll picket my horse out behind then, if that's all right," I said.

"Suit yourself. Nobody there to watch him for ya. It's your risk, not mine," she replied with a screech.

More of a storage closet than a room, Bill's digs consisted of a narrow plank bunk along one wall with some ragged blankets piled on it for a mattress. A saddle and tack took up nearly half the space remaining in the room. Some wooden crates, built to ship potatoes, held whatever possessions Bill required in his simple life. I had looked into bigger jail cells. At least the place did not stink. A real, wooden-plank door shut off the outside world from Bill's little enclave instead of a piece of holey canvas like I had noticed draped across the entrances to the working cubicles of the whorehouse. Some occupant of this monastic cell had pried out a big knot from a plank in the exterior wall, about a foot from the bunk's head, so that the sleeper might get a little fresh air in good weather and a view of the night sky. I could see my horse's tail flick into view now and again if I turned the right direction. A discarded, worn-out miner's pan spun down on the nail it was impaled on by its rim to cover the hole, if a wooden peg was pulled out from between the planking of the wall bracing the pan up out of the way.

I pulled off my boots and my gun belt, tucking the muzzle end of the holster down into a boot within easy reach, flipped my hat onto the saddle, and stretched out on the meager bed. My hide-away rested with me by my right knuckles. When I folded my hands across my chest in preparation for the temporary hereafter, the little sky-blue ribbon brushed my fingertips from my shirt pocket. My sister, Alison, had worn ribbons like that in her yellow hair so long ago in Centralia, but Missouri was long dead and gone, like Alison. I wasn't fit to have such a thing as that ribbon on my person. What right Bill had to it was none of my business. Reluctantly, I pulled it from my pocket, smoothed it out, and hung it from the tin pan so that moonlight from the knothole glinted softly from its satin curls. With that vision of a life lost to me, I finally dozed off.

In that tense hour before daylight, the sounds of a man and woman going at it on the other side of the wall from my bunk woke me. He was a gruntin' and she was rootin' him on pretty intense, but the whole affair didn't last long. I've seen hummingbirds take longer. As soon as he'd given his last wheeze and spasm, she was done with her performance and ready for him to leave the stage.

"If you're done, then pull up your britches and get out. I want to catch a little sleep," she said, cold as a dead fish.

"Move over. I'll think I'll stay for a snooze myself," he said in a growl.

"The hell you will! I'm not listening to your snoring! You paid for the piece of tail, not the piece of mattress. Now get the hell out!" I heard her yell, followed by a meaty thump and a groan from him. This was followed by the unmistakable crack of a fist against jawbone, then absolute silence.

"Kick me, bitch! That'll teach you. You could of just laid still without all the fuss. Now you'll have a sore lip to remember me by when you come to. And no point in you sharing this bed cause I don't think you're gonna' come to for a while," he muttered, followed by the sound of her body thudding to the floor.

Well, it was a whorehouse, and whores take their chances to earn their money on their backs in bed. I laid there mulling that over in my head, trying to drop back to sleep. That damn blue ribbon kept fluttering gently over the knot hole, bothering me. After about a quarter of an hour, I obviously wasn't dropping back to sleep. That woman on the floor in the next room must have been somebody's little girl once upon a time, no matter what she was now. Maybe her daddy was a better fella than that scum sack in the bed, inches from where I lay. I could hear the bastard snoring away contentedly already. His happy racket pissed me off enough to finally make up my mind.

After pulling on my boots, cinching up my pistol belt, and dropping on my hat, I gathered up Bill's keepsake ribbon into my shirt pocket and eased the door open without a squeak. The whores worked fast with little time for privacy. They barred the world's view of their labors with nothing more than a scrap of canvas pulled across their portals on a string. It was easy to enter the room of bliss and battery without a sound. The whore's silent form was wadded halfway under the iron bed frame while her satisfied client snorted away facedown in the filthy bedding. I snatched hold of his foot and yanked him off horizontal into thin air next to the bed, mid-snort. He lit face down with a satisfying thud on the plank flooring.

"Ahhh! Son-of-a-bitch!" he roared, struggling to his knees.

When his bare ass got about the right level, I planted a solid boot tip into his ball sack, hard enough to make applesauce. He probably would have squealed a lot if he hadn't went head first into the iron bed post and dropped face first into the chamber pot. The spilled, busted chamber pot made a hell of a stench, and he was as docile as the whore beside him, so I figured it was time for me to go. As I exited the whorehouse, who should be coming across the street in the pale, gold light of the morning but Wild Bill Hickok himself.

"Morning, Timmons. How did you sleep?" he asked as he stepped up to the entrance. "What is that smell!"

"Thanks for the bunk, Bill. It got a little noisy next door about an hour ago. Things are quieted down nicely now though," I said.

"I never put my feet up until after daylight. Business is much too brisk here to have any guarantee of sleep. Things will be quiet as church around here until noon at least. So you see you were no inconvenience at all," Bill explained. "What is that smell?" He pushed by me to follow his nose to the source of the odor. I followed him to the scene of my handiwork. He surveyed the mess on the floor in silence for a moment with his hand over his nose. "This some of your work?" he asked.

"'Fraid so," I admitted. "He belted her a mean one, threw her on the floor, and stole her bed, and what's more, he disturbed my sleep and he snored."

"I would have shot him," Bill said.

"That might have been cleaner."

"Use a shard of that chamber pot to scrape that mess up into his hat. Wipe the piss up with his shirt, while I skid his bare ass out into the street. It is better treatment than Mad Molly will give him for smacking up one of her girls and fowling a room. He'd be singing soprano in the church choir if he survived at all."

Bill backed up between the man's bare feet like a horse between wagon shafts, grabbed ankles, and skidded him out face down with little regard for any splinters the unconscious man might suffer on the way out. I made a half-assed effort to clean up the mess as he had requested, then carried the filthy hat, shirt, and other clothing out behind Bill. The woman never moved from her place on the floor. Perhaps the bastard had killed her.

"Looky here!" Bill exclaimed as he rolled the man over by twisting his feet. "It's our old pal Broken Nose McCall. That's Broken Nose twice now, it looks. Didn't you recognize his voice?"

"Now that you mention it, he did sound familiar. But I was half asleep and he sounds a lot different when he is humping than when he is playing cards."

"Complains a lot less I imagine," Bill speculated. "Go around back and find a pail to fill with water from the horse trough, will you? We should throw some water on that floor and Beatrice in there. Maybe she will come to. We'll get her up on the bed and get a blanket over her anyway. This stupid bastard can lay right where he is at."

A couple of wooden buckets rested near the back wall of the whorehouse, probably for filling the horse trough and washing out the rooms. I filled both buckets and returned to the whore's room. Bill stood looking into his little bit of heaven next door.

"You still got that little scrap of cloth I gave you last night as a ticket in, Timmons?" he asked.

"Sure, Bill, right here," I said, pulling it from my pocket and handing it to him. Picking up one of the pails, I flushed down the floor and whore at the same time. Beautiful Beatrice stirred a little and moaned.

"Help her get up on the bed would you, Timmons. Watch out though. She may be groggy, but she'll think you are trying for a free toss maybe, and she'll scratch or bite or worse. I guess I will take this other bucket out and sluice McCall down after all. He is such a disgusting sight in the state that he is in."

"Take these too," I said, handing Bill the boots that still remained in the room.

"We will leave the pistol belt with Molly. She may want to sell it for damages to her girl. Even Broken Nose should be smart enough not to come looking for it until she's had a few days to settle down."

Beatrice had risen to her knees and elbows so I got a hand under her arm to help her to the iron bed. She was still barely conscious and didn't give any resistance. An ugly, swollen bruise deformed her left jawline, as if a mouse were burrowed under the skin. A blanket was folded over the footboard of the bed. I spread it over the naked woman and left the building.

McCall had apparently begun to regain consciousness on his own before Bill arrived with the bucket. He lay on his side, curled up into a ball with his hands on his privates, or what was left of them. "I'll kill you for this, Bill," he croaked.

Bill took careful aim and flushed him down well with the cold bucket of water. "You won't be killing anybody for a while there, McCall. You'll be lucky if you're able to walk by this evening. If I had known that you had enough money for a whore and whiskey enough to get so stinking drunk, I would have let you stay and play some more cards. Now that you're awake, get your britches on and get the hell out of my dooryard before I throw a rope around your neck and drag you out of here. Never mind about your boots and other things. You can carry them outta here," Bill growled.

McCall struggled to his feet and began to wobble down the street bent over as if he too spent all of his days stooped over a gold pan or crawling down a mine shaft. "I'll kill you for this, Bill," he moaned. "Watch your back, you son-of-a-bitch!"

Bill's eyes narrowed to slits. His face went cold and flat. "Don't say that a third time, McCall, or you'll not say another word–ever again."

Broken Nose turned away in silence and stumbled down the crooked street until he pitched around a corner to crawl under whatever particular rock he called home.

Bill relaxed. "How is Beatrice?" he asked.

"Well, she'll have a damn sore mouth for a few days, but I imagine she will mend," I replied.

"I'll look in on her before I stretch out and again in a few hours. I am done in, Timmons. I'm going to bed. I'll see you around," he said and turned into the quiet building with a feeble wave.

I never played cards again.

—*Brian Keith Day lives with his wife Joelle, three dogs, and a cat in a small town at the base of the Big Horn Mountains in Wyoming. Writing has long been a hobby of his. He has retired recently from a heating and air conditioning service and installation career, allowing him more time to pursue his writing. A few of his stories have been published in various small press in the past. He has two books currently in publication:* Wyoming Trivia *and* Red Horse, and Other Supernatural Tales of the Sage. *Both books are currently available on Amazon. Other hobbies of Brian Keith Day include hunting, fishing, camping, and hiking.*

THE MAGIC WATER MACHINE

BIG JIM WILLIAMS

"THE MAN SAYS he can get water out of the air," said Dutch Higgins.

"Rain's been doin' that since before I was born," replied Eli Bloom. "Happened last winter cuz I got wet. Expect it to rain again... sometime, even here in Jacktaw."

"The water man ain't talkin' rain," said Dutch. "It's better."

"Better than rain clouds?"

"Yep."

"Dutch, ya gotta stop chewin' loco weed."

The two Double-ZZ cowboys' chairs were tilted against the outside of the Jacktaw Saloon, their customary Saturday morning spot marked by their shadows, cracked boots, scuff marks, tobacco smoke, and cigarette butts.

"The stranger has a big water-makin' machine on a wagon at the other end of town," said Dutch. "Wanna go see it?"

Eli Bloom slowly leaned forward in his captain's chair, shielded his eyes, squinted down the dusty street, and then went back to his willow stick. "Nope, cuz whittlin' this stick is gonna be takin' up most of my busy day."

"The man turns a crank," said Dutch, "and fresh, clear drinkin' water flows out of his miracle machine––takes it right out of the air––like a mountain spring. I done seen it."

"If his contraption produced beer, or whiskey, I'd go see it," said Eli, slicing more thumb than wood.

"That miracle machine produces gen-you-*wine* wet water."

"I can do that with a water barrel. Just turn on the spigot."

"No, that ain't it," said Dutch.

"Or," said Eli, "lower a bucket and pull up gallons from our Double-ZZ well. You might try it some time, Dutch. But your doin' anythin' except eatin', sleepin', drinkin', smokin', or ridin' a horse ain't your work style."

"Eli, yer momma should have learned you better."

"I never had a momma, we couldn't afford one."

"That's an old joke."

"Speakin' of old things, " said Eli, "where's the five dollars I loaned you three years ago. You ain't never paid it back." He did some quick calculations on his fingers. "I figure, with quad-ripple bank interest, you now owe me two-hundred thousand dollars."

"Eli, your greedy attitude 'bout lendin' money to your best friend, Dutch Higgins, shocks me. I read about you evil money lenders in the Bible."

"And whatever happened to that pair of socks I let you borrow two years ago?"

"I'm still wearin' 'em," said Dutch.

"Ain't it about time you gave 'em back?"

"Been thinkin' on it, cuz they're gettin' holes in 'em."

"Well, those socks didn't have holes when you borrowed 'em. They was mail-order, store-bought, all-the-way-from Chicago, Ill-uh-noise."

"Eli, you should buy better socks. I hate borrowin' cheap stuff."

Eli continued sharpening his stick and thought about jabbing Dutch.

The two cowhands enjoyed the morning sun while waiting for the Jacktaw Saloon to open. Saturday mornings in Jacktaw was quieter than a deaf convention. Today's only action was watching two stray dogs sniff each other and christen a hitching post.

"Gettin' back to this travelin' feller's Magic Water Machine," said

Dutch. "He just turns a crank and sucks water right out of the air. It's the strangest dang thing I've ever done seen. But he needs money to make more machines so everyone can have one, and never run out of drinkin' water, especially cattle ranchers. I been thinkin' of maybe investin' two-hundred dollars in it." Dutch cleared his throat, turned to Eli, and said, "Can you loan me two-hundred dollars?"

"Maybe if you gave me back my five dollars and socks?"

"Eli, I thought we were friends?"

"Dutch, friends like you, I don't need." Eli whittled some more, and then asked, "Does this miracle machine make whiskey, beer, or lemonade?"

"Nope," said Dutch, "but the man says he's workin' on it."

"I'd prefer whiskey or beer," said Eli, "or gettin' my money and socks back."

"That's about as unlikely as being attacked by a prairie dog," said Dutch.

"I've never seen a mean prairie dog."

"That's cuz they don't like showing it. It shatters their puppy image. Last one I saw was chasin' a steer. Was angry about somethin'."

"The prairie dog or the steer?"

"That tiny prairie dog was growlin' and kickin' dust, snarlin' and bitin', like your ex-wife when she threw a hissy fit."

"I've done told you a thousand times I ain't never been married."

"With your terrible attitude about socks and money I can see why."

"Findin' a mean prairie dog in Texas," said Eli, "is as rare as me gettin' my money and socks back."

"You said that a minute ago. Eli, I'm worried about you, since you keep repeatin' yourself." Dutch leaned back in his chair and studied some white, fluffy clouds. Watching clouds was a habit that didn't interfere with his talking, smoking, eating, drinking, or napping.

Eli thought about rolling another smoke, then remembered Dutch had his makings. "Dutch, can I have my tobacco back? I'd like a smoke."

"You're gettin' low," said Dutch, shaking the thin sack. "I wouldn't want you to run out."

"I'll try and remember that." Eli wanted to kick the rickety chair out from under Dutch but didn't.

"Eli, you need to buy two Bull Durham sacks next time so we don't run out."

"*We?*"

"'Plan ahead' my daddy always said. Eli, it's one of your many shortcomings."

Eli rolled his eyes, and thought, Someday I'm gonna... He carefully twisted another smoke, licked the paper, and struck a match. He took a puff, exhaled, and coughed.

"And you should give up smokin'," said Dutch. "Ain't good for your health."

"Dutch, if I give up smokin', where'd you get your free tobacco?"

Dutch sat up. "Then maybe it's best you keep smokin'."

———✦———

LATER, ELI ASKED Dutch, "Did you once say you made it through the third grade?"

"Ain't braggin', but graduated top of my class in our one-room schoolhouse."

"How many were in your class?"

Dutch slowly counted on his fingers. "Two. Me and Sally Lou. The teacher made me the class valley-dick-a-torrian and the main speaker at our third-grade graduation. Had punch and cookies."

"You gave a speech? About what?"

"How to fix the world's problems."

Eli stopped whittling and stared at Dutch. "What in the heck do you know about fixin' the world's problems?"

"I've been around."

"How old were you when you graduated from the third grade?"

Dutch again slowly counted on his fingers. "Eighteen-and-a-half goin' on nineteen."

"Almost nineteen years old?"

"Yep."

"How old was Sally Lou?"

"Eight-goin'-on-nine."

"And you were the valley-dick-a-torrian... whatever that was."

"I was smarter than Sally Lou."

"I would hope so... you bein' a solver of world problems and all."

"I've traveled a lot too."

"The only time I've ever seen you travel is when you were herdin' cattle, hurryin' to an outhouse, or runnin' to the Jacktaw Saloon for nickel beer and the free lunch."

"Well, little you know, Eli Bloom," said Dutch. "Been to the Alamo twice. Saw Pikes Peak once, and read the Police Gazette whenever I can find a free copy in an outhouse."

"Dutch Higgins, a reader... speaker... grammar school graduate... and world traveler?"

"Rode the train to Chicago once, but I don't brag about it."

"The Chicago stock yards are unforgettable," said Eli, "especially downwind in the summer heat."

Dutch rolled another of Eli's smokes and strained his neck watching a new cloud change from a herd of stampeding longhorns to a tall full-chested woman. He preferred the new cloud.

Then....

"You boys got the makins?" It was Curly Robbins, another Double-ZZ wrangler. He slid off his horse and stepped forward. "I'm plumb out."

"Curly, if there's one thing I can't abide," said Dutch, "it's people moochin' Eli's tobacco. He can't be givin' it to every Tom, Dick and Mary that comes along. Buy some yourself."

"The expression's, every Tom, Dick and Harry," said Eli to himself.

"Eli," said Curly, "I see you've got a Bull Durham sack. Surely you can spare some tuh-bac for an old bunkmate?"

Eli tried to talk, but Dutch interrupted: "Eli, can you imagine this moocher?" Dutch slammed his chair down on the plank sidewalk. "Curly wants to smoke your tobacco when Jacktaw's general store sells five cent Bull Durham twenty feet from here. I'm ashamed of you Curly Robbins. Didn't know you was that cheap?"

"Just figured you'd––"

"Well, you figured wrong."

Curly muttered something and walked toward the store.

"Tarnation," said Dutch with a sigh. "Eli, it's a good thing you've got me to look out for you. The gall of some people." He again pulled the near-empty Bull Durham tobacco sack from Eli's shirt. "You're almost out of cigarette papers too. Better get some before Curly buys 'em all up. Wouldn't want you to run out."

"Dutch," said Eli, shaking his head, "you've certainly been mighty considerate of me, and my money today."

"Consideration is my middle name," said Dutch, rolling tobacco into a smoke.

It was several minutes later when Dutch said, "Eli, you sure you don't wanna see that miracle water-makin' machine down the street?"

"Nope. If you've seen one miracle water-makin' machine, you've seen 'em all. It's probably a fake."

"You might change your mind if you got a gander at the curvy, tall lady in red tights prancin', dancin' and swishin' her tail on the tailgate. A real attention getter. Prettier than a June bug."

Eli stood and looked down the rutted street where a crowd had gathered. The big water machine rested on a wagon covered with wind-snapping, high-flying colorful flags and banners. On top were big funnels that could suck the water right out of the air, claimed the inventor, who looked like a sideshow barker. "You never mentioned a woman before," said Eli. "What's she doin'?"

"Lookin' beautiful to suck in a crowd of cattlemen and potential investors," said Dutch. "Take a look."

"Nope." Eli returned to his chair. "My day's complete cuttin' on this stick, watchin' clouds, and protectin' my tobacco."

"The travelin' feller's about to suck more water out of the air. Just saw him turn a crank and fill a bucket with crystal clear drinkin' water. Eli, ain't you interested in seein' a miracle?"

"If you've seen one miracle you've––"

"It's a big machine with flashin' lights, rotatin' wheels, a million pipes, and spinnin' tops."

"Dutch, my life's full just sittin' here talkin' with someone as smart as you." Eli whittled his stick into a toothpick, stuck it in his mouth, and grinned as he studied new clouds that looked like two full-breasted women.

The uneventful morning remained uneventful until it blew apart when a pregnant woman with young twin boys confronted the alleged water wizard. Claimed she was the man's abandoned wife. She showed the potential investors and ranchers how water from the Magic Water Machine actually sneaked through a hidden, under-the-wagon, thin pipe from a secret storage tank. Her angry words quickened her con-man husband's tar-and-feathering, rail-riding departure from Jacktaw.

The tall, curvy young woman in red tights left town on the afternoon stagecoach. She was bandaged and teary-eyed after coming-in second in a hair-pulling catfight with the pregnant wife and shin-kicking twins.

Dutch, Eli, and Curly Robbins smiled and watched.

"Don't know about you, Eli," said Dutch, "but all this water talk makes me thirsty."

"For water?"

"Nope. A big schooner of beer, especially if you're buyin'."

The Jacktaw Saloon was now open.

But first, Dutch grabbed Curly Robbins' new nickel sack of Bull Durham tobacco and cigarette papers.

"What you doin'?" said Curly.

"Makin' a cigarette."

"That's my tobacco. Just bought it. It ain't yers."

"I know that."

"But...?"

"Tarnation, Curly," said Dutch, lighting up and blowing a lopsided smoke ring. "What kind of a cheap friend are you if you won't share a smoke with an old bunkhouse buddy like me? A man who'd give you the shirt right off Eli's back."

Curly rolled his eyes and shook his head.

Eli groaned.

The water machine story made the front page of the weekly Jacktaw Banner in 1885. People even read about it in New York City, and Tupelo, Mississippi.

* * *

IT WAS WRITER Mark Twain who said, "A gold mine is a hole in the ground with a liar on top."

Inspired with such knowledge, Dutch Higgins decided to go into the water-seeking, well-digging business with him supervising from the top of the hole, while Eli dug at the bottom. That was Dutch's plan. However, Eli, un-consulted in the decision, preferred to return to shorter eighteen-hour workdays on the Double-ZZ Cattle Ranch.

* * *

—*Big Jim Williams' imagination wanders from Westerns to published stories of pirates, crime, mayhem, suspense, ghosts, and humor. "It's a kick to sit at my computer," he says, "and let my mind tumble through the universe, picking up ideas, and finally settling on something to write about." Big Jim is also the author of 11 Western novels, including three short story collections,* Tales of the Frontier. *His book,* A Desperate Cattle Drive, *won the Western Fictioneers' 2014 Peacemaker Award for Best First Novel. He's also produced four books in his Texas Ranger Jake Silverhorn series, and contributed stories to many anthologies, from* Greed, Gold, and Gunsmoke *to* Through Western Storms. *He's a lifelong broadcaster, former Voice of America news stringer, and native Californian. His radio play,* Close Encounters of the Confederate Kind, *aired on over 100 NPR stations. "I'm 93 and never plan to stop writing," he says. (bigjimwilliams2@cox.net)*

THE CHARITY COIN

BEN HENRY BAILEY

"FOR YOUR NEXT meal, son." The metallic spinning of the charity coin on the bar top rang through my ears as anger churned my insides. How dare that son of a bitch treat me like some peasant who has their hand out. The night's festivities had not turned prosperous for me outside of a couple small pot wins. I got cleaned out in that last hand, and an empty belly was the only thing I was walking away with. Then, as if the bastard who cleaned me out could hear the rumbling in my stomach, he leaves money on the bar to remedy just that.

Looking down at the charity coin, I had to bite my tongue to keep from yelling at the top of my lungs as I turned and watched the tall, well-dressed figure walk out the saloon door. A slight chuckle left my lips followed by a low groan as my hand shot out and snatched the spinning charity coin. My eyes could not help but dart around the room as onlookers gawked at me like some damn circus animal. Sneering back at them, I made my way for the door to the street.

I left the No. 10 Saloon, not even seeing where I was going when I ran right into a well-sized woman on the boardwalk. To say that we collided would be an understatement because I doubt that I even slowed her pace down a little. For me however, I went flying off the boardwalk and landed ass deep in mud. Laughter came from all around and the portly lady turned as if to see what all the commotion was about even though she had caused it. I recognized her from the other night when she had thrown me out of her crib. Apparently, she only saw high paying customers.

I tried to get up, but the mud made it difficult to stand. I ended up on my hands and knees, my face inches from being drowned in the filth. Not seeing another choice, I crawled my way to the boardwalk. "You better watch where you step, boy," the oversized whore said. "You never know who you may run into that you are not man enough to handle."

More laughter erupted as I pulled myself up and out of the mud. Rising to my feet, I pushed through the crowd, wanting to get away from all the shame that I felt.

───────※───────

LATER THAT NIGHT, I found myself over a bowl of stew in some cheap café. The meaty aroma was too much to handle as I dug in with the spoon almost as soon as the owner of the joint dropped it on the table. It had been a few days since I had a substantial meal, mainly just filling myself up with whiskey and playing cards. If your money holds out, you could be at a table for hours, holding on to that hope to win big.

To win big and finally be somebody with some financial backing. Not some nobody who gets laughed at and pushed around by a fat whore. Someone who could lay down cards with confidence to win and who wouldn't lose to a fancy dandy who rakes in all his winnings and treats you like a poor child holding out for charity. Every time I relive that interaction in my head, the anger returns. I see red, thinking of the bastard, dying in the mud, bleeding out as everyone around laughs at him. Every time I feel that way I come up short and feel a sense of gratitude toward the man. He is a serious poker player but also had the sense of someone that would help his fellow neighbor. Like something I would hear from a sermon back when I was a child.

Then the metal swivel sounds of the charity coin return, ringing in my ears. The gratitude is drowned out, and the anger returns.

I slurped down the remaining stew and let out a large belch. Some other patrons stared at my dreadful wear and lack of manners. I dropped the bowl to the table and stumbled to my feet. "You all can kiss my ass." I dropped the charity coin on the table and made my way back to the street, slamming the flimsy door to the café.

THE ANGER IN my stomach had slowly turned toward annoyance and embarrassment. To make such a stupid decision, to go all in on a hand that I had felt was a winner to then instantly be slapped in the face with the reality of the other man's cards. That excitement to the amount of money I would be raking in turned into a sour emptiness. In my mind, I had already spent that money, and to be sent packing with nothing but a dollar to buy my next meal with was overwhelmingly depressing. I was never one to take losing well, and that fancy dressed gambler added oil to the flame by giving me that damn charity coin.

The air outside felt good on my face, but I couldn't help but feel that everyone I passed was silently judging me. They might not have been, but the mindset I was in made the whole damn world feel like it was against me. Walking around the mining camp called Deadwood did nothing to lift my mood as everyone seemed to be having a rip-roaring time. The mud in the streets was not the only thing that was filthy in that place. You could feel all sorts of sin in the air being explored in the brothels and saloons. A ways down the street I was even surprised to see a man and a woman getting very well acquainted with each other in an alleyway. Realization came to me like a sledgehammer breaking stone. Even if I wanted to partake in certain activities with a lady of the night in an alleyway, there was no way in hell that I could have even afforded it.

Further into my walk, a figure stepped out of the shadows. Wobbly on his feet, he wase not able to stand in one spot for very long. Stepping around him, I heard him mumble something incoherent followed by the sound of a loud splat. Turning, I saw that the figure lay sprawled out, face down in the mud. I tried to turn away but that small part of my brain that houses my conscience got the better of me. Stepping out into the mud, I grabbed the drunkard by the back of his pants. As my fingers grabbed ahold, I felt something metallic and hard, tucked into his waistband. Lifting his shirt, I could see metal shining from a nearby lantern. It was a pistol, and the drunk was lucky he didn't land in the mud on his ass otherwise it would have been hell to get it cleaned to firing condition again. Taking the pistol from the man's pants, I tucked it into my own and managed to grab the man by his trousers and shirt collar.

The man was heavier than I had imagined and dragging his sorry carcass out of the street damned near made me reconsider the whole thing. Finally, getting him to the boardwalk, I slumped him over on his back, his legs still halfway out on the street. "Next time, find a better place to sleep one off you damn fool." As I walked away, I didn't think twice about not giving him back his weapon.

As the night went on, the more I felt suffocated by the mining camp and just wanted to get away. The stench of human filth was enough to make any man shudder at the smell. I made my way from the structures and went back into the timber. What I would do when I got away from the camp, I didn't know, but the cool night air was refreshing.

I had walked into the trees for a good thirty minutes, my mind elsewhere. When I stopped to take in my surroundings, I couldn't see much besides the shining stars and the black silhouettes of the pine trees around me. I cursed myself for stomping off into the wilderness with no blanket, much less supplies. Not that I could afford them anyway.

I walked a little further and a flicker of light caught my attention, realizing there was a campfire not far off. I made my way carefully among the rocks and fallen tree limbs, coming upon a man sitting at the fire, roasting a small sized rabbit.

"Hello, the camp?" I hollered over to the man, who didn't seem a bit surprised at a stranger coming in from the dark.

"Well come on in if you're comin'."

The man had a great white beard and beady little eyes that were behind a small pair of spectacles. He was dressed in clothes that looked as if they had seen many a mile with him.

"You lookin' for some grub?" I sat down across from the man, who was turning the rabbit over the fire.

"I was just walking, and I saw your fire. I don't mean to intrude." Feeling kind of sheepish for walking into this old timer's camp.

"Well, I don't have much to say for the rabbit, but you can help yourself to a cup of coffee."

I took the cup he handed me and filled it. I had tasted better coffee before but didn't say anything to the man.

"You look like you been missin' meals regular." The old man studied me through his glasses.

"I just had a meal in town."

The beady eyes held onto me for another moment before the man went back to cooking his scrawny rabbit.

"Been in town you say? You see Hickock yet?"

I sipped the hot coffee slowly and looked back at the man. "I have heard of him but don't know what he looks like."

"Just the best damn frontiersman you will find. I rode with him a spell back in sixty-seven. Can shoot the eye of a hawk a mile away."

Thinking of how that would be damn near impossible, I tossed out the coffee grounds at the bottom of my cup into the grass near the fire.

"Yes sir, Hickock is a good pard to have on the trail. He can outdraw any lowlife and plant him in the dirt."

"Sounds like a real dangerous man." I was losing interest in this man's fascination with Hickock.

"Nobody dresses prettier than he does either. Hell, I would even dare to say he out-dresses most women." The old timer began packing a pipe he produced from his breast pocket. "Wears two pistols with the butts forward and is lightning on the draw. I saw him gun down three buffalo hunters without so much as breaking a sweat. 'Course those boys had it coming, insulting that fine woman like they did."

The old timer struck a match and began lighting his pipe. The crack and sizzle of the match lighting the tobacco seemed to vibrate my senses. I had stopped listening to the man's story once he mentioned the two pistols. Not many people wore their guns like that, and so far in camp, I had only seen one person that did.

I turned back to the man who was now surrounded by a thick cloud of smoke from the pipe. "This Hickock, he have long hair, tall, and lean?"

The man only nodded which I was glad for because I was done listening to him talk. My mind began to race with many different thoughts. Hickock was the son of a bitch who had given me the charity coin. Hickock was known near and far as a frontiersman who had done just about everything and even traveled with Buffalo Bill's Wild West Show.

As if lightning came down with an idea and struck my brain, I began wondering how big the name would be of the person that sent Wild Bill to hell. The thought of fame and glory as the one who took down the best surged through me. I could see people practically bowing down to me as I walked down the street. Women fanning themselves from the flushed feelings they got as I winked their way. I would finally be someone who had standing in the world. I was going to kill Wild Bill Hickock.

"What did you say?"

Turning toward the man, I realized that I had said my last thought out loud. Embarrassment grabbed hold but only for a second as I felt the reassurance of the pistol, tucked in the back of my waistband.

"He would chew you up and spit you out for fun." The man had gotten to his feet, anger taking hold of him. "I would even wager big money you never even killed a man, you little runt. You know how hard it is to end a life?"

The old timer started walking toward me but went rigid as an echoing crack pierced the night. Crimson grew across the front of his shirt, and blood spurted from his mouth. Looking over the smoking barrel of my pistol, I saw the man begin to stagger a couple steps before falling into the fire. A slight grin crossed my face. "How hard could it be?"

THE EXCITEMENT THAT I had from the night before had remained strong, but as I searched for Wild Bill in the different saloons of Deadwood, nervousness started to chip at the excitement. Even though I was sure this was going to go through without a hitch, I couldn't help but think about what the old man had said the night before. I had envisioned myself getting the pistol stuck in my waistband and then feeling Wild Bill's bullet strike me down.

It was in the middle of the afternoon when I entered the No. 10 Saloon, and as my eyes adjusted, I took in the people who were trying to stay out of the summer sun. My eyes made it to the back of the room, where a poker game was in play, and settled on none other than Wild Bill.

I immediately walked up to the bar, trying hard not to make eye contact with anyone. The nervousness took hold, now much stronger than the excitement and determination had been. My stomach started flipping and I felt that I might throw up. Leaning on the bar, I laid my head down for a second to try and calm my nerves. Breaths came shallow for a few minutes before they started to slow. Turning my head to face the back of the saloon, I saw that no one seemed to take notice of me, probably just assumed that I was already on a bender.

I stood up straight and slowly made my way down the bar, keeping my eye on the poker game. Hickock looked over at me, and I saw recognition on his face. He nodded ever so slightly at me and then looked back down at his cards. The bastard thought we were on friendly terms because of his good deed that he did in giving me that charity coin. I gave a slight smile back and looked over at the balance scales at the end of the bar.

The scales were used to weigh gold. I pushed down one of the pans which suspended the other in the air. I soon realized that I couldn't do it as sweat broke out on my forehead. Turning, I made my way toward the backdoor.

"The old duffer, he broke me on that hand."

Those words had stopped me in my tracks, and the anger returned. The nervousness went away as if burned up by a flame. He is going to die a loser I thought and immediately pulled the pistol from my waistband. In the same motion, I pulled back the hammer and brought the pistol up, pointed right at the back of Will Bill's head, pulling the trigger. Gunsmoke erupted from the barrel and the loud bang echoed off the wood walls of the saloon.

"Take that damn you!"

Little did I know at the time, there would be no celebrating this deed, and I might as well have been aiming at my own head to be sent out of this world. It was like those scales in the saloon. The right pan held the charity coin, and the left pan held me, Jack McCall. The charity coin turned out to weigh more than I could have ever imagined, pushing the right pan down to the bar top, whereas the left pan was held up leaving me suspended.

———◦◦◦◦◦———

—Winner of the Will Rogers Medallion Award 2025 for his short story, "My Friend Tom," Ben is a native to Colorado and grew up watching westerns at the early age of three and started writing westerns at the age of seven. He wants to tell stories that come from different points of view and explore the triumphs and tragedies of his characters who reflect the brave men and women from all walks of life that called the west their home.

BIG SKIES. BOLD FLAVORS. REAL RANCH COOKING.

Will Rogers Medallion Award-winning author **Sherry Monahan** takes you on a delicious ride through the kitchens of America's most iconic dude and guest ranches in the first volume of her new Culinary Treasures cookbook series. From sun-up sourdough flapjacks to sundown skillet suppers, *Dude & Guest Ranches of America* delivers recipes straight from the trail, the chuckwagon, and the family table—each served with a side of Western heritage and hospitality. Learn the secrets of perfect cowboy steaks, campfire beans, and flaky ranch pies, all while exploring the untold stories of the families who keep these living legends alive. Fire up your range and rediscover the spirit of the West—one unforgettable bite at a time.

www.sherrymonahan.com

HAT CREEK

THREE-TIME SPUR AWARD WINNER

DUSTY
RICHARDS

Presents the Award-Winning Novels of

THE
BRANDIRON

Prepare to embark on a thrilling adventure into the heart of the untamed Old West, where the spirit of ranching collides with the pulse-pounding allure of the frontier. Brace yourself for a wild ride through rugged landscapes and daring escapades that will leave you breathless. Experience the adrenaline rush as resilient ranchers battle against the elements, outlaws, and the untamed wilderness itself. Feel the exhilaration as they push the boundaries of their courage and skill to new heights. From high-stakes cattle drives to treacherous encounters with outlaws, these gripping tales will transport you to a time of danger, resilience, and unyielding determination. Get ready to lose yourself in a world of thrilling action, vivid imagery, and unforgettable characters who embody the spirit of the Old West. Are you ready to saddle up and join the adventure? The frontier awaits, and the excitement is just beginning.

A BRIDE FOR GIL · THE CHEROKEE STRIP
GOLD IN THE SUN · RANGE WAR OF CALLIE COUNTY
BOUNTY MAN & DOE · OUTLAW QUEEN

*Catch Up on All the Action Today
At Your Favorite Bookseller*

"A man only learns in two ways, one by reading, and the other by association with smarter people."
—Will Rogers

WILL ROGERS
MEDALLION

RECOGNIZING EXCELLENCE IN WESTERN MEDIA AND STORYTELLING AND COWBOY POETRY

www.willrogersmedallionaward.net

THE HAUNTING NEW WESTERN MYSTERY

SHARON FRAME GAY

WHERE THE CROWS FLY

WHERE CROWS GATHER...
DEATH AIN'T FAR BEHIND.

NOW AVAILABE EVERWHERE BOOKS ARE SOLD

TRICKS FOR A TRADE

TRICKS FOR A TRADE

Lloyd Johnson

Diamond Lake Publishing

DEDICATION

This book is dedicated to the angels who believe in me, and the devils who don't.

DISCLAIMER

This book is a work of fiction. Names, characters, businesses, organizations, places, events, and incidents either are the product of the author's imagination or are used fictitiously. Any resemblance to actual persons, living or dead, events, or locales is entirely coincidental.

OTHER BOOKS BY THE AUTHOR

The Dog Catcher (a gritty contemporary novel)
The Best Possible Angle (a thriller...coming soon)

CHAPTER ONE

Friday, June 6, 2008

5:40 AM

"You're on your period, now? Really?" Karen turned her back to Armando in bed. He didn't know why she would even bother telling that lie. *Was a time when I'd fuck that pussy out of place and ol' girl would be so tired, she couldn't talk mess or ask a lot of questions,* he thought to himself. Now, Armando was getting nonsense excuses but no sex. He wondered if he was losing his touch.

Karen wasn't drop-dead gorgeous, but she was cute to look at. Medium brown, with long-lashed, warm eyes. She kept her hair done–always permed and together. None of that new-growth-busting-through stuff.

There was a gap between her two front teeth, but it didn't make her teeth look wrecked. You had the feeling her smile wouldn't have been as beautiful if she ever got her teeth fixed. God must've skipped out on her in the self-esteem department, though. It seemed like everyone but Karen knew she was a good woman. Sure, she'd tell you that she was, but it's not like she really believed it. Every time Armando stroked her hair, he was stroking her ego.

He was a good man who'd found his good woman. He was just waiting on her to believe it too.

"So, I guess I can't get none before work, huh?" Armando asked, his thick arms crossed, his gray eyes seductive.

She sat up in the bed, intentionally allowing the bed sheet to fall from her breasts. "Boy, you better stop playing with me," she said, unfazed by his eyes' magic. She'd seen them before.

Armando jumped from the bed and stared at Karen with both anger and lust in his eyes. His boxers fell to the floor. Karen couldn't help but steal a glance of him stroking his girth. But it changed nothing.

Determined to remain strong she asked, "Have you given any more thought to what we talked about?"

He stopped stroking. "Karen, don't start this again, all right?"

"No, Armando. I'm going to keep on it. I'm getting tired of hearing my mama suck her teeth, telling me how I'm living in sin."

"I don't know why you gotta tell your mama everything in the first place," he said.

"Because she's my mama!"

"Oh, please. Y'all don't even get along."

"Don't try and change the subject," Karen said, shaking her always well-manicured hands and rolling her neck.

"When are we getting married?"

"I gotta go to work."

"Yeah, that's right. Take your black ass to work. But we ain't finished with this conversation. Believe that. But I know one thing; I better not find out that you're screwing

some other woman, Armando. Because if you are, you better take a good look at that ding-a-ling of yours, baby."

"What, you're gonna go Lorena Bobbitt on me?" he asked with a chuckle, trying to lighten the mood.

"Hell yeah. But in your case, they won't find it in no bushes."

"Why is it every time you hear something you don't like, I gotta be messing around?"

Karen didn't care how many times he claimed his whoring days were over. He hadn't proposed to her yet, so he must be out laying every female who would let him. She gave him the iciest of stares, her arms folded, like she was expecting a full confession to some bogus crap he'd been doing.

Instead, Armando went to the bathroom; his jet stream of piss turned the toilet water yellow as Karen stood in the doorway. Her words began sounding like Charlie Brown's teacher's *"Wah wah wah wah, wah wah wah wah!"*

Armando flushed the toilet, hearing her say, "Enough of the dumb shit!" He slammed the door in her face, which was met with angry pounding. He locked the door and turned on the shower, jumping in quickly. She didn't deserve his ding-a-ling anyway.

After his shower, Karen had quieted down. But he wasn't going to risk starting her up again, so he avoided eye contact and put on his underwear, undershirt, black work pants, and white golf shirt in record speed. Karen sat on the side of her bed with her back toward him.

Karen had told him a thousand times–she felt used and abused. He got it. And he was sorry she felt that way, but it wasn't going to change who he was. He did want to marry her...someday. But since leaving home at eighteen

to get away from his mother and her boyfriend drama, he'd been in survival mode, always thinking, "Be loyal to yourself. Everything and everyone else comes after." Freedom pulsed through his blood, and Armando wasn't ready to give that up.

Why couldn't she just relax and enjoy the orgasms he put on her? But maybe that was the problem. Maybe she wasn't strong enough to handle the sex. It spun her around and left her out of breath...and paranoid.

Armando walked up to Karen, kissing her on the side of her temple. "I'll call you later," he said.

"Whatever."

He left for work, not feeling too badly about any of it. She was twenty-seven, just like him. They were both grown and she knew how he was. Armando had to do things on his own timetable. He had told *her* that a thousand times.

One thing was certain, he loved Karen. On a good day, he loved that she encouraged him not to be afraid to dream, and seize opportunities. But as he drove to work, he was reminded of just how many of these opportunities he'd allowed to slip through his grasp: journalism scholarships offered by the Urban League, offers to learn a trade at Job Corp, work as an apprentice with a landscaper, and even modeling. He knew he had an intelligent mind but he was lazy. He'd gotten off easy with his looks. With gray eyes that contrasted brilliantly against his dark skin—the color of a Brazil nut's shell, and hair cut tight to the scalp, Armando knew he was a gift for the ladies. But it only took him so far. After working everything from janitorial to McDonald's, Armando was now a busboy at the Peterson Hotel. He hadn't exactly set the world on fire.

He pulled into the employee parking lot of the hotel.

When he stepped out of the car, the Minneapolis humidity hit him so fiercely, he was bleeding sweat. Entering the employee entrance, Armando found no relief from the heat. The back corridors were just as hot as it was outside, which meant the AC system was busted again. *Great, I'm gonna be sweating all damn day long! They need to invest in a decent system that works,* Armando thought to himself, though for a brief moment he thought he'd said it aloud. This is what he'd been reduced to; passing time in a dead-end job. There had to be a better way to make money.

Even if he were ready for marriage, how was he supposed to marry the woman he'd been blessed to have if he was always living hand to mouth? Day after day, busing dirty dishes, cleaning up busted sugar packets, and scraping cereal from a carpet wasn't going to provide them with any kind of decent life. Maybe Karen didn't mind, but Armando was a man. He minded a lot.

By the end of his shift, Armando was so drained he walked out of the hotel without the obligatory good-byes. The heat outside was as strong and determined as ever, and his skin was already damp and rubbery. He got into his car, pulled out into the street and made his way toward home.

At the corner of Franklin and Hennepin, his cell phone rang. It was Karen. The light at the intersection turned green, he made a right turn and found a spot on the neighboring city street to park so that he could take the call.

"Yeah," Armando said, impatiently.

"You need to stop off and get something for dinner," Karen told him.

"I wasn't planning on stopping."

"Look, I just walked in the door my damn self, I'm tired, and I'm not cookin.'"

"What do you want?" Armando was getting agitated.

"I want some chicken."

"Karen, I'm almost home. You better think of something else to eat because I'm not searching high and low for chicken."

"Boy, you asked me and I'm telling you. Bring me some chicken!" Karen screamed as Armando hung up on her.

The phone rang again and Armando ignored it. He checked around to see if anyone was coming. When he pulled out to head to the nearest KFC, he heard the chirp of his voicemail. He knew it was Karen, calling to curse him out for hanging up on her.

Once he pulled up to the restaurant, he realized he didn't know what Karen wanted. So he ordered a 10-piece bucket with biscuits and mashed potatoes. If she didn't like it, too damn bad. She should've gotten the food herself, he reasoned. After picking up the chicken, he stopped at a gas station for cigarettes. The woman cashier was cute, he thought.

"How you doin'?" she asked him.

"I'm cool. Just trying to get home, ya know?"

"I heard that," she said. As she scanned the price of the cigarettes, she leaned in coquettishly and said, "You know you need to leave these cigarettes alone. Didn't your mama tell you they're bad for you?"

"We all need a vice," he said, smiling back at her. He could feel himself falling into flirt mode.

Just then, the manager stepped out from the back area. But the cashier didn't see the manager when she said,

"Just be glad you ain't my man. Cause I wouldn't kiss any man with stank cigarette breath."

"Benita, what did I tell you about your mouth?" the manager admonished.

Armando paid the cashier, tossed her a parting wink and left quickly, not wanting to get her into more trouble. When Armando got home he found Karen in the kitchen on the phone. He walked over to her and set the bag of food down in front of her. She looked up, telling the person she was on the phone with she would call them back and promptly hung up.

"I'm sorry, baby." Karen looked at him with doe-eyed innocence. She wrapped her arms around his waist and planted the side of her face to his chest.

"Next time, get it yourself," Armando said, pushing her away.

"Armando, come on now. I'm trying to be nice so quit trippin.'"

Armando rolled his eyes. "Do you even know why you're sorry? Just eat your bucket of grease and leave me alone," he said, leaving the kitchen to go into the bedroom. Karen got up and followed him.

"Armando, I know I'm acting crazy. It's just that I love you and I'm scared you're gonna mess around and find a better offer with someone else. I don't want to lose you."

"You're too insecure, and it's getting old, okay? The way you talk to me is foul. And I'm getting tired of coming up in here and not knowing which mood you're gonna be in."

"I know, baby, and I'm sorry. I promise I'll work on that."

Karen ran her hands along his chest, and down his stomach, resting them on his crotch.

"You gonna give me some later?" she asked suggestively.

Armando turned to look at her. *Now* she wanted the dick? Typical. They'd argue one minute, and then behave as though nothing happened the next, usually after her mood shifted. Things between them had always been spicy and explosive. He remembered their fourth date...

"I saw you staring at that bitch in the movie theater," Karen said once they'd made it back to the car.

"Wow, Karen. How in the hell was I gonna be checking out another female when it was pitch black in the theater?"

"Boy, you had all that light coming from the screen. You could see."

"Babe, you need help," Armando said, putting the key into the ignition.

"You think that bitch can do this?" Karen said, reaching over to massage his crotch.

Armando's body jolted at the sudden touch. He nervously looked around the garage to see if anyone was watching them.

"We're parked back here in the corner. Ain't nobody gonna see us. Now, you tell me if the bitch would do this," Karen said as she pulled Armando's growing girth from his unzipped pants. He watched helplessly as his hardened inches disappeared into her mouth. He pulled his underwear and pants down farther to give her easier access.

"I asked you a question," Karen said, stroking him suddenly. She looked up at Armando, who appeared lost in a dream.

"Hell no, she can't. You got this, girl!" Armando

sounded out of breath, his voice thick with anticipation for Karen to place her heavenly lips on his manhood once more.

"Yeah, I know this," Karen said, secure in her skills. She may not have known if this man was truly hers, but she knew enough to introduce him to her inner freak. She judged by Armando's response that he was glad to make its acquaintance.

She reclined back into her seat, hiking up her skirt. She pulled her panties off and threw them in Armando's lap.

"Smell 'em," she instructed. Armando did so obediently. He sniffed her panties deeply as though he were taking in oxygen; her natural scent mixed with the jasmine and vanilla body spray. While his face was buried in her panties, she jumped on top of him, took her panties from his face and tossed them into the passenger seat. She forced her tongue into his mouth, kissing him hungrily.

"Recline this seat back," she said.

Armando fought with the side latch to get the seat to fall back as far as it would go. When it did, he turned to see Karen had unbuttoned her blouse. Her breasts were firm, nipples hardened by her own desire. He grabbed them and began to suck on them. She threw her head back, enjoying the pleasure. Then she lowered herself onto his dick, which had been aching for her. She rose and fell on it, at first slowly, throwing in a few pelvic swirls just to get used to him being inside her.

"Naw, girl, you're playing with me," Armando said, his voice filled with the same wanting as before. He grabbed her ass and brought her down hard. She screamed out.

This wasn't the way Armando had envisioned their first

time together. He assumed Karen would've wanted more from the experience...perhaps a little romance. He respected her waiting until their fourth date. Most women he'd been with had thrown themselves at him on the first night.

Karen's riding him in that driver's seat would set the tone of their relationship: they'd love as hard as they fucked, buffered down by the commonality of having wrecked home lives with mothers who didn't understand them.

"Armando, you hear me talking to you," Karen said, drawing Armando back into the present moment. "I said, are you gonna give me some later?"

Armando smiled as he thought about the miles traveled in their relationship. He drew her near him. They stood in the middle of the bedroom, admiring themselves in the mirror across from the bed. Armando knew the sex with Karen was off the charts. As usual, all was forgiven. He knew her heart. She wasn't perfect, and neither was he.

"Go eat, baby. Afterward we'll take a nice, hot shower, and then I'm gonna lay it on you," he said, his eyes sparkling.

She could be in the world's worst mood as she often was, but all he needed to do was smile, and all of their problems faded away at least for a moment.

Karen went back into the other room to eat her chicken, leaving Armando to relish the thought of becoming one with her. They had cleared the air just enough so he could enjoy being with the woman he loved, and the happiness she brought to his life.

CHAPTER TWO

Friday, June 6, 2008

7:30 PM

"You better sit still and let me finish setting this wig," Cabrien said.

"Boy, how many bobby pins you gotta put in it? It hurts, you know. You're mutilating my scalp," Don said, clutching the wig so tightly that he was ruining the curls Cabrien had just put in.

"I'm sorry, but I gotta make sure it's on tight so I can finish styling it. Boy, you just messed up the curls! Now I'm gonna have to redo them all!"

"Well, hurry up with those damn pins. I can't take no more!"

Cabrien fastened the last of forty pins through the wig into Don's real hair. "There. Now what were you telling me before?" Cabrien said, reaching for the large curling iron.

Don wiped the tears from his eyes, sitting for a moment to wait for the pain to subside. "I was saying how that drag queen, Glenda Dupree, took off her hoop earring and straightened it out before she stabbed some dude in the neck with it."

"Are you serious? Why in the hell did she do that?"

"She was probably with a piece of rough trade and he found out she had the same business between her legs that he did. I done told that bitch that just because she can give good face and realness, doesn't mean she ain't got to tell these straight dudes she messes with that she's still a man."

"Especially these thugged-out brothas. I don't care how good she tucks her twig and berries," Cabrien said, twirling the curling iron in his hand. He caught a glimpse of Sheronda, another stylist, who shook her head in disgust. Cabrien rolled his eyes, and went back to curling.

"I see our neighborhood bible thumper over there can't take a little punk bar storytelling. Let me hurry up and get done with you before I have to go in on somebody."

"Some kinds of talk ain't appropriate, Cabrien," Sheronda said.

"Then I suppose you're talking about your gossiping too, right?" Then Cabrien leaned into Don's ear. "If this rotten fish don't stop pushing me, I'm gonna push back. Hear me talkin'?" he whispered.

"I know that's right," Don replied, giving Sheronda the evil eye.

Cabrien continued working in silence. When he finished, he whirled the chair around to reveal the curled updo to Don through the large mirror.

"Ooohwee! Go in, bitch, and let have!" Don said with a snap of his fingers. "Ladies, I don't know what y'all stylists call themselves doin' to y'all heads, but *this* is how it's done, hunties. Cabrien, this is *beyond*, honey!" Don sprang up from the chair and began sashaying around the room, which was met with mostly smiles and some stony faces. Cabrien smiled at his own handiwork.

"I was gonna put my baseball cap back on, but you're giving me life with this ol' nasty style! I'm fixin' to wear it out the salon."

"That's fine. I appreciate you advertising my skills! And I know you'll be turning it tonight, too!"

"Hell to the yes, you best believe I will be rocking this wig tonight. I'm about to let the children have it, hunty!"

Cabrien gave Don a peck on the cheek. "See you later, boo. And thank you!"

"No, thank *you!*" Then Don left.

The woman seated at Sheronda's chair shook her head and said, "Instead of going out to the club, they need to take their asses to church."

"Amen, walls," Sheronda said.

Cabrien rolled his eyes again. "Yeah, okay, Sheronda. You do realize that Asa, your boss, is gay, right? Try telling *him* that he needs to go to church and see if your behind still has a job, since you wanna be over there judging folks."

As if on cue, Asa Barkley came sweeping grandly into the salon. He breezed past everyone with a quick, "Good evening, ladies," stopping in front of Cabrien, who had begun sweeping up hair near his station.

"Cabrien, can I talk to you in the backroom, please?" Asa asked.

Cabrien Jacobs noticed the other hairstylists look away and busy themselves with their clients.

"Anything you have to say to me, you can say right here," Cabrien said.

"No, I need you to come in the backroom with me. Right now!"

As Cabrien followed Asa, he noticed Sheronda staring

at him with a smirk on her face; a smirk that told him he was in trouble.

"We have a problem," Asa said.

"Who's 'we'?"

"The other stylists feel uncomfortable working with you."

"Why?"

"They feel you have some objectionable personal habits."

"What kind of habits?" Cabrien asked, folding his arms.

"Let's take your attendance, for example. You're barely here. And there's talk that the reason you're not here is because you're off somewhere selling your body. Plus, Sheronda claims that you've been inappropriate with her fiancé."

"And you believe that bullshit?"

"Are you denying it?"

"Asa, you know me. I've worked here for four years. I don't do messy stuff like trying to take somebody's man."

"So you're not out there selling yourself, either?"

Cabrien just looked at Asa.

"Well, are you?"

"That's none of your business. Y'all have been cutting my shifts like crazy, so I have to do what I have to do."

"I've been cutting your hours because you've been showing me that you don't want them. And you're right, what you do outside of work isn't my business, but what goes on *here* is, which means having stylists who can perform the job I ask of them. You do great styles, and the customers love you—when you're here."

"So what's the problem? That appointment book is full

because of *my* talent. That Hair Show Award sitting out there is because of *my* designs."

"I wouldn't go so far as to say all of that. Anyway, I don't want drama in my salon. Please, just clean out your station and leave."

"I can't believe y'all are doing me like this. Asa, you're gay too, and you're gonna stand up here and side with Ms. Holy-Is-the-Lamb? Her ass would love to see both of us tossed into a lake of fire." Cabrien said, his eyes tearing up.

"You think I'm going to side with you just because I'm gay? I'm not out selling *my* ass when I should be at work. Besides, why would you want to work in an environment where people don't want you? Where's your self-respect?"

"You know what? I tried to tell the devil to go on about his business, but y'all about to see him use me!" Cabrien stormed from the backroom and walked out into the busy salon and over to Sheronda, who was trying to look as though she knew nothing about the situation.

"So, did God tell you to finish the dirty job?" Cabrien asked.

"Cabrien, why don't you take your disease-infested ass on outta here?"

"Disease infested? You're sure you wanna take it to that level?"

"Yeah, I said it. So what? You sissies are always trying to take other people's men away from them, when y'all know there's hardly any *decent* black men left. Y'all too busy trying to turn 'em out!"

"I see. So is that why your dirty-dick fiancé tried to hit on me outside the Gay 90s club? Is that why Mr. Down Low told me he can't stand fucking you because your pussy smells horrendous?"

"Cabrien," Asa shouted. "Watch your mouth!"

"Sheronda don't know what she started, Asa. Tell her to douche her stuff with some bleach!"

"Cabrien, there's kids in here!" Asa yelled.

"I ain't thinking about these kids, Asa. You wanted to see my self-respect? This is it!" Cabrien grabbed his Louis Vuitton messenger bag, his body humming with adrenaline, and walked out of the salon, slamming the door behind him. *Asa's monkey-ass needs me, I don't need him,* he thought to himself as he strutted down the sidewalk. Cabrien knew he'd bounce back. After all, he was a twenty-three year-old pretty boy, with high cheekbones and a lean, muscular dancer's build. Cabrien was a resourceful young man who knew how to play the hand he was dealt.

By the time Cabrien got home, much of his anger had burned off, replaced by the sobering reality that he was unemployed. He called Don and told him what happened. There was no sharp-tongued wit tossed back and forth, nor was there two- snaps-and-a-clap glee, but very real sobs from Cabrien, and words of support from his friend.

"You listen to me, Cabrien LeAnthony Jacobs. I'm gonna say this to you one good time, and then we're going out cocktailing. There are other salons out there killin' for someone with your skills. Tomorrow, you're gonna take your ass out and get yourself a gig with an even better salon, and you're gonna make sickening coins, and let these bitches who thought they knew the tea have it! Then you'll be saying, 'Asa Barkley? Who?'"

Cabrien smiled at the prospect. With renewed hope he said, "All right, chile, if I'm comin' out tonight then you're buying the drinks, because a bitch is strugglin.'"

Tuesday, July 1, 2008

2:30PM

Cabrien stood in the middle of his small studio apartment, furnished with mismatched low-end items from IKEA. He wore a matching yellow gauze shirt and pants that brought out the hues of his chocolate-brown skin. Cabrien gazed at the sunlight beaming through the window, as though it could answer the question of how he was going to pay rent. For three weeks, Cabrien tried getting hair styling jobs with other salons. He may have felt good about the scene he caused at Asa Barkley's salon, but Sheronda wasn't going to just stay embarrassed. She told every salon that called for a reference that Cabrien was unreliable, and a male prostitute. After that, he never received a single call back from any of the salons.

The landlord had been more than patient. He'd even taken a liking to Cabrien. So much so that the two of them spent many evenings in their mutual loneliness, sipping wine together as they tried one-upping each other as to who led the more pitiful existence. Some of those evenings ended with Cabrien giving the landlord a mercy blowjob, which paid the rent for the month completely. But now the landlord had met a woman online—willing to give him her heart and a blowjob, while Cabrien's savings dwindled fast.

Just as the feeling of helplessness was about to swallow him whole, Cabrien heard a knock at the door.

Ralph Sorrentino stood in the doorway, smiling with big, lustful eyes. He was the UPS man who made deliveries to Cabrien's building, and quite a few visits to Cabrien's apartment.

His uniform looked as though it were made with him in mind. Ralph's shirt hugged every muscle of his upper body, with tufts of black chest hair peeking through, while his tight shorts showed off his firm bubble butt.

"How you doin'?" Ralph asked.

"I've been better. Been waiting on you to make one of your deliveries, though. I see that it's arrived in great shape as usual."

"Yep. I got your package right here," Ralph said, clutching his crotch.

"Well, come on in, then. Shit," Cabrien said, backing away to allow himself a full view of Ralph's rock hard body as it entered his apartment. "How's the wife doing?" Cabrien asked, looking at Ralph's solid calves as he walked toward the platform bed.

"She's fine. Still pregnant."

"She should've had that baby by now. In fact, to hear you tell it, she should've had at least two," Cabrien said playfully.

"Hey, ya got me. She slaps me in the face whenever I try to touch her. She won't even blow me. But she never could suck a dick like you, anyway," Ralph said, laughing.

"Honey, *nobody* can suck a dick like me."

Ralph sat down on the bed. Cabrien remained by the door, waiting to be beckoned. He liked it when alpha male types like Ralph took control.

"Why are you standing over there? Come sit by me," Ralph ordered.

Cabrien did as he was told. As he sat on the bed he could feel Ralph's large hands caressing him. He leaned in to kiss Ralph.

"I don't kiss," Ralph said, turning his head away. "You know that."

"I forgot. Sorry."

"Show me how sorry you are."

Cabrien knelt before Ralph, who looked at him with anticipation. Cabrien started by removing Ralph's boots. He placed his hands beneath the arches of Ralph's socked feet, rubbing them.

"Damn, you got big feet."

"You know what they say, baby; Big feet, big cock."

"They weren't lying in your case, were they?"

"Nope."

"What else do you want me to do for you, Ralphie?"

"Why don't you get started on this dick?" Ralph said, unzipping his zipper.

Cabrien could see the outlines of Ralph's dick through his shorts. As he continued massaging one of Ralph's feet, his other hand moved up towards his cock and began rubbing it. Ralph let out a deep moan as he began to pull his shorts and underwear down. Cabrien licked the head of the rock solid dick. Ralph closed his eyes and leaned back onto the bed.

"Aw, man," Ralph said, as Cabrien took the head into his mouth.

"I love the taste of your cock, you know that, don't you?"

"You're teasing me."

Cabrien held the cock at the base and spit on it, then he engulfed it with his mouth, alternating between stroking it with his hand as he sucked it.

"God, you're killing me!" Ralph exclaimed as he grasped handfuls of Cabrien's bed sheets.

Cabrien continued sucking Ralph's dick, changing his rhythm every few seconds as Ralph whispered, "Wanna ride me?"

"You ain't tearin' me up with that," Cabrien said, looking down at Ralph's thick, uncut penis as he came up for air.

"Aw, come on. My ol' lady is real bitchy lately. She won't let me fuck her."

"Too bad for you," Cabrien said, before putting all of Ralph's cock back into his mouth, trying to get Ralph's mind off fucking him. Ralph lay back on the bed.

"That feels so fucking good, dude."

Cabrien lifted Ralph's massive legs into the air as he sucked him off, deep throating like the pro he knew he was.

"I'm gettin' close, man," Ralph said, breathing heavily. "Where do you want my baby batter?"

Cabrien began to laugh. He had never heard that term for semen before. But before he could respond...

"Aw, shit! I'm comin'!" Ralph unloaded a flood inside Cabrien's mouth.

Cabrien's cheeks inflated as he received the heavy gush of Ralph's semen. He spit as much of it out as he could before wiping his mouth with the back of his hand. He glared at Ralph, who was still lying on the bed, his chest rising and falling as his body shook from the explosive orgasm.

"Motherfucka, don't you *ever* come in my mouth again!"

"I'm sorry. It's just that it was feeling so good. I didn't know where you wanted it."

"That's disrespectful!"

Cabrien got up and went into the bathroom and ran the

faucet. He scooped cold water into his mouth, followed by mouthwash. He looked into his mirror and could see Ralph pulling up his underwear and shorts. When he came back into the room, Ralph looked up at him sheepishly.

"Are you mad at me?"

"I know I'm good, but damn!" Cabrien said, trying to lighten his anger. He didn't want Ralph to say that he wouldn't come back again.

Ralph reached for his boots and began putting them on.

"Well, I gotta run. I got some more deliveries to make and, well, you know...."

"Yeah, okay. I got it." Cabrien smirked.

"Next time, I want some of that tight ass of yours," Ralph said.

"I'll think about it. But I should tell you, my cookie is so good, you won't be able to handle me."

Ralph got up from the bed and walked up to Cabrien, looking him right in the eyes and said slyly, "Dude, I'll break your fuckin' back." His five-o'clock shadow gleamed with sweat.

Cabrien shivered at the image of Ralph fucking him.

"Ooooh, you better stop."

Ralph laughed, tucking in his shirt as he walked to the door. "I guess I'll be seein' ya," Ralph said.

Cabrien followed him to the door. "Only if I'm lucky." He watched Ralph leave; his body was considerably more relaxed than when he first arrived.

Cabrien's afternoon suck-off was an unexpected pleasure. He couldn't charge Ralph his usual price of $250 because Ralph was too gorgeous in his own mind to pay it, and probably couldn't afford it. But Cabrien knew that somewhere in the Minneapolis streets there were those

that would pay the price, and do so gladly. Rent money problem solved.

CHAPTER THREE

Tuesday, July 1, 2008

6:00PM

Bruce Hedrick stood before fifty people at the Pearl Park Recreations Center. His smile was lazy at best as he tried to hide his own discomfort with the unbearable heat.

"Stay with me people, I know it's hot. But if Christ could die for my sins on that blessed cross, I can withstand a little heat," Bruce said as he hunched over the podium, wiping the sweat from his forehead with a crumpled handkerchief. His assistant, Bernice, sat directly behind him, drinking slowly from her cup of water. Turning to her, he put his hand over the microphone so others could not hear what he said to her.

"Bernice, did you call down to engineering?"

"Yes, Mr. Hedrick–twice, and they said they would be up to fix the air. That was an hour ago."

Bruce turned back to face the audience. "Ladies and gentlemen, I want to extend my sincerest apologies. When we reserved this room weeks ago, it was my understanding that we would have adequate air-conditioning. You've been most kind and patient despite this obstacle." Bruce searched the room for a forgiving glance and found few.

"Before I read the names of my two picks, let me remind you that you'll receive a full dossier on each candidate to enable you to make a wise choice when it comes down to the vote. We will have a formal dinner to congratulate the person voted in to take over when I step down three months from today. I know the time frame may appear long, but whoever fills my position has to be the best option."

He was confident that either candidate could tackle many of the problems the Black Republicans for Change faced in getting political clout to move Congress into action, and to welcome middle-and upper-middle-class black Republicans to the political table.

At that moment, Bruce began to cough. Bernice bolted up from her seat to hold him up as a male member of the audience poured Bruce a cup of water. After drinking a few sips and taking a few breaths, Bruce graciously thanked those who had helped him and proceeded to announce the candidates. "The nominees are Gary Walsh and Isaac Walterson."

A polite applause rose from the audience. Gary, looking elegant like Sidney Poitier, and Isaac, looking as though all his fat would unfurl if he removed his tight fitted suit, joined Bruce Hedrick on stage, while a couple of ushers handed out information packets about both candidates. The packets contained glossed-over profiles that served to highlight the achievements of both Gary and Isaac, and superficial question-and-answer sections called "Getting to Know Your Nominees."

As the ushers passed out the packets, Bruce spoke again. "The packets are meant to help familiarize you with both Mr. Walsh and Mr. Walterson. It will ultimately be

their responsibility to best articulate their vision of moving the BRC forward."

Gary Walsh stood on stage, his knees locked, his jaw clenched. The sweat that appeared on his brow had more to do with his thoughts than the heat in the room. He looked down to his wife, Wanda, who looked stunning in a black-and-white blocked sleeveless dress. Her hair was pulled back into a classy chignon. He winked at her, mouthing the words, "I love you."

Wanda smiled back, but mouthed nothing.

"Dear Lord, if it be your will, please give me this promotion. I'm tired of living in my wife's shadow," Gary murmured to himself. He loved his wife more than anything else in the world, but her success had long ago eclipsed his.

Tired of seeing bad weaves and synthetic wigs you had to throw away after one use, Wanda created her store Wanda's Wig World, offering moderately priced, high-quality human hair wigs, weaves, and other hair care products. After achieving that goal, she opened Wanda's Elite Experience, a chain of high-end salon and day spas featuring her own hair straightening and maintenance system. Despite her good fortune, she remained in Gary's corner, attending the same boring affairs month after month, year after year. For that, Gary was grateful. Still, he wanted to meet her halfway. This was a golden opportunity for him, and he needed this.

While Isaac beamed a bedazzling smile, and Gary struggled to nullify his thoughts, Drake Hill sat in the audience, with his coffee brown eyes fuming. He wasn't sure what made him angrier—not being considered for the position or the fact that Gary Walsh was standing up on the stage. Their rivalry started when the Star Tribune did an

article about up-and-coming African-Americans and their road to success in politics.

Drake was quoted as saying, "Gary's wife, Wanda, is very charming. Their relationship is inspiring on many different levels. It takes a strong man not to feel outshined by a woman who makes all the money."

When Gary confronted Drake about the article, Drake said he'd been misquoted. But Gary never believed that. Since that time, there was tension whenever they had to deal with each other.

While all of the well-wishers congregated, Drake went into the bathroom, locking the door behind him. Jealousy gnawed at him as he splashed cold water over his face and Caesar-style haircut. He looked up and stared at his reflection in the mirror. Once again someone had decided he wasn't good enough to be chosen; once again he'd tried to play the game and lost. Drake's father had been a surgeon at Hennepin County Medical, and his mother a respected professor at the University of Minnesota. Despite graduating at the top of his class at the University of Minnesota, he could never measure up to a bar set so high. Becoming president of the BRC might have been that opportunity to continue the Hill family's history of success. His parents were dead now, but their disappointment in him still haunted him.

A knock at the bathroom door pulled Drake out of his thoughts. He dried his face with a paper towel and gathered his composure. After a second, more forceful knock, Drake opened the door to find Gary Walsh standing on the other side smiling. But when he saw Drake standing there, his smile faded fast.

"Congratulations are in order," Drake said.

Gary walked past Drake, saying nothing.

"Did you hear me? I said congratulations."

"I heard you, Drake," Gary responded, standing at the urinal. "You know you don't mean a word of it."

"Why is it every time we're near one another, there always has to be conflict, Gary? I was simply congratulating you. That's all. I thought you'd gotten past all that other stuff, especially now. I mean, tonight is *supposed* to be your night, yours and Isaac's."

"Drake, I'm taking a leak. We can talk later."

"I simply meant to..."

"Later!" Gary said and turned his back, signaling an end to the conversation.

Drake shook his head and said, "Fine. Have it your way." He went into the hallway and left through a back exit. As he walked toward his car, Drake's eyes began to burn from the salt of his sweat. He paused in the parking lot to wipe them with the back of his hand, catching a glimpse of Gary and Wanda. Gary looked over in Drake's direction, and then looked away quickly. Drake shoved his hands into his pocket, holding his keys so tightly they dug into his palm. Inside his car, he started the engine and drove off into the night, not really knowing or caring where he was going.

CHAPTER FOUR

Tuesday, July 1, 2008

7:30 PM

Karen and Armando lay entwined in a loving embrace on the bed, the cool air kissing their moist skin. The scent of his maleness and her womanliness filled the room like invisible aphrodisiacs. Armando was proud of himself; never before had he heard Karen cry out so often with such intense pleasure. Their passion and tenderness were unlike anything he'd experienced before.

"Why are you with me?" Karen asked him, spoiling the afterglow.

"Because I love you."

Karen stared up at the ceiling as if she could look past it into the heavens. "Yeah, but, I mean, you could be with anybody you want to be with. I've seen some of the girls you used to mess with. I don't look like any of them." Tears began to well in her eyes. She shifted her focus, looking directly at Armando, who began to rub her shoulder as she lay nuzzled close to him.

"Yeah, but you have my heart. I chose you because while those other females are about the games, you keep it real with me. You encourage me to be a better man. I

never got that from any of them. I ain't goin' anywhere. And that's why, no matter what I have to do, I'll take care of you." His tone was soothing, almost paternal.

"Some of those other women are so pretty, though."

"Yeah, but they ain't got shit on you. You're the one I'm with. You're the total package." Armando lightly kissed her forehead.

The mere sensation made Karen shudder. She felt closer to him than she had in a while.

Armando was silently in awe of the woman lying next to him. She made him feel blessed every day and night. Despite their foolish squabbling, they were devoted to each other. Each had become the other's strength.

"Why can't you just accept that you're enough for me? My player days are long gone."

Karen's tears flowed freely. "You don't understand. I don't wanna end up by myself. My daddy fooled around on my mama like it was his job. After he died, my mama..." She couldn't continue. She abruptly freed herself from Armando's embrace and sat at the edge of the bed. The moonlight created a glow around her naked body. She wiped the tears from her eyes. "I wanna go out. You ain't got to work tomorrow, right?"

"Nope."

"Right, so I wanna go out." Her mind was already made up.

Armando, puzzled, said, "Yeah, sure, whatever you want, baby." He watched Karen slip into the blackness of the bathroom, and when he heard the shower, he pulled the pillow over his eyes to keep out the light from the bathroom.

"Eh, you want me to come in there with you?" Armando

called out. But the shower water beat down with such force that it drowned out his words.

A doorbell ring broke the calm. Armando jumped from the bed, searching for his jeans, then poked his head into the bathroom. "Are you expecting anyone?"

"It's probably Cabrien. He's joining us." Cabrien was Karen's favorite cousin. She loved that he was true to himself. Armando opened the door and Cabrien stood there decked out in tight blue jeans and an Abercrombie & Fitch muscle shirt.

"Oh, hey, Armando! Is my girl ready to rock?" Cabrien asked enthusiastically.

"Wassup, Cabrien. Naw, she's in the shower." Armando gave Cabrien the once over and invited him in. He didn't have a problem with gay people; he just believed that men should behave like men regardless of their sexual orientation. He found effeminate men difficult to relate to. "She'll be out in a minute."

"What do y'all have to eat up in here?" Cabrien asked, entering the apartment.

"There's some KFC in the kitchen. Help yourself," Armando said, hoping to sound hospitable.

"Uh, boo, I can't do chicken. I'm trying to watch my figure. I done told Karen about eating that mess!" Cabrien walked over to the bathroom door and, without looking in, called out, "Karen, your ass ain't ready yet?"

"I'll be out in a minute!" Karen hollered.

"Girl, hurry up! You're steamin' up the place and shit. It'll be hotter on the inside than it is on the outside." Cabrien turned to face Armando, who had taken a seat on the couch.

"Oh don't mind us," Cabrien said, smiling his most dazzling smile.

Armando managed a smile as Karen came into the living room in her bathrobe.

"Hey, boo. How you doin?" she asked happily.

"What's wrong with your hair? You need to let me do something to it," Cabrien said, backing away from her.

"It's wet, Cabrien. I just washed it. Dang."

Cabrien leaned in to give Karen a hug. Armando watched the exchange between Karen and her cousin, and found himself a bit envious. He never had that easy, affectionate give-and-take with his family.

"Yo, Cabrien, you want something to drink?" Armando asked, wanting to be included in the conversation.

"That depends. What have you got?" Cabrien replied as he broke his embrace with Karen.

"Uh, I got a beer," Armando said, holding up a green bottle as Cabrien's face turned disapproving.

"Y'all must think I'm one of these butch queens. No offense, but I don't drink beer. I don't like the taste and it leaves my stomach feeling heavy. What else do you have?"

"You know what, Negro? Nowhere does it say 'liquor store' here, okay? You take what we have or wait till your ass gets to the club," Karen chirped.

"Damn girl, you don't have to say it all like that," Cabrien said.

"No, I mean it, Cabrien. Save the diva act for the club, okay?" she said, snapping her fingers exaggeratedly.

"Karen, it's all good," Armando said, trying to smooth things over.

"No, it ain't all good. He knows better than that."

"Ain't no kids in here, Karen. I don't take what I don't want. You're tryin' to force beer on me now?"

"No, Cabrien. But a simple, 'No thank you' would've worked."

"Oh, get *this* bitch. The queen of the ghetto is gonna try and tell me how to speak to people!"

"Look, goddamn it," Armando said, "This is the beginning of my two days off and I'm not spending it listening to corny mess! Now, I said it was cool. If Cabrien doesn't want the beer, he ain't got to drink the beer. I mean come on, y'all!"

Cabrien smiled a slightly superior smile.

"Don't get happy. We really don't need you for a good time," Karen said, squashing his small triumph.

"Karen, go get ready," Cabrien said dismissively.

Armando followed Karen out of the living room and back into the bedroom, and closed the door. She began to put lotion on her body from head to toe as he kneeled down to pick up the sheets from off the floor. "I thought you guys were cool. Why are you yelling at each other like that?"

"I ain't thinkin' about that limp-wristed fool! He always has to be the center of attention. He can do that in the clubs. He ain't diva!"

Armando threw the sheets onto the bed. "I mean it. Nobody asked me what I wanted to do tonight. Don't get me out here if y'all are gonna be clowning all night."

Karen folded her arms and was silent for a moment. "Tell him to get in here," she said, looking as though she wanted to laugh but was trying to stay angry.

"You talk nice to each other, and put this back on." He handed her the robe and left. "Cabrien, man, she wants to

talk to you. But, I'm gonna to tell you like I just told her: you need to talk nice."

Cabrien walked past Armando as if he were prepared for a major fight. He went into the bedroom and closed the door. Armando sank back into the couch, emotionally spent as though he'd spent the entire day with bratty children. As he listened to the faint sharpness of voices, he got up and went to the bathroom to shower. They were so crazy, he thought, to quarrel about something so ridiculous and allow it to spoil the evening. If they were still at it by the time he got out of the shower, he'd tell them both that the evening was done and he was going to bed.

As Armando scrubbed his body, he began to get hard again, remembering the pleasure Karen's sweetness had given him. Her outburst with Cabrien had ruined his feeling of completeness with her.

When he finished, he turned off the water and dried off. He tried to hear if the hollering had subsided. It had, replaced with faint murmurs. He walked up to the closed door and knocked, "Are you guys finished in there?"

"We're still talking," Cabrien shouted from inside the bedroom. He and Karen erupted into laughter.

"Yeah—well can you finish that out here? I'm standing in the hallway, butt-ass-naked."

The laughter turned into wild cackles as Karen opened the door.

"Come on," she said to him, motioning him in with her index finger.

"Can I get some privacy?" Armando asked, clutching his towel closed. He glanced over Karen's shoulder at Cabrien, who seemed to be enjoying the view.

"Oh don't mind me, honey. I've seen many a dick

before."

Looking back at Karen, Armando said, "I bet you have, but still."

Karen smiled broadly, turning her attention to Cabrien. "He doesn't know you like that, boo. Come on. Let the man have some privacy."

"Thank you, appreciate it," Armando said, closing the door.

Karen stopped him halfway and said, "Don't be in here all night." And then she closed the door.

Armando finished drying off and threw the towel on the floor, burying his head into his hands. "Man, I don't wanna do this," he whispered to himself. After a defeated sigh he got up to get dressed.

In the living room, Cabrien sat with Karen. There was no hint there had been tension moments before. The air-conditioner stopped working. Both Karen and Cabrien looked over at the worthless machine, hearing water drain from it.

"Back when Mama decided she wanted to be friendly for a couple of seconds, she gave me that raggedy-ass machine. It was just sitting at her house so it wasn't like she was using it. Anyway, I had to act nice because you never knew when she was gonna get mean again."

Cabrien rolled his eyes at the mere mention of Karen's mother, Thelma. "Girl, your mama is Ms. Dial-a-Mood. I don't know how you took it for all those years." Karen gave Cabrien a high five as he spoke. "Your mama is supposed to be all saved and sanctified, but she's steady throwing daggers at people."

"Why you think me and my mama don't speak now?"

Karen ran her fingers through her damp hair. "What should I do with my hair?"

"Girl, you better throw some grease on that bad boy and call it a day, because it's too late to start messing with it now," Cabrien said.

"But you said that I should let you do something to it," Karen said. Armando walked out into the living room. Karen looked up at him and smiled.

"You ready?" She gave his outfit an approving look. He wore a blue oxford shirt and khaki slacks. He nodded yes.

"Well, let's hit it, y'all. I need to get my drink on!" Cabrien said.

"Hit the lights, Negro," Karen said, adjusting the short, black-and-purple swirl printed halter dress she wore.

"Girl, that dress is fierce, and the shoes are workin,'" Cabrien said.

They all went outside, Armando closing the door behind them. Cabrien had been correct; it was cooler outside. The moon lit the path to the vehicles.

"Who's driving?" Karen asked.

"I don't care who's driving as long as I'm drinking," Cabrien said.

"I'll drive. Where are we going, by the way?" Armando asked with disappointment in his voice. He knew his own fun would be curtailed. Since he was being dragged out, he at least hoped to catch a buzz and now wouldn't be able to do that.

"Oh, it's a place for my kinda folks, called Sir Martin's," Cabrien said, his lips shaping a mischievous grin. "Don't worry, nobody will bother you." He disappeared into the backseat and closed the door. Armando gave Karen a worried look but said nothing. After all three were buckled up

Armando started the car and drove off into the summer evening, doubtful he'd have any fun at all.

CHAPTER FIVE

Tuesday, July 1, 2008

8:30PM

"We're home, so you can hang up now," Gary said to Wanda as the massive, stained-oak garage door opened. There was an edge in his tone that made her take notice.

"Ray, I don't care what it takes. It should've been handled by now!" She clicked off her cell phone with a flourish. "Boy, I tell you. Some people."

Gary turned the car off and got out in one swift motion. Wanda followed Gary into the house. She stood back and watched him stomp into the darkness of the house.

Flicking on the foyer light, Wanda asked, "What's wrong?"

"What do you mean?" he asked, tossing her an icy glance. His movements were brisk. He threw his keys onto the small credenza in the foyer and slammed his briefcase down.

He's such a big baby, Wanda thought to herself. She knew she'd soured his mood by not spending another half-hour disingenuously engaging people at Pearl Park. And she didn't want to sit quietly in the car and listen to Gary's brainstorms. The ride home was an ideal time to call Ray,

who'd promised her property permits months ago, and was holding up progress. Time was money as far as she was concerned. The time she'd put into her businesses afforded them the lifestyle they'd grown accustomed to. Gary was just *now* playing catch-up to her.

"It's too hot to play guessing games, Gary. Are you going to tell me what's wrong or not?"

"Did you have to rush off like that?"

"Were we not at the same place? It was too hot in there. Ray is driving me crazy with his incompetence, so I had to get a hold of him before he shut his phone off like I know he likes to do. So excuse me for wanting to get my business in order."

"But this is *my* opportunity, don't you get that?"

"How many opportunities have you had, Gary? First, you wanted to run for city council; then you wanted to run for mayor. *Then*, you completely dropped politics altogether and said you wanted to become an owner operator of a fast-food franchise. Now, we're back to politics. Don't get me wrong, I love to see your face light up about something. But you don't think things through. Either that, or you never follow up."

"Can't a man change his mind in life?"

"Of course, but at some point you need to make a decision! Stick with something! I get so sick of all the talk of big dreams and then you walk away from it all when it becomes difficult. Sometimes things have to be difficult, or they're not worth the time."

"You think I like drifting? You think I like following you around like some puppy dog?"

"I don't know, Gary. You tell me."

Gary stared at her. Why pick this moment to tell him

how she really felt? He'd been more than supportive when it came to her aspirations. As he recalled, she'd had some tearful nights when everything that could have gone wrong before the opening of her first store went wrong. At one point she didn't think there would even be a store.

"If I remember correctly, that damn store wasn't an overnight success either, and yet I stuck by you. I didn't kick you when I saw you trying so hard."

"You're absolutely right; you were there. And yes, the store didn't take off right away. But you were there every step of the way when it did. Listen, I know all of that. I love you for all of that. Believe me; I'm not trying to discourage you. I'm just trying to be real about this. I just want you to find *some* kind of success."

"I'm through with this conversation." He left Wanda standing in the foyer, went into the kitchen and poured himself a glass of wine. *How long had she felt this way?* he thought to himself.

"Gary, don't be like this. I'm just being honest," Wanda said, her voice entering the kitchen before she did.

"You're not the only one around here who made sacrifices. I let you talk me out of having a brother or sister for Abbey. You promised once things settled down that we could try for more children."

Wanda looked as if she'd been slapped. "When did it ever settle down to where I could lay down and get pregnant again? Things got crazy. I thought you understood all of that!"

"Yeah, right. There never was going to be another baby because you were intent on never having another! You're just throwing in the whole 'I was busy' thing to justify it to yourself!"

"Do you, or do you not, love our daughter?" Wanda demanded to know.

"What kind of question is that? Of course I love our daughter."

"She's turned into an amazing young woman who's about to finish at the top of her class at university. I don't know about you, but I'm proud of that. Some people can't even have children. We should be praising God for the amazing one we have!"

"You could've just said you were fine with just one so you wouldn't have gotten my hopes up," Gary said quietly.

Shaking her head, Wanda moved to pour herself a glass of wine. Truthfully, as her success grew, plans to expand their family took a backseat, and then eventually disappeared. She hadn't planned it that way. But it was what it was.

She wanted to say something, but she gulped her wine instead and allowed the words to die on her lips. The libation thawed the chilliness in her voice.

"Clearly we're both holding on to some things," Wanda offered.

"Clearly."

"I don't want to go to bed angry with you."

"Me either. So what now?" Gary said, loosening his tie.

"Let's go out to eat."

"You wait until we get all the way home to figure out you want to go out to eat?" he thought to himself before saying, "Sure. Figlios?"

"Perfect. Let me freshen up a bit. Are you going in what you have on?"

"I'd planned on it."

"Okay, I'll be quick," Wanda said, turning around the-atrically and leaving the kitchen.

Gary poured Wanda's remaining wine into his own glass. He turned on the small TV and caught a rerun of *A Different World*.

By the time he'd finished the wine, the TV credits rolled. He looked at his watch. Between his laughter and the wine, fifteen minutes had passed. He made his way toward the bedroom, calling out to Wanda. "Listen, we should get going if we're..." Gary found Wanda standing in the middle of the bedroom. As he stood in the doorway, she let her black-and-white, Michael Kors summer dress fall to her feet. She stared at him with beckoning eyes. It was tried and true; an easy way to make things right.

His manhood surged inside his pants. He walked toward her slowly, taking in her sensuality. He reminisced on the first time he laid eyes on her at Howard University. She looked like a young, *Julia*-era Diahann Carroll as she placed a tapioca pudding cup on her lunch tray. Tapioca was his favorite pudding.

Now, he stood before her in her *Dynasty*-era incarna-tion; just as ambitious, just as sophisticated, and just as sexy in her own right.

He placed his hands firmly on her breasts, something he hadn't done in a while. He relished the rare opportu-nity, unsheathing them from her bra. Then he kissed her tenderly. It had been a while for that too. Their affection had become forced in recent years; closed, pressed lips at the start and end of their days. But now, he sucked the softness of her tongue, pushing her into the vanity. He pulled the expensive pin from her chignon, unfurling her store-bought tresses. He turned her around to face the

mirror above the vanity, so she could see him lick and kiss her silky neck. He brought his other hand to her opening, touching it, almost deep massaging it, letting loose her sexual pulses. She rolled her head back, feeling the best, the most desirable she'd felt in months.

Hearing her purr with appreciation, he dropped his pants and underwear, sliding his dick inside her as she writhed against him. Though Wanda usually conducted herself as a lady, she allowed her inner whore to savor the experience.

"That all you got? You playin' with it," she whispered.

"I ain't done with it yet," Gary said like an old pro, throwing the tie from his neck to the floor. He pulled open his shirt, sending popped buttons flying about.

He swirled his hips deep, savoring the way she felt from the inside and out. Even as she bent before him, hair tussled, sex-speak whorish, there was something still very lux about her, like an expensive object he was proud to own. Gary let go of her waist and slid his hands between her inner thighs. As he pounded away, the carnal sounds of their blissful moans and melding of flesh heightened their arousal.

Later, Wanda stood in the doorway of the en suite bathroom, wearing a diaphanous cream-colored robe. Gone were the false eyelashes and expensive makeup, but her natural beauty remained.

"You know what I keep thinking about?"

Gary was where she had left him, lying on the bed, spent.

"I don't know."

"How you and I used to be so frisky in school. Suddenly, here we are, in the beginning of our fifties, taking

ourselves way too seriously. Do you even remember the last time we made love like that?"

Gary propped up his pillow and rested his head. "I want to say, the night before finals week."

Wanda sat on the edge of the bed. "I think you might be right. That's a damn shame, actually."

Gary pulled Wanda onto the bed, holding her from behind. They were silent for a moment. Then she said, "I guess it wouldn't have hurt me to congratulate you for your nomination. I'm sorry."

Gary shook his head. "And maybe you have a point. If I followed through more, you'd find it easier to get behind me."

"I am behind you. My workload is no excuse to toss off what matters to you. You're going to get that promotion. If you believe it, then so do I," she said.

Gary squeezed her lovingly to show his forgiveness. Soon he began to snore. He'd fallen asleep with a renewed spirit.

Wanda got up and made her way to her side of the bed. She stood, staring at Gary's back as he slept. She shook her head and whispered to him, "All right then. Show me."

CHAPTER SIX

It was Retro Night at Sir Martin's. Psychedelic pulses flashed across six flat-screen televisions placed around the bar and dance floor.

The bartenders—all gorgeous, with muscles busting out from their tight, fitted black shirts—were shaking their asses as they shook drinks behind the sleek, stainless steel bar.

Cabrien, Karen, and Armando put their IDs away as they entered, and scoped out the scene. Cabrien salivated at the male eye candy while Armando positioned himself closer to his girlfriend.

Boy, calm your nerves, Cabrien thought, sensing Armando's nervousness. Cabrien began to fan himself dramatically. He felt at home, and was ready to let loose. "What are y'all drinking?" Cabrien shouted to his companions once they had all gathered at the bar.

"What do they have?" Karen asked, freeing herself from Armando's grip.

"Whatever you want, but I should warn you, chick, this *is* a classy joint. You better not order any of that Alize stuff. I gotta maintain my reputation," Cabrien said, only half-joking.

"I'll have a glass of white wine, then," Karen said, trying to look demure.

"Armando, what do you want?" Cabrien asked.

"Uh, I'll have the same."

The music began to segue from "Incense and Peppermints" into The Who's "My Generation." While Cabrien busied himself trying to flag down a bartender, Armando noticed a sharply dressed, older African-American man with a graying low-cut haircut watching him from the bar.

"Yo, why is this dude steadily staring at me?" Armando said as he took a sip of his wine.

"Who are you talking about?" Cabrien asked, looking around the room.

"Don't be obvious, just follow my eyes."

"Oh him, that's Drake. I had him before," Cabrien said, once he recognized him.

"You know him?" Armando asked.

"I don't think you heard me, I *had* him," Cabrien said proudly.

"Well, your boy keeps looking over here at me," Armando said uneasily.

Cabrien became exasperated. "Well, where do you think you are, Armando? I mean this *is* a gay bar. Just be flattered, and don't start, all right?"

Karen looked at Armando as if to underscore Cabrien's request that he behave himself.

"Yeah, okay. But nobody better get the wrong idea," Armando said.

"Armando, Drake is a nice guy. Ain't no tea there. Why don't you go over and meet him?"

"So he can try and hit on me? No, I'm good on that one."

"How very straight of you," Cabrien replied, shaking his head. Then he turned and disappeared into the throng of people, making his way over to Drake.

"Try and relax, please. I don't want to hear from Cabrien how homophobic he thinks you are, okay?" Karen pleaded. She took a sip from her wine glass as she watched Cabrien talk to Drake. "If Cabrien is talking to him then he couldn't be too bad."

"I guess," Armando said dryly. He nodded toward Drake, who never took his eyes off him, even as Cabrien talked to him.

"Here, change places with me so that my back will face him. That guy is bugging me out," Armando said as he angled Karen's body.

"Why do you have to act like this?"

"Karen, it's his eyes. It's like he's stripping me naked."

"Armando, please," she rolled her eyes. "You act like you can't go anywhere without somebody wanting to sleep with you."

"I can't," Armando said under his breath, shrugging.

On the other side of the room Cabrien was trying desperately to get Drake to go to bed with him. Drake had paid Cabrien for sex many times, and Cabrien welcomed the opportunity to make money for just an hour of his time. He was quietly thankful when he noticed Armando change his position.

"Your friend appears out of sorts," Drake said, looking up at Cabrien for the first time.

"He's not my friend. That's my cousin's boyfriend."

Drake squinted to get a good look at Karen. "She's pretty," he said simply.

"Yeah, she is, isn't she? So, Drake, I was wondering if you needed some..."

"Is he gay?" Drake interrupted.

"No, he's straight," Cabrien said annoyed. *"Very straight."*

"Why is he here, then?" Drake asked, ignoring Cabrien's agitation.

"Because I wanted to go out, and so did my cousin and he's kind of along for the ride." Cabrien knew then that he was losing the battle.

"And you're sure that he's straight? I mean, he's gorgeous, Cabrien."

"Yes, I'm sure, Drake. Damn!"

Drake turned back to Cabrien as if coming out of a daydream. "Oh, I'm sorry; you were meaning to ask me something?"

Cabrien's feelings were hurt. He never had to work this hard at getting Drake's attention before, and it was a slap to his ego.

"I was just asking if you wanted some company tonight," Cabrien said, his eyes downcast.

"I would love some if you can bring him along," Drake said, ignoring Cabrien's hurt feelings.

"I told you he's straight," Cabrien repeated. This is what Cabrien liked least about Drake– the way he would become fixated on what he wanted. Cabrien sensed he'd need to bide his time and wait. Let Drake become a little more intoxicated before he brought up the subject again. Drake was hornier when he was drunk.

"I'm going back to my cousin over there. Are you gonna be around later?"

"Tell him to come over here," Drake said.

"I don't think so." Cabrien walked away. He knew he had to come up with a way to get Drake to take him home. Making his way through the crowd seemed harder than before—as if the bar had exceeded capacity in those few minutes he'd spoken to Drake. The crowd swallowed Cabrien as he fought his way to his cousin and Armando.

Armando was watching the interaction of those around him and was a little bit intrigued by what he saw. Besides coworkers, the only gay people he knew were his aunt Beatriz and her partner Yvette. They'd been together as far back as he could remember. His mother never bothered to explain the nature of their relationship. It wasn't until he became older he understood that his aunt and Yvette were life partners and he was impressed that they'd managed to stay together for more than thirty years. Lesbians he could understand. After all, they liked what he liked. But he couldn't understand the dynamic of two dudes getting down.

Cabrien finally pushed through the crowd and stood in front of Karen and Armando, his face in a grimace.

"What's wrong with you?" Karen asked.

"Too many bitches in here. I've spilled half my wine trying to get back over here!" Cabrien screamed over the music.

"Well, you picked this place, and anyway, you can always get another glass of wine. It is a bar, after all."

Cabrien gave her a *don't go there* look. Turning to Armando, his expression changed to one of mischievous glee. "I think Drake was wagging his dick at you underneath that bar."

"Did you tell him he was wasting his time?"

"Yes, but I think that turned him on even more," Cabrien said, getting a kick out of Armando's uneasiness.

"Whatever he likes is fine for him. Just tell his ass to keep it over there," Karen chimed in.

The beginning sounds of Rose Royce's "Car Wash" distracted Karen long enough so that Cabrien didn't need to respond. Karen looked as she always did when a particular song that she liked came on the radio. She would close her eyes and begin smiling broadly as if the singer was singing just for her.

"Baby, I feel like dancing," Karen informed Armando.

"I don't have a buzz yet, so I don't feel like it. Give me a little time," Armando said, watching the tiny dance floor become engulfed with men.

"Cabrien, let's go dance," Karen said.

"Come on, girl. But if a cute guy wants to dance with me, let him. I don't need you killing my action," Cabrien said, grabbing Karen by the hand and leading her to the crowded dance floor. He looked over in Drake's direction one last time and found Drake staring down at the bar. Something was wrong, he guessed.

Armando looked for an empty seat and found one next to a young woman who appeared very masculine. Smiling at her, he asked if anyone was sitting in that seat.

"Yeah," she said with no warmth in her voice.

Armando didn't respond to her rudeness. Instead, he went and stood in a spot against the wall by the entrance. He soon found himself having an inner dialogue with himself, "Yo, his punk ass better quit staring at me, for real! I mean, I'm not trying to hate on anyone for what they like. There are gay dudes at the job I get along with just fine. But they know better than to be coming at me like this. They

know better. This dude right here is gonna mess around and get his grill busted if he keeps playing with me!"

The lights began to rotate and the tiny disco ball twinkled. Sweat dripped from the bodies on the dance floor. Karen had caught the fever too, and was in her element as she danced with her cousin.

Just then, the drag queen diva Divinia Butterfly sashayed into the middle of the dance floor, fanning herself theatrically, beckoning everyone to move back to give her room. She was wearing a spectacular fuchsia and silver colored sequined mini dress with a high neck and dolman sleeves that glittered dazzlingly under the light.

The crowd quickly created a circle around Divinia, and she danced in six-inch, black ankle boots as no one else there dared to– high kicks and splits that shook the wig of wild curls on top of her head.

"You better go in, diva, and let have!" Cabrien squealed in delight.

The mob erupted into wild applause at Divinia Butterfly's antics. Karen was caught in the moment as well. "I hate it when guys look better than me when they dress in drag," she said while applauding. While Divinia continued to strut, Karen looked to see if she could find Armando, but the bodies standing in the circle had closed off her view.

Armando's silent talk to himself ended in time to realize he wanted another glass of wine. Finally there was space to move so he wouldn't have to elbow anyone or be elbowed out of the way. When he got to the bar, he looked over and was able to see Divinia's commotion from that angle.

"What can I get you, sweetie?" the bartender asked him.

"Another white wine, please," Armando said with a forced smile.

While waiting for the wine, he tried to avoid making eye contact with Drake, who he was sure was still looking at him. But his curiosity won out. He looked to see if Drake was looking at him, but Drake wasn't sitting there. A wave of relief came over him and he began to sway to the music of "Car Wash", which seemed to go on and on.

"Can I get that for you?" a voice said from behind Armando. He turned around and saw Drake standing, looking intensely at him.

"No, thank you, I got it," Armando said, quickly turning back to face forward.

Drake stepped from behind him and stood at Armando's side. "I insist." Drake placed a twenty-dollar bill onto the bar. When the bartender came back with the glass of wine Drake forcibly pushed the bill at the bartender and told him to keep the change.

Armando took a big gulp from the glass. "Thanks, man," he said, his eyes looking downward.

"You're a very good-looking man," Drake said matter-of-factly.

"Thanks," Armando replied, still looking down.

"What's your name?"

"Why do you need to know my name?"

"You don't have to tell me now, but I guarantee I'll find out before I walk out that door tonight." Drake was captivated by the brilliance of Armando's gray eyes. Time stood still for him for just a moment.

"I see you got jokes," Armando said, taking another gulp of the wine. He looked away from Drake once more

to search the dance floor for Karen and Cabrien. "You boys with Cabrien, right?"

"Yes, Cabrien and I have a history," Drake said, looking over at the crowd himself. He spoke as though he were referring to a very distant memory.

"And now?"

"Well, if you were watching, then you'd know that I find you far more interesting."

"Yeah, I caught that. I don't appreciate you staring at me," Armando said, trying to posture aggressively.

Drake smiled. "You know, I'm always fascinated at you straight brothas who think you're doing all of us fags a favor by coming into our establishments. Instead of kicking back and enjoying yourselves, you all spend the entire evening trying to prove your heterosexuality. Your male ego is telling you that I want you so badly, as if I couldn't possibly get anyone else in this bar."

Armando was taken aback. "Yeah, but dude, it's not every day I'm in a place like this; dudes staring at me, wondering how big my johnson is, or how good I'm gonna lay it in the bedroom. It makes me a little nervous."

"Oh, I think more than a little nervous. In any event, have no fear. I'm not going to support your narcissistic self-image that everyone in this place wants you to bang them, or possibly wants to bang you. Perhaps you should steer clear of these places until you can relax."

Peep this uppity fool, Armando thought to himself.

The music changed to Barry Manilow's "Copacabana". Karen and Cabrien found their way back to Armando before the rest of the crowd had dispersed. When Cabrien saw Drake next to Armando, he looked on disapprovingly.

"Well, Cabrien, you didn't tell me that you know such charming individuals. Imagine my surprise," Drake said.

"This is Armando's girlfriend, Karen," Cabrien said, pushing Karen forward to shake Drake's hand.

Drake smiled and then winked at Armando, having learned his name. Armando averted his eyes. "Karen, I must say you're beautiful. You two make a great-looking couple."

Drake looked again to Armando, who was now looking at the pulses on the flat screen television on the wall nearest him.

"Thank you," Karen said happily.

"You all have a good evening, I'm sure I'll be seeing you very soon." And he was gone.

"What did I miss?" Cabrien asked. His tone was laced with resentment.

"Not much, he just came and offered to buy me a drink. I didn't see you guys so I figured I'd have another one."

"You knew we were over there dancing," Karen said.

"What was going on over there anyway?"Armando asked to change the subject. "All of a sudden I look up and there's a huge crowd over on the dance floor, and I saw just little glimpses of someone twirling in the middle of the circle."

"That was just a drag queen over there acting crazy. She's a friend of mine," Cabrien said. He quickly looked around. None of the other men looked in desperate need to pay for a pretty young thing to warm the bed. It wasn't Armando's intention to steal a potential client from him, but his jealousy still wouldn't fade. The rent was due in a few days and he was at a loss as to what to do.

"What's wrong with your face?" Karen asked Cabrien.

"Drake was supposed to loan me some money for my rent."

"Hey, babe, maybe you can loan him some money," Armando said.

"Boy, I don't have that kind of money," Karen replied, feeling put on the spot. "Anyway, I'm working all kinds of doubles at the bar and we're still struggling. I love you, cousin, but I can't help you. Not today."

"That's cool," Cabrien said with a shrug. "I got one other person I can ask. I'm going out to have a cigarette." Cabrien left, not waiting for a response.

"I should've stayed at home. I'm bored," Armando said, pulling Karen close to him.

"Well, you're just standing off by yourself, not dancing or anything. No wonder you're bored." Karen welcomed his embrace in the midst of all the energy around them. She continued, "So what do you think of my cousin?" She felt now was a good time for Armando to be honest, with Cabrien outside.

"He seems like a whole lot to handle. I mean, he seems cool, but a little too girly for my taste. Does he actually go walking down the street acting like that?" he asked.

Karen nodded.

"Well then, I give him mad props for being bold enough to do that, because I know that if I swung that way, I'd keep it on the down low. Nobody would know but me and God."

"His mama doesn't really talk about it with him, and you know how *my* mama is. I'm really the only family he has who accepts him. When everyone else kicked us to the curb, we bonded. He's like my brother."

"Hey, whatever makes him happy," Armando said.

Exhaling cigarette smoke, Cabrien stared inside

through the bar's window at his cousin and her man, their arms around each other, their eyes focused only on each other, looking very much in love.

CHAPTER SEVEN

When Drake arrived at work that Monday, he was less than happy to be there. He'd brooded all weekend about what he felt was a snub by the organization. He was determined to get answers from Bruce Hedrick as to why he'd been overlooked, especially considering all the help he'd given to politicians affiliated with the Black Republicans for Change.

As Drake walked the hallway, the walls seemed to close in on him. Colors flattened and the people walking around him seemed as if they were moving in slow motion. He paused for a moment to get his bearings. Bernice was sitting at her desk when he arrived outside Bruce Hedrick's office.

"Good morning. Is he in yet?" Drake asked, his eyes looking past her to the closed door.

"He had a breakfast meeting and then a personal errand to run. He should be in at about 11:00, no later than 11:30."

"Thanks, I'll try him later," he said, and turned toward his office.

When he passed Gary Walsh's office, he heard laughter. His entire body tensed. He didn't want to even look into that room. Once he arrived in his office, the room felt hot

and stale. He cranked the air-conditioner up to high. Yeah, it was costly to cool the entire building, but it was the least the organization owed him.

After dropping his briefcase, he sat in his swivel chair and closed his eyes. The only image that brought a smile to his face was the good-looking man he'd met at the bar two nights ago. The likelihood of him seeing him again was nil, but the image was still a welcomed distraction.

Eventually he heard Bruce Hedrick make his way through the corridor, graciously saying good morning to all of his staff, as he did every day. Bruce was savvy to know that if he treated his staff well, they would in turn work hard for him.

Drake put aside the folder of documents he'd been half-heartedly reviewing, and proceeded to follow Bruce the short distance to his office. When Bruce noticed Bernice looking over his shoulder, he realized that he had company. Judging by the stern look on Drake's face, it was obvious to Bruce that there was a problem.

"Good morning, Drake," Bruce said.

"Good morning, Mr. Hedrick." Drake's tone was surly.

Bruce placed his briefcase on the floor near the file cabinet in his office and opened the blinds of his window that faced the street. The rumble of traffic was barely audible.

"Well, you sound and look pissed about something," Bruce said, deciding to cut to the chase.

"Can you please explain why you didn't consider me as a candidate for the promotion? I've been here longer than Gary and about as long as Isaac. All three of us lobby. But *I'm* the one you come to over and over again when you want the politicians we deal with to play dirty. And after all of that you deny me a nomination?"

"Drake the organization recognizes—" Bruce instantly rephrased his answer. "I recognize all of your contributions to the BRC and most importantly to me."

"Okay. So what gives?"

Bruce slowly sat down in his chair, hoping his uneasiness was not apparent. "To be totally honest, I really had no idea that you were interested in the position."

"With all due respect, sir, don't insult my intelligence. You know perfectly well that I had and still have an interest in being president of the BRC. I have a vision that can bring all Republicans together."

"I can appreciate what you're saying, Drake. When you've collaborated with our politicians out in the field, they've won every single time. That has always made them indebted to us. You're very good at what you do here. No doubt about it," Bruce said, smiling wryly.

"So why am I not a candidate?"

"All right, Drake. Do you want an honest answer?"

"Yes please." Drake felt he was finally getting somewhere.

"I did and do believe that you've done wonderful things for us in your current capacity. However, your lifestyle choice would be a liability that we can't afford at this point. It flagrantly contradicts many of the values of our constituents."

"Ah, here we go," Drake said bitterly. "Mr. Hedrick, I work, travel, pay my taxes, and go to the theater every now and again. All of those things are my lifestyle, not just who I have consensual sex with. Let's not be one-dimensional here."

"Drake, let's be realistic. Most of the people who work here and the folks we do business with are church going

folk—Baptists, Pentecostals. Now that's just a fact. What you do in your private life doesn't take away from the fact that you do wonderful work here. Your job has never been in jeopardy, and you know that. But putting you as the face of what we're trying to build here would ruin everything I've—*we've* worked so hard to achieve. You think I'm going to let you mess that up?"

"Wow. I guess I didn't know being gay was such a liability. I don't flaunt it."

"Brotha, look. I don't give a good-goddamn what you do. I really don't. That's between you and God. But I do care about the legacy of this organization. Like I just said, the people we get elected are church going folk."

"And do you remember how we got them elected? It was due largely to my digging up dirt on the opposing side. I can still hear the poor liberal politicians crying in the wings because I've ruined a career or two. That's what you've paid me to do, and that's what I've done."

"Still, having a practicing homosexual leading a black Republican organization with roots in the church? How in the hell would we explain it?" Bruce's voice had become agitated.

"Well, I guess now you won't have to." Drake rose from the chair and left Bruce Hedrick's office. He tore through the corridor like a hurricane, ignoring those in his path. His face was sweaty, his breathing ragged.

"All of 'em can go ahead and kiss my naturally black, naturally gay ass!" Drake muttered, slamming his office door behind him.

CHAPTER EIGHT

The telephone was ringing when Karen unlocked her front door. "Hello," she said, kicking her shoes off after sitting on the couch.

"Girl, why are you all out of breath?" It was Cabrien.

"Because I just got done climbing three flights of stairs. What's up?"

"Girl, I am not having a good couple of days."

"What happened?" Karen slid her shoes to the side of the couch.

"Well, you know my rent is due. Hell, it's been due, and I can't find anyone who can help me."

"Okay. And?"

"I went out last night, and I saw this guy I knew named Paul. He said he could loan me the money."

"So what's the problem?"

"I didn't get it. He ditched me for some boy-bitch. And a nasty one at that."

"Wow, you called the boy-bitch nasty?" Karen began to chuckle.

"Well he is. He tries to act like he's diva. All he knows how to do is mooch off people. He can't even pay the twenty-five dollars a month for his low-income housing. Dude came over to my house many moons ago because he

didn't have a place to stay and you know I'm always trying to help other people out. Girl, he was so funky; I literally threw a wash rag and an unopened bar of soap at him and told him to wash his ass."

"No, you didn't!" Karen's chuckles flowed into wild laughter.

"I sure did, huntie. I don't play when it comes to hygiene."

Karen doubled over into the couch, her face buried into the cushion. "Cabrien, you ain't said none of that!" She was laughing so hard that her eyes began to water.

"That doesn't make any sense, somebody stankin' like that! But I'm sure Paul found out. That's what his ass gets trying to ditch somebody."

Karen tried to get serious for the moment. "I wish I had it, cousin. I truly do. What little money I have, I need."

"I know it. That's why I feel bad even talking to you about this," Cabrien said, in a somber tone. All of the humor opening the conversation was gone.

"I worry about you, though," Karen said. "I know I'm not your mama, but I worry you're gonna mess around and get AIDS, or get killed by some crazy person."

"Well, if I ever tested positive for HIV, I would get on the pill cocktail quick fast," Cabrien said.

"Yeah, well, a girl at work said that her brother went on that cocktail and it ain't working for him."

"Too bad for him," Cabrien said, trying to sound unaffected by her statement.

"Cabrien, I'm serious! Those drugs don't work for everybody, and I'm not even gonna ask if you're practicing safe sex. But if you aren't, then I advise you to start."

Cabrien was silent on his end. All of a sudden the tone

and theme of the conversation had gone into a direction he hadn't anticipated. "Karen, you're tired so I'm going to let you go," Cabrien said.

"No, Cabrien, don't be mad."

"I'm not mad. I was just about to walk out the door but thought I'd give you a call before I did," he explained.

"All right then, I'll talk to you later. I love you."

"Yep. Me too." Cabrien hung up quickly. He didn't really have anywhere to go, but he stood in his kitchen and began to sob out loud. He had to do something but at that moment, he felt as though he was losing against something not easily beaten.

Karen hung up her phone and sank back into the sofa. She closed her eyes, hoping he was protecting himself, but with Cabrien one could never be sure. He was the only family member she'd grown to count on and couldn't imagine life without him.

Karen began to pray silently, "Precious Lord, please bless my cousin, Cabrien. He's doing the best he can. I just pray that You don't take Your merciful and watchful hand off him. In Christ's name I pray, amen."

***

Armando's day had gone from bad to worse. The restaurant was filled to capacity with bratty children and impatient adults. Armando was determined to make it out of the dining room with his sanity intact.

"Um, excuse me, but can I please have a cup of tea? And while you're at it, can you get a rag and clean this table off? It's disgusting," a woman said to him.

Armando looked at the woman and the other two peo-

ple sitting at the table, shooting them all a look of consternation, but said nothing. He went over to the side station where Octavia, a server, was busy pulling up a check for another table. Without thinking he leaned into the side station.

"You have a bitchy joiner over at table 37," Armando informed her.

"Why, what happened?" Octavia asked, turning from the screen in front of her to look at Armando.

"There's a lady over there talking about how nasty the table is, and can I get her some tea. And she wasn't nice about it. Maybe you should go over there and see what else she needs, if anything. And don't forget that lady's tea," he said, trying to be helpful.

"She'll be all right for a few minutes." Octavia went back to retrieving the check for another guest.

"I'll bus the table when they're finished, but I'm not going over there unless you go and check up on those people, because I'm not tryin' to hear people's nonsense today."

"I'll be done in a minute."

When Octavia emerged from the side station, check in one hand and a teapot in the other, Armando followed her to the table where she dropped off the check. He then followed her to table 37.

Armando took the dirty plates and napkins away from the table as Octavia placed the tea pot in front of the woman. She asked if there was anything she could bring them.

"I don't do English breakfast tea. Don't you have green tea? It might've been nice if someone could've asked what

type I like instead of just bringing what you think I'd like," the woman said curtly.

Armando shot Octavia a knowing look as he finished taking the dishes off the table.

"Oh my God! This table is just nasty, I can't believe it," the woman said as she ran her hand along the table.

"You know, Armando, it's really bogus how people sit down at a dirty table that two other people just vacated when we have clean tables available, and then want to cop an attitude." Octavia looked down at the snooty woman to make it known she was talking about her.

"May I have a cup?" the woman asked, ignoring Octavia's speech. The two other individuals at the table squirmed uncomfortably.

"If you'd be patient, I will bring one to you," Octavia said, trying not to match the level of spite in the woman's voice.

"It should've been here in the first place. And never mind about the green tea. If you go to fetch it, you probably won't come back," the woman said as she placed the tea bag into the pot.

"Look, nobody told your ass to come and sit at a dirty table. I would've been over here to bus it earlier, but I was in the kitchen getting food for another table because believe it or not, other people do exist besides you," Armando interrupted.

The woman shook her head and said, "Whatever."

"Naw, don't 'whatever' me! I'm sick of people like you bringing your asses in here, acting like you're better than everyone else!"

Octavia began to look around in embarrassment as

Armando's voice rose. She appreciated what he was doing but didn't think it was all that serious to lose a job over.

The food and beverage director was standing at the hostess stand and had witnessed the entire episode. He walked over to the booth, noticing the look of incredulity on the woman's face.

"Are you the manager?" the woman asked.

"Yes ma'am. My name is Ben Travis, food and beverage director here at the hotel. Is there a problem?"

"You didn't just see that?" the woman almost shrieked.

"Ma'am, I'm sorry that your experience here has been unpleasant."

"That young man is downright rude. All I asked for was some tea and he comes and bites my head off. I mean, *really!*"

Ben turned to face Armando, who glared at the woman's misrepresentation of what happened.

"Ma'am, please calm down. I wouldn't want to disturb the other guests."

"Calm down? You're too late for that because this young man's attitude is the problem."

"Bullshit, lady! *Your* attitude is the motherfuckin' problem!" Armando screamed.

Ben whirled around to face Armando. The anger in his eyes almost made him lose his professionalism. "My apologies, ma'am. Your entire meal will be complimentary. Armando, go into the office and wait for me. Octavia, find something else to do!"

Octavia passed Armando an apologetic glance and left the scene obediently.

Armando went outside to the hotel's loading dock and lit a cigarette. He'd had it with the hotel. He knew the end

of his job was a sure thing, but he didn't care. He stood outside in the heat, his body trembling.

Beverly, another server, came outside with a look of shock on her face. "Oh my God, Armando what happened in there?"

"Bullshit happened! And it's gonna keep on happening because none of you people wanna stand up for yourselves!"

"Armando, I told you weeks ago that they have been inching closer and closer to firing you. And now you've gone and acted stupid."

"Stupid my ass, Beverly! I'm not gonna sit there and just let someone talk crazy to me!"

"Well, you've just got yourself fired. I hope you know that," she said to him, shaking her head.

"I don't give a shit," Armando said, staring out into the parking lot.

"I hope you have something else lined up."

"I can find another job."

"Not acting like this you won't. I get why you're upset, but if you don't rein it in, you'll keep cutting off your nose to spite your face! There are ways to handle things like this, and I'm telling you, what you did in there was not one of them!"

"Yeah okay," Armando said, flicking his cigarette from the dock and turning to leave.

"No, let's talk about this," Beverly pleaded.

"What's to talk about? This place is a dump and a joke!"

"That's nothing new."

"Look, Ben's waiting for me in his office. Thanks." Armando left Beverly standing alone on the dock. When he got to the office, Ben was fuming.

"I thought I told you to come into the office and wait for me!"

"I'm here now, aren't I?"

"That's not the point. I asked you to wait for me here and you went off and did your own thing. Week after week it's the same thing with you."

"Y'all been treating us like shit all these weeks. That's the problem."

"How do you feel we've treated you badly, Armando? Just because we hold you accountable for what you do wrong?"

"The fact is, y'all have no idea how to run a hotel, and you don't know how to treat the employees either," Armando shot back. It was as if a million bricks had been swept from his shoulders. The floodgates opened, allowing any and every point of contention that once lay dormant to boil to the surface.

"Since Groveman Group took over this property, y'all been flexing your muscles to show us who the big boss is, and look what's happened."

"Don't try to take away from the crap you just pulled out there," Ben ordered.

"That's just it. You don't understand that what happened out there is just a small part of a bigger problem."

"Armando, that doesn't cut it. You had no right, I repeat, *no right* to speak to that lady the way you did. Have you forgotten the Respectful Workplace form you signed regarding this? Have you forgotten that it requires immediate termination if you violate it?"

"Man, fuck that form! You'd take that lady's word over us any day, and that's why this raggedy-ass hotel is getting run into the ground!"

"I'm not going to go back and forth with you on this. The bottom line is that you broke one of the rules, so, I have to let you go."

"Then you know what, Ben? You can take this job and shove it up your ass!"

Ben nearly burst a blood vessel. He had never had an employee talk to him with such disrespect. "I'll need to escort you out!" Ben said as his ears turned red, and began to twitch from the tension.

"You're just mad that someone had the balls to tell you what *you* did wrong." Armando turned and left the office, not acknowledging anyone in his path. He was proud of himself that he stood up for his beliefs and his integrity. He figured that they needed him more than he needed them. Surely he'd find another job.

CHAPTER NINE

"What the hell just happened?" Armando's question traveled the distance it took to drive from the hotel to the bar. He was still angry, but mostly humiliated, in a fog of disbelief. Armando detested the Peterson Hotel like a sickness, yet still assumed one day he'd walk away of his own volition, not be forced out. As he got out of the car, he was no closer to answering the question.

Armando stopped into the Red Dragon restaurant and bar once every few months to flirt drinks out of Pamela, a cute Asian-American woman with spiky red hair. He was impressed and flattered that she remembered his drink as sharply as she remembered his beauty. It was all innocent fun: they'd play their game of flirtation, he'd pay for only two of the dozen drinks he'd consume and leave her a little something to make it worth her while. But today Armando didn't carry his usual swagger. The pained expression on his face told her there would be no suggestive glances or innuendo.

"Hey, handsome. Rough day?" she asked, removing the cap from a beer before placing it in front of him.

Armando nodded without looking at her. Pamela was disappointed she couldn't see his eyes. She could stare into them all day and night.

"Wanna talk about it?"

"Not really."

"Well, I'm here if you change your mind. I'll just be down at the end of the bar rolling silverware."

"Fine. Thanks." Armando finally looked at her, but the coldness in his eyes was a warning.

When Armando finished his beer, he threw money onto the bar and put the empty bottle into the bar's well. He gazed at the bottles of liquor lining the bar, then stared at the blank space on the walls, wondering what he was going to tell Karen. He needed a cigarette.

Armando went out front of the building and stood with his back to the wall, inadvertently exhaling smoke into the faces of people walking past. It wasn't just the fear of Karen hollering, it was the promise he'd made. He wanted to be ten times the man to Karen that his mother's boyfriend was to her. Real men didn't beat their women, or suffocate them with fear. They didn't belittle, or think just bringing the thunder in the bedroom made them men. Real men honored their commitments; they didn't run from their responsibilities. Armando knew Karen could take care of herself, but Armando wanted to provide for the both of them. He couldn't do that while unemployed or even underemployed. The thought of Karen coming home from a long shift only to shake her head in disgust at him, or question his manhood, made him depressed. He wanted to go back in and drink until he couldn't drink anymore. Throwing the cigarette out, he went back inside. There was a fresh beer waiting for him when he returned.

"That's on the lady at the end of the bar," Pamela said.

Armando glanced down at the older woman. He nodded, forcing a smile. She took the smile as an invitation

to join him. Even in the dimness of light, Armando could tell the woman's blonde hair color came from a box. Her eye makeup seemed to have been applied with a trembling hand. Her lipstick looked pulled against her wrinkled skin and too bright a shade of red for her age. Armando guessed she was a woman who thought she still had some party left in her.

"You're cute," she said, trying to resist the inclination to slur her speech.

"Thank you."

"I bet you've broken a lot of hearts." The woman propped herself against the bar for support. Her breath smelled of black licorice. Sambuca.

Armando offered a fuller smile even though she had him pegged. *Who this bitch been talking to?* he wondered. "No, ma'am," Armando said, stifling a guilty chuckle.

"The name is Sharly," she said, determined to make it up onto the stool. She extended a bony hand that felt like gathered branches when Armando shook it.

"I know you probably think I'm too old for you, but I could show you some things."

Armando knew where Sharly was going. He imagined her becoming even more brazen as the afternoon went on. Armando winced. He hated Sambuca.

But then Karen snuck back into his consciousness. What would he say to explain being out of a job? Or drunk in the middle of the day?

"Don't think too hard. Keep it short and simple," he thought, taking a swig of the beer.

"I don't suppose you'd be interested in coming home with me? You sure could give an older gal a thrill." Sharly said, taking Karen's place on Armando's mind.

Armando looked at her. Sharly seemed pitiful; clearly lonely. He wondered how many beers it would take to even consider plunging into her. He imagined creaking joints and clouds of dust.

"You probably could teach me some new tricks, but I have a girlfriend."

Sharly looked let down, then embarrassed. "I figured. Well, you can't fault a girl for trying."

Armando finished his beer, pushed Pamela's tip money into the well, and leaned in to give Sharly a kiss on the cheek.

"You have a good one," he said, and left.

Karen came home to a dark apartment. She noticed Armando's silhouette as he exhaled cigarette smoke through the screened window.

"Why are you sitting here in the dark?"

"I got a headache, and the lights were bothering my eyes."

"I can't see."

"I'm good. Go ahead and turn the lights on."

Karen flipped the light on. She noticed seriousness in Armando's face. "Is that it? Anything you wanna talk about?"

"How was your day?"

"Long. What about yours?"

"Rough."

"Why?"

He looked directly into her eyes. In them, he could see she was ready to be there for him. Armando took another drag of his cigarette.

"You ain't gonna answer the question?"

"Naw, it's my moms. She's not doing too hot. I'm gonna call out tomorrow and swing on by her crib." The lie took seconds.

"You gotta call out for the whole day? Why can't you go by her house after you get done with work?"

"What does it matter?"

"What's it matter? We need every bit of money we can get."

"I know all of that, but my mother comes before that job."

"What's wrong with her?"

"She's been missing me."

Karen did a double take. "Boy, you better take your ass to work. If she ain't seen you in all this time, another eight hours ain't gonna hurt her."

"Yo, just cuz you and your mama got beef don't mean me and mine do!"

"Fine! Don't go to work. But when the lights get cut off, you'll know why."

"Baby, nothing's about to get cut off. Why you trippin'?"

"Because we need all the money we can get and I'm working myself to death. You ain't doing your part."

Armando had wondered what would happen if he allowed himself to be just a little vulnerable. He got his answer.

***

"All right, I'm out," Armando said, carrying a duffle bag.

"Where are you fixin' to go? What's in the bag?"

"I'm going in. I hate wearing my uniform to work. I'm gonna start changing there."

"I thought you were hanging with your mom all day."

"I told her I'd come by after my shift. Besides, like you said, we need the money. I'm out." He kissed her quickly on the forehead, and left her standing there.

Thankfully he still had a few hundred dollars in the bank, but that would be gone soon. There was no time to explain himself, but he knew it would be just a matter of time before he'd have to.

Armando went to a gas station and changed into the business casual clothes he'd packed away. He would devote the day to filling out job applications and possibly meet with employers for interviews. He went to various stores, companies, the loading docks, the post office, and even other hotels. By the end of the day, when he returned to the gas station to change his clothes again, the balls of his feet burned from all of the walking. Still, he felt he'd spent the day well. He was positive that eventually someone would call about a job.

"Hey, honey. How is your Mom doing?" Karen asked when Armando returned home.

"I couldn't get over there today. They had me go from the restaurant to banquets afterward because the banquet manager didn't bother to schedule enough people. Like he didn't know he had a function for 480 people!"

"Damn, that many?"

"And they didn't even bother to ask me if I wanted to help, they forced me to go over there. Then I got stuck. I'm tired as hell. I hate that damn job."

"Well, maybe you should start looking for another job," she said, spooning some yogurt into a dish of fruit.

"Yeah. Maybe."

"Just don't quit the one you got until something else comes along."

"No. I won't."

The lies came almost too easy.

Weeks passed, and after finding out the hotel was contesting his request for unemployment insurance, Armando had devoted his time to trying to find another job, even branching further outside of Minneapolis. Still nothing. He decided he needed a break from all of the doors slamming in his face. He owed himself a day off just to sit and regroup. It was cooler than it had been in a while. He was glad to be able to sit without being drenched in sweat as a breeze passed through the apartment.

Armando tried calling Karen, but got voicemail, which meant she was probably in the middle of a lunch rush. It didn't matter; he could always call again later. As soon as Armando put the phone down there was a knock at the door.

"Yeah," Armando shouted from the couch.

"It's me, Cabrien."

Armando got up and went to open the door.

"Hey, Armando, is Karen here?"

"Naw, man, she's pulling a double today."

"Oh," Cabrien said. He appeared disappointed and out of sorts.

"I don't know when she's coming home, but you can come in and chill for a minute if you want. Come on."

Cabrien walked into the apartment and looked around as though it were the first time he'd ever been there. He

tried not to look at Armando's sex, which seemed ready to leap out at him when Armando adjusted his boxers.

"You want something to drink?"

"I'll take whatever. Oh my goodness, I don't know how y'all can walk up and down those stairs like that."

"You get used to it," Armando said, walking into the kitchen. Opening the refrigerator reminded him to go to the grocery store. Usually Karen did the shopping, but with all the extra hours she was working, she didn't have the time. There were several cans of a 24-pack of beer left, and some red Kool-Aid he wasn't sure was cherry or fruit punch. He'd also forgotten that there was still half of a pizza left in its box which he could eat for dinner.

"I just have some Kool-Aid and beer. And I know you don't drink beer."

"Honey, I haven't had Kool-Aid in I don't know how long. Is it red?" Cabrien asked.

"Yep."

"I'll have some of that."

"You want ice?"

"Only if you have it, I don't wanna put you out or anything."

"I think we have a tray of ice cubes in here." Armando went into the freezer and saw a single cube left. "Damn! I told that girl about taking the last of the ice and not filling it back up. How in the hell is somebody gonna leave just one cube of ice in the damn tray?"

Cabrien started to laugh. "She didn't fill the tray back up with water?'

"No. She does shit like that all the time. But that's my girl, though."

"So, you must be off today," Cabrien said as Armando came back into the living room.

"Yep," Armando said quickly, averting his eyes.

"Is it that bad?" Cabrien took the glass from Armando.

"I don't wanna get into all of that."

"Oh I'm sorry; I'm just all up in your business."

"No worries, bruh." Armando joined Cabrien on the couch.

There was a moment of silence.

"Hey, I better put on some shorts," Armando said.

"No need to get all formal on my account." The two men laughed together.

Armando went to his bedroom. After a couple of minutes he returned and sat back down.

"That's better," he said before taking another swig of his drink.

"Can I ask you something?" It was Cabrien.

"Sure," Armando said, meeting Cabrien's glance.

"You don't like me very much, do you?"

"Who told you that?" Armando said, taken aback by Cabrien's directness.

"Nobody told me that. It's just a vibe I get from you."

"Well, I ain't gonna lie; I don't have any gay friends. I have a gay aunt, and we're cool. I worked—I mean work with gay people at my job." He thought for a moment on how to phrase the rest of his response.

"I just get the feeling that you only tolerate me when Karen is around."

"I mean, it's like, I don't dislike you. I don't know you. You seem cool to me. A little out there, but you're cool."

Cabrien studied Armando's face to see whether or not

he was lying, and decided he was comfortable with Armando's answer. His shoulders relaxed.

"You know it's a damn shame that I get more hate coming from my own race and people. Women are generally okay. They tend to be more open-minded. But the men? Chile, you can forget it."

"The brothas give you problems, huh?" Armando chuckled.

"Hell yeah they do! You would think that we as a people would be *less* homophobic given that our people have known so many struggles."

"Yeah, but a lot of folks come from the church. Karen used to tell me stories about how her mama was."

"Ain't that the truth? The church used to bond us together, and now it's tearing us apart." Cabrien shook his head.

"I ain't gonna lie, I've been uncomfortable. I think that's just a guy thing. You have to remember that a lot of dudes don't know gay people, so all they have is a stereotype to go by."

"I know, but still. Do you know how many times I walk down Hennepin Avenue and people yell 'Fuckin' faggot!' out the car?"

"Wow! Really? Folks be trippin'!"

"Boy, please, I mean look at me. I'm a walking full tank of sugar." Cabrien smiled.

"I don't understand two men being together, but I'm not gonna go out my way to make people feel bad about it. As far as I'm concerned, that's your life, not mine."

"Thank you! I just wanna tell some of these folks that are out late harassing me, to go home and read a book to

their kids. Hell, pay your child support! Better still, go to school and get your hours for a degree!"

Armando laughed.

"I'm serious as a heart attack. I mean, I really don't know how my being gay affects anybody else. Worry about your shit before you come talking to me about mine."

"Who you fuck is your choice," Armando said.

"I'm sick of people thinking I woke up one day deciding to be this way. I didn't choose this shit! No more than y'all choose to be straight!"

"Calm down, man, damn!"

"For real, though. Do you think that I would deliberately choose to be something that I have to worry about being discriminated against for? I'm already black. Why would I want to give people something else to work with?"

"I feel you," Armando said thoughtfully.

"I have to worry about what family and friends think. I have to worry about getting beat down when I come out of a gay bar. And on top of that, I have to hear all that fire-and-brimstone church mess! If I chose that, then that would be pretty masochistic."

"Yeah, but man, things are changing. Most people don't get wrapped up in that crap. Don't let it bother you," Armando said, getting up to get more Kool-Aid. When he returned, Armando looked at Cabrien cautiously. "So can I ask you something? I don't want to get too personal but..."

"Just spit it out."

"Did you ever get the money you were looking for?" Armando asked.

"No. I couldn't find a date."

"A date? Man, that sounds like you're out there..."

"Selling my time?" Cabrien said with a crafty smile.

"Your what?" Armando looked on with confusion.

"My time. It's illegal to sell myself as a sexual object. But, how I *spend* my time with a gentleman? That is purely up to us, and consensual."

"Come on," Armando said, "That's fooling around with words. Whether you out-and-out say you're a prostitute or you gloss that shit up, it doesn't change the fact that you sell your ass, so why not call it what it is?"

Cabrien was suddenly defensive. "*Anyway*, Karen doesn't know. Don't tell her, okay? I don't wanna hear her mouth."

Armando nodded. He was silent for two beats before asking, "How long have you known you were gay?"

"Hello, I came out my mama's coochie like this! But I officially told her back when I was sixteen."

"What happened when you told her?"

"She probably knew and didn't care, but all her boyfriends would call me names."

"And she didn't say anything?"

"Nope. I didn't want to embarrass her, or hear it from her man of many, so I left home. And, that was around the time that my aunt Thelma started talking Jesus talk to her. I wouldn't be surprised if my aunt told my mama to dis-own me, because my aunt would do some mess like that. But that's fake Christians for you."

"I can see why you and Karen are so close. She doesn't get along with her mother, either," Armando said.

"Me and my mom are cool now, but look how long it took. I mean, I'm twenty-three now, and I left home when I was sixteen. It took seven years before she got Jesus burnout. Guess she woke up and realized living the

'blessed' life would put a damper on how she was living *her* life."

Armando laughed. "I left home young, too. My ma always picked her knucklehead boyfriend over me. Toward the end I wanted to kill him!"

"Chile, I can't begin to count how many of my mama's dumb-ass boyfriends I've wanted to put in the ground. That's why I try not to think about that shit, because in the end that's all it all is. The important thing is that I've been taking care of myself for a long time now. Sure, I'd rather be doing hair. Hell, I've even had dreams of becoming a hairstylist to the stars one day. But nobody will hire me now. So, I turn tricks. Instead of doing a client's hair, the client is doing me. And I know people always have something to say about it. "

"Yeah, well, people are always gonna feel they can put their two cents in."

"I know. But unless you're planning on making sure my bills are paid on time, then you best mind your business."

The clouds hid the remaining sunlight. The breeze was still nice and Armando and Cabrien continued their conversation until Armando finally looked at the time.

"Man, I don't know what I'm gonna do with myself all night?"

"Yeah, and your girlfriend ain't comin' home anytime soon," Cabrien said, as he looked at his own watch.

"I need to call her."

"For what? She's working."

"I know. I just wanna hear her voice, see how her day is going." Armando quickly grabbed the cordless phone from its stand and dialed Karen's cell phone. It rang twice before a male voice answered the phone.

"Who is this?" Armando wanted to know.

"Who are you trying to call?" the voice said impatiently.

" Naw, tell me who this is!" Armando yelled into the phone.

"Hello," Karen said, her voice appearing suddenly.

"You've got dudes answering your phone now?"

"Oh, that's Craig; he's always playing on my phone."

"Who's Craig?"

"Look, don't get bent out of shape. Craig is one of the other bartenders."

"I don't care if you work with him. Why is he answering your phone?"

"Okay, don't let me get started on all the females you've had calling the apartment. Craig is just a friend."

"Yeah, but those females don't call here anymore."

"Damn right. You keep those bitches in the streets where you find them!" Karen said.

"All right, fine, I don't want to get into an argument. I was just calling to see how your day was going."

"Crappy. We're short-staffed because Meagan called out again. That bitch is always calling out. I'm surprised she still has a job."

"Yeah right," Armando said, nervously thinking about his own situation again.

"Anyway, baby, I gotta go, I got a whole bunch of drinks to make."

"Okay. When do you think you'll be home?"

"Pretty late. Are you gonna be up?"

"Yeah."

"Okay, baby, I'll see you when I get home."

"Okay," Armando said sadly as he put down the phone. "She's working herself to death."

"I know, right? It almost makes you feel bad for sitting up here when you could be working."

"What the fuck is that supposed to mean?" Armando snapped.

"All I meant was that it must make you feel a little guilty that you're lucky to get the day off from your job, but Karen has to work," Cabrien said, puzzled by Armando's sudden defensiveness.

"Oh, yeah, right." Armando leaned back into the couch.

"Boo, you need to chill out. You seem tense all of a sudden."

"Naw, man, I'm cool."

Suddenly, Cabrien's face brightened. "You know what? Let's go out," Cabrien offered. "It'll get your mind off things."

"Naw, I was just gonna chill here at the house." Armando looked down again.

"Is she on her way?"

"No."

"Well then, it's not like you have shit else to do. Come go with me. You can keep me company."

"Man, don't tell me we're going to that gay bar again."

"You didn't enjoy yourself? I saw how you and Karen were toward the end of the evening."

"What?"

"When I went out to smoke, I saw you two all hugged up with one another."

"Oh yeah. But, I don't wanna be bothered, and people don't seem to respect the fact that I'm straight."

"Who else bothered you besides Drake?"

Armando was silent.

"Uh-huh, that's what I thought. Anyway, you can tell them you're with me if anybody asks."

"Yeah, you'd like that, wouldn't you?" Armando said, smiling.

Without missing a beat Cabrien replied, "You better believe it. Go on, get dressed!"

Armando looked at Cabrien, who for a moment began to bat his lashes in hopes of getting his way, then stopped, realizing that wouldn't work on him.

"Okay, fine, but I don't want to be out all night. I want to be home when Karen gets here."

"Fair enough. Now go find something halfway decent to wear. And don't get too cute because I want the boys to know that *I'm* the available one."

"You'd leave me by myself if a trick came your way?"

"You best believe it. Don't worry, you're driving. It's not like you're going to be stuck if I happen to meet a gentleman."

"Okay, give me a minute," Armando shouted over his shoulder as he made his way to the bedroom to change. After what seemed like an eternity, he emerged from the bedroom wearing a white golf shirt and khaki shorts and brown sandals.

"Damn, were you back there sewing?" Cabrien joked.

"Man, you just scared I'm gonna steal your thunder," Armando said, picking up his set of keys from the table.

"That's really doubtful, my dear."

The two of them emerged from the apartment complex, enjoying the early evening air. It was crisp, fresh, and long overdue. As they got into the car, Armando looked up at the window of his apartment, hoping that when he returned he would find the lights still on.

He definitely wanted to talk to Karen. He had some explaining to do.

CHAPTER TEN

Drake was focused on writing a proposal for Bruce Hedrick when Isaac Walterson appeared at his door, drawing Drake back.

"Mr. Hill. How are you?" Isaac said, smiling.

"What do you want, Isaac?" Drake asked curtly. He and Isaac were cordial enough, but the extra sweetness in his voice meant he wanted something.

"Just wanted to talk. You look like you could use a good sit-down."

"What's that supposed to mean?"

"Well, I noticed you weren't thrilled about not being named a candidate for the BRC president. Thought you might want to vent."

"I went to Bruce about it," Drake said, flipping through his proposal.

"And how did that go?"

"I vented," Drake said.

"But it didn't go as well as you might've wanted?"

"What are you driving at, Isaac? I'm very busy."

"I'm worried about you. You've been walking around here on edge."

"Oh, and you think you might be able to help me?"

Drake said, matching the level of phoniness in Isaac's voice.

"I just might. May I come in?"

Drake nodded in the direction of an empty chair.

"You know, I don't blame you one bit. I'd probably be pissed too. Walsh being considered over you? I'm thinking that you might want to fix that."

"Actually, I've already congratulated Gary."

"Yeah, and you were about as sincere as a pusher advising a junkie to kick the habit," Isaac said sneeringly.

"Bruce had his reasons for picking Gary. Just as I'm sure he had his reasons for picking you."

"Yes, but I'm not the one you have a beef with. Look, let me get to the point..."

"Yes, please do," Drake said brusquely.

"I like Gary less than you do. He's weak, and people like that shouldn't be running anything, much less this organization. Correct me if I'm wrong."

Drake relaxed in his chair, his lips curling into a smirk. Entertained, he decided to give the conversation his full attention. "If you feel that way, Isaac, then maybe *you* should talk to Bruce."

"Oh no, I couldn't do that. You can't convince someone of somebody else's shortcomings if they don't want to see it, and I *know* that Bruce doesn't want to see it."

"If you have some sort of vendetta against Gary, then maybe you should do something about it."

Isaac's smile turned malevolent. "I'm so glad you feel that way. That's why I came to you."

Drake crossed his arms, his interest piqued.

"You see, Drake, I know that you're very good at what you do."

"And?"

"Think about it, Drake. You have the little fundraising thing that you do, there's the occasional proposal, but what do you really excel at?"

"Getting other people elected."

"By...?" Isaac was coaxing.

"Generating negative publicity on opponents."

"You destroy people's careers, Drake. And that's what I want you to do to Gary."

"What makes you think I want to do that?"

"Come on, let's not be coy. If you help me, he won't get elected, and you would have solved your problem and *mine*."

Drake began to smile at the prospect of ruining this opportunity for Gary, but he wasn't sure that he wanted to align himself with Isaac.

Drake started to speak slowly. "If it were your intention to exploit my alleged animosity toward Gary, then, you're not very bright."

"What are you saying, Drake?" The smugness in Isaac's voice faded.

"I'm saying that I never told you I was pissed with Gary. But I'm glad you're aware of what I could do for you or *to* you." He looked menacingly at Isaac, who shifted nervously in his seat.

"To me?"

"Yes, to you. I look at it as a situation where I could be of assistance to him or I could be of assistance to you. You think I would do such a dirty job just to take an opportunity away from Gary? To be perfectly honest, I'm put off by your audacity."

Isaac's eyes grew hard. "What is it you want?"

"There's a lot riding on this, Isaac. I'm going to have to sleep on that question."

Isaac bit his tongue so that he wouldn't say anything that he would later regret. He rose from his seat and backed slowly to the door. He paused, almost as though he'd been quickly spun around and said, "This isn't how I imagined this conversation would turn out."

"I bet."

"Please think this over carefully, Drake. I think we both could stand to benefit from this," he said as he left the room.

Drake started rifling through the papers in the basket on his desk until he found what he was looking for: a copy of Isaac's proposal of what he would do once elected as president of Black Republicans for Change. He scanned the document quickly, his eyes narrowing when they came across certain passages on the paper. He took out his red pen and began quickly circling various words and phrases. When he was done, he smiled and whispered, "That should do it," then placed the document in the top drawer of his desk. He had reached a decision as to how he was going to handle Isaac Walterson's proposition. He wasn't going to deal with it that day however, because he had a scotch and soda with his name on it waiting for him at Sir Martin's.

While Cabrien flirted with the bartender, Armando watched videos playing on the flat- screen television nearest him. He wasn't jumping for joy at returning to Sir Martin's, but he didn't hate the idea either. He felt more relaxed. The bar was almost empty. No one had disrespected him.

Chuckling, Cabrien patted Armando on the back. "Wow. Can you believe it? You've been here a whole twenty minutes and nobody has grabbed for your dick. *Yet.*"

"Shut up, dude," Armando said, sipping his beer. "How long do you want to stay here?"

"I don't know. We don't have to be here all night, but I would like to get a little buzz before we leave. You're driving anyway, so I don't have to worry about drunk driving." Cabrien reached into the little drink garnish box behind the bar and helped himself to some maraschino cherries. The bartender gave Cabrien a disapproving look. "Honey, you need to eat before you get here. This isn't a buffet," he said before snapping the garnish box closed.

"I can't help it, I love those things," Cabrien whined.

"You're not the one who has to run to the back to stock them, are you? Here..." The bartender reopened the little box, put four cherries on a cocktail napkin and slid it in front of Cabrien as though he were giving a small child an afternoon snack. "Now that's it." The bartender closed the box up again and moved it to the other side of the bar and continued his conversation with another patron.

Cabrien looked over to Armando, who was shaking his head.

"Don't judge me," Cabrien said jokingly.

Armando turned his attention to the television that had *MadTV* playing.

"Aw, shit! This is the show! Karen got me watching the repeats."

"Oh that? Yeah, it's funny," Cabrien said, munching one of the remaining cherries.

Armando continued looking at the screen as Cabrien looked about the room, trying to decide how he should

best position himself that evening. He wanted to appear available and didn't want Armando cramping his style. Armando took notice of Cabrien's eyes as they darted about the room. He became curious as to what was drawing Cabrien's attention.

"What are you looking at?"

"I'm just trying to figure out where I need to be tonight when it starts jumping off."

"You're looking to hook up with some dude tonight for real? Seriously?" Armando asked. He thought Cabrien had been joking. "Listen, if you really have your mind set to hook up, maybe I need to bounce."

Cabrien had become so transfixed by his image in the mirror across the bar that he barely heard Armando.

Armando flicked Cabrien's arm to get his attention. "Eh, bruh."

"I'm not going to ditch you. What kind of person do you think I am?"

"Yeah, but you're all up in the mirror and shit. Anyway, you told me that if something else came along..."

"That was a joke," Cabrien said, almost in disbelief that Armando had taken him so seriously.

Armando pushed his beer away. The bartender looked down at the beer and then at him.

"Did you want something else?" he asked, taking the bottle from the bar.

"Could I get a screwdriver, please?" Armando replied politely.

"You betcha," the bartender said, and threw the bottle in the garbage

Armando took out a ten-dollar bill and placed it on the

bar. He began looking around at the other people in the place.

"Man, some of these dudes in here, I wouldn't even think got down like that," Armando said to Cabrien, who was sucking on a cherry stem.

"We come in different packages, boo. You actually think they can all be as fierce as me? Thank you, but there ain't that much fierceness to go around."

Armando rose from his bar stool and announced that he was going to the restroom.

"Do you want help holding it?" Cabrien joked. Armando shook his head no.

Drake Hill entered the bar and immediately saw Cabrien sitting by himself. He nodded in acknowledgement to the bartender and made his way over to him.

"Hello, Cabrien," Drake said.

"Oh, you know me now?"

"Of course I know you. Try not to be too ridiculous, will you?" Drake said, noticing the drink sitting to Cabrien's side. He took off his suit coat and put it on his own bar stool and sat down. "Don't tell me you're still pissed about the other night. That feels like such a long time ago."

"I came to you in need and you totally blew me off," Cabrien said as he folded his arms.

"Cabrien, we get together from time to time and I feel as though I've been more than generous with you. The idea here isn't that I'm going to fund whatever lavish lifestyle you feel you're deserving of. You ought to get a job and make your own money. It's what *I* do."

"Honey, let's not get it twisted, okay? You propositioned *me*, remember? You had to have my, oh how did you say it, 'exquisite' ass, remember?"

Drake chuckled. "I'm here *now,* aren't I? Let's play nice, Cabrien." Drake lowered his voice so that he wouldn't make a scene. The bartender finally came back with Armando's change and laid it next to the screwdriver.

"Your usual, Drake?" the bartender asked. Drake nodded.

Cabrien's arms remained folded. "I could've used your help, Drake. That's all I'm saying."

"As I said, I'm here now. I wish you would talk nicely to me," Drake said, looking intently at Cabrien.

Cabrien turned to see Armando returning from the restroom. Rising from his chair, Cabrien nodded in Armando's general direction. "Maybe *he'll* talk nicely to you," he said.

"Gladly," Drake said under his breath.

Cabrien drifted further away, passing Armando on his way. "My turn to use the little boys' room," he told Armando when they crossed paths.

When Armando got close enough to the bar, he froze. He wasn't expecting to see Drake there and immediately became nervous. Before sitting down, he pushed his bar stool further away from Cabrien's and Drake's. He offered a feeble smile and looked straight ahead.

"Hello, Armando," Drake said, aroused just by looking at him.

"Hey, wuz up?" Armando said, still looking straight ahead. Drake got up from his seat and walked to an empty bar stool near Armando and leaned in closely.

"Fancy seeing you here. *Again.* Comfortable yet?"

"I'm out for a drink with Cabrien and that's it. Maybe you ought to talk to him if there's something you think you need."

"I'm not a bad person, Armando. Has our friend been telling lies about me?" Drake turned and looked in the direction of the departed Cabrien.

"As a matter of fact, no, he hasn't," Armando said, looking at Drake for the first time.

"I'm going to cut to the chase. I like what I see. And I want what I see. Name your price. And don't tell me you don't do this sort of thing. I'm sure that's the same thing Cabrien said, and now he can't get enough of the green." Drake took out his wallet and placed his business card in front of Armando. "Just in case," he said to him.

Drake noticed Cabrien returning from the bathroom. He patted Armando on the back. "I'm sure we can and will become very close friends," he said, and walked back to his seat.

Cabrien wasn't happy with what he saw. Sensing a Cabrien storm brewing, Drake decided to go the nice route.

"You know, I was thinking about you today," Drake said, putting his hand on Cabrien's knee.

"Yeah right."

"You really shouldn't be so cynical, Cabrien," Drake said, lifting his scotch and soda to sip.

Cabrien looked Drake squarely in the face. "Give me a reason not to be."

Drake squeezed Cabrien's leg and then began to massage it softly, moving his hand to his crotch very slowly. Cabrien had been longing for Drake's masculine touch. When he was with Drake, he found himself transported from the world and all of his problems. He wanted to be with Drake, and not just for the money. Drake was the smartest man he knew, and he wished that some of Drake's smarts would rub off on him.

Their time together was special. It was a bond that Cabrien didn't share with any of the other men he had been with. He liked the way Drake spoke; how he didn't just offer an opinion without knowing something about the subject first. When they were together, Cabrien loved to surrender himself to Drake. He loved being picked up and carried to the bed. Cabrien liked how Drake held his hands during sex while looking deep into his eyes. He didn't think of it as work, or even fucking, but rather, making love.

Cabrien felt his face flush and his heart beat more rapidly remembering their encounters.

Armando tried to ignore what was going on with Drake and Cabrien, but glanced down at the card. He swallowed hard and slipped the card into his pocket.

Cabrien's back was to Armando now as he leaned in and gave Drake a hug. Drake welcomed it, hugging Cabrien tightly. He felt Cabrien relax in his arms, and heard him sigh softly. Then he kissed Cabrien lingeringly on the neck. The two of them behaved as though there was no one else in the room. Drake kissed him gently and Cabrien received his kiss openly, feeling his anger fade away.

If he was clever—and lucky, Cabrien thought, maybe he could get Drake to fall in love with him, maybe even make Drake his only lover. He was beginning to feel like the luckiest person on the planet.

Drake nestled his chin onto Cabrien's shoulder, allowing himself a view of Armando. When he glanced down at the space immediately in front of Armando, he noticed that the card was gone. Drake winked and Armando looked away in embarrassment.

Drake pulled himself from Cabrien's grasp, smiling vic-

toriously to himself. He got up quickly, grabbed his suit coat and headed for the door to wait for Cabrien.

Cabrien turned to Armando. "I know I said that I wasn't going to ditch you, but we're going to take off, Armando. Is that all right with you?"

Armando got up and gave Cabrien a hug. "Handle your business. Thanks for getting me out the house. I had fun."

"You did?"

"Yeah, it was all right. I got to know you a little better today. I'm sure Karen will love that."

"Yeah, I'm sure she will," Cabrien agreed.

"But, I don't want you to think I did it for her. Like I said, this is all kinda new to me," Armando said, playfully jabbing Cabrien on the shoulder.

"So you would come back?" Cabrien asked.

Armando paused for a moment. "Well, I'd like to go to some straight places, too, but yeah, I'd come back again with you...and Karen," Armando said, smiling as he looked over at Drake, whose back was to them.

"I'll see you later, then. Tell Karen I said hello." And Cabrien walked away to join Drake.

"Aren't you going to say goodbye to Armando?" Cabrien asked.

Drake looked over Cabrien's shoulder to see Armando getting up to leave.

"No. I'm sure I'll see Armando again soon enough."

CHAPTER ELEVEN

When Armando came home, Karen was already asleep. He was surprised she was home so early. The conversation about his employment situation would have to wait for another day. Perhaps by then he'd have won his unemployment, or better still found a job. He grabbed a beer from the kitchen, sank into the couch, and pulled out the card Drake had given him. He didn't know what possessed him to take it in the first place. As he closely examined Drake's name in bold, glossy font on the card, he thought back to Drake winking at him.

There was a power in Drake's eyes that seemed to ask Armando if he was man enough to play a game. Could he go the distance? Armando wasn't attracted to Drake, but he wondered if he could continue using his own good looks to get what he needed to survive. It would be nice not to have to choose which bills got paid, and which didn't. Armando got up, threw the card in the kitchen garbage and headed to the shower.

Afterward, he wrapped the towel around his midsection and watched Karen sleep from the bedroom doorway. "How the hell am I gonna take care of her when I can't even take care of myself?" He stood there for a few moments

feeling less than a man. "Why didn't I go to college? Why didn't I learn a trade that actually pays something?"

As he watched Karen shift position, he envisioned her taunting him. "See, if your ass had a job like me, it could be you laying here trying to get some sleep. Instead, you probably out fucking some bitch. Can't keep a job, but you can always keep some stray pussy around!" he imagined her saying. Just a few weeks ago he'd promised that they wouldn't struggle, and he was no closer to making good on that promise.

"Who am I kidding?" he muttered, moving out of sight. Armando's shame ran so deeply he didn't want to wake her.

Armando went into the bedroom, threw the towel down, quietly put on a pair of shorts and T-shirt, and slipped into bed with Karen. He wasn't planning on going to sleep; he just wanted to be next to her for awhile, relishing her being there. He thought about different ways he would break the news to her, rehearsing possible dialogues in his head. "She will forgive me," he muttered. Fatigue overcame him, and he fell asleep.

Early the next day, Armando awoke to the smell of bacon frying in the fry pan. Still tired, he sat on the edge of the bed and slipped on a pair of socks. He caught his reflection in a small mirror leaning on the dresser. It was either now or never to tell Karen about the job situation. He took a deep breath before going into the kitchen. Karen stood with her back to him, the latest issue of *Vibe* magazine resting on the counter.

"Good morning, baby," Armando said. A weak smile crossed his mouth.

"Hey. You know, this don't make no kinda sense." She

jabbed her index finger into the magazine. "These celebrities make all this money and they are some of the most messed-up people in the world."

"What those fools doing now?" Armando asked as he wrapped his arms around her waist and kissed the side of her neck.

"Acting clownish," she said, quickly closing the magazine to resume turning the bacon. "I know one thing, if I had a choice between having money and going through all that drama, or not having any money but being right in the head, I'd choose being right in my head."

"I hear you," Armando replied, unwrapping his arms.

"Oh, some lady called for you this morning. Said she was calling from The Mall of America. You put in an application to work in the food court?"

"Yeah." His stomach dropped.

"I know you ain't happy at the hotel, but I thought you would've told me you had started putting in applications other places."

"I was going to mention it to you, but you've been killing yourself at the bar and I didn't want to burden you with all my drama."

"You're my man. If you got problems, I wanna know about it so we can work through them together. It's as simple as that."

"I feel you," Armando said, going in for another hug.

"Wait a minute, I gotta finish turning this bacon or it'll burn." Karen turned back to the stove. "Anyway, a second job would be good. I'm getting my ass kicked down at the bar and the extra money could help out around here."

"Yeah, a second job," Armando agreed. "I guess I

should get ready to go for the interview, then. What time did she say it was?" Armando's tone was hopeful.

Karen looked down and began to shake her head. "No time. She called to thank you for your interest, but they didn't need any help at this time. But she said that she'd keep your application on file just in case something else opened up."

Armando's facial expression became sad. Another rejection.

"I'm sorry, baby," Karen said.

"Hey, it is what it is, right? I'll just go apply somewhere else."

"Well, look at it as a blessing. You know good and well you don't have it in you to work no two jobs. Shit, as hard as I work, you see how I am at the end of the day."

"But I don't want my woman to work harder than me. *I'm the man.*" Armando looked away in shame. Now was the time to admit he'd lost his job and that he had diligently tried to find another, but the words became caught in his throat.

"We're in this together, baby. I thought you knew that," Karen said, touching the side of Armando's face.

"I know," Armando said.

Karen turned her attention back to the bacon, now on the brink of burning. She turned the fire off and moved the pan to the rear of the stove.

"Speaking of work, I'm gonna have to leave here soon myself. You're off today?" Karen asked.

"Yep." Armando watched Karen flutter about the kitchen.

"Oh, okay. You know that you don't have to find a second job, just don't lose the one you got," Karen said laugh-

ing, hoping to lighten the moment. Armando didn't laugh back.

"Armando, look at your face," she said sadly. "Here, eat some bacon, honey, and try to cheer up." She left for the bedroom.

Standing alone in the kitchen, Armando looked toward the trash can, knowing what lay inside it.

I should've left it at the bar, he thought to himself. His nose began to flare with anger as he thought about the business card. How dare Drake even think he'd be down with that?

Do I look like a punk? He wondered, feeling his masculinity take a hit.

Drake's presumption incited an aggression in Armando. Suddenly he had something to prove.

When Karen ran the shower, Armando followed her into the bathroom. As she undressed, he did also and came up behind her. He began to kiss her neck and shoulders. Karen let out a sigh as Armando began to descend with his kisses and licking down her back.

She tilted her head to the side and closed her eyes as the sensation seemed to spread throughout her body. Armando stood tall again, placing his large hands on her shoulders and worked them downward toward the small of her back. As his fingers dug into the tenseness of her back, he pressed himself against her and began to gently nudge her toward the basin. Then, he held her there as his breath warmed her neck.

Karen turned around slowly to face him. He looked almost angry. His body was desirable; strong. Her tongue swirled around his nipples, then moved tantalizingly down Armando's stomach. Karen kneeled in front of Armando,

taking his penis in her mouth, feeling it come to life. Armando put his hands on her head as she began to tease his cock and stroke his balls. First slowly, then quickly. Armando licked his lips as he watched her go to town on him. She looked up at him, her eyes expressing a desire to please. He leaned back into the basin, his body shuddering. He pulled out, waving his dick in front of her. Karen kept her eyes locked on it.

"No! Gimme!" she said, reaching out for it.

Armando grabbed her by the wrists and pulled her up. "Naw, I want some of this pussy," he said, touching it as though taking ownership of it. "Get your ass in that tub," he instructed. He got into the shower and Karen followed him in. She stood at the front of the shower and the warm water beat down on her body as Armando reached for the sponge that hung on the neck of the shower head. He put small amounts of body wash soap on the sponge and lathered it on her back with one hand while reaching around with his other hand to squeeze her breasts.

"Damn, Armando, that hurts," she said.

"Shut up," he said, turning Karen around completely before kissing her hungrily. He dropped the sponge. As he went to pick it up, her womaness in his face, he wasted no time attacking it with his tongue, first swirling his tongue on her love button, then burying his nose and tongue deeply. Water continued to roll from their bodies. Armando swung one of her legs over his shoulders, forcing Karen to struggle on one leg as sexual rapture passed through her. The taste of wet pennies lingered on his tongue. He removed her leg from his shoulder and slowly ran his hands all over her water-slicked body as he rose to stand. He pressed her against the sliding glass door,

flattening her breasts, and then rammed himself inside of her. He shuddered as her moans became louder. The falling shower water and the deep suction sounds created by Karen's own juices almost hypnotized Armando. He then started ramming deeper. Karen's head lightly banged against the glass sliding door while she gripped the towel rail with both her hands.

See? Can't no punk make no female do or feel what I do, Armando thought to himself as he worked to bring pleasure not just to himself but Karen as well. Their bliss ended as the hot water became cooler. Armando pulled out, allowing his load to fall and be washed away. Before the water became completely cold they held each other tightly, listening to their heartbeats over the beating water.

Later, when Karen was dressed and ready to leave, she said, "Now, I got lucky last night and came home earlier than I thought. But don't wait up tonight because I'm probably gonna be late."

"Oh, yeah?" Armando said. He lay on the bed with the sheets partially covering his nakedness.

"Yep, but I'll call you later," she promised.

"Cool," Armando said to her as the light caught the glint in his eyes.

"God, your eyes are beautiful," Karen said, almost melting at the sight of him.

"That's because you're giving me something beautiful to look at."

"You're so silly," Karen said, laughing. "Oh, before I forget. We're gonna have to figure out these bills because the cell phones, electric, and the water are all due. You're gonna have to run me some money for your share if we're gonna get them paid on time."

Armando's stomach did a flip. "Damn, why do they all have to come at once?"

"They just do. Anyway, we can talk about it later. I was just letting you know so you can get your half ready. I love you," Karen said, turning to leave.

"I love you more," he shouted behind her.

Almost immediately after Karen left, Armando was on his feet, putting on a pair of jeans and a T-shirt. It was too hot for underwear, he reasoned, and so he didn't put on any. He went into the kitchen and stared at the trash can again. He reached in and pulled out Drake's card. There were a few speckles of grease on the card but he could still make out the name and number. He went over to the couch and took the cordless phone and sat down. He looked at the card and then at the phone, scared to go down this path, but feared he had no other choice. A job may or may not be around the corner, but Armando couldn't just pass the days waiting for a call back. Now there were bills that were due, and having paid the whole rent, he was down to $2.47 in his account, with the threat of an overdraft hanging over him.

Then Armando thought of Cabrien, and figured if Cabrien could do it then certainly he could. But unlike Cabrien, he wasn't gay. He wouldn't be taken advantage of. He was no one's bitch.

"Ain't no way I'm gonna let another dude pump dick in my mouth or ass. He can forget that," Armando muttered. With shaking hands Armando dialed the first of the two numbers. He guessed that the first was the office number and figured that Drake would be at work. The office answering service picked up.

"Good morning, BRC, how may I direct your call?" The cheery voice on the other end said.

"Uh, hello, may I speak with Drake Hill, please?" Armando asked, using his professional voice.

"One moment, please." The operator put him on hold.

Armando fidgeted as he waited for what seemed like forever.

"I'm sorry, but Mr. Hill isn't in yet. Would you like to leave a message on his voicemail?" Relief passed through Armando.

"Um, no, thank you. I'll just call again another time. Goodbye." And without waiting for the good bye from the other end, he hung up the phone.

"You better find your ass a job, boy," Armando said out loud as he buried his face into his hands.

Armando sat for twenty minutes pondering what to do. Even the temp agencies had no leads. No, he had found the courage to call Drake and he would see it through. If the money was right, then Karen wouldn't have to know anything about the hotel situation. He picked the phone up again and dialed the second number. It rang only once.

"Hello," the voice said.

"Yes, hi, is this Drake?" Armando asked.

"Speaking."

"Drake, this is Armando. We met through Cabrien."

"Ah yes, Armando. I was expecting your call. But not this soon."

"Yeah, well, I was thinking about your idea and I want to take you up on it."

"I see."

"Are you still interested?"

"I'm always interested, Armando. I actually have a

short day at the office today. Why don't you fly on by later this afternoon?"

"You want to do it today?" Armando wasn't expecting to do anything right away.

"Sure, why not? I just have to stop in at the office to get an important document and then I'm free."

"Oh, okay," Armando stammered.

"You're sure you're up for this?"

"Yeah, I'm sure," Armando snapped back, his stammer gone.

"Do you know where the Greenwich Towers are?"

"Yes."

"I'm on the 24th floor. Apartment 2403. Shall we say 3:00 PM?"

Armando looked at his watch. "Yeah, I can make it."

"Sounds good. I'll see you when you get here."

Armando went into the kitchen to eat, but the grease around the bacon had solidified; he didn't want to eat that. He settled for a bowl of cereal instead.

In a few hours he hoped to seal a deal that would make enough him money to pay his share of the bills and if he was lucky, spoil the woman he loved.

CHAPTER TWELVE

At 2:50 PM, Armando parked his car a little ways from The Greenwich Towers. He looked into his wallet for the scrap paper on which he'd written Drake's apartment number. While digging deep for it, he caught a glimpse of Karen's photo. He brought the photo of Karen's smiling face to his lips, kissed it, and braced himself for what he had to do.

In order to get through this, he'd have to separate himself from the act of having sex with Drake; his body would be doing it, but his heart and soul would be somewhere else. He wasn't looking to lay pipe like he did for Karen, so if Drake thought he was getting his back blown out, he was mistaken. Still, in the larger picture, he knew he had to do at least a decent job in order to get paid.

The clouds rolled in dark overhead as Armando made his way down the cobblestone street to Drake's condo. Many of the stones were chipped, others completely lost. Withered grass lay where stone had been.

Just as he faced the glass doors of the condo building, the first drops of rain fell. A scattering of wetness stained his pale blue golf shirt. No one was at the reception desk, which was just as well, because he didn't want to have to say who he'd come to see. He strode briskly to the elevators

and waited, listening to the thunder and then the torrents of rain outside.

The floor, walls, and ceilings of the elevator were all mirrored. Seeing his reflection, he noticed the half heartedness immediately. Whatever mask of bravado he had put on before had slipped. Money or no money, this would be his first sexual act with a man. He decided he wouldn't permit any trace of shame or guilt to appear on his face when he entered Drake's apartment. He ran his hands over his head, catching beads of sweat. With a pasted tough-guy smile on his face, Armando took a deep breath and straightened his shoulders. "This here is strictly business. He's buying what I'm selling. That's all it is."

It was a short walk to apartment 2403. "Let's do this," he mumbled under his breath and rang the doorbell.

Drake answered the door with a warm, welcoming smile, holding a glass of what looked like orange juice. "Thank you for coming."

"It's raining pretty bad out there," Armando said, entering Drake's apartment.

"You don't look too wet," Drake asked, touching the back of Armando's shoulders as he walked past him.

"No, it started to come down once I made it inside," Armando said, looking around the living room. The interior, bathed in earth tones and recessed lighting, was decorated with high-end comfort. An Italian light-brown leather couch faced the window with a triangular glass coffee table fanned with men's fashion magazines. At an angle was a matching chaise lounge, all sitting on a beige and brown area rug. Chocolate-brown framed mirrors and large framed movie posters hung all around the living

room. Armando especially liked the black-and-white movie still of Diana Ross from her film *Mahogany*.

"Nice posters," Armando said.

"Yeah, it's become kind of a hobby of mine, collecting old movie posters. The one that you're looking at now was extremely hard to find."

Armando continued looking at the picture of Diana Ross, transfixed by her glamour and frank sexuality.

"I take it that you like it," Drake said, walking up to Armando and standing by his side. "I do, too—very much."

"She's a legend." Armando smiled.

"Indeed. Would you like something to drink? Orange juice, perhaps?"

Armando nodded yes. Drake quickly walked into the kitchen, which could be seen from the living room. The kitchen had all-granite counters, an island, state-of-the-art stainless steel appliances, a light-green glass backsplash, and espresso cabinets with silver hardware.

"Straight?" Drake asked.

"What?" Armando asked as he walked over to the poster of Joan Crawford in a still from *Mildred Pierce*.

"Do you want the juice straight? I tend to take mine with a little vodka. I also have wine if you'd prefer."

"Uh, no, juice is fine *without* the vodka."

"Sure."

Armando watched to make sure Drake didn't add anything to his juice.

"Would you like to sit down?"

Armando nodded and sat down on the chaise lounge. Drake sat on the sofa.

"To be perfectly honest, I didn't think you were going

to come, not right away, I mean. Cabrien wouldn't be too happy about it." Drake chuckled.

Armando looked sharply at Drake. "He doesn't need to know that I'm here and I wanna keep it that way."

Drake smiled. "Of course."

"You have a nice apartment," Armando said, trying to avoid Drake's stare.

"Thank you. It's taken some time to get everything the way I like it. I like to think of it as my sanctuary."

"Yeah, I like to think of my place like that too, except for when there's drama going on over there."

Drake said nothing but continued to stare unashamedly at Armando's body.

"So, what do you do for a living? Can I ask that?" Armando said, trying to keep the conversation going so he could put off the real reason he was there.

"I work for an organization that's kind of on the conservative end of the political pendulum. I've done a lot for them by way of getting certain officials and politicians elected by exposing unpleasant secrets about their opponents." Drake had a self-satisfied smirk on his face.

"What kinds of things do you dig up?" He took another sip of the juice.

"Some of the things that I've had to bring to light tend to be sexually unconventional."

"What kind of conservative organization?" Armando asked, shifting away from the sexual turn in the conversation.

"It's called Black Republicans for Change."

"I didn't think there were black Republicans. None that weren't Uncle Toms, anyway."

Drake was pensive for a moment, not knowing immedi-

ately how to respond to the comment. "We—um, the organization feels that the black voting block is of value to the Republican establishment. We're trying to seat ourselves at the table. Some of the people I work with think there are a lot of social ills in our society today. The organization seeks to change society, bring it back to better times."

"What needs changing, though? For example...?"

Drake was stuck for something to say. "Oh, things like Roe v. Wade, welfare reform, and the so-called 'homosexual agenda.'"

"Wait a minute, what homosexual agenda?"

"They happen to believe that homosexuality is being promoted as a 'positive alternative lifestyle.'"

"But aren't *you* gay? How could you be a part of an organization like that?" Armando noticed Drake shift uncomfortably.

"It's work, Armando. That's all it is."

"But aren't you sending gay people up the river?"

"I believe that the best revenge is to live well, and do it right under the nose of those who despise me. And as you can tell, I live *very* well."

"Oh, so because you have yours, then everyone else can get theirs the best way they can?"

"I think you're oversimplifying the issue." Drake was becoming agitated.

"Seems hypocritical to me."

"Would you like another glass...?" Drake asked, changing the subject. His tone was almost hostile.

"Yeah, thanks. You can put a little vodka in it this time."

Drake forced a laugh, which broke the tension. He rose from the couch, taking the empty glass from Armando. He

made sure that his hand touched Armando's as he took the glass. Armando didn't flinch.

Drake went into the freezer and took out an ice tray. As Drake put cubes into the glasses, the phone rang. Caller ID flashed Cabrien's name. He rolled his eyes, muttering to himself, "Not right now." The phone was still ringing when Drake went back in the living room with fresh cocktails for he and his guest.

Before sipping it, Armando looked out the window and noticed that the rain was falling harder than he'd ever witnessed in his life. The thunder and lightning followed one another as he rose to take a closer look. He watched people down below racing to get out of the storm.

"Damn, this don't make no kinda sense," Armando said, looking at the rainfall.

Drake took that opportunity to stand next to him. Desire throbbed through his body. "You're safe from it now." Drake's voice fell away into the silence of the room. He put his hand on Armando's shoulder. As his grip tightened, Armando's body tensed up. Armando couldn't pretend he wasn't being touched and turned to face Drake, whose own face was flushed from vodka.

Armando studied Drake's face closely. "Anybody ever tell you that you look like Wayne Brady?" He smiled hesitantly.

Drake chuckled. "I've heard that before, yes."

Armando's smile lasted all of two seconds. "I've never done anything like this before. I'm not like you," Armando said quietly while averting his eyes.

"I know you aren't. Just relax and enjoy it. Don't think too much about it." Drake placed his screwdriver down on the end table by the couch and began massaging

Armando's shoulders with both hands. The strokes were deep and worked to take away Armando's trepidation. "Damn, my woman doesn't even do me like this," Armando whispered, as though he'd been transported out of himself. "Fuck, that feels good."

"Oh, you like that?" Drake asked seductively. "Move over to the couch so I can get a better angle," he gently commanded.

Armando walked over to the couch as he was instructed to do.

"Take off your shirt," Drake said, his own excitement brewing within him.

Armando suddenly stiffened. "I don't think I can do that just yet," Armando said, straightening the collar of his golf shirt.

"I thought it was feeling good to you. Wasn't it?"

Armando didn't answer. He just took huge gulps of his drink until he finished it.

"I think I need another drink, please. In fact, keep 'em coming." Armando's eyes were soft and almost unfocused. He handed the glass to Drake without looking at him.

"Fine," Drake said with slight irritation in his voice. He realized he'd have to work harder at trying to keep Armando calm and not appear so forceful in his advances toward him.

"I mean, I just need a little more time, we'll do it—you know—the thing, but I just have to catch a buzz first, you know?" Then Armando met Drake's eyes and Drake smiled.

"Of course," Drake said as he rose yet again to fill their glasses. "You're doing well," he said, walking toward the kitchen.

"I'm sorry, dude. I told you I haven't done this before."
Inwardly Armando felt his control of the situation fading.
He had stoked himself into believing that he would be in
charge of what would happen with Drake, but it wasn't
working out that way. He hadn't counted on enjoying
Drake's hands massaging his back. He had to stop himself
from wondering how Drake's hands would feel on his
naked body.

Drake returned with the drinks and made the decision
to sit further away from Armando so that he wouldn't feel
so insecure. Drake had been aware of the bravado
Armando displayed when he first arrived, and sensed that
it was an act. Still, he let Armando do whatever it was
he needed to do to get into and through the moment,
although it seemed having sex with him was becoming a
distant possibility. He looked only briefly at Armando and
then turned away, smiling slightly.

"Hey, I didn't mean to upset you about your job earlier," Armando offered.

"What? Oh, don't worry about it. Like any job, they can
piss me off sometimes, but I do like it for the most part."

Armando leaned back, allowing the nape of his neck to
recline against the top of the couch. The liquor was beginning to take effect and he thought it better to go for the
moment now while he was feeling good. He began to take
off his shirt as Drake had told him to. Drake was aroused
but tried not to appear too obvious about it.

The light in the room captured the sharp angles of
Armando's chiseled body. He was slightly warm because
of the alcohol and his nervousness, but his sweat added
sweetness to his scent.

Drake's hands were wet with perspiration and he ner-

vously wiped them alongside his pant legs before putting his hands back on Armando's shoulders. Armando began to sigh softly. "Aw man, that feels amazing. Right there, dude." Armando became lost in the feel of Drake's hands, allowing himself to enjoy the pleasures offered him.

"Want more?" Drake asked.

"Mmm hmm," Armando responded, his breathing getting heavier.

"Where does it hurt most?" Drake asked, trying to appear as though this was a simple massage.

"Lower back," Armando said, taking another sip of his drink. Drake reached over and took it from him and placed it on the coffee table.

"You can have more of this later," Drake whispered closely into Armando's ear. He made sure that his upper lip touched Armando's ear when he spoke.

Armando let go of the glass and his head drooped forward as Drake began to massage Armando's lower back, starting in the middle and moving his hands lower and lower.

Ten minutes passed before Drake finally pulled away, aware that Armando was becoming more and more relaxed. Armando finished his drink; the warm feeling had become stronger. He felt amazing. He stood up, waiting for Drake's next move. Drake rose, taking Armando's hands in his. Armando looked down. He had dreaded this moment, and couldn't help but show a little apprehension. He released himself from Drake's hands, but followed him. His eyes were half open but sparkled still as he looked Drake directly in the eyes.

"Drake, what am I doing?"

"You're about to let me suck your dick," Drake said as

he began to guide Armando out of the living room toward the bedroom.

"Oh, that's right," Armando said before bursting into laughter.

"I'm glad to see you're into this," Drake said, grinning broadly at the realization that the time had finally come.

"No, I'm not. And I'll *never* be into this,'" Armando stopped for two beats before continuing. "But I figure a mouth is a mouth, right?" He passed Drake and entered the bedroom first.

Drake's smile faded. "I wouldn't have phrased it quite so crudely, but you're right. It is what it is—just sex." With that, Drake also entered into the bedroom, and closed the door behind them.

He watched as Armando began to strip. When he was down to his white Calvin Klein briefs, Drake pushed his hand away.

"Here, let me take care of that," he said, slowly easing them down Armando's body. "God, you're really smooth! I like that!" he murmured as his mouth watered in anticipation of what he was about to do.

"Get your ass down on your knees!" Armando shouted. Drake was more than happy to comply. He watched Armando's dick quickly lengthen and thicken as he tugged on it a little. Then, taking a deep breath, he took it slowly into his mouth inch by inch, teasingly, licking and sucking it.

"That's 100% black Dominican dick, motherfucka!" Armando said, gasping with pleasure as he watched more and more of his penis disappear into Drake's hot, hungry mouth. "Damn, your mouth is all warm and shit! I bet you like it hitting the back of your throat, don't you?"

Armando closed his eyes, imagining the dirty talk he'd say to Karen. He tried imagining her soft lips pressed around him, her tongue licking his shaft. But as Drake worked him over, he gave up trying and surrendered to the delight pulsating through his body.

The phone rang again, bringing Armando out of his euphoria. Drake looked over to the phone on his night-stand as the ringing became almost incessant. He looked up at Armando, who also stared at the phone.

"Shouldn't you get that?" Armando asked, exasperated with the ringing.

Drake looked back at Armando's throbbing dick just as the ringing stopped. He smiled. "See, it stopped. It wasn't anyone important anyway."

CHAPTER THIRTEEN

"Drake, answer the damn phone!" Cabrien threw his cell phone onto his bed, and then buried his face into his hands.

Three times he called Drake's place of work, much to the annoyance of the receptionist. Then he called Drake's cell, but the calls went immediately to voicemail. Drake's home? Still, no answer. Cabrien never had to work so hard to find Drake before, and he was filled with an aching feeling that Drake was avoiding him. It was far easier to take ten inches of a stranger's penis into his mouth than deal with being made to feel like a yo-yo in Drake's head games.

It hadn't always been that way. Cabrien thought back to that spring evening over a year ago. The two were lying on the bed, moonlight illuminating the room.

"Do you know what I like most about you, Cabrien?"

"No, what?" Cabrien asked, burying his face into the crook of Drake's neck. He could smell the faintness of sweat and Issey Miyake cologne.

"Your rawness."

"Hey, I give you me. If a person likes what they see, then fine. If not, they can kick rocks."

Drake chuckled. He kissed Cabrien on his temple, and then climbed on top of him, taking Cabrien's hands into

his own. Drake began to kiss him passionately, while Cabrien allowed himself to be washed away, clenching Drake's moist back. He loved the feeling of Drake's masculinity—his powerfulness on top of him. The sex that night hadn't felt like work at all. The intense passion in Drake's eyes evoked new feelings in Cabrien.

"I like you, Cabrien. I think I'm going to keep you around for a while," Drake said as he rolled off him.

"Aw hell, that's all you had to say, then," Cabrien said, erupting into giggles.

That summer, Drake treated Cabrien to a trip to Los Angeles. Because he'd started considering a relationship with Drake, Cabrien didn't accept any money for his time, although Drake paid for everything. They stayed at The Élan, an ultra-modern hotel located between West Hollywood and Beverly Hills. As soon as they checked in, they were in bed together. With the passionate sex, the sophistication of this disarmingly handsome, fifty-year-old man, and the excitement of being in California for the first time, Cabrien couldn't resist his descent into love. After showering and dressing, they had dinner in Beverly Hills at an intimate Italian bistro. Drake gazed unashamedly into Cabrien's luminous eyes.

"So what do you want to do after dinner?" Drake asked after sipping his Pinot Grigio.

"Honestly, Drake, I really don't care what we do. I'm just happy to be here with you. No other guy ever thought to take me out of town, so this is golden for me."

"You know, this is kind of like a pseudo anniversary. It was exactly a year ago we met in Loring Park," Drake said, pouring more wine into Cabrien's glass.

"Yeah, you found me when I was young and innocent."

"Hardly. There's never been anything innocent about you, Cabrien."

Cabrien stared at Drake, trying to figure if the moment was right to get something important off his chest. Drake noticed a sudden seriousness in Cabrien's eyes. He put his glass down and folded his arms. "You look so serious all of a sudden."

"Oh, it's nothing bad. I mean, I don't think it's a bad thing."

"Okay, say what's on your mind."

"I think I could see myself with you, Drake."

"Uh-oh."

"No, I'm serious. No one's ever made me feel the way that you do. You know we have a great time together, in and out of the bedroom."

Drake began to fidget nervously. "Listen, Cabrien, I like you. But, I'm not the settling down type. Why don't we just enjoy this moment."

Cabrien brought his face up from his hands. His eyes were filled with tears as he recalled that memory. He was foolish to let his mind wander back there.

"I should've kept my big mouth shut," Cabrien moaned.

Drake had grown distant and cold after that trip to Los Angeles. It became a task to get Drake to spend any time with him at all. Last-minute meetings kept cropping up. And now he couldn't even get him on the telephone.

Cabrien got up from the bed and made his way to the bathroom. There, he stared at himself in the mirror.

"I ran his ass away," he sobbed to his reflection. "Nice going, you needy bitch!"

CHAPTER

FOURTEEN

Gary and Wanda Walsh, along with Tony and Samantha Cannon, had just finished an incredible meal: filet mignon and seafood pasta were washed down with spectacular red and white wines. The mood at Opal Restaurant had been a jovial one, with lively conversation shared equally among the four adults. It wasn't until Tony began asking questions about Gary's nomination that the conversation hit a wall for the two wives at the table.

"Jesus, who would have thought that Gary Walsh, a kid I watched grow through the ranks, would one day become president of one of the soon-to-be most powerful organizations in the state of Minnesota," Tony beamed as he poured himself another glass of wine.

"I haven't won the presidency yet, Tony, but I plan to."

Wanda rolled her eyes. Gary hadn't even gotten the job yet, and as far as she was concerned, he probably wouldn't. Listening to pipe dreams was the last way Wanda wanted to spend the evening.

"Wanda, why don't we head over to the bar and let the boys talk shop?" Samantha said.

"Yes, let's. I'm sure we can find something else to talk about."

Without even looking at her husband, Wanda left with Samantha. Gary seemed unnerved at Wanda's leaving without speaking to him.

"They'll be fine," Tony said as he tried to bring Gary back to the discussion. "So, tell me about your vision for the BRC."

"Well, I'm thinking about taking the group in a completely different direction."

"Oh?" Tony said, putting down his glass.

"I'd like to tap into a group that the Republican Party is ignoring."

"And who might they be?"

"The moderates. The way the country is shaping up, we're too far to the right. I think moderation is the key to the future."

Tony began to fidget in his seat. "Yeah, but isn't the main reason for the group's success is that it has catered to the far right? You plan to undo what it has taken the BRC years to accomplish."

"I'm not going to undo anything. I'm simply going to build on what we've already established, and reach out to more moderate conservatives."

"Yes, but you'll piss off a lot of people who've been with you guys from the beginning. Are you sure you want to do that?"

"Yes, I'm sure. Look, don't you remember George W.'s campaign for his first term? He spoke of 'compassionate conservatism,' won the election, and then it got lost somewhere. I want to try to find it and use it."

"What do you mean?" Tony was intrigued.

"Let's face facts. The party doesn't have a great track record with courting the black vote. Republicans are being seen as a pack of morality watchdogs and *that* ,Tony, is pissing off a lot more people on a larger scale then a few nut jobs in the organization."

Tony smiled as he said, "Go on."

"Why should I care if honest, hardworking people who pay their taxes decide to terminate a pregnancy, or want to marry each other if they happen to be of the same sex? At the end of the day it doesn't affect me."

Tony became stern. "Because abortion is murder, and the gay thing, don't even get me started." Tony picked up his glass again and drank from it.

"See, it's that kind of moral superiority that gives the Republican Party a bad name. With abortion, I happen to be pro-choice, because I, as a man, don't feel I have the right to tell a woman what she ought to do with her body. Now does that mean that I think abortions should be used as a form of birth control? No, because I think that a man can use a condom or the woman can use some other form of contraception. But I don't think it is realistic to tell people that abstinence is the only way to go," Gary said.

"You know that abortion is wrong, Gary," Tony shot back.

"Look, I'm not out here advocating that people run out and get two for the price of one. But I'll be damned if I'm going to tell a woman who has been brutally raped that she ought to carry that child to full term and be reminded every day of what happened to her."

"Okay, but what about the gay thing. You mean to tell me you've actually bought into what those perverts are saying about equal rights? Okay, so now I'm going to

divorce my wife and marry my first cousin? I mean, we've always had a thing for each other."

"Come on, Tony. I'm talking about consenting, non-related adults."

Tony was quiet for a moment before smiling. "Gotcha," he said.

"What?" Gary asked, confused.

"I'm pulling your chain, Gary. I actually agree with you, but what I was saying before is the same kind of stuff that people are going to be screaming in your ear, except they won't be kidding about it. Are you prepared for that kind of resistance? You ought to think really hard about it, because only the strong can survive in this line of work."

"I just know that Isaac's vision doesn't reflect where most people are in their politics. Grown people don't want other grown people telling them how to live their lives."

"Well said, my friend," Tony said, and the two men raised their glasses.

At the bar, Wanda and Samantha talked spiritedly about anything that didn't center on their husbands' work. Wanda rarely enjoyed the wives she'd met over the years, but she did like Samantha, and wished they could get together more often than they did.

"You know, Samantha, I wonder how you do it. I really try to stay out of the whole politics thing because I think it's phony."

"What can I tell you, girl? You get used to it. You see your husband up there doing great things. So what if you have to waste a couple of hours with dreadful people at a cocktail party? It's to support your husband."

"It would be easier to support him if I knew he was going to go the distance."

"The distance?" Samantha tilted her head in confusion.

"Yes. He's always been flighty. But I wonder if it's because of the pressure I've put on him to succeed. Maybe he jumps from one thing to another because he's looking for something he can really excel at." Wanda brushed back the hair that fell over her shoulder. She was absolutely devastating in her Naomi Campbell-inspired weave, black pantsuit and simple diamond necklace.

"Do you think he's jealous of your success?"

"I don't know. Gary holds a lot of stuff inside."

"Well, have you talked to him? The one thing I learned is that no matter how busy Tony is, I make him talk about everything."

"I do. But he's very proud. He won't tell me anything. I just get an 'Oh, it's nothing. I'm just stressed from work.'" Wanda turned and could see her husband with Tony in the dining room. Gary looked up at Wanda and smiled broadly.

Samantha followed Wanda's eyes toward their husbands. Then she leaned in closely. "Wanda, have you ever heard the saying that behind every great man, there's an even greater woman?"

"Of course."

"Maybe you might want to get involved a bit. Use whatever you can to help him out."

"Help him out how?"

"Let me put it this way; Tony used to be like Gary. He'd be on the brink of getting something going and then drop the ball. When I married him, I took a huge risk because my parents didn't approve. They had what they thought was my ideal man picked out for me. But they couldn't

dictate my heart. I was determined for them to see that I hadn't made a mistake with Tony."

"What did you do?"

"I had to get involved. I was the one who got Tony his job. He doesn't know it. And you better believe I'll be sure to take that to my grave."

Wanda looked at Samantha, waiting to be told that she was joking.

"Sometimes we ladies have to help our husbands. Wanda, you have the money and the creativity. I'm sure you can find a way to make things happen for Gary."

"I wouldn't know where to begin."

"Listen, do you love him?"

"Of course I do."

"And I love my husband. But sometimes we have to do some very strange things to get the things we want. It's part of the sacrifice."

"I suppose you're right. I'll think of something," Wanda said, noticing Samantha's sinister smirk.

Gary decided that perhaps now would be the right time to ask Tony for his help in fundraising. Tony Cannon was a genius when it came to inspiring people to reach into their pockets for worthy causes. He hoped that Tony would deem his cause worthy enough.

"Listen, Tony, I know that you know a lot of people. With you behind me on this thing, I could really hit the ball out of the park."

"I don't know, Gary. If I lend a hand to you I would lose future opportunities with someone else."

"I don't know what that even means," Gary said quietly.

"But, I have to hand it to you, though; you have a lot

of balls to want to propose such a drastic change in direction."

"What's so drastic, Tony? George W. sat in front of a camera and spoke of compassionate conservatism. I believe in that."

"I know you do. But you can't walk away from the fact that a lot would be at stake if you came in all of a sudden saying that we were no longer interested in the moral lives of the American people. Bruce Hedrick would tell you to fuck off if he knew what you were planning."

"I disagree. I think Bruce knows what he'll get with me running the show. I think he knows his way is losing steam."

"Just as long as you know that you have one hell of a fight ahead of you on this one. I hope you know that."

"Yes, I do."

Tony looked at Gary intently for a moment. The silence made Gary uncomfortable.

"I'm not prepared to discuss specifics with you tonight, but you can call my office tomorrow and we'll set something up."

Gary began to smile. "So does this mean you'll help me?"

"I don't want my name on this, Gary. I believe in your vision, yeah, but I don't want to alienate the wrong people either. Actually, do me a favor. Call me at the end of the week and I'll tell you what I've come up with."

"Thank you. I appreciate it. You won't be sorry," Gary said, raising his glass again to toast Tony.

Laughing nervously, Tony raised his glass too, hitting it lightly against Gary's. "God, I hope not."

The women rejoined their husbands and the couples

chatted about how splendid Barcelona was in the wintertime. They said good night and promised to get together soon. Gary was immensely happy as he drove home.

"Why are you so happy all of a sudden?" Wanda asked.

"I think Tony is going to help me raise funds."

"Really?" Wanda said as she reached for the seat recline button on her seat.

"Yeah, he really threw me for a loop though. When I told him my vision for the BRC he pretended to be offended by it."

"Why would he do that?"

"That's Tony for you. He's such a kidder. We're going to raise so much money, Wanda."

"He actually told you that he would help you?"

"Well, he has to come up with a strategy so that his fingerprints aren't on it, but yeah, I think he's going to help me."

"I'd be careful, honey. If he hasn't given you a clear-cut answer, don't presume anything," Wanda cautioned him.

Gary said nothing.

"Anyway, I'm thinking that maybe Samantha and I should get together more often. I was telling her earlier that we don't need our husbands as an excuse to socialize."

"That sounds nice," Gary said as he visualized his victory.

"It would be nice to not always think of work."

"I totally agree. You work too hard as it is."

"Yeah, I wouldn't have gotten these lines around my eyes if I hadn't worked so hard. I need some touching up."

"Are you kidding me? You look incredible, Wanda. Tony was going on and on about how great you look."

"Oh really? That pig," Wanda said with disgust.

"What?" Gary said, turning to look at her.

"I don't like Tony. He seems phony."

"What? Wanda, trust me, I've known Tony for quite awhile and he's completely legit. He's a little rough around the edges, true. But trust me, he tells it like it is. He's a native New Yorker."

"Oh, and I guess New Yorkers don't lie," Wanda said, her words dripping in sarcasm.

Gary pulled the car over and placed it in park. He looked at Wanda, who was taken aback by his barely suppressed anger.

"Why are you trying to burst my bubble?"

"I'm not, but I'm pretty damn good at judging character. I'm telling you—be careful with that one."

"But you want to go have dinner with his wife?"

"Samantha is a wonderful woman. We have a lot in common. She and I think alike."

"Oh, she's your friend now, huh? Well, did your friend tell you that she was caught fucking one of Tony's interns and she had to beg Tony not to divorce her when he found out?"

Wanda, shocked, said nothing. As Gary put the car into drive and pulled back onto the street he said, "I didn't think so."

The rest of the drive home was quiet. Gary turned on NPR to escape the quiet. When they arrived home Wanda entered the house first, still saying nothing to Gary.

When Gary went into the living room, he noticed the red light on the answering machine flashing. He went into the kitchen and poured a glass of wine from the half-full bottle sitting on the counter. He took off his suit jacket, slung it over a stool, then went back into the living room to

retrieve the message. Gary Walsh almost dropped his glass when he heard the voice on the recorder.

"Well, howdy stranger! This is Stewart McKillen calling. Don't ask how I got your number; you know I've always been creative at finding out information. Listen, I was calling for two reasons, the first to see how you were doing. It's been a long time. Secondly, I'm calling to tell you that I'm in town on business. I'm speaking at a convention and was wondering if we could get together later. I'm here for a week but the convention's only three days, but I really wanted to talk to you and maybe see you. Jesus, I don't know if I should be doing this over the phone, but Sarah and I got a divorce. Do you remember Sarah? Oh that's right, I don't think you ever met her but.... (Bleep)" That was the end of the message.

Wanda came into the living room wearing a revealing robe that teasingly displayed her full, beautiful breasts. "Was that the answering machine?" Wanda asked, breaking her silence.

"Hmm? Yeah, it was."

"Who was it?"

"Stewart McKillen," Gary said, smiling suddenly. "Talk about a blast from the past."

CHAPTER FIFTEEN

"Can I get my money so I can go?" Armando asked, rising up to sit on the edge of the bed. He needed separation from Drake.

"You're in a hurry?"

"Yeah. I need to get home to my girl, and I got a lot of shit on my mind."

"What are you thinking about?" Drake asked, noticing the pensive look on Armando's face.

"Naw, man, I'm just thinking about what I'm gonna do for work."

"What do you mean? What are you doing now?"

Armando was silent for two beats. Until that moment, no one knew of his secret. He felt like a noose was tightening around his neck. "I used to work at a hotel, and I got fired. And my girl doesn't know."

"Why didn't you tell her? You can get another job, right?" Drake said.

"Aw man, you don't understand. I promised her I'd take care of her, and she'll think I'm a sorry excuse for a man if I tell her I got fired."

"What was their reason for letting you go?"

"I talked back to a guest. She was mad out of line and I told her so, and my supervisor let me go."

"So, you'll get another job." Drake repeated.

"I've been trying. It's been over a month, and nothing. This economy is jacked up!" Armando became tense again.

Drake lay on his side and stared at Armando, who became self-conscious at being looked at.

"Dude, why are you staring at me?"

Drake broke from his trance. "I was just thinking that perhaps you could continue to do this."

"You got jokes."

"I'm serious. You're a great-looking guy. I'm willing to spend money on beautiful things, or in this case, beautiful people."

"Naw, dude. I need a job. Karen wouldn't go for this if she found out about it."

"Then don't tell her. You already have a secret, so it's not like you're a stranger at keeping them. I won't tell if you don't," Drake said.

"I'm not a whore. This ain't gonna be an ongoing thing."

Drake stood up and went into his closet for his robe. Armando turned away so he wouldn't see Drake's dick swinging between his legs.

"Okay, look. If Karen doesn't know that you're not working, she'll be very surprised when your money starts to run out. Keep looking for jobs like you've been doing, and just do this until you find something."

Armando said nothing but continued staring forward. His shadow began to dance along the wall of the candlelit room. Rose Royce's song "Wish Upon a Star" played softly in the background, but Armando was so deep in thought, he didn't notice.

"Armando, did you hear me?"

"Yeah, I hear you. But I don't wanna be one of those people that get caught up in this shit. Years pass and they can't get out." Armando got up to search for his clothes.

"Oh, I wouldn't worry about that. I won't let you get caught up. It would cost too much," Drake said, laughing. Armando began to laugh as well and became relaxed again. He was still buzzing from the alcohol but he was lucid enough to know what he'd done.

"Don't freak out, but what do you think about what we just did?" Drake asked. He went over to his pants, which he'd slung over the back of a chair. He pulled out his wallet and took out some money.

"I don't really have an opinion. Like, what do you want to know?"

"Did you like it? Were you repulsed by it?"

Armando noticed Drake flipping the bills slowly. "No, I wasn't repulsed by it," he said carefully.

"So, you would do it again?"

"It isn't something I'd go looking to do. But you're paying me. A mouth's a mouth."

"Well, you were great at this! My fantasy made flesh," Drake said, handing Armando money. "Is five hundred okay?"

"Yeah, cool. Thanks, man," Armando said, stuffing the money away into his pants pocket before Drake had a chance to change his mind on the amount.

"I tell you what. Put me down as a reference and say that I was your boss from the hotel, and when they call me I can give you a glowing review."

"You'd do that?" Armando asked.

"Sure, why not. You give me what I want and I'll give you what you want. It's only fair, right?" Drake's words

oozed from his lips like syrup running down the side of pancakes.

"Hell yeah!" Armando beamed. He suddenly looked at the clock on Drake's nightstand. It was almost 11:00 PM. He couldn't believe that he'd been at Drake's all that time.

"Shit, I gotta bounce!" Armando said, bolting from the bed. The candlelight highlighted every muscle on his well-defined body. Drake looked sad for a moment, as though a dream that he'd been enjoying was coming to an end.

"Aren't you going to take a shower?" Drake asked in disbelief.

"Oh yeah, you're right. I should probably do that." Armando didn't wait to hear where towels were located. He darted into the bathroom and hit the light, his eyes trying to adjust to the sudden burst of light.

Drake lay down again, putting his hands behind his head and smiled. *If the people in the office could see me now.*

Armando was almost literally in and out of the shower, nearly breaking his neck to get dressed and leave. When he rushed back into the bedroom his naked body still dripped with beads of water. His penis swung heavily as he began to dress.

"Where the hell are my shoes?" Armando asked in irritation.

"Look under the bed," Drake suggested, admiring Armando's well-cared-for feet.

"Thanks again, man, for the cash. Not bad for eight hours of work. Plus, I got to bust a couple nuts..."

"You know good and well I didn't suck your dick for eight straight hours, and it was three nuts, not a couple. But you were a perfect lover. I'm sure it wasn't easy for

you, but you rose to the occasion–pun intended, and you did very well."

"And thanks for the help with the job reference. I really appreciate it." Armando eyed the clock again. "I hate to bust and run, but I gots to go. I have to tend to some damage control at home."

"No problem at all. I'll call you?" Drake asked as he reached into the nightstand for a pad and paper.

"Why don't we keep it like it is? If I need you, I'll call you, okay?" Armando said cautiously.

Drake took in Armando's eyes one last time for the evening. "You have nothing to worry about, but that's fine. If you want to do that, we can do it your way."

"Yep." Armando reached in and gave Drake an awkwardly stiff hug and then left.

When Armando stepped outside, the night looked and smelled fresh, as though the rain had washed everything clean. The light reflecting from the streetlamps looked like melted pools of butter on the cobblestoned streets. Armando drove home with the windows down, the cool summer air lightly touching his face. The day had gone better than he'd planned. Nothing to make him throw up like he thought he would. He wished Drake hadn't touched him so much, but the five hundred dollars and reference made them even.

When Armando got home, Karen was sitting in the living room, holding a can of beer. Seven beer cans were laying crushed on the coffee table in front of her.

"Where the fuck have you been?" she seethed.

"What?"

Karen threw the can of beer at him. It missed, hitting

the door instead. Beer suds splashed over the side of his face, shirt, and forearms.

"You heard me! Where in the hell were you at?"

"Bitch, what the hell is wrong with you?" Armando yelled, wiping the beer off his face. His heart was racing.

"Nigga, I know you didn't just call me no bitch!"

"My bad, damn! I was at work," he rambled nervously. "They called me in because they needed help tonight!" Was this the woman he'd made love to early this morning?

"Oh really? Then why is it that when I called the hotel they said you weren't there?"

"I had to work a banquet tonight. We had a large function," Armando lied.

"Then where's your uniform?" Karen asked as she stood up from the sofa.

"I needed a different uniform, so they lent me one to use for the night," Armando said, looking down again at the empty beer cans.

"And you didn't bring it home to wash it? You just left a sweaty-ass uniform for somebody else to use?" Karen asked as she stood on the opposite side of the table.

"Karen, what's with the third degree? I was tired and wanted to get home, so I wasn't thinking about no uniform, all right?"

"As a matter of fact, I've noticed that for about the last month when you've left up out of here, you don't have a uniform with you."

"I told you that I don't like to wear it to the job. I put it on when I'm there and take it off before I come home," Armando said, glaring at her.

"Is that a fact? Okay, maybe you can explain to me why

for the past month I ain't seen any of your uniforms in the dirty clothes basket when I've done the laundry."

"Karen, how many beers have you had?"

"Don't try and change the subject. You *know* where I'm going with this."

Armando tried to gather up the empty cans from the table, but Karen knocked them out of his hands onto the floor.

"I talked to your former boss, Armando. What's his name? Ben Travis? He told me your black ass got fired. You ain't been working all this time? " Karen screamed.

Armando's heart began to pound till he felt it would jump out of his chest. Suddenly he felt dizzy. Armando fell onto the sofa, hoping everything would become still. He looked down.

"Your goofy ass got fired, and you ain't said squat to me about it! What happened to trust, Armando? And you might have gotten away with it if my mama hadn't called my job today." She began to cry.

"She called your job?" Armando asked softly, his heart still beating fast.

"Yes, my mama called my job to tell me that my older sister, Ruby, is in the hospital fighting for her life, Armando. Some Mexican hit her with the car and ran! And I came home because I needed you and when you weren't here, I called your job thinking that yeah, maybe you went in after all. And then Ben tells me this crap about how you ain't been working there for about a month!"

Armando looked up at Karen and it was as though his breath had been stolen away from him. It was breaking his heart to see her in such pain. He was angry with himself for allowing this lie to go as far as it had.

"Baby, come here," Armando said to her. His eyes began to moisten.

"Hell to the naw! I don't hug liars! I've called my mama and she's coming to get me. I'm gonna go stay over her house and then go to the hospital in the morning."

"Let me come with you," Armando said, reaching in to hug her.

"Where the hell were you tonight?" Karen asked, returning to her original question.

Armando's words ran together in a panic. "I was with Cabrien. He came over looking for you, and he convinced me to go to that damn bar with him!"

"I thought you hated that bar."

"I don't hate it. Cabrien was there. You were gone and I didn't have shit else to do."

"Yeah right. You were probably out there fucking. Your ass can't work, but you can find the time to fuck." Karen's cell phone rang and she answered it. She told the caller she'd be right down. "I gotta go. You best believe that this ain't over. I just can't do this tonight, but you better have your ass here tomorrow so we can talk about this." And she was gone.

Armando felt like a rock was tied to his neck, and he was sinking quickly to the sea's floor. He wanted to hush the drama. Climbing into bed, he hoped to fall asleep, but his mind raced.

The next day, despite little sleep, he chose a positive outlook and use of his day. He planned to pay some bills, fight for his unemployment, and put in more applications, using Drake Hill as a reference, and that reference would be so amazing that somebody would *have* to hire him.

As far as doing anything else sexual with Drake,

Armando hoped Drake had enjoyed the evening with him this one good time, because he wasn't planning on doing it again.

Later, Armando was enjoying a bowl of cereal when Karen entered the apartment, slamming the door. He bolted up, looking like a child awaiting punishment.

"Hi," Armando said timidly.

"Hi," Karen said. She put her purse and keys on the coffee table.

"How's your sister?"

"The doctors said that she's going to make it, but she looked all messed up. I barely recognized her."

"But she's alive. That's the important thing. You gotta think positive," Armando said.

"Yeah, but it's still hard. And what makes it so bad is that there were a couple of cops buzzing around trying to ask her questions. I kept trying to tell them that she wasn't in any condition to talk about that shit and that they should wait."

They were silent for several minutes before either spoke. It was as if neither knew where the conversation should go.

"Look, I'm sorry I didn't tell you about the job situation, okay? I don't want it to be this way with you."

"I'm gonna stay with Mama for a few days. You know, just chill out over there," Karen said, averting her glance to avoid those gray eyes of Armando's that always weakened her will.

"Karen, you hate your mother. I bet y'all can't go two days without some kinda drama starting." Armando said.

"I don't hate my mother."

"We both know y'all don't get along."

"Yeah, well, at least my mama doesn't tell lies. She may get the truth twisted about some things, but she doesn't straight up lie to me. And you do."

"I made a mistake, baby. And you have to believe me when I tell you that I've been out there beating the pavement trying to find another job. When I found a new one I was gonna tell you that I lost the old one. That's the way it was supposed to go."

"I don't care why, because it all ends up the same–you lied!"

"Why are you being so cold? Okay, I didn't tell you straight out, but I didn't lie to you. You never asked me 'Armando, are you still working?'"

"Now that's a lie! Last night, did you or did you not sit there and tell me you were working banquets when I asked where you were?"

He had nothing to say to that, so he put defensive on like a pair of shoes. "Just do what you gotta do because I'm through arguing with your ass," he said, his shoulders hulking. "If you don't wanna accept my apology, then fine. Run home to your mammy!"

"Yeah–all right, I'll run to my 'mammy' because I'm living with a boy who is too afraid to be a man: open his mouth and tell me the truth. Don't reverse this, Armando. All you had to do was meet me halfway and you couldn't even do that!"

"You won't last a week at your mama's house, Karen. But like I said, you do what you want. I'll be here when you come back. But right now, I'm gonna go out to get a job."

"That's all you have to say?" Karen shot back, beating on his chest.

"I ain't got nothin' else to say."

"Yeah, I bet if I was one of your sluts you could sit and talk till the cows come home! But with me the cat's got your tongue."

Armando shrugged, then shook his head.

Karen watched as Armando sat down again. She sat too, so that they could be at eye level. Once upon a time, one look from him would extinguish her anger. This time was different. It was as if she'd built an imaginary wall to keep him and all of his charms from breaking her down.

"Baby, I want things to be right between us. I was wrong, okay. I admit it. I shouldn't have put you through what I did. Get mad if you want to. Get it out of your system."

"It hurts," she said flatly. "I'll need time." She dared not look into his eyes.

Suddenly, Armando changed his tone and was upbeat.

"I think my luck is gonna change with the job situation, though. For real."

"That lady from the mall called you back?" Karen asked as she reached for her keys.

"No. But I know my luck is about to change. I'm gonna make it change."

"You have a lead?" she asked, fidgeting with the keys.

"No, but I'm gonna put in a whole bunch of applications, and Beverly from work is gonna pretend to be my boss from the hotel and give me a positive review so that someone will want to hire me."

Karen acted as if this changed nothing. "That's good, I guess."

"Yep, we're going up, baby. Everybody has problems and we're gonna work through ours."

Karen stopped fidgeting with the keys. Armando

reached over and took the keys from her hands and placed them back on the table. He then leaned over, put his hand on her face and directed her to look at him. When she looked into his eyes, her defenses were swept away.

His vulnerability struck Karen as sincere and she again saw the man with whom she had fallen in love. Tears fell from her eyes. She believed everything would be all right with them.

Armando leaned in and kissed her gently on her lips. "I need to get going. I hope you'll be here when I get back. Are you still going to your mama's house?"

Karen shrugged.

"Come on, baby. I'll be back in a few hours. Then, we can talk, whatever you want. "

"If I stay, you promise we can get down to the nitty-gritty? No more lies? Only the truth, no matter how bad it might hurt? Can you promise that?"

Armando's throat felt like it was filled with rocks. He swallowed big. "I promise."

"Fine. I'll stay."

Armando quickly got up and headed to the shower. When he was ready to leave, he kissed Karen on the forehead. Karen sat alone in the stillness of the room, but she didn't feel alone. She just knew that they would work through this.

CHAPTER SIXTEEN

"Damn it!" Gary yelled at the computer monitor. He clicked the computer mouse again, and again the same warning box popped up– *The file you are trying to open cannot be found.*

Gary had been struggling to pull up an unedited video outlining the BRC agenda to improve the lives of lower- and middle-class black families. He had one more day until he had to show the video to the board members, and now the file wouldn't open.

Angrily, he picked up his office phone to call his assistant. "Yeah, I need you to come in here right away!"

Ten seconds later the assistant arrived with pen and notepad at the ready, completely prepared for the tirade he was about to endure.

"Have you been messing with the files?" Gary asked while repeatedly trying to gain access to the video.

"What's the problem?" the assistant asked as he crossed the room to look at the monitor.

"I can't get the video file, that's the problem! Look at this!" Gary clicked the mouse on the document again: *The file you are trying to open cannot be found.*

"It was working fine yesterday. Have you been in here?"

"No, Mr. Walsh. I remember you telling me that you

had some last-minute touches to make on it, but that you were going to do it later. That was last week some time."

"Well, it couldn't have erased itself!" Gary said, pushing the mouse away.

"Did you save it to the backup drive?" the assistant asked, trying to appear helpful.

"No, I didn't save it to the backup drive," he growled back. "It wasn't finished."

Gary got up and began to pace the room. The vote was coming up soon and he was back at square one. "How did this happen? Was someone in my office?"

"No, Mr. Walsh. I mean, Mr. Hill asked me for a box of paper clips yesterday and I told him there was some in your desk..."

Gary's glare stunned his assistant into silence. He darted out of his office toward Drake Hill's office.

"Did you go into my office without my permission?" Gary asked, bursting in.

"Gary, I'm on the phone, I'll talk to you when I'm finished," Drake said brusquely.

"Get off the phone, now!"

Drake sat in disbelief. He excused himself from his caller and hung up. "Don't you ever come into my office again and embarrass me like that. Do you understand me?" Drake said.

"I want to know why you were in my office, Drake!" Gary demanded.

"When was I in your office, Gary?"

"You asked my assistant for paper clips, and he said you went in there to get them."

"You're pissed over some paper clips?" Drake took out

a box of paper clips from his desk and threw them to the edge of his desk. "Here, take 'em."

"And that's all you took from my office?"

"Yes–that's all, Gary. Jesus Christ. What's your problem?"

"A very important file is missing from my computer. In fact, it keeps saying that it can't be found."

"And what does that have to do with me?" Drake said.

"My assistant told me that you were in my office— so I figured..."

"You figured that I'm so eaten up with jealousy that I'm trying to sabotage your lil promotion?"

"Did you?"

"Gary, let's get something straight right now. I did not go into your office and delete anything from your computer."

"Swear you had nothing to do with it."

"What is this, grade school? I didn't erase your document; it's as simple as that. And I'm sorry if you're not satisfied with that answer."

"You're not sorry at all," Gary said, glaring at him.

"You're right, I'm not sorry. You really ought to get your information straight before you go around accusing people of things."

"Whatever you say, Drake." Gary was about to leave until Drake threw in a parting remark.

"I think you might want to ask Isaac if he knows anything about it, considering the fact that he came in here not too long ago practically begging me to help him find dirt on you. I actually would've considered it too, but you don't have any worthwhile dirt to expose."

"Oh, and I guess you expect a thank-you for that."

"You just win this thing first, *and then* you can thank me."

"When did Isaac ask you to do this?"

"A few days ago."

"I guess I should go talk to him. You'd better not be lying to me, Drake."

"I don't have to lie. And I think you should talk to him. But he's not in his office today."

As Gary left Drake's office he said, "Stay out of my office."

"Asshole," Drake said under his breath. Gary went back to his office and sat down in front of the monitor and began to ponder what he would do next. The phone rang, and he answered it immediately.

"Hello," Gary said, irritated. There was a pause before a voice spoke up.

"Gary Walsh?"

"Yes."

"Hi, this is Stewart McKillen. How the hell are you?"

Suddenly Gary's demeanor shifted to upbeat.

"Hey, how are you doing? Sorry I missed your call the other night."

"No problem. I called your office and begged some woman to give me your home number. She said she was doing it against her better judgment, but that she hoped I was who I said I was."

"Who did you say that you were?"

"I just said that I was an old friend of yours and that you'd probably want to hear from me."

"I guess that worked, then, didn't it?" Gary said, smiling into the phone.

"Are you free this afternoon?"

"Sure. What did you have in mind?"

"I was thinking we could get something to eat and catch up. My convention let out early today."

"What time were you thinking?"

"How about 1:00 PM. What's good to eat downtown?"

"Meet me at Stella Bar and Grill on Nicollet Mall, okay? There's a big sign. You can't miss it."

"See you then." And then Stewart hung up.

Gary smiled as he leaned back in his chair. It had been seven years since the last time he saw Stewart.

When Gary approached the restaurant, he saw the familiar face smiling broadly at him.

"Stewart?" It was as though time had stood still for Stewart. He was as attractive as he was in college, with the exception of a few crows' feet and a slight peppering of gray in his hair.

He had the elegance of a black Cary Grant, and his eyes sparkled with wit and intelligence.

Gary knew he was a very attractive man in his own right, looking younger than his fifty-three years. But time had been even more generous to Stewart McKillen.

"Well, shall we?" Stewart asked, opening the door for Gary. The two men were escorted by the hostess to a table near the open window. A busboy scurried over to place bread on the table and quickly began to pour water into their glasses.

"You look really good, Stewart," Gary said.

"Thank you. You look great too, Gary."

"Oh, please. I'm old."

"Hardly."

"So when you called the other night, the answering

machine cut your message short. You said something about getting divorced?"

Stewart's expression became serious as he put his glass down. "First off, I can't believe you still have an answering machine picking up your messages. But yeah, I'm divorced."

"Well, I spent a lot of money for it, so I'm going to keep using it until it croaks. So what happened?"

"Shortly after we graduated, Sarah and I got married and moved to Thousand Oaks, California. Everything was fine, I thought, until I started spending a lot of time in New York City working with the United Nations Secretariat. The nights started to become lonely. And there was this other side of myself. I met someone. A man."

Just then, the waiter came to them with an order pad at the ready. The two men looked quickly over the menu and decided on Cobb salads and iced tea.

"How long ago did this happen?" Gary asked as he pulled a small piece of bread from the hunk in the basket.

"Oh, Jesus, I'd say 1983. That's the first time. But I've dallied a bit over the years. The last time I cheated with a guy was two years ago in 2006."

"Wow," Gary said, trying not to sound judgmental.

"It's funny, I wasn't sure that I even wanted to get married. But that's what you did back then: you met a girl, you called yourself falling in love, and you got married. But I was hiding stuff I didn't want to deal with. I tried to tell myself she had forced me into getting married, but I went along with it because I knew I could hide who I was."

Stewart stared past Gary as though he was reliving a memory for the first time in years, and the recognition of that memory frightened him. He began to shake his head.

"Anyway, we tried to work on our marriage. Actually, *she* tried to work on it, but I acted like I couldn't be bothered." Stewart dropped his gaze and whispered, "I should never have gotten married."

"You know, we don't have to talk about this," Gary said, putting his glass down and reaching for more bread.

"No, no. Believe it or not, it's better to get it all out. Bottom line, she caught on to the cheating and paid me a visit in Manhattan. Imagine her surprise when she found me with a guy."

"Does that really happen? That sounds like something from a soap opera."

Stewart gave Gary a hesitant smile. Just then the salads came and Gary couldn't wait to begin eating and abandon this depressing subject.

"So enough of my doom and gloom, what have you been up to?" Stewart asked as he stabbed into his salad.

"Well, right now, I'm up to my eyeballs in work. I've been nominated to take over as president of a political organization called the Black Republicans for Change.... Well, I shouldn't have to tell you, since you called there looking for me."

"Yeah, good for you, though."

"Thank you." Gary caught himself looking at Stewart. The golden light from the sun lit up Stewart's otherwise melancholy face. Gary stopped eating his salad and watched Stewart force large gobs of salad into his mouth without any consideration for dining etiquette.

"Hungry?" Gary asked good-naturedly.

"God, this is good." Stewart continued to devour the salad.

Outside the restaurant, the sidewalk was alive with

people walking in pairs to get something fast to eat, and others walking briskly back to their offices with takeout. People were chatting on their cells, sometimes bursting into laughter. It was summer and people were out in large numbers.

"Stewart, do you remember our junior year at Howard? I felt like you had distanced yourself from me."

"That's because I had the biggest crush on you. I didn't think you'd understand. Anyway, that was a long time ago."

"You had a crush on me?"

Stewart looked sharply into Gary's eyes. "Yeah. But do you honestly think you'd have been able to handle it if I'd told you?"

"Why not? We were friends. We *are* friends. You're just being honest about how you felt," Gary reasoned.

"Well, you're being pretty calm about a man having a crush on you."

"I mean, how else do you want me to act? I'm a fifty-three-year-old man. I'm not going to get bent out of shape over something like that. Now, would I have understood in the past? I don't know. Maybe."

"It was a good thing that we had that time apart, though. I couldn't have taken seeing you on a day-to-day basis. I felt like damaged goods."

"Why?"

"I had my issues that I was dealing with, Gary, issues I didn't want to deal with, and still don't."

"I know now, that all of those times that I thought about you over the years weren't for nothing. You were obviously going through a rough time."

"You thought about me?" Stewart asked in a whisper.

"Sure I did. Look, I'm not going to pretend to understand those feelings. As far as you liking me in college, I guess I'd say that I'm flattered. But, I know I could never reciprocate those feelings. But I can still be your friend. We still have our friendship, right?"

"Yeah, some friendship. Last time we even saw each other was seven years ago."

"You know what I mean. I just wish that you would've believed in our friendship enough to tell me whatever it is you wanted to."

Stewart put his fork down and looked out the window. "It's not that simple. It was *never* that simple," Stewart muttered. He didn't know if he had the strength to accept rejection, real or imagined. "We don't have the time to do this here," Stewart said cautiously.

"Yes, I guess you're right," Gary said as he wiped his mouth with the napkin. "I should get back to the office."

"Do you *have* to go back to work?" Stewart asked as his tone became hopeful.

"Yes, I need to go back and do some things. But we should get together later."

"Sure, sure, and you know you need to tell me more about this potential promotion."

"I can do that," Gary said, signaling to the waiter that he wanted the bill.

"Hey, listen, about all that stuff I said earlier about having a crush on you…"

"Don't even worry about it."

"Yeah, I know. It's just that I wanted you to understand that was how I felt a long time ago. I don't feel that way anymore." Then he smiled, "Don't worry, I got over you," Stewart said, breaking into laughter.

"Well, it's been a lifetime, so I should hope so," Gary replied with a few chuckles of his own.

Stewart stopped laughing.

When the bill came, Stewart gave the waiter his credit card on top of it. As they waited for the waiter to return for Stewart's signature, the two of them again looked out toward the sidewalk, the sunshine beckoning them. Stewart decided he would walk around downtown and take in the sights until he could re-connect with Gary later.

When the waiter returned with the credit card, Stewart took it and signed the bill. When they got up to leave, Gary's curiosity got the better of him.

"Listen, I know that we said we'd talk about all of that old history stuff later, but I have to know something. You can call me nosey if you want."

"What is it?"

"The person you were seeing in New York, how did you meet?"

"I met him at that Diana Ross concert in Central Park."

"Oh, yeah, the one in the rain. I remember she received a lot of press for that concert. She did two of them, didn't she?" Gary asked.

"Yes. I went to both, but left early because of the rain. The next day, we had to deal with all of those thugs coming at us trying to mug us. Not a good time to be in New York City," Stewart laughed.

"Who was the guy?"

Stewart's face looked as though he'd just swallowed something tart. "His name was Drake Hill." Suddenly, Stewart paused at the door; a certain darkness filled his eyes. "If there was ever anyone who broke my heart, it was him."

Then Stewart walked out first and into the sunlight. Because he never looked back, he didn't see the blood drain from Gary Walsh's face.

CHAPTER
SEVENTEEN

Drake Hill marched to the beat of his own drum, never answering to anyone but himself for anything he did.

When Drake graduated from the University of Minnesota with a degree in Political Science, he convinced his parents to let him take a year off before dealing with the real world and all its responsibilities, such as finding a job and paying bills. He had always wanted to go to take an enormous bite out of the Big Apple and, he wanted to distance himself from family and the slow pace of Minneapolis.

When Drake got to New York in June 1983, an adventure funded largely by his parents and money he had set aside from a part-time job, he felt like the proverbial kid in an incredibly big and tempting candy store. Manhattan sang a sweet song of freedom for Drake and he gladly responded to it.

He quickly acclimated himself to the New York vibe, spending his days walking the long city blocks, checking out museums, and eating at cafes. Nights were for reveling on Christopher Street, then the Mecca for gay nightlife.

A dizzying parade of mustached men walked up and

down the street with their mops of curly hair, small afros, or jheri curls. Their lean, muscular bodies moved with feline grace yet captured the exaggerated masculinity of the lion. Most nights he wandered west until he came upon the Christopher Street pier, a popular meeting spot for gay men. Those escapades satisfied his appetite until he met someone who was totally unlike the men who cruised the piers.

On July 21, Drake made his way to Central Park to see Diana Ross. He had gotten there early. Vendors were setting up and the diehard fans had begun to congregate. There were even Diana Ross impersonators braving the heat in full Ross regalia, spreading love and a sense of togetherness. The show started out well. Diana was a sight to behold, the winds whipping through her luxuriant mane of black hair. She wore a glittering orange bodysuit and red diaphanous cape that billowed in the wind. As the sun died away, the clouds turned dark and the crowd was pelted with rain. Love or no love, Drake wasn't going to get drenched for anyone and so he ran away before the rain became too heavy and caught the first downtown subway train he could.

The next day he heard that the star was going to give another free concert and decided to make the trip uptown again. But Drake became disappointed with the mood of crowd, which had changed dramatically from one of peace and love to rowdiness.

Then, La Ross graced the stage in a white, bugle-beaded gown with fur cuffed sleeves, which Drake had not seen the previous evening. To the left, he noticed a handsome man who was a few years older standing by himself. The two men made eye contact several times.

As Diana blew kisses and pointed the microphone at the audience for a sing-along, the man inched closer and closer to Drake. As the energy of the show increased, so did the rowdiness of the crowd. As a result of all the pushing and the shoving, Drake found himself standing next to the man.

"What's your name?" the attractive man asked.

"Drake. What's yours?"

"I'm Stewart. Listen, it's pretty obvious that we're attracted to each other, so, why don't we beat this crowd and get out of here?"

"Lead the way," Drake said, following close behind.

They managed to avoid the street thugs that had begun to descend upon the unsuspecting audience, quickly hailed a cab and headed to the sublet Stewart was staying in.

That first night, full of passionate kisses and bedspring-squeaking sex, set the pace for their affair. Stewart lived in California (with a wife), but he was in New York on business, sent there to work with the United Nations. He saw Drake whenever the opportunity presented itself.

Drake enjoyed the summer fling. Borrowing a woman's husband and offering Stewart something she could not was an incredible high for Drake.

When the summer ended, Drake was ready to move on to a new conquest. Stewart had fallen in love and seriously considered leaving his wife, Sarah. Drake discouraged him at every turn.

"Don't ruin the time we share now by making plans. You and I both know you're going to have to go back to your wife. We're two people living in the moment. Relationships tie people down. It's better this way," Drake would say.

At first Stewart went along with it; Drake was simply a sexual release from his sham of a marriage. As long as no one found out about it, no one would be hurt. However, as time went on, Stewart began giving serious consideration to ending his marriage.

On August 25, Sarah flew to New York to surprise her husband. She arrived at the apartment Stewart rented for extended stays in the city. She lied to the super of the building, begging that he open the door because no one had heard from her "friend" who lived there in days and she feared the friend lay dead inside. As soon as the super put the key into the lock and turned it, she pushed him out of the way and burst into the apartment to find her husband and Drake in the 69 position on the living room rug, sucking each other off; their underwear and pants bunched around their ankles. A gay porno was playing muted on the TV.

"I knew it!" she exclaimed.

Drake's eyes had been closed. He'd been enjoying the length of Stewart's manhood inside his mouth. Suddenly, it was snatched away.

"Sarah, wait. Let me explain!" Stewart jumped up immediately, scrambling to pull up his underwear and pants.

"Now I get it! You can't keep it hard for even a minute for your *wife*, but this faggot can lay up in here and suck it all goddamn day long! You'll stay hard for that, won't you?"

Drake continued sitting on the floor, making no attempt to pull up his own clothes. He eyed the strange woman as she flailed her arms, her tan raincoat flapping about.

"What are you looking at, pervert?" she said, meeting Drake's gaze. "I ought to kick you in your damn throat for this filth!" Sarah screamed at Drake.

"I can explain," Stewart said.

"Explain what? Why I caught you with another man's dick in your mouth?"

"Sarah..."

"Now I see why you've been rushing off to New York City every chance you get!"

"I have this thorn in my flesh—this *sin*. He made me do this," Stewart said, pointing at Drake, who looked up at him with bewilderment. "Please, just come into the bedroom so we can talk."

"I ain't going in there! You probably haven't even made the bed after screwing on it, or whatever nastiness you two do."

"Sarah, please."

Sarah stomped through the hallway, her coat billowing behind her. She imagined stained sheets and used sex toys strewn throughout the room. Upon entering the bedroom, she stood with clenched fists at her side. Stewart backed into the dresser, fearing she'd lunge at him.

After an hour, she came out of the room, walking briskly, and stood in front of Drake, who had fixed his clothes and was sitting on the sofa.

"You can have him. You two fruits deserve each other!" And she left.

Stewart came out of the bedroom, his face stained with tears. Yet he looked relieved.

"What did you tell her?" Drake asked.

"I told her the truth; that you and I are in love, and that I can't be with her anymore."

"Wait just a minute. I'm not in love with you, Stewart. What, you think because we're sex buddies that we're in love? And another thing, I don't appreciate you telling her that I made you do this."

"I had to, Drake. It was the only way I could get her to talk to me."

"But why do I sense you actually believed what you said?"

Stewart looked away, not answering the question.

"I advise you to pack and run after her."

"You know that's not what I want. I want to stay here with you," Stewart said, reaching out to hug Drake.

Drake laughed, easing away. "Hey, is it true what your wife said? That your dick stayed soft with her?"

Stewart's face looked pained. "Is that even anything to joke about?"

"I'm just asking. You never seemed to have that problem with me."

"That's because she doesn't have what you have. All the more reason why I can't be with her. I want to be here with you."

"Well, you know I can't give you that kind of commitment."

"Why not? The truth is out, we can start fresh. No more secrets."

"But see, that's kind of a problem. Part of my fun was knowing that I was doing it with a married guy. Now that everything is out in the open, I don't know if I'll be able to get *my* dick hard from now on."

Stewart's eyes narrowed, his brows becoming furrowed. "Why are you playing with me?"

"I'm being truthful with you. I told you before, I don't settle. There are too many cute men out there to be had."

Stewart felt his blood pressure rise. "Are you making fun of me?"

There was an edge to Stewart's words that made Drake uncomfortable. "I'm gonna go."

"I asked you a question," Stewart said, slowly walking toward Drake. He stared at him with a deathly seriousness.

Drake's smile faded. "I'm not making fun of you. This whole thing with your wife barging in was a little heavy. I was just trying to lighten the mood. Honest."

"Then why were you laughing at me?"

Drake gulped. "It was just nervous laughter."

Stewart cocked his head, squinting his eyes as though he were trying to read Drake's face. Drake became self-conscious being watched so closely. He could feel his heart beating in multiple rhythms.

"Hey man, I'm sorry. I wasn't trying to disrespect you. I made a joke, and I guess it wasn't very funny. Like I said, I laugh when I'm nervous."

Suddenly, Stewart's face brightened. His eyes warmed with possibility again. "Fine. So, you want to grab something to eat?"

"I wish I could, but, I promised my folks that I would have dinner with my aunt Louise at least once while I'm here. And she's leaving for Paris tomorrow for the rest of the summer," Drake said.

"I really didn't want to be alone tonight. Can you come over after?"

"Uh, probably not. She said she's got all my cousins there at the apartment who I haven't seen in God knows how long. I'll probably wind up staying the night."

Stewart shrugged in disappointment. "Well, I guess if you gotta go, then you gotta go, right?"

Drake walked up to Stewart and kissed him on the cheek.

"But tomorrow, I'm all yours."

"I'm working late tomorrow. A huge meeting that'll last forever and a day, and then an important dinner I can't miss."

"Oh, that's right. Totally forgot." Drake was thoughtful for a moment, and then said, "Well, I'm sure we'll think of something. I'll call you," Drake said, now standing in the open doorway.

"Okay, have fun with your family."

"I will. Again, sorry about before."

"Don't worry about it. Just glad you weren't playing games with me. Because then both of us would have had a really bad day," Stewart said, leering at Drake.

Drake nodded, offering a lazy smile before closing the door behind him. As he began to descend down the flight of stairs, he heard a door opening. He looked up to see Stewart watching him.

"I love you," Stewart yelled down with a wave.

"You're so sweet. What did I do to deserve you?" Drake yelled back, quickening his steps.

Once he made it outside of the apartment, he stood against the building and let out a *real* nervous laugh. The evil in Stewart's eyes gave Drake the impression he'd narrowly escaped something dangerous. The feeling gave him a chill. He inhaled deeply, taking in the aroma of hot dogs and knishes from the corner street vendor. Then, heading below street level toward the 1 train subway platform, he exhaled a sense of relief. He hoped to find someone to

spend the night with, touch him in the morning, and then gladly walk away. There was no auntie Louise waiting with dinner. And Drake had no intention of ever calling Stewart again.

After dropping off Stewart's radar, Drake began to up the ante and go to the bathhouses. What he couldn't find at the St. Marks Baths, he found at Man's Country, which he ultimately made his permanent stomping ground.

He was determined to become his own person, and detach himself from the image of the perfect son that his parents had foisted on him. With every man he slept with the summer of 1983, he felt his parents' power over him fade. But then reality hit him.

One evening when Drake was at a bathhouse, he overheard a couple of men talking about a mutual friend's rapid deterioration. They spoke of Kaposi's sarcoma lesions, and a wasting disease, and something known as "Gay Cancer."

There was alarm in the men's voices as they spoke of "Rick," who they'd seen transition from a healthy, body-conscious stud to an emaciated skeleton, and nobody knew why. There was talk that "poppers," a cheap inhalant used to get high, was a possible way to catch the Gay Cancer.

The conversation made Drake's stomach churn and he began to question why he was there in the first place. After the voices of the two men became whispers in the distance, Drake decided to leave. While in the locker room getting dressed, he noticed a man hunched over on a bench tying his shoelaces. The man hadn't yet put on his shirt, and Drake saw that his back was covered in purple splotches. The man turned and looked over at Drake. His gaunt face offered a weak, hollow smile. Drake averted his eyes and

finished dressing quickly. He could sense that the man was looking at him, and didn't want to return the glance. The lesions had burned themselves into his memory forever.

When he went out to the disco that evening, he stood in the shadows, watching the mob of sweaty, shirtless men dance with careless abandon. As the throng pulsated to the strong beat of Donna Summer's "I Feel Love," Drake imagined another type of shadow, one from which he could not hide: a shadow of death looming across the stretches of that place, randomly touching the men's shoulders. Some of the cruising men would go home with carriers of the unknown plague. They would look back and remember the night Donna Summer sang to them.

For Drake, the sickness that was going around seemed to bring a free-floating anxiety to the city, and he decided to return to Minneapolis a week later. His parents were happy to have him home, and didn't ask any questions. But Drake had changed in ways that were too difficult to explain, even to himself.

It would be two years before Drake would dare be intimate with anyone, although things were just as dangerous, and by then everyone knew what AIDS was. It was time for him to buckle down and get serious about his career. He became a little wiser, embarking on a journey that would take him to the level of success that he would soon enjoy.

CHAPTER EIGHTEEN

When Gary returned from his lunch with Stewart, he found the Post-it note he placed on his computer to remind him to call Tony Cannon regarding fundraising. He reached for the phone and dialed.

A monotone male voice answered the phone. "Harper Institute, how may I direct your call?"

"Tony Cannon. Please."

"One moment, please." Silence was followed by what sounded like elevator music.

"This is Tony Cannon," said a rushed voice from the other end.

"Tony, this is Gary Walsh. Did I catch you at a bad time?"

"Oh gosh, Gary, I was actually on my way out. Listen, I called around and I was able to get some people willing to back you, but most of them insisted on anonymity."

"Why don't they want their names on it?" Gary sounded hurt.

"I don't know, probably wanting to protect their interests. You gotta expect that."

"Well, I was hoping we could get together and discuss this in further detail, just so I have an idea of what I'm dealing with here."

"Yep, I just can't right now. I looked at my schedule and I'm free late next week. How's that?"

"I guess I don't have much of a choice, do I?"

"I'll call you next week and we can set something up. It looks pretty good."

"Okay, I'll talk to you then. Take care." Gary hung up the phone.

Wanda suddenly appeared in the doorway to Gary's office, looking ravishing in a white pantsuit. She carried several bags of clothes from the most exclusive dress boutiques in the city.

Gary looked at her and smiled. He hadn't been expecting her, but her visit was a nice diversion.

"Hello, my dear," Wanda said.

"Let me help you with those," Gary said, jumping up to help her with the bags.

"I came by earlier to see if you wanted to have lunch but they told me you had already gone."

"Oh yes, that friend of mine from California came and we had lunch. Do you remember Stewart McKillen?"

Wanda shrugged. "Well, since you weren't available I did a little shopping instead."

"Glad to see you've finally made time for yourself to enjoy some of the fruits of all that hard work."

"Yeah, well, I figured taking the day to buy a few things couldn't hurt."

"A few things," Gary said, unbelievingly.

"Are you going to be done soon?"

"I don't know. I have to find this damn file."

"What file?"

"It's a video I'm using to summarize what I intend to

accomplish as president of the BRC. The computer keeps saying it's been deleted."

"Oh. Maybe you pushed something by mistake."

"No! There was no mistake; I know what the hell I'm doing!" Gary snapped.

"Well, you've been under a lot of pressure, and people make mistakes when they're under pressure. I was just saying..."

"I'm sorry, baby. It's just a lot to deal with right now. Been a long day."

"Well, we can end the day with a relaxing dinner at Palomino. How does that sound?"

"That sounds perfect. But I told Stewart that I would call him when I was through here. He got a divorce from his wife, and although it's been a couple of years, I still think it's eating at him. He's got some other stuff going on as well and I think he could use a friend right now."

"Then I guess you have to do what you have to do," Wanda said, rising from her seat.

"But I'll see you when I get home."

"Yeah, okay." Wanda walked over to Gary and leaned in and kissed him goodbye.

Gary saw Wanda out on his way to the men's room. When he walked through the corridor he came upon a handsome, light-skinned man coming toward him. Gary nodded hello to the young man, who looked squarely out of place. "Hello, may I help you, young man?"

"Yes, thank you. I'm looking for Drake Hill's office."

"You need to go the other way. He's around the corner just as you come into this section of the building."

"Oh, okay. I came down too far, then. Thank you, sir."

"Sure, not a problem," Gary said to the man and went on his way.

Armando found Drake at his desk, looking seriously at something on his computer monitor. He knocked on the wall outside Drake's door, which was open.

"Hey, Drake," Armando said, smiling halfheartedly.

"What are you doing here?" Drake snapped.

Armando blinked twice before replying. "I was in the neighborhood because I had to see about my unemployment. They denied me, so I decided to come and tell you that I'm going to start filling out more job applications. Since you said I could use you as a reference, I wanted to warn you that you'd start getting calls, just in case you forgot."

"You can't come here ever again. Do you understand?" Drake said less intensely, but still sharply.

"Dude, you need to check the tone, for real." Armando's face became red with embarrassment and frustration at being talked to in the imperious voice that Drake was using.

"What can I do for you, Armando?" Drake asked as he went to close his office door.

It took Armando a moment to calm himself before he responded. "I wanted you to know you're gonna start getting calls for a reference. When they call you'll know what these people are talking about."

Drake went back and sat down. "You look great, by the way."

"Thanks."

"Are you free for dinner?"

"My girlfriend is back at home waiting for me, so I can't be out tonight."

"Since you're here, I think maybe you should have dinner with me. We can discuss what you want me to tell the people."

"What do you need to know? The people call and ask you what my work habits were like, and you tell them they were good." Armando said. He sensed Drake's ulterior motive and didn't want to go back there again.

"That's it? That's all you want me to say?"

"What else do you need to say?"

"Employers don't just ask cookie-cutter questions like that. They need to know dates of employment, how much you made. How am I supposed to tell them when I don't know what you put down on the applications? You don't want me to tell them something that differs from what you wrote on your applications, do you?"

Armando sat down, putting his backpack on the floor. He didn't like feeling as though he were at the mercy of anyone, even if a job was at stake. But he needed work if he had a prayer in making things better with Karen, and right now, Drake held all of the cards.

"I can't go out to eat with you tonight, Drake," Armando said firmly.

Drake began to shake his head. "That's too bad. I was more than prepared to help you with your dilemma, but I don't want to be a sucker here. You can't get something for nothing, you know."

"I'm not asking you to do something for nothing. You got what you wanted the other night."

"Armando, you're changing midstream on me. I asked you if you were okay with what we did and you said you were. At least it was okay enough for you to accept five hundred dollars."

"Yeah, and I had to hear it from my girl when I got home, too. I almost lost her because of this," Armando said, his voice heavy with contempt.

"Not my problem. You need to do a better job of covering your tracks and then you won't have a snarling woman waiting for you. Anyway, this isn't an extension from the other night. If you need me to do something you want, then you'll have to do something I want," Drake said. His voice was cold as a winter wind.

"Wow. You were the one who offered it in the first place, and now you're not going to help me out?"

"I changed my mind. See how it is when someone changes midstream?" Drake said as if he were scolding a small child.

"Dude, you're messing with the wrong one!"

"Will you keep your voice down? I have to work here, remember? We shouldn't even be having this discussion here."

"Whatever, man. I'm gone. I'll do it on my own." Armando jumped up from the chair, grabbing his backpack from the floor. He opened the door and stormed out without saying another word. Drake wasn't the least bit fazed. He only stared into the space where Armando had just stood, and smiled. "He'll be back." He wadded up a piece of paper on his desk and sent it sailing through the air, hitting the inside of the wastebasket by the door.

CHAPTER NINETEEN

Cabrien's afternoon had been filled with errands and browsing up and down Nicollet Mall. After stopping in to a bar during happy hour to say hello to a few friends, Cabrien decided to head home and sat down on a bench to wait for the bus.

Across the street was Broadway Books and Video, an adult bookstore. And making his way inside was a vessel of swagger, dressed in a green Celtics jersey and shorts, with a white do-rag peeking out from beneath a backwards-turned Celtics basketball cap. The man turned to look over his shoulder, caught Cabrien looking at him, winked and disappeared inside.

Cabrien took the wink as an invitation. He got up and looked both ways before he ran across the street. Stepping inside this video store meant stepping into the sleaziest of the sleaze. Cabrien was no stranger to the place. Inside he'd found some of his tricks among the cast of freaks and sweaty, fat old men who couldn't get laid any other way. But he never suspected the Celtics man would find such a place appealing.

The store was bright, with shelves stacked high with the latest adult erotica. Straight or gay, the horny could find anything for his or her taste. To the left was the checkout

booth, where a man stood with pale white skin and painted black fingernails. He wasn't smiling and looked as though he would rather be somewhere else. The glass wall that separated the checkout booth from the door had a mannequin on top of it wearing lingerie, and looked as though it hadn't been dusted in many years.

Cabrien's eyes darted around the room, searching for the mystery man. He did not see him, but was intrigued by four large rectangular bins that had been spray-painted black over in the corner. In these bins, he saw every conceivable "toy" known to man, mixed in with old VHS porn movies. He put his hand in, pulling out a twelve-inch rubber dildo. Cabrien raised it and looked over at the salesclerk, who broke out into a smile having seen the look on Cabrien's face, before going back to thumbing through *People* magazine.

Cabrien then glimpsed an illuminated staircase with walls painted red and black. He stood at the top and peered down it. Because of the low ceiling in the staircase, Cabrien could only see the bottom halves of men walking around down there. He knew that was where the young man must have gone.

The downstairs area was completely different aesthetically from the upstairs. The floors were covered with black rubber mats and the light was dim. There were four aisles of twenty-five-cent movie booths and red paint on the back wall of each of the aisles, contrasting to the black booths and black curtains. On a wall facing the aisles were pressed VHS covers showing the movies being shown that day.

Men sought sex down in this space; within the small confines of these booths, men would get oral sex, and, if they could get away with it, anal penetration. Some men

stood with their backs to the walls just watching; others were more determined to join in. One man in a business suit placed newspapers down on the ground before kneeling in front of another suit-clad man.

The air was ripe with moans and gasps from both the movies being played and the live action enjoyed by some of the men. The booths were mere fronts that both inspired and covered the many sexual liaisons taking place. Cabrien squinted, looking for the prize he had come in for. He walked through the aisles trying to select the right booth to check. He opened the curtains on one of the booths, and was met with the sight of a middle-aged man leaning forward, with his left hand pressed squarely on the TV monitor, and his right arm and hand moving frantically. The man turned around suddenly, alarmed and embarrassed that he was caught masturbating. Cabrien watched as a tissue fell from between the man's legs to the floor.

"Close that damn curtain!" the man yelled, sounding like someone's ornery grandfather. Cabrien snickered as a tall figure stepped directly behind Cabrien.

"Yo, you gotta name, man?" The voice was incredibly deep.

Cabrien turned around quickly to see the handsome man who had enticed him. The Celtic man's eyes were stern and narrow; the color of coffee beans. His massive arms were tattooed with the scales of justice and horoscope sign of Libra.

"It's Cabrien," Cabrien said, his eyes demurely downcast, like a teenage girl gushing over a teen idol.

"Your mama gave you a white boy's name? I ain't never heard of no brothas named Cabrien."

"What's *your* name, since you wanna talk shit?" Cabrien said, smiling broadly.

"Trevor."

"Oh, now that's *real* black," Cabrien said, imitating Trevor's tone.

Trevor smiled.

"So, you like creeping up on dudes while they're getting their freak on?"

"No. I was looking for you." Cabrien looked down, almost too shy to look at Trevor again.

"Fo' real?"

"Yeah." Cabrien heard the quiet muffled sound of someone reaching his climax. His shoulders straightened, knowing that the sound was coming from behind him.

As Cabrien and Trevor fell silent, they heard a soft "Jesus," being muttered like harmony beneath a melody of moans. Cabrien's eyes directed Trevor's away from the booths and out near the wall with the empty, pressed VHS movie covers.

There were more men there, walking around like restless spirits, drifting in and out of the shadows, almost shadows themselves. Trevor looked uneasy as he caught a few of the men looking lasciviously at him. Their eyes were calling silently to him as though they wanted to make what was being seen and heard from the videos real.

Cabrien stepped back into what little light there was. He wanted to make sure that Trevor could see all that he had to offer. He repositioned himself, standing tall with his tight ass out, trying to tempt Trevor with the allure of his backside.

"So, wuz up? You want some of dis?" Trevor grabbed his crotch and bit his lower lip as his eyes softened. The

scene looked like something LL Cool J might have done were he a tad bit raunchier. He grabbed Cabrien's firm ass, then threw his hands on the back of his head as though he were about to pluck the most tempting of fruit. "Damn, I wanna see how dis' booty works! Ya heard?"

"If you got the paper then you can have it," Cabrien said, grinding his juicy ass into Trevor's crotch. He could feel the instant stiffening of Trevor's dick.

Trevor pushed Cabrien away, causing him to almost trip. He reached down and re-adjusted his dick, which had begun to slip from behind his boxers and rub against his shorts. He gave Cabrien a stern glance.

"Yo, I ain't never had to pay fo' no ass, ya heard? You got me twisted."

"My bad, boo," Cabrien said, wishing to take back what he said.

"Make no mistake; I like some boy pussy once in a while. But, I'll take a nice piece of woman over this any day!"

"If that's true, then why are you even here?" Cabrien wanted to know.

"It's been a bad couple of months."

"Well, since there ain't any females around, you wanna get in this?" Cabrien asked as he touched his own ass. Trevor arched his eyebrow. His eyes were contemplative.

"Hell, yeah," Trevor said, cupping a hand over his fist.

Cabrien sized up his conquest. *There ain't no way in hell I'm gonna get two hundred and fifty dollars out of this fool!* Cabrien thought to himself.

"You can stick me for a hundred dollars. My rules are that you use a condom, and no pain, or blood."

"Listen, I'll give you fifty," Trevor said as he looked around to make sure no one was listening.

"Chile, please! I should be charging you my normal rate of two-fifty. But I recognize that you probably a struggling brotha, so, I'll do it for one hundred."

"Wow! You be gettin' niggas to give you two hundred and fifty dollars? Is the ass *that* good?"

"Boy, don't play with me. Hell to the yes. My stuff is all of that. I wouldn't embarrass myself and charge what I charge if it wasn't. You just better be glad that your ass is fine as hell, because I don't usually give discounts."

"Where you wanna go?"

"We could handle our business over there." Cabrien nodded in the direction of the booths.

"Hell naw, man! Did you look inside those booths? There's dried cum and shit everywhere! I ain't goin' in there!"

The two were silent.

"We could go back to my crib," Trevor finally offered.

Cabrien beamed. "That's all you had to say in the first place."

"I stay over at Matson House. I rent a room for pretty cheap over there."

Cabrien nodded. The Matson House was a place where some of Minneapolis' under- privileged resided until they were able to get on their feet. Most came from either Chicago or Gary, Indiana, and from what Cabrien knew of the place, many of the people living there took their precious time getting on their feet.

He had a transsexual friend named Deena who worked there, and he went there sometimes to keep her company

while she watched the front desk. He never knew anyone who actually lived there.

"Dude, I ain't trying to be funny or nothin', but you need to harden up once we get outside." Trevor spoke with caution as his eyes melted into a soft concern. "You know how dudes are around here, yo. I don't wanna have to break my foot off in some knucklehead's ass cuz they wanna disrespect us."

Cabrien straightened his back and thrust his chest forward. He dropped his chin and managed a menacing glare. "Eh, I'll break 'em off too, *yo!*" Cabrien exclaimed, his voice dropping two octaves, causing Trevor to chuckle.

When Trevor and Cabrien arrived at Matson House, Cabrien became worried that his friend Deena would be behind the front desk. But then he decided that it would be okay if she was there. After all, he had a good-looking piece with him, and it was a refreshing change from the older, out-of-shape men he normally went with.

All of this internal dialogue became moot when he realized that Deena wasn't there. Instead, there was a tall, lanky white man with a buzz cut, and wearing a wifebeater. Cabrien was struck at how much the man's eyes looked like Uma Thurman's. The man smiled and nodded at Trevor who nodded back quickly and kept walking. Cabrien stared straight ahead, following his afternoon delight upstairs.

Trevor lived on the second level. When they turned the corner, three people were impatiently waiting outside a closed door at the end of the hall.

"What's going on there?" Cabrien wanted to know.

"That's the bathroom."

"Y'all don't have private bathrooms in your rooms?"

"Nope," Trevor replied, not thinking anything unusual about it.

Trevor opened the door to his room. A pungent odor of sweat and dirty clothes hit Cabrien in the nose like a fist. Behind the door, was a closet that had a rusted rod with two shirts hanging from it. Further into the room on the left was a queen-size bed, dressed with dingy, stained sheets that looked hastily made, leaving the fitted sheet to hang pushed down from the corner of the mattress. To the right was a small cart where the TV rested. On top of it was the DVD player, with stacks of DVDs balanced precariously. Next to that was a large pile of dirty sheets and clothes.

Trevor walked over to the bed and sat down, removing his shoes. Cabrien turned his attention from the mess, to see Trevor's large and arched feet. His socks were brilliantly white. Why the room couldn't be as clean, Cabrien didn't know.

"You live here?" Cabrien asked incredulously.

"Naw, this is just a place I come when I don't want to be found," Trevor said with a smirk.

Cabrien looked around the room again. "Clearly you're never here long enough to keep it clean."

"I could clean up a bit," Trevor offered, as he got up and snatched the sheets from the bed and threw them into the already existing pile of dirty items. He looked around frantically for clean sheets, while Cabrien continued eyeing of the room. Over on a card table sat a hot plate, with a sauce pan sitting on it. Along the side of the pan was encrusted tomato sauce which had dripped down and dried on to the coils of the hot plate.

As Trevor continued his vain search for sheets, Cabrien

noticed the many *Playboy* magazines lying near the bed, along with a navy blue washcloth that was rumpled and stiff. At the foot of the bed was a spaghetti sauce jar, with its label partially torn, and filled with what looked to be urine.

"What's that?" Cabrien asked, already knowing the answer, and not wanting to get too close to it.

"Oh, that. Man, sometimes I can't get to the bathroom, cuz these fools around here are always hoggin' it."

As Cabrien looked at Trevor with bewildered eyes, Trevor sensed he was being judged harshly. It was a cruelty he'd come to know in his life as a black man, but one he didn't expect in the bedroom, and not from another black man.

"Dude, it ain't that deep. I bring fools back here all the time," Trevor said.

"Are you serious?"

Trevor nodded. Cabrien didn't know what was worse; the fact that Trevor had the nerve to bring someone to his room in such disarray, or that Trevor tried to justify it.

Cabrien stood in silence, shaking his head. The thrill of the moment had ended as soon as Trevor opened the door. Now he really wanted to go home and wash the filth from his body.

"Man, you're trippin'," Trevor said, losing any further motivation to spot clean. "I thought you wanted me to smash you?"

"Nope. I don't like this."

"What were you expectin,' the Waldorf-fuckin'-Astoria?" Trevor asked.

Cabrien covered his nose, as the strong stench tapped it again. He thought about being too good for this scene. At

that moment he wished he had a man of his own, someone who wouldn't make him take chances like this.

"Yo, why you actin' all high and mighty? You ain't no better than me. You're tryin' to get your lil hustle on just like the rest of us! Here's your funky lil' two-hundred and fifty dollars. Bet you thought I couldn't even pay it."

Cabrien shook his head.

"Let's make the shit rain," Trevor said, tossing the bills into the air in Cabrien's direction, who watched as the bills scattered on the bed.

Cabrien looked at Trevor, whose eyes reflected the slight of Cabrien's rejection of him. Cabrien had certainly turned many tricks in less than ideal surroundings: the backseat of cars, and behind dumpsters, to name a few. Yet those places seemed like heaven in comparison to the squalor he now stood in. Still, there was something pure about Trevor. Cabrien could tell his tough guy behavior was just a front, and under it all was a guy longing to connect with another human being.

Cabrien reached down and picked up the bills and counted them. Then, he stuffed them into his pocket. Trevor began playing with his dick again, which seemed like it was desperate to be released from captivity. Cabrien walked up to Trevor, pressing himself into Trevor's chest. Trevor leaned into his neck and began to deeply inhale Cabrien's scent of Dolce and Gabbana. With his nose still buried in Cabrien's neck, Trevor moved his hands down to the small of Cabrien's back and squeezed a handful of Cabrien's ass. Cabrien used both of his hands to lift Trevor's jersey over his head, tossing it to the floor. He circled both of Trevor's nipples with his tongue, making Trevor's eyes flutter.

Trevor sat down, and leaned down on the bed to peel his shorts and boxers off. His manhood stood at attention. As he sat up, he spread his legs open, offering an invitation for Cabrien to begin sucking on his prize.

Cabrien didn't waste any time, taking all of Trevor into his mouth in one gulp. He rolled back his lips over his teeth as his tongue brushed over Trevor's swollen shaft. Trevor threw his head back, closing his eyes tightly, again licking his lips as though he were going to enjoy a feast of all feasts. He placed his large hand on top of Cabrien's head and gently guided him to and fro. Cabrien ran his hands along Trevor's chiseled chest, using his index fingers to gently rub his nipples. He deep throated all of Trevor right down to the base, his lips slightly touching Trevor's bush of pubic hair.

Cabrien retreated from the dick for a moment and began to massage Trevor's calves up to his thighs. He leaned in, running his tongue from the shaft all the way to the head and sucked the head. Trevor outstretched his hands, gripping both sides of the bed. He began to moan with a simmering sensuality that made Cabrien's own dick rock hard.

Trevor got up and forcibly pushed Cabrien down on his stomach, grabbing his ass, slapping it and massaging it in rough circular motions. He parted Cabrien's ass as though he were parting the Red Sea, letting his manly girth slip in between the cheeks. He rubbed himself up and down along that ass, writhing like a stripper. Trevor leaned forward, wrapping his legs around Cabrien's, his hot breath moistening Cabrien's back. He kissed his back with small, wet kisses, running his tongue all the way down to the small of

Cabrien's back. Cabrien shuddered as the tingling sensation spread throughout his body.

Trevor moved his tongue down further toward the area where the back meets the ass, and he paused.

"Damn, yo. Dis' ass looks good, yo. I wanna taste you."

"Do it, Daddy," Cabrien said, breathily.

"I ain't gonna get no doo-doo on my tongue, am I?" Trevor asked, chuckling a bit.

"Never that. My boogina is *always* clean, trust." Cabrien turned around the best he could since Trevor was on top of him. His hole was so welcoming, pulsating as it beckoned Trevor to come closer. Holding Cabrien's cheeks apart as far as they would stretch, Trevor began licking each cheek, biting them playfully. He moved his tongue in long lines toward Cabrien's center, and then, he went in. Cabrien's body began to spasm. It felt so good having Trevor's tongue discovering his hole.

"This ass tastes so damn good, yo. You gonna let me hit dis?"

Cabrien remembered that he had some lube packets and condoms that had been offered for free at the happy hour. He leaped from the bed and dug in his pants pocket. He tore the lube packet open with his teeth, the cool gel gushing from the pouch. He let it fall onto his fingers as he applied it to his hole. The anticipation of having Trevor in him, looking so fine, overwhelmed him. Suddenly, the mess of the room no longer mattered. He had two hundred-fifty dollars and a gorgeous specimen of man in front of him.

Trevor took the condom that had fallen from Cabrien's grasp when he opened the lube. His cock wagged stiffly, as he took the condom out of the wrapper. Cabrien had

thrown himself back on the bed, his legs spread and his ass waiting to be entered.

Trevor crawled onto the bed, kneeling in front of Cabrien as he slid the condom on his cock. He took the remaining lube and lathered it on to the condom. Then he brought Cabrien's legs to his chest, slapping his member against Cabrien's opening. He slid his dick in slowly, muttering, "Aw, fuck yeah," as he did so.

Trevor started out slowly, with long deep strokes. Cabrien arched his back, lifting his ass to receive Trevor's thrusts. Trevor closed his eyes as he held onto Cabrien's legs, nuzzling his face along Cabrien's smooth calf muscles.

"Damn, dis' pussy feels good," Trevor whispered, savoring the sensation the head of his penis felt as he slid in and out of Cabrien's warmth.

"Don't play with it, Daddy. Pound that pussy," Cabrien instructed as he put his own hands on Trevor's ass, drawing him close while wrapping his legs around Trevor's waist.

That was all the encouragement Trevor needed as he began to fuck with a staccato rhythm, grinding his pelvis as he went in deeper. He kissed Cabrien's neck, sucking hard as though he meant to draw blood. Cabrien whimpered softly, moving his hands along Trevor's solid biceps.

Cabrien knew this was not going to be a "sit-thru" encounter. Trevor confidently delivered his sex. He took command.

"You're all man, baby. Hit this ass like you own it."

"Oh, you want me to tear it up?"

"Take what you want."

Trevor pulled out and placed Cabrien on his stomach. He tightly wrapped his arms around Cabrien as he entered

him again. His thrusts were forcefully supreme, causing the two of them to bounce on the bed. The lube became frothy as the slickness of his dick went faster and faster. His balls, which hung low like bagged marbles, slapped against Cabrien's ass, and he became even more turned on by the slapping sounds.

Cabrien pulled away from Trevor's embrace. "Get on your back," Cabrien ordered. "I gotta surprise for you."

Trevor did as he was told. He looked on as Cabrien lowered himself onto his rock hard manhood. Cabrien began to slowly rise and fall on it, picking up his pace as Trevor held onto his waist. Cabrien smirked as he saw the effect he was having on Trevor, who was biting his bottom lip, breathing heavily. It was the same effect he had seen hundreds of times. He felt empowered in his talents. Anyone who said it took a woman to make a man feel good had never dealt with him before.

Cabrien began to gyrate his hips, as Trevor thrust upward. Cabrien arched his back, grabbing onto Trevor's ankles as he rode him.

The air seemed thin to them as they gasped for air. Trevor pulled Cabrien toward him, grabbing his ass and slamming him onto his dick. Cabrien began to moan ugly moans.

"You workin' this ass, ain't you, Daddy?"

"Hell, yeah," Trevor responded as his toes curled.

"I got some good ass, don't I?"

"Hell yeah, baby. Gimme dat ass!"

Cabrien continued bouncing up and down until he could feel Trevor's balls stiffen beneath him. Trevor's eyes remained closed as he felt himself getting closer. He

allowed the sensation to wash over him. His body tensing as it climbed that orgasmic mountain.

"I'm about to bust, yo!" Trevor said as his tongue became dry.

"You wanna bust that nut, baby?" Cabrien cooed.

"Yeah, I wanna bust!"

"You worked hard for that nut, didn't you?"

"Hell–y-yeah, I worked h-h-ard!" Trevor stuttered.

"This the best ass you've had, though, right?"

"Oooh, yeah, baby!"

"You wanna bust real bad, don't you?" Cabrien asked, grinding it home.

"You gonna let me bust?"

"Tell me when."

"Aw, shit, I'm gonna bust!" Trevor screamed, pushing Cabrien off of him just as he began to explode inside of the condom. His body shook as he filled the condom with cum. Cabrien sat and watched, running his fingers lightly over Trevor's sweaty chest. The tingle of his touch heightened the release of the orgasm. Trevor opened his eyes as sweat rolled down his temples. It was as if color had rushed back into the room, everything was so vibrant. He looked over to Cabrien, who smiled, knowing he had just completed a job well done.

"Yo, I can see why you be chargin' two-fifty. You definitely know how to drain a nigga, ya heard?"

Cabrien smiled and then looked at his watch. He needed to leave to get home and shower. He didn't trust the bathroom at the Matson House. It probably had doo-doo floating in the toilet and months worth of ring-around-the-tub that could've used a good scrubbing.

"I gotta go. Thank you. It was fun," Cabrien said as he began putting his clothes back on.

Trevor remained on the bed, still trying to catch his breath. "Yo, you think I could get your phone number so we can kick it fo' real?"

"If you're gonna pay me, sure."

"Oh, what, so we can't get together and just kick it on the DL? You must have a man."

Cabrien could only smile. "I don't really get involved with clients. It's a rule I have."

Cabrien finished dressing and went over to Trevor and kissed him on the forehead and left. As he walked down the corridor, he knew that he had just told a lie. He was emotionally involved with someone else who paid for his sex, and his name was Drake Hill.

But of course, Trevor didn't need to know that.

CHAPTER TWENTY

When Gary arrived at Stewart's hotel room later that evening, Stewart answered the door, looking very different than he had at lunch. There were dark circles under his eyes; his eyes were red from crying, and his clothes appeared as if he'd rolled around on the floor all afternoon.

"What in the hell happened to you?" Gary asked. The sight of Stewart in this condition was shocking. Suddenly, enjoying that dinner with his wife seemed like a better alternative.

"I shouldn't have come. I just shouldn't have come," Stewart muttered.

"To Minneapolis? Why shouldn't you have come?" Gary asked, gently nudging Stewart back into the room.

"I'm so messed up," Stewart said. He reached for a plastic cup from the desk. Gary noticed empty mini bar liquor bottles lying on their sides all over the floor and on the desk.

"Why?" Gary asked, taking the cup from Stewart's hands.

The look of sadness in Stewart's eyes was pitiful. "I feel like I don't have anywhere else to go. Sarah has turned everyone against me."

"How did she do that?" Gary asked. The stink of liquor on Stewart's breath was nauseating.

"She told everyone I was living a lie."

"You didn't mean to hurt her. I'm sure she knows that."

"It's like I told you today at lunch, I shouldn't have married her."

This again? Is Stewart going to repeat himself all night? Gary wondered, then thought of the succulent Chilean sea bass and garlic mashed potatoes he could have had for dinner.

"Maybe you shouldn't have." Gary chose his words carefully. "But you can start from this moment and go forward. You can be truthful *now*. The world is a much different place than it was thirty years ago. I certainly won't turn my back on you."

Stewart sobbed loudly, collapsing into Gary's arms. Gary began to think Stewart needed more than his presence to get back on the right track. But what could he do for him?

"So, when are you going back to California?" he asked, helping Stewart erect himself and stand on his own feet.

"I'm not sure. I was hoping we could spend some time together," Stewart said.

"This is a really busy time, Stewart. I'm sorry, but it is. I'll see what I can do. I have to go, but will you please promise me that you won't drink anything else tonight? God knows you don't need any more alcohol."

Gary felt like a babysitter who was desperately awaiting the return of the child's parents. He still didn't know what happened to his video file, and Drake's insinuation that Isaac Walterson had done something to it piqued Gary's

interest. The quick thought of Drake reminded Gary about what Stewart had said earlier that afternoon.

"You seem to be working through a lot. Did you ever talk to anyone about this?"

"I went to counseling with Sarah, but other than that, no."

"So you said earlier that Sarah caught you with Drake?" Gary asked, knowing he'd foolishly prolonged the conversation. Despite his own problems, he knew he had to at least appear to be present for his friend.

"Yes, she did. I was elated actually, because then it meant that I could stop all of the lying and I could be with Drake. You know that I was in love with him. I don't even think he was in 'like' with me."

"So, the two of you didn't continue your relationship after Sarah found out?"

"Hell no. After that day I never heard from him again."

"That was it?" Gary asked, though he really wasn't too surprised Drake had behaved that way even back then. *People don't really change,* he thought to himself.

"Pretty much. He told me that I'd be better off trying to work things out with Sarah, and after he vanished, that's what I did."

"Were you still in love with her?"

"Not really. I figured if I couldn't be with the one I loved then I would try to love the one I was with. I put everything into my marriage after that, but nothing worked." Stewart's voice was clearing up, and aside from his face looking worn out from crying, he sounded normal again.

Gary looked at his watch. There was still time to call and have dinner with Wanda. He opened his mouth to

invite Stewart but thought better of it, given Stewart's condition.

"I really want to keep going with this, but I really have to get going because I have dinner plans with Wanda," Gary fibbed. "Maybe I can swing by tomorrow."

Stewart became very alert, "Oh, okay. That's fine. I guess I shouldn't expect much company at this pity party anyway. I mean, you *have* someone."

"I do want to hear what you have to say, I just have a lot going on right now."

"I understand," Stewart said, bowing his head.

"I want to be here for you. I promise to come by tomorrow. Will you be around?" Gary didn't want to appear so abrupt.

"Yeah, I'll be around. It's not like I have anywhere else to go tomorrow," Stewart said. At least with Gary gone, he could resume his drinking.

"I'll be by tomorrow evening after work. Are you going to be okay in the meantime?" Gary asked.

"I'll be fine. I have this," Stewart said, raising the plastic cup to Gary.

Gary walked to the doorway of the hotel room and paused for a moment. The last thing he wanted to do was be responsible for anything destructive his friend might do.

"Let that be the last one for the night, Stewart, okay."

"I told you, I'll be fine." Stewart looked at the contents of the cup and then back at Gary. Raising his cup he said, "Here's mud in your eye."

CHAPTER
TWENTY-ONE

"Hunty, he had some of the meatiest dick I think I've ever had!" Cabrien exclaimed to Karen on the telephone.

"It sounds like he had a nice stroke goin' on," Karen said.

"Girl, he tore my boogina up! I mean, I've been home a half hour and my insides are still shook."

Karen lost herself in a fit of laughter. "Boy, your ass is wild! I just hope you're careful."

"Girl, I don't play with that unsafe stuff. Condoms always!"

"I'm glad to hear that. Oh, before I forget, how was the bar last night?"

The sudden change in subject confused Cabrien. "What do you mean?"

"You and Armando went out last night, right?"

"I don't know what you're talking about. I didn't go anywhere last night because *Cleopatra Jones, Coffy,* and *Black Belt Jones* were on TV back to back."

Karen's face tingled with anger. "You're sure you didn't see Armando at all yesterday?"

"Not unless he made his way into my TV and was pick-

ing lint out of a nappy-ass afro. Girl, I said I didn't leave my house."

Just then, Armando came through the door.

"Honey, I have to let you go. Armando just walked in."

"Ooooh, did he tell you he was with me? Girl, I wasn't trying to get anyone into trouble," Cabrien said, realizing what was happening.

"You didn't," Karen said as she made eye contact with Armando. "He did that to himself." Without saying good-bye, she hung up the phone.

Armando sensed there was going to be yet another argument. Instead of partaking in it, he decided to go into the bedroom.

"So, that's it? You're gonna do your dirt and then go hide in the bedroom instead of facing me, huh?" Karen yelled at him.

"What, Karen? What?" Armando said, turning around quickly. He had spent the entire day going from place to place, putting in applications and paying bills. But being denied unemployment and his meeting with Drake Hill had soured his mood. Whatever Karen was trying to say, he wished she would get to it.

"Do I have 'Dummy' printed on my forehead?" Karen asked, running her freshly french manicured-nail along her forehead as she followed him into the bedroom.

"You told me that your black ass went out with Cabrien last night when you and I both know that's a damn lie, so you may as well come clean. Where were you?"

Armando saw a fire building behind Karen's eyes that he'd never seen before. Something told him he would be unable to charm his way out of this.

"I think I should step for a few days. I need to clear my

head. With everything that's gone down, you might want some time away from me, too." He began taking papers out of his backpack to make room to pack a few things.

"That's what I was trying to do with your sorry ass! Now, because *you* want some space that makes everything all right?"

"I think you want me to admit to something I don't wanna say," Armando said. The backpack was too small for what he wanted to take, so he went inside the closet to get his black duffle bag.

"I don't believe this," Karen said, collapsing onto the bed. "You're gonna walk out of here without telling me what you were doing? Hell, I know what you were doing, I just don't know with who. But, I know one thing: if you walk out that door, don't bother coming back."

Once Armando packed the few things he needed, he paused outside the bedroom door, contemplating whether he should just leave or say goodbye. He watched as Karen began to sob. He ached inside. He wanted to say something, anything to ease her pain. But silence was better than telling another lie.

"If anyone calls here about offering me a job, can you tell them to call my cell?"

"Why are you lying, Armando?" Karen sobbed. "You know good and well you ain't out there looking for no job! Just take your ass on if you're going!"

"I know you don't see it now, but it's better like this. I need to clear up some shit before I come back here."

"You ain't coming back up in here. You can forget that!" Karen yelled.

"I love you. I want you to believe that. I just can't be with you now, and I can't explain it now."

Karen stood up, the salt of her tears staining her cheeks, her hair a tangled mess as though she had been pulling at it.

"Is the bitch you're laying up with pregnant?"

"Karen it's nothing like that. I know that I'm a dick for not explaining things, but you gotta believe me that it's better this way."

"No, you're not a dick. You're *dickless*." She slammed the bedroom door in his face.

Armando clenched the handle of his duffle bag and went into the living room to get his cell phone charger. After that, he took one last look around the apartment, as though he'd never see it again.

Armando got in the car and drove, all the while wondering how things had gone so wrong so quickly. Why had he lied about losing his job? How could he ever admit to Karen that he'd become a prostitute like Cabrien?

When he finally stopped the car, he found himself in front of his mother's house. He reached over to the passenger seat, grabbed his duffle bag and walked slowly to his mother's door. Armando had no idea what he'd say to Gloria about why he needed to spend a few days over there. But, he knew she would allow him to stay. Hopefully, his mother's boyfriend, Lamont, wasn't home.

Armando heard the faint sounds of Miles Davis coming through the front door, just before he knocked.

"Hey, honey!" Gloria opened the door with a mixing spoon in her hand and a greasy kitchen cloth slung over her shoulder.

"Hi, Ma," Armando said, trying to convey cheerfulness that would match his mother's.

"Well, come on in," Gloria said as she went back around the corner to the kitchen to finish cooking.

The amazing smells of fried chicken and collard greens filled the home.

"Did you eat?" Gloria called out from the kitchen as Armando looked around at his mother's latest acquisitions. He knew she was an avid collector of black baby dolls, so he wasn't surprised to see boxes of even more dolls at the door.

"No, I ain't ate yet. You offering?"

"Boy, don't act stupid. Of course I'm offering," Gloria said, laughing.

"Ma, you know what I mean," Armando said with a smile.

"I'm just mixing this cornbread batter," she said, fiercely stirring the mix in the bowl.

"You got a beer?" Armando asked.

"I got some Corona. But those belong to Lamont. Oh wait, go out onto the breezeway and look in the cooler for a couple of Heinekens."

Armando went out through the dining room and found the little rickety cooler that had about eight beers in it. The door leading into the garage was open. Armando peeked in and saw Lamont's old Buick with the hood up.

"Is Lamont here?" Armando asked. His change of tone made it obvious that he was hoping he wasn't.

"No, he's not, so don't you start," Gloria warned her son.

Armando returned to the kitchen just as his mother put the baking pan into the oven. He handed her a beer, and opened another for himself.

"Thank you," she said, wiping the sweat from her brow.

"How are things between you two? He acting like he got some sense?" Armando said, taking a huge gulp of the beer.

"You know how he is. He's been all right this week. He's still moody, but he ain't been putting his hands on me. Not after I hit him upside the head with a pot."

Armando's eyes widened. "You what?"

"I sure did. You would've been proud of your mama, boy!"

"What happened?"

"He just came in here acting all crazy. Acting stupid as usual and, I don't know, that particular day I must've been in a not-giving-a-shit kinda mood. So when he slapped me, it made me think about all the times he used to put his hands on me and that shit he did to you with that extension cord."

"You thought about all of that?"

"Boy, you just don't know. It was like a flood of memories came over me, but real speeded up like. Anyway, he came at me so I popped him with the pot. Then, I ran outside and started screaming and the neighbors called the police."

"They did?"

"Yep," Gloria smirked as she sipped her beer.

"And y'all are still together?"

"Yeah."

Armando shook his head. With all that was going wrong with his relationship however, he knew he didn't have room to talk.

"I need to stay here for a few days," Armando said.

"Why? What's going on with you?"

"I just need some time to myself. Gotta lot of stuff I'm trippin' on that my girl won't understand."

"You ain't messin' around on her, are you?" Gloria's words were stern.

"Naw. It's nothing like that. I just need some space to breathe."

"You and Lamont are like gasoline on a fire. You really think staying here is a good idea?"

"Well, last I checked, this was *your* house. I don't remember you putting that fool's name on a deed or mortgage payment. He shouldn't have anything to say about it. I mean, I am your son after all, in case you forgot."

"Boy, ain't nobody forgot! Shut that noise up!" Gloria thought for a moment, even working in a couple of sips of beer before saying, "Fine, just keep the peace with Lamont. That's all I ask." She checked her watch to remind her when she put the cornbread into the oven.

Armando decided not to tell his mother that she ought to tell Lamont to try and keep the peace with him, though it would have been the least she could do, since she tended to side with Lamont on everything else. Armando knew she wasn't scared of Lamont, not if she was going upside his head with pots. He wondered why his mother kept him around. Probably had something to do with sex, though it was gross to think of his mother as a sexual being. But Armando knew from his own sword wielding that a dick laid down right could get women to put up with damn near anything. His mother was just another one of those females who forgot her common sense once she had a man inside of her. And the worst thing about it was that the dick keeping his mother stupid belonged to Lamont.

After dinner, Armando sat with his mother and listened

to Natalie Cole singing "Mr. Melody." The house was still warm from her cooking. Armando went around opening windows and doors to get the air circulating.

"I'm gonna go lay down," Gloria said, disappearing down the hall into her bedroom.

About a minute later, Lamont came into the house. He had a scowl on his face, looking like a man who was working himself to death and still not getting ahead. It was the same scowl Armando remembered as a child, and he usually received the brunt of the anger that fueled the scowl. On Saturday mornings, he was Lamont's punching bag, a way to release all of his stresses from the week. He told Gloria it was his way of making her son into a man. She bought it, and Armando hated them both for it.

Armando pretended not to notice Lamont standing in the doorway, a mass of muscle in work clothes. He pretended to have difficulty opening one of the living room windows, but could see Lamont staring at him through his peripheral vision.

"Can't you speak, boy?" Lamont asked.

"Wuz up," Armando said, returning an icy glare.

"Where's your mammy at?" Lamont asked, ignoring Armando's attempt to be hard. He kicked off his work boots by the front door.

"My *mother* is in there lying down," Armando said.

"She put a plate in the fridge for me?" Lamont asked, walking past Armando into the kitchen.

"You know she always does. Why would today be any different?"

"What, boy?" Lamont poked his head out from the kitchen.

"I said that you know she put a plate in the fridge for

you, so why are you acting like you're brand new and don't know the routine?"

"Listen, you cocksucker, I've been working all goddamn day. You get me? I don't need any of your sass!"

"Yo, man, don't come over here with that, all right? That's my mother in there, not my *mammy*, okay? Don't get it fucked up!" Armando shot back.

"Nigga, I will stomp you up in here!" Lamont slammed the refrigerator door shut.

"Look, don't you two start that shit!" Gloria screamed from the bedroom.

"Gloria, you better come in here and check this son of yours!"

Armando walked closer to meet Lamont eye to eye.

Gloria walked around the corner just in time to see Lamont's heavy hand slap Armando in the face. She jumped in between the two men.

"Armando, please! I didn't want this foolishness in my house today," Gloria said.

"Well, tell that to his punk ass! He's the one coming in here with his usual attitude problem!"

Gloria's eyes spilled over with tears. "Armando, you gotta go."

"You're throwing me out? He stays, but you're throwing *your son* out? Okay, I got you." Armando stormed toward the front door where his bag was still sitting next to.

"Where are you gonna go?" Gloria asked, running after Armando.

"What difference does it make?" Armando said, then slammed the door behind him.

For the second time that day, Armando was sitting in his car without a clue where he was going. He wasn't going

back to the apartment to argue with Karen, who would only demand answers he wasn't ready to give. He'd taken the five hundred dollars from Drake and paid bills. Now, he only had thirteen dollars left in his wallet, not even enough for a motel room.

Armando pulled away from his mother's house and drove aimlessly for hours. The color of the sky had gone from looking like a melted Turbo Rocket Popsicle sunset to black and starry. He finally pulled into the parking lot of a Target store just as it was closing. He parked as far from the building as possible, finding a corner under some trees. He saw an employee walk a train of shopping carts from the cart park back to the store. Armando was exhausted, both in mind and body. His head ached from all the fussing and arguing. He'd had enough to last him a lifetime.

His mind drawing a blank as to what to do next, he fixed his attention on the McDonald's across the street. People came and went, no doubt on their way to welcoming houses. He stared at the bright golden arches, wondering how long until its light went out. Reclining his seat, he fell asleep wondering.

The next morning, Armando awoke feeling the same way he'd fallen asleep...alone. The early morning birds singing did nothing to improve his mood.

All of the tossing and turning through the night rewarded him with a stiff neck. He lit a cigarette. His first exhale brought him back to ponder the question from the previous evening: what would he do next? The possibilities weren't endless, he knew. Maybe he could wait for Karen to leave the apartment for work so that he could sneak a shower. He'd be sure not to get too comfortable.

Then Armando had a thought that made him shudder.

The paltry thirteen dollars he had wouldn't last the day. He knew that amount wouldn't even get a decent amount of gas for the car.

"Ma's ass should be giving me some money for putting me out like she did," Armando thought out loud. He looked at his watch. 8:30 AM. He took out his cell phone and dialed his mother.

"Hello." Lamont's voice croaked into the phone.

"Put my ma on the phone, man," Armando snapped.

There was a willful silence from Lamont.

"Eh, man, I know you're still on the phone. Quit playin' and put my ma on the phone, nigga!"

"Gloria, it's your faggot-ass son!" Lamont said, passing the phone to Gloria as they lay in bed.

"Where are you?" Gloria asked.

"I'm parked outside of a Target. I slept in my car last night. You satisfied?"

"Ain't nobody told you to do that. You shoulda took your ass home."

"I told you I can't go home. Karen is trippin' hard. I got too much to think about without being caught up with her insecurity shit. And anyway, this wouldn't have happened if you would've let me stay the night like you said I could."

Gloria sucked her teeth. "Now, don't think you're gonna call my house and make me feel bad. Speaking of which, what do you want?"

"I need some money."

"What? Lamont, do me a favor and hang this up."

Armando heard Lamont's maniacal howl before the line went dead. "Fuck!" Armando threw his phone to the passenger seat and pounded the steering wheel repeatedly with his fists. His body buzzed like an electric live wire.

"Forget both y'all," he muttered, turning to the sidewalk to see a group of people who were waiting for the bus staring at him.

The point was being made clear: the only person who could give him what he wanted was Drake. But that would mean giving Drake what he wanted in return. Armando's stomach fluttered as he thought of the smirk that would appear on Drake's face when he asked for help.

"Why do I feel like I gotta kiss ass every time I need something from him? I'm gonna bust him in the mouth if he acts up!" Armando said to himself. But he knew it was an empty threat. To get money, he'd have to do whatever Drake expected of him, or find another way to get it. He swallowed hard before dialing Drake's number.

"Hello?"

"Yeah, Drake it's me, Armando."

Silence.

"Did you hear me, Drake? It's Armando."

"What do you want?" Drake asked coldly.

Armando decided to sweeten his voice. "I was thinking that since I'm free today, you might want to have lunch or something."

"Well, of course you're free. It's not like you're working or anything."

"Nope. I guess not," Armando said, straining to maintain a respectful tone.

Drake chuckled. "I knew you'd come crawling back."

"Yeah, fine, whatever. You win, okay? Are you happy? We need to talk about some stuff. Can you have company?"

"Not right now."

"So, I can't talk to you?" Armando asked. He feared his last resort was slipping from his grasp.

"I didn't say that. We just aren't going to do it now. Meet me at Albert's downtown. Noon-ish."

Armando gulped as though he were accepting an impending doom. "Fine. I'll see you there."

"Don't sound so disappointed. You called me, remember?" Drake said. A yawn escaped his mouth.

Armando hung up the phone in disgust over Drake's condescending tone and started the ignition.

CHAPTER TWENTY-TWO

Gary was at his desk when he heard the sudden eruption of cackles coming from down the hall. He followed the sound to Isaac's office, where he was cracking jokes with his assistant.

"Isaac, I'd like a few words with you."

Isaac and the assistant exchanged quizzical glances for a few seconds until she got up and left the office, closing the door behind her.

"What's up?" Isaac asked.

"I want to know if you've been in my office."

"Not recently," Isaac said, shifting in his seat. "Why do you ask?"

"I'm missing a very important file from my computer, and I was wondering if you had anything to do with it."

"Why would I mess with your computer, Gary?" Isaac asked, sounding deeply offended.

"I know that you would do anything to get this damn position. You can hide behind your faith all you want to, but your dirty work will come to light."

"This is what you came into my office to do? Call me dishonest and attack my integrity?"

"If you had nothing to do with it, then I suppose you won't have anything to worry about."

"Maybe you erased the thing accidentally, Gary. It can happen, you know. It doesn't always have to be someone else's fault."

"I didn't erase it," Gary said, shaking his head.

"Then, I don't know what else to tell you." Isaac stood up to signal the end of the conversation.

When Gary left the office, Isaac sat back down, thought for a moment, and then leaned over and called Drake's office.

"Yeah," Drake answered.

"Did you ruin Gary's video file?" Isaac asked.

"You mean to tell me you couldn't walk the few paces it would take to get to my office? We're reduced to playing games on the phone?" Drake said, laughing.

"Drake, I had Gary Walsh storming into my office and accusing me of erasing some file. The whole thing smells like something you'd do."

"I'm flattered," Drake said.

"Don't be. I'd appreciate it if, when you want to be on my side, you would tell me so. That way I know how to fend off accusations of wrongdoing. I didn't see that one coming."

"First off, Isaac, make no mistake, I'm not on your side. But while we're on the subject, there is something that I believe you ought to do for me if I am to proceed with phase two of my plan."

"What's that?" Isaac asked.

"You'll have to drop all of that hate speech toward gays."

Isaac was silent on his end.

"Isaac, did you hear me? I want that portion out."

"I don't know if I can do that," Isaac said cautiously.

"Then the missing video file will reappear as mysteriously as it disappeared and if any questions are asked, I'll make sure the answers point to you."

Isaac's nostrils flared. "How so?"

"Well, if I told you that, I'd be showing you my hand."

"You son of a bitch," Isaac hissed into the phone.

"You're too kind," Drake said.

"Look, you know that the gay lifestyle goes against everything I stand for."

Drake chuckled. "Okay, well, maybe you can explain to me how helping you sabotage someone else's career represents 'family values.' Don't forget, you came to me, Mr. Sanctimonious."

Again Isaac was silent.

"Oh, and by the way, how is your mistress?" Drake asked cheerily. "Has she met your wife yet?"

Isaac stifled an anxiety attack at the mention of the word "mistress."

"I can't promise to eliminate the gay thing from my proposal, Drake, it's too important to those with whom we do business. You knew that when you began working here. Go somewhere else if you don't agree with us. You're the one selling out, political whore that you are."

"Well, I'll just have to make sure that Benita and your pretty lil' mistress become acquainted with each other. I'm sure they'll find that they have plenty to talk about."

"Okay, fine. You win," Isaac said in almost a whisper.

"Excellent. We'll begin by working on a rewrite of your speech. Those references you make regarding a 'gay agenda' and 'lifestyle' won't be necessary."

"I don't understand why you aren't rallying behind Gary. He's a lot more moderate on social issues."

"I have my reasons. Anyway, I'm done talking about this for now. I have to meet someone for lunch. But we'll talk later."

"Yeah, later," Isaac said, hanging up the phone.

Drake sat back in his chair, grinning from ear to ear. He not only smelled victory, he could taste its sweetness.

CHAPTER TWENTY-THREE

When Armando entered the apartment, he felt happy to be in a place which held mostly happy memories. Instead of going in to shower and change for his lunch with Drake, he collapsed onto the bed and closed his eyes.

Later, Armando awoke from a hard sleep. He glanced over at the clock on the nightstand and saw that the clock read 12:00 PM.

"Damn!" Armando exclaimed, shooting up from the bed. He knew Drake was going to be waiting for him at Albert's, and that a battle with traffic awaited him.

Without much thought as to what kind of place Albert's was, he pulled out a fresh pair of underwear and socks, followed by a pair of jeans and a blue oxford shirt. After choosing his new outfit, he stripped naked and found relief in the shower as the water peeled away the sweat and faint scent of cologne from the previous evening.

Armando arrived at Albert's at 1:15 PM. Drake was sitting by himself at a table tucked into the farthest reaches of the room.

Albert's was not just another restaurant. Historically, Albert's had seen more deaths and shady business transac-

tions than any other eatery in the Twin Cities. There was nothing aesthetically pleasing about Albert's. Dents and scratches covered practically every piece of furniture. The ambience was drenched in doom and gloom, what little light there was came from the tackily wired brass fixtures that were mounted on the worn, maroon velvet walls.

The only other patron there was an elderly woman who had such advanced osteoporosis, that her back had become a hump. She sat next to the door, not speaking, scrawling on a napkin what she wanted to eat. Armando approached Drake, who was flipping hastily through the newspaper.

"Wuz up?"

"You're late," Drake said simply. Armando hated Drake's flat response and surmised correctly that he was in for a lecture.

"I was heading down 35 W northbound and it was backed up. You'd think all of them uppity mofos would be at work by now."

Drake was exasperated. "Armando, you've lived here all of your life. You know about these conditions. You must plan for these things."

"I know, Drake, but..." Armando began softly like a child trying to avoid a whipping from an angry parent.

"No buts, Armando. You may have gotten away with arriving late when you were working for the hotel, but I expect you to be on time. Am I understood?"

Armando averted his eyes, allowing a meek "yeah" to escape from his lips.

"Good. Then I trust we won't need to have this conversation again."

"No."

Turning his gaze from Armando to the menu, Drake's tone began to soften and became upbeat.

"I suggest the crab cakes, they're pretty good."

Armando raised his eyes back at the man who sat before him. Drake wasn't going to let Armando forget that he held all of the face cards and could trump Armando's hand every time. However, with little else going for him, Armando endured it. He forced his facial muscles to form the most convincing smile that he could. Swallowing his pride downward into the bowels of his stomach, he responded, "Then I guess I'm having the crab cakes."

Lunch limped along the best way it could from that point on. After they finished eating, Drake methodically wiped his hands and his fingers. He studied Armando's face—which looked miserable—then announced, "I have a few hours to kill before I have my meeting. I'd like to go back to my apartment and..." Drake's cell phone rang, cutting him off. He looked at the caller ID and saw that it was Cabrien. He sighed wearily and answered it.

"Hey, I can't talk right now."

"If I didn't know any better, I'd say you were avoiding me," Cabrien said, half joking.

"No, don't be silly. Now's just not a good time. But we'll talk soon, okay?"

"When, Drake?"

"I'll call you. I promise." And he hung up.

"Sorry about that. Now, where was I? Oh, so I've got some free time and..."

Armando didn't want him to continue. He interrupted with, "Fine, let's go!"

Drake threw some money down on to the table to pay for the meal and they headed for the door. As they passed

the old woman sitting in front, Armando locked glances with her. Her eyes looked vacant and haunted.

"You can follow behind me to my place," Drake said.

Trailing behind, Armando muttered, "I figured as much."

When they arrived inside Drake's apartment, Drake leaned in to kiss Armando on the lips. Armando turned his head and Drake's lips fell gently against Armando's cheek.

Drake became exasperated. "You're going to fuck me!" he demanded. "It's time."

Armando peered into Drake's eyes, the gray of his own eyes turning like ice. In a flash of a second, Armando transported himself inside of a porn movie. "You want this, huh?" Armando taunted as he began to touch himself. "Get down on them knees! This ain't nothin' new. If you want me to fuck you, start suckin'. And you better make this shit hard, too!"

Drake smiled as he dropped to his knees. He unzipped Armando's fly and pulled down his shorts, digging around for Armando's cock. Armando closed his eyes and allowed Drake to take all of him into his mouth. His body trembled as he thought about Karen doing to him what Drake was doing right now. But it didn't work; Armando knew Karen wasn't in the room. He knew it was Drake sucking him, making him hard, and it made him angry.

"Get yo' bitch ass up!" Armando ordered to Drake, who did as he was told. "Get in that bedroom and pull them clothes off, bitch." Armando's voice was low and commanding.

Drake began to undress, locking eyes with Armando.

"Hurry this shit up, I ain't got all day!" Armando

yanked at Drake's shirt, ripping the fabric from his chest. Drake's concentration was broken from the moment.

"Hey, are you crazy? This is Ferragamo!"

"Oh, you wanna cry about it, bitch? If you got the money to pay me, then you got the money to buy another one. Now shut up and pull them pants off!" Armando pushed Drake onto the bed. Drake stared helplessly at Armando as his pants were torn away.

There would be no lovemaking. Armando was going to impale; punish him for having everything, and being like everyone else in Armando's life who refused to believe that he was anything beyond a handsome face. He wanted Drake to feel his pain, if not emotionally then physically. He wanted Drake to feel the humiliation Armando felt day after day as a man who had offered his woman the moon and never delivered it.

He took a condom from Drake's nightstand drawer, remembering where Drake kept them. As Armando rolled the condom into place, Drake said, "Make sure you use plenty of lube."

Armando laughed at him. "Hell naw, you ain't getting' no lube, bitch. Spread them ass cheeks and be quiet!"

Armando rammed himself into Drake furiously without allowing Drake's body any time to relax. Drake's body grew rigid as he was being penetrated.

"Hold on! Hold on! Give me a minute to get used to you!" Drake pleaded as he panted for breath. Sparks of pain spread through his body as his hands grasped for the sheets.

"What did I tell you to do? Didn't I say be quiet?" Armando remembered the time Karen had allowed him to anally penetrate her. He had enjoyed the tightness of her

ass. Surprisingly, being inside Drake felt just as familiar. And it felt good, despite Drake's squirming beneath him.

Armando glared at Drake, holding him down by the back of the neck, his face pushed into the pillow. "Yeah, you ain't got all that mouth now, do you?" he said, hearing Drake's muffled moans. "That's right, shut yo ass up and take this dick!"

Armando kept his strokes hard and deep, moving past Drake's prostate. As the older man bucked, whimpering in agony, Armando knew he was hurting him. The glare on Armando's face dissolved into a smile as his dominion over Drake served as the perfect aphrodisiac.

"Damn, you about to make me lose my breath. C'mon, man, hold on!" Drake begged.

Armando began to fuck Drake even harder. In his mind he saw Drake becoming unconscious from the unbearable pain of being torn open. But then, Drake bucked again, he turned around, his face determined.

"All right, then! Give it to me, nigga!" Drake braced himself. "Fuck me with that club dick!" he demanded, slamming himself into Armando's thrusts.

Armando forcibly turned Drake onto his back and held his legs in the air, allowing them to rest on his shoulders. He pounded Drake harder and harder. Armando tried to hold on to the mental image of Drake crying out incoherently, waiting for him to stop. But in reality Drake was enjoying every minute. As Armando's face strained and contorted, Drake reached up and brought Armando's face closer to his and kissed him on the lips, which only infuriated Armando. Drake was supposed to feel degraded, writhing in pain from the relentless force of Armando's nine pounding inches of sexual dominance.

Once again Armando felt defeat.

Later that afternoon, Armando rose from the bed. The curtains were drawn, allowing little light into the room. The shadows crawling through the room made Armando uneasy. He walked into the bathroom, his body feeling cool as the sweat from his fast and furious fucking evaporated.

Armando turned on the bathroom light and ran the faucet, splashing cold water on his grainy face. As he dried himself with a facecloth, he caught his reflection in the mirror. A malevolent grin stared back at him.

"Wuz up, Armando!" the reflection said cheerfully. Armando stumbled backward into the doorway.

"Who are you?" Armando demanded.

"I'm who you'll become when you allow men to stick their dicks up your ass!"

"Naw, I don't do that. I stuck him. He NEVER penetrated me. And never will! Get that straight."

"Yeah, sure—for now. That's how it starts. It'll be just a matter of time before you've got your bitch T-shirt tied up above your bellybutton, walkin' around here begging for a dick to sit on!"

Armando's reflection morphed into an emaciated, demonic form. Its mouth and eyes stretched open wide.

"What's wrong, Armando? You don't look too good," the demon taunted.

Armando began to feel faint. The phantom continued, "Do you still wanna give Karen the moon? How you gonna do that when you ain't even got a window to throw your piss out on some grass? Let me know, cuz if you do, you'll give it to her looking like this!"

With that, the reflection laughed maniacally, lifted its

torn T-shirt to reveal open sores oozing with pus and blood. Armando ran from the bathroom, the laughter's haunting echo in his mind. He ran back into the bedroom where Drake slept.

"Drake, get up!" Armando shouted.

Drake was still.

"Drake, wake up!" Armando shouted even louder. He began to shake Drake's body. Drake's eyes opened to reveal empty sockets. His body began to sink inside the bed, remaining motionless as the bed swallowed him.

Armando awoke dripping in perspiration. It was evening now and Drake slept quietly at his side. Armando looked down at Drake and shook him gently.

"Drake?"

"Hmmm," was Drake's sleepy reply.

"I have to get going. You need to run me my money."

"There's an envelope inside my briefcase. Whatever's in it is yours."

Armando got out of bed and went to look inside the briefcase that was slightly opened.

He found a bank withdrawal envelope.

"Drake, this is $1000," Armando said incredulously.

"Yeah. Take it."

"What?" Armando was perplexed.

"Take it, and there's a whole lot more where that came from," he said with a touch of kindness in his voice. He looked at the clock; it was 7:00 PM. "Well, I guess I'm not going back to work today," Drake chuckled.

"Man, are you sure?" Armando asked, not taking his eyes off the ten, crisp hundred-dollar bills.

"Armando, I want you to listen for a moment." Drake sat up in the bed. "All of my life I've had to be in control

of myself and other people. You don't make any headway in this world if you let people disrespect you. You have to seize the reins and take control, and never lose it. You know what I mean?"

Armando nodded.

"My parents are rotting in a couple of boxes in the ground, looking up at me from their places in hell. To them, my achievements still don't amount to much. But to the assholes still here, I showed them all. I may be a fag, but damn it, I'm a successful one."

"Yeah, I can see that," Armando said.

"I've hurt and ruined a lot of people to get to where I am today. And deep down, I know I deserve to be punished for what I did to them. When you came hard at me, I got to be the bitch. It was probably the best lay I ever had." His voice was rough and breathy. "I've been waiting for someone like you all my life; you're my fantasy come to life. You and I aren't done yet."

Armando thought the relationship he had with Drake was an open contract that either party could walk away from freely with little or no consequence. He bristled at the thought of being beholden to Drake indefinitely. He'd barely been able to perform sexually for Drake twice, but a third and fourth time?

CHAPTER TWENTY-FOUR

Gary sat inside the Minneapolis Café waiting for Tony Cannon.

It was a slow evening at the restaurant, maybe twelve or thirteen diners at the most, all enjoying their food and wine and laughing raucously. Not Gary. He was worried whether anyone would back him and his vision for the Black Republicans for Change.

Since its founding by Bruce Hedrick, the BRC had been socially very conservative. And the entire state of Minnesota was becoming more conservative too, as evidenced by the election wins of Governor Tim Pawlenty and Senator Norm Coleman. Gary didn't want to accept the status quo, but realized that it was going to be an uphill battle to create change and move the state and the nation to the political center. Hopefully, Tony would bring news that would help toward his objective.

Tony arrived wearing a navy suit with pinstripes, his jet-black hair slicked back severely. He walked in with a deep frown creasing his face.

"Good evening, Tony," Gary said.

"Hello, Gary," Tony said flatly.

"The waiter just went to get me a glass of water. I haven't ordered anything yet."

"I'm gonna cut to the chase. It doesn't look good for you. The people who were willing to give you money anonymously have backed out completely," Tony said. His voice was low and tense.

"What happened?" Gary asked. His stomach began to turn violently, and his hands began tingling.

"They just thought better of it, I don't know," Tony said, waving at a waiter who had made eye contact with him.

"What am I supposed to do?" Gary asked, his voice drying up.

"Maybe you should rethink your platform and not veer too far from what the organization is doing."

"No, I can't do that," Gary said firmly.

"Then Isaac Walterson is going to become the new president of the BRC."

Tony didn't wait for Gary to respond. He became frantic trying to wave down the waiter, who, after making eye contact, merely rolled his eyes and turned his attention elsewhere.

"That's not our waiter, Tony," Gary said finally, getting irritated watching Tony wildly flail his hands about.

"Then where in the hell is *our* waiter?"

"I told you, he's getting my water."

"What is he doing? Pumping it from a well?" Tony shot up and went to the bar himself.

A couple who had witnessed Tony's impatience from another table, murmured audibly about how rude people could be.

At this point, Gary was ready for something stronger

than water. He watched as Tony returned to the table, with two drinks, placing one in front of Gary.

"Make no mistake; I'm not pleased to have to bring you this news. Anyway, it is what it is."

"So, no one gave you any explanation?"

"Well, yeah, more or less. They said that they didn't want to get involved with someone who didn't stand a chance anyway. That was the bottom line. Drink your drink"

"Thanks, but I'm having a colonoscopy tomorrow, so I shouldn't."

Tony shrugged, "Suit yourself," he said, putting the second gin and tonic next to his. The waiter finally came back with Gary's water.

"I don't understand it; Bruce nominated me because he thought that I stood a chance," Gary said, trying to make some sense of what he'd just been told.

"Are you sure about that? I mean, Bruce is a good guy and everything, but he's still very business minded. How do you know that he didn't set you up to fail?"

"What?"

"How do you know that Bruce didn't set it up like this? He could've just made Isaac his successor and that would've been that, but it wouldn't look good to the staff. What if he put you up knowing full well that you didn't have a prayer of beating Isaac Walterson out of the position? That way, when the staff voted, it would look as though he was elected because it was what the *people* wanted, when in actuality it was what Bruce wanted."

"That would be a despicable thing to do to someone."

"Yeah, well, this *is* politics; not a profession where people always play fair."

"But I know Bruce; he wouldn't do that to me. And besides, he has a lot of health problems to worry about. Why would he take the time to play these kinds of games?"

"Good question." Tony started on the second gin and tonic. "Look, Gary, I like you. I think you're great. I wasn't lying to you when I told you that you had the values and the vision that would appeal to most rational people. But I'm just one vote. And that means nothing."

When Gary walked through the door of his home, Wanda knew the meeting with Tony Cannon had not gone well. He was despondent. She swept across the room, looking glamorous in her vintage, stark-white dressing gown with ostrich feathers.

"They all bailed on me. Can you believe it? They all dropped out." Gary tossed his briefcase aside and collapsed into the reading armchair in front of the bay window.

"Tony told you that?" Wanda asked.

Gary stared out of the window into the night, only nodding in response to Wanda's question.

"I'll bring you a glass of wine," Wanda said, leaving the room to go into the kitchen.

"I don't want any wine," Gary said in a strangled whisper. But she had left the room and didn't hear him. He kicked off his loafers just as Wanda returned with a glass of Chardonnay. He took it but didn't drink from it.

"Wanda, have you any idea what it's like to feel as though you're fighting a losing battle. And no matter what you do, you watch the faith that people had in you just disappear?"

"I have faith in you," Wanda offered. "I always have, and always will."

"He told me that I didn't stand a chance in hell to get this job because I'm too moderate. I don't want the humiliation of losing." Then Gary erected himself in the chair, holding the stem of the wineglass tightly. "I'm going to drop out of the whole thing."

"So I married a quitter now?"

"Wanda, they don't want me. Maybe now just isn't the right time."

"Now is the *perfect* time. You think change is easy? Huh? Do you? I almost blame myself for this mess because I've been pushing you so hard."

"Wanda, you have nothing to do with this. Tony thinks I was set up," Gary said, taking a small sip from the glass.

"Who set you up?"

Gary sat there silent, instantly regretting his words. He wasn't sure he even believed Tony's conspiracy theory.

"Who set you up?" Wanda repeated, kneeling in front of him.

"Nothing, I shouldn't have said anything," Gary said as he caressed her cheek.

Wanda pushed his hand away. "Tell me."

"I don't know if it's true or not, but Tony thinks I was set up to lose, and then with the deleted file and everything..."

"What deleted file?"

"Remember the day you went shopping, and you came to my office afterward? That was the day I found out that someone had deleted the footage I was going to use of black families doing well under Republican power."

"I remember."

"I think either Isaac or Drake had something to do with that."

"Why would they do that?"

"Hell if I know."

Wanda's eyes grew hard. "You want this promotion, Gary. You know you do, so don't give up."

"What I want is to not talk about this anymore tonight. Now, I love you, and I appreciate what you're trying to say. But I've made up my mind. I'm finished."

Wanda moved away from Gary. Her husband was intent on growing weaker by the minute.

"Fine, if that's what you've chosen for yourself. I just don't want you waking up a year from now asking yourself, 'what in the hell did I do?' Because then, Gary, it will be too late." Wanda started to leave the room to leave Gary to his solitude, saying over her shoulder, "Remember your colonoscopy with Dr. Fortier tomorrow."

"I know it. I have to drink that stuff to clean me out," Gary said, remembering suddenly.

"Where's that stuff I have to take. I don't know why I even sipped that damn wine. You shouldn't have given it to me."

"I wasn't thinking either. I saw you looking so sad. I'm sorry. That liquid is on top of the refrigerator."

"Thanks." Gary left Wanda standing there.

As she watched her husband walk into the kitchen, she muttered, "Don't break down on me, Gary. Not now."

CHAPTER
TWENTY-FIVE

"Open up the door, bitch!" Cabrien screamed as he pounded on the door.

Don answered, wearing a honey-blonde spit curl wig on his head. The tresses swung dramatically over his eyes.

"Boy, why do you have that thing on your head?" Cabrien said, "And what the hell? What happened to your eyebrows?"

"I had to shave 'em off. Getting ready for a show tonight. I have to draw them in to get the right shape." Don said. He snatched the wig from his head and brushed it while he held it.

"Oh, you're working the Gay 90s tonight?"

"No, chile, I am not working that club. Those messy bitches? When I was in the audience tipping those heifers with my hard-earned money, I was honey, boo, and sweetheart to them. Now that I want to share their stage, they get to acting funny. I ain't thinkin' about those late and antiquated fools."

Cabrien watched as Don stood in front of the closet door mirror. He put the wig back on, and started talking to his reflection as though he were talking to someone else,

practicing how he would swing the hair in front of his eyes. It was what Don called "climbing inside the mirror." Cabrien, for all of his flamboyancy, thought Don was nuts to do some of the things he did, but that was Don.

When Don walked into the salon two years ago, Cabrien initially didn't take to him. He'd come whirling through the shop like a cyclone, taking all the focus off Cabrien. He couldn't understand why the ladies who worked at the salon were so quickly amused by Don, but took longer to warm up to Cabrien.

Then one afternoon, Don brought in a plastic bag stuffed with wigs he wanted dyed black. Cabrien said he could do it but wanted to be sure that all of the wigs were human hair. Don was in a rush and gave Cabrien a, "Yeah, yeah, sure they are. I know what I have, I brought them to you, didn't I?" and then dashed out the door.

When Don came back he discovered one of the wigs had been badly burned by the dye, and all that was left was the underlying scalp net with a few patches of wet hair attached. Don was horrified and demanded to know what Cabrien did to the wig. The salon became so quiet you could hear the bristle of one of the beautician's brushes hit the floor.

Cabrien responded calmly, "Did I, or did I not, ask you if all of those wigs were human hair? And what did you say to me because you were just too busy to be bothered? Well, you slipped me a synthetic wig, so you get what you got. But fair is fair. Synthetic or not, I will reimburse you for what the wig is worth."

Everyone stood or sat in stony silence as Cabrien reached into his wallet.

"You have change for a dollar?"

The aroma making its way from the kitchen quickly pulled Cabrien back to the present. Don had been cooking beef tenderloins in peppercorn gravy and boiling bowtie pasta.

"I know you're gonna let me get some of that food."

"Boy, you ain't company. Get in there and fix you a plate. And fix me one too," Don replied.

"Oh, I see how you are. You cook and I serve, huh?" Cabrien said, making his way past Don toward the kitchen.

Don winked. "You better act like you know."

Soon Cabrien emerged with two plates of food. He took his place at Don's small dining room table. "Can't believe you made me fix you a plate," Cabrien said, feigning upset.

Midway through the meal, Cabrien looked thoughtfully at Don, who was busy eating, his teeth clacking against the fork after every bite.

"Don, I'm thinking about telling Drake that I love him," Cabrien said as he searched Don's face for approval.

"Does Drake feel the same way?" Don asked, tearing pieces of white bread and soaking them in the gravy left on his plate.

"I guess I'll find out, won't I?"

"I wouldn't bother, chile. I know all about Mr. Drake, okay? So believe me when I tell you that he ain't tryin' to get serious about your ass."

"I think I could make him serious about me. We have the best conversations. I mean, we talk *a lot*."

"That's awfully nice, Cabrien," Don said sarcastically. "Let me tell it to you like this, because I'm tired of messing with you."

"Tell it then," Cabrien said.

"Your friend Drake is one of those unfortunate children

who don't look at other black men as their equal. He has made his way through every gay bar of the Twin Cities, my dear. And unless you're fine as hell, with dick or booty to spare, he won't talk to you. And since you two like to chitchat, ask him why not nary one black man is to be found in his social circle?"

"Drake is a little snotty, yes, but he's not racist against his own kind."

"You can cut him all the slack you want to. Drake is just as bad as some of these white gay children out there. All they're interested in is our so-called Zulu dicks and All Night Long sex mythology. I'm telling you. I think Drake has an issue with his own blackness," Don said, pushing the plate away.

"No, Drake ain't like that. I think I would know that if it were true. And I *know* I can make him a one-man man. You should've seen us back when he took me to Los Angeles. He was so wonderful, so tender. That's when I really got that he digs me like that."

"Yeah, okay. You keep on thinking like that. Who cares that you lasted past a couple weeks with him? I'm surprised he dealt with you *that* long. You're still just a flavor of many to him, baby. You're not the first and you will not be the last. But don't let me try and tell you the tea. You do you, hunty. That's your prerogative."

Don got up from the table and Cabrien followed. Both put their empty plates into the sink and made their way to the bathroom. They washed their hands and Cabrien stood in the doorway as Don pulled out his huge makeup kit.

"You wait. I'll be sending you an invite to our commitment ceremony," Cabrien said with absolute assurance.

"If you say so." Don moved back in front of the mirror

and started to put his show face on, signaling the end of the conversation.

"Don, I think you hide behind your drag persona because you're afraid to connect with a man. In fact, when's the last time you even *had* a man?"

Don began drawing his eyebrows as he waited for the rest of his makeup to set before blending. "I don't hide, but there's too much going on out there. I ain't ready."

"That's it?" Cabrien asked, expecting deeper revelations.

"That's it. I'm perfectly happy being alone. I mean, when I give my love to a man, I want it to be forever. I'm not having any of this bed hopping mess. AIDS is *still* real, and these young kids today, who don't know their buttholes from a hole in the wall, or their penises from a stick in the mud, are runnin' around here actin' like it's a thing of the past! Believe it or not, I'm quite happy with myself, *by myself*. I'm the happiest queen in Minneapolis."

"Your black ass doesn't have to bed hop, but you can date. I mean can't you at least do that?"

"I get all the love and adoration I need from the people when I perform every night. And when you're *Divinia Butterfly*, honey, that's all you need!"

CHAPTER
TWENTY-SIX

"You know you can't go back there," Drake called to Armando through the bathroom door.

"Watch me. I gotta fix this. And the longer I stay here, the harder it'll be." Armando opened the door, put his shirt on, and began shoving his belongings into his bag.

"I suppose you think that Karen is just going to welcome you back with open arms, right?"

Armando was silent, acting as though he hadn't heard Drake. He knew what he had to do, and wasn't in the mood to justify himself to Drake.

"Maybe you should stay and sleep on it."

"Why, so I can lay it on you one more time before I leave? Naw, man, we've done enough of that. And I mean *enough*. I've got to get my head together."

"I'm not trying to get you to do anything you don't want to do. I was simply suggesting that you wait until the morning at the very least. I mean, I don't think that you even know what you want to say, much less what you *should* say."

Armando paused for a moment. He needed to come up with something. Maybe it would be better if he slept on it.

"Maybe you're right," Armando conceded.

He put the bag on the floor and sat on the bed. Drake was cautious not to appear too happy about Armando's sudden change of plans.

"I can leave you alone to think if that's what you want," Drake said. "I know you've got a lot on your mind. I don't want you to be any more frustrated than you already are."

Armando didn't say anything, but with the immediate disappearance of worry lines on Armando's face, Drake knew he was doing the right thing.

Armando leaned back on the bed, the black satin sheets wrinkling around him. He thought about getting down on bended knee and telling Karen, "I'm an asshole, please forgive me!" He visualized seeing a smile break her frown. He thought about the money in the envelope; paying ahead on some of the bills, even buying Karen something special.

When Armando emerged from the bedroom twenty minutes later, Drake was watching an episode of *Ellen* on one of those "chick and fag" channels.

"You know Cabrien likes you, don't you?" Armando said.

Drake muted the volume and looked at Armando for the first time since Armando entered the room.

"And?"

"And I think he's really into you, Drake. You should look into what's happening with that. I mean maybe you two could hook up or something."

"Hook up? Armando, Cabrien and I have already *hooked up*. More times than I care to even talk about. My wallet breathes a lot easier now that I'm not seeing him anymore."

"Yeah, but you gave me money for sex. What's the difference?" Armando asked, crossing his arms.

"You're a lot more interesting," Drake smiled slyly.

"Have you even taken the time to get to know Cabrien? He's been through a lot in his life. But he's survived."

"Listen, we all have our sad stories, Armando. It doesn't always translate into chemistry. I get so tired of his finger snaps and the girlish behavior. I never would've fucked him so many times if he weren't so gorgeous."

"So it was just a piece of ass to you? You don't care that Cabrien is catching feelings for you?"

Sensing that this conversation was going to take longer than a minute or two, Drake turned off the television. "I think that we as adults should look out for our own self-interests. Cabrien knew what the deal was; if he got attached, there really isn't too much I can do about that."

"Dude, you have this superior air about you. And it's foul. Know what? I think you get off being the rich guy that can come in and sweep us lowly niggers off our feet. Then, once you've got us wanting more, you lose interest. Matter of fact, I don't think you even like being black. I think you see somebody white staring back at you in the mirror!"

"Okay, so now I don't like being black? You really think you've got me pegged, don't you? I'm sorry if I don't fit your limited scope of what blackness is. I'm educated, speak properly, and don't blame other people for what's not working in my life; that doesn't make me less black than you. I worked my ass off. I took advantage of every opportunity given me and am successful. I'm just as black as you ...*brotha*!"

"Man, drop all that off somewhere. I'm talking about Cabrien, now. I really think he's feeling you. And if all you

can say is that he shouldn't be, then maybe you should've done a better job getting that through to him," Armando said.

Drake rose from his sofa and went into the kitchen. He looked inside of the refrigerator for something to drink.

"Oh, so now you're gonna pout like a little bitch?" Armando called out.

"No, I'm going to get something to drink. Am I allowed?"

"Do what you gotta do. It doesn't change the fact that there is a kid out there who sells his ass because he doesn't have anyone to love him. That hour or so of affection he gets from tricking is a lot more than he's seen in his whole life."

Drake closed the refrigerator and walked back into the living room to read Armando's face.

"You don't really believe that crap you just said, do you? Or, is this some nonsense Cabrien fed you one evening when you girls were up late doing each other's nails, or just doing each other?"

"Naw, man. That sounds like some shit *you* do. In fact, you keep doing what you gotta do, and I'm gonna do what I gotta do."

"What? More of that 'tell Karen that I'm sorry' crap?" Drake asked sarcastically.

"I thought you understood that I had to do it. Isn't that why you so-called left me in the bedroom with my thoughts?"

"Wait just a minute." Drake slammed his water onto the coffee table, and sat on the edge of it. "You really are naïve. You created this problem the day you lied—and *this*—you actually think she's going to take you back after

you made it with a fag? You kept your dick pretty hard, I'll give you that much. If I didn't know any better I'd say you even enjoyed it."

"I did what I needed to do to get through it. I just imagined that everything I was doing to you I was doing to Karen," Armando said.

"Hey, if that's what it takes to get you through the night, buddy, that's fine with me. Still, I think you and I will be seeing a lot more of each other." Drake smiled; he had the whole scenario perfectly played out in his mind.

"I'm serious, Drake. You watch and see. If I can convince her that what I did was for her, I'm sure she'll forgive it eventually. We'll be all right."

Drake chuckled as he picked up his water and took a big gulp. "You *actually* believe that; that's what's so sad about it. I'll tell you what; I'll leave the door unlocked for you. How's that?"

Drake's know-it-all answers fell on deaf ears. He knew nothing about Armando's past with Karen and all they shared. Drake was lucky he had given Armando the money, because were it not for that, Armando would tell him to go to hell. Ignoring Drake's gall, Armando quickly went back to talking about Cabrien.

"I'm serious, Drake. You should think about Cabrien. I think he'd be good for you."

"I'm sorry, but Cabrien is just going to have to discover the one lesson in life that people learn everyday: sometimes some people don't get what they want."

Then with a big grin Drake added, "But then, the more fortunate among us *always* do."

CHAPTER
TWENTY-SEVEN

When Stewart got to The Black Out, it was well on its way to being the place to be. He walked through the crowd of beautiful and not-so-beautiful bodies, finding his way to the almost totally dark backroom, and discovered why the place had earned its name.

He barely walked five feet into the room when, from out of the shadows, eager hands groped the already swelling crotch of his jeans. One very insistent pair of hands pulled down the zipper on his fly and pulled out his hard-on. Before he could push the hands away, he felt a tongue licking it from the bottom of its shaft to the swollen head, while the hands stroked and teased his heavy, hairy balls. He heard cries and moans of pleasure all around him as men released themselves into mouths, or onto the floor. The man giving him the blowjob paused for a minute to catch his breath and tell him how much he enjoyed his task, and in that moment, Stewart pulled away from him. He didn't want to come. Not just yet.

As he moved deeper into the room, Stewart felt something warm fall on top of his hand. Blindly lifting the substance to his nose, he sniffed the unmistakable scent of

freshly spilled semen and quickly wiped it on his jeans. He just stood where he was for a moment, responding to the erotic sounds of horny men, enjoying the feeling of his last inhibitions fading away.

Suddenly, a slight bit of light entered the room, which made it possible to see only the outlines of bobbing heads and shoulders of men servicing other men. He inhaled the room's high testosterone energy that blended with the smell of raw denim and leather and sweat-soaked T-shirts and jockstraps. The grunts and groans of orgasms, the slurping, gagging sounds of nonstop sex aroused him almost unbearably. His body felt as though it was on fire. Once again his cock strained against his jeans, demanding release, and he began to unzip his fly. He felt a pair of hands push his hands away and begin to finish what he started. He felt someone on his knees shove against his leg and felt that man's tongue begin to lick every hair on his sack. Involuntarily, Stewart began face-fucking the cock-sucker working on his hard-on, first slowly, then faster and deeper. When he could hold back no longer, he shot his load, almost fainting from the intensity. Then, he pulled his jeans back up and walked slowly out of the backroom.

Back in the shadows, he was forced to accept what he really was—a gay man. He knew he would have to live with it—or *did*? He'd think about that later.

Cabrien arrived shortly after, and saw Divinia Butterfly take to the stage to begin "her" lip-synching number, Rihanna's "Disturbia." Divinia was wearing the same wig she'd tried on as Don earlier that evening. "She" was serving the audience female illusion, looking amazing in a sil-

ver sequined midriff and skirt and thigh-high stiletto boots. The crowd on the dance floor immediately stopped what they were doing, acknowledging that a true diva had arrived. A long line, three people deep, gathered at the stage. All of them waited with dollar bills in their hands and mouths, ready to pass their tips to the drag queen superstar.

Cabrien watched Divinia perform with cyclonic energy. By the end of the song, after her dramatic bows, Divinia walked away from the stage with fists full of money.

Cabrien ordered a Cowboy Cocksucker shot from the bar. He'd been craving one all evening. Divinia made her way effortlessly through the crowd as people simply moved out of her way. She clenched her money in one fist, graciously shaking hands with the other, and kissed well-wishers along her path to the bar.

"Hey, baby! When did you get here?" Divinia said, towering over Cabrien in her stilettos.

"I just got here. Came in right when you were on stage. Chile, you look sickening!"

"Thank you, baby. You gonna get a 'girl' a cocktail?"

"Sure, what do you want?"

"Just get me whatever you're having. And ask for a straw, I'm not trying to mess up my lipstick."

"I'm just doin' a shot."

"Oh, in that case what kind?" Divinia asked, fluttering her fake eyelashes.

"It's called a Cowboy Cocksucker."

"Is it fruity?"

"No, it's creamy."

"I'm never one to turn down anything creamy. I'll do one," Divinia said, still fluttering.

Cabrien ordered the shots, amazed that only a few hours earlier he had seen Divinia as Don, looking so plain. Now a goddess stood before him.

"That outfit must be the first time out," Cabrien said, looking Divinia up and down.

"It is. How could you tell?"

"Baby, you showed your goddamn ass off! You hear me? You were workin' it!"

"Thank you."

When the shots came, they clanked their glasses together.

"I gotta get ready for my next number," Divinia said, blowing an air-kiss at Cabrien.

"Have you been in the back room tonight?" Cabrien asked, not sure whether he should check out the action there.

"Honey, you know I don't do back rooms. If I can't see it, then I don't eat it, okay?"

The evening was winding down for Cabrien. He'd achieved his objective to catch a buzz. Like any good friend would, he stayed until the end, watching Divinia close the drag show. There was dancing for those who weren't ready to leave yet, and judging by the loud chatter over the music, there was plenty of party left. But Cabrien had had enough.

Divinia, in her fifth outfit of the evening, came sweeping by grandly wearing a sensational off-the-shoulder, beaded black gown, with body glitter glistening on her shoulders. The long fall wig cascading down her back remained intact from all of the hairspray she'd used.

Cabrien squeezed in between the small crowd of people showering Divinia with compliments.

"I'm about ready to go. How are you getting home?" Cabrien said as the group of fans began to walk away.

"I was going to cab it," Divinia said, screaming over the music.

"I can give you a ride home, but you have to leave now. Are you ready?"

"I just need to grab my things. It won't take any time."

"You don't have to change, do you?" Cabrien asked, hoping Divinia could wait until she got home to turn back into *Don*.

"I'm cool like this. Why don't you pull the car around? By the time you do that I should be ready. I just have to get my bag, and say goodbye to a few people."

"Don't be in here all night, Don, or you'll get left," Cabrien warned. Ordinarily he called Don Divinia when he was in drag, but he used his real name to underscore the importance that they leave soon.

Ten minutes later, Don emerged from the club. He had taken off his wig and dress and put on his shorts and LA Lakers jersey. His face was still painted, but he had taken off the false eyelashes.

"I'm sorry, Don, but I had to get out of there. I was starting to get a headache."

"Are you all right to drive?" Don asked, concerned.

"I'm good. I didn't have too much."

"Okay, then. Let's hit it."

"I want some White Castles," Cabrien said as the White Castle came into view.

On a normal evening, there was usually a long line of waiting cars backed into the main street. This particular

night there were only three cars ahead of them. Hopefully the other customers' orders would be quick and simple.

"Do you want anything?" Cabrien asked, fishing his wallet from his back pocket.

"What can I get?"

"Get whatever you want."

After they received their food, Cabrien pulled back out into the street. As he drove, he greedily dug his hands inside his bag, pulling out a fistful of fries. He began to bite at them from all sides. Don looked at Cabrien and shook his head.

"I guess I should tell you now before we get there," Cabrien sounded as though he were about to make a confession. "I'm gonna take you home, but we have to run somewhere first."

"I thought you were eager to get home, Cabrien."

"Don't be like that. I just need you to go inside with me and act as a kind of witness."

"Witness to what?" Don asked suspiciously.

"I'm gonna tell Drake that I love him."

Don's eyes became big with incredulity. "Are you serious? Boy, turn this car around and take me home. I'm not gonna be part of any of that foolishness. You can do all that on your own time."

"All you have to do is stand there. You don't need to say anything."

To Don, the whole scenario seemed immature. If Cabrien wanted to avoid conflict with *him*, then he'd abide by those wishes. Cabrien drove silently, occasionally wiping the fry grease from his hands onto his pant leg. Cabrien made up his mind. Don was coming along for this ride, whether he wanted to or not.

"I'm sleeping on the couch," Armando announced.

"I don't care. I'm just happy that you're staying the night."

"Yeah, well, don't get too happy. I'm leaving first thing in the morning."

"Do what you have to do. Just make sure when you come back as a gay boy in your next life, you don't lose my number," Drake said with a smile.

Armando didn't want to be set up for another one of Drake's psychological games. He was getting tired of his air of superiority and entitlement. He was going to go and get Karen to take him back; he'd beg if he had to.

"I don't know. I don't really feel like going to sleep now. Maybe I'll sit and watch TV."

"Just make sure you keep the volume low." Drake left to go brush his teeth.

Armando sat back against the sofa. He glanced up at the posters of the celebrity women and had a flashback to his first time at Drake's apartment. Why couldn't he have let that be the only time he messed with Drake? At least then he could say he'd had a lapse in judgment in the event that Karen found out. But as far as he was concerned, she was never going to know about this.

Armando heard voices coming from the hallway. The volume increased as the voices came closer. He was hoping they'd pass by. It was late and he didn't want to hear other people's drunken jibber jabber. But no luck. The voices stopped in front of Drake's door.

"He better be home," one of the voices said impatiently.

"Will you relax? He'll be here," the second voice hissed.

Armando sat on the sofa, hoping that Drake would hear the rapping on the door and answer it himself. He was surprised that Drake was having guests this late at night.

"Drake, get the door," Armando called out.

"Who is it?" Drake said, poking his head out of the bathroom, his mouth frothy from the toothpaste.

"Dude, don't you know who you have coming to your house so late?"

"I wasn't expecting anyone." Drake disappeared back inside the bathroom. When he reemerged, he was wiping his mouth with a facecloth.

"Why couldn't you answer the door?" Drake asked him, shaking his head.

"It ain't my house. I don't answer other people's doors," Armando whispered.

Drake opened the door to find Cabrien and Don standing there.

"Cabrien, what are you doing here?" Drake said, startled.

"Don't be rude. You can't say hello?" Cabrien asked, miffed.

"Hello, Cabrien." Drake's tone made it perfectly clear that he was not happy to see him. He repositioned himself in the doorway so that he could block Cabrien from entering, and totally ignored Don.

"What? You got trade over here?" Cabrien nudged his way into the apartment to see a startled Armando looking up at him.

"Oh hell no!" Cabrien screamed at the top of his lungs, spit spraying from his lips. He hoped to awaken everyone in Drake's building.

"Cabrien, damn it, calm down!" Drake ordered.

"Cabrien, it's not what it looks like," Armando said feebly.

"Bullshit! You're in here fucking Drake when you got a girlfriend, *my cousin,* at home not knowing where your ass is at?" Cabrien yelled as he approached Armando.

"Chile, let's just go, okay? You know he ain't no damn good," Don said, trying to grab the fabric of Cabrien's shirt.

"Uh, playa, I don't think you know me," Armando said as he stood up and faced Don.

"Naw, brotha-man, you ain't gonna ignore this by trying to check my friend! Does Karen know you're into men now?"

"I ain't been fucking anyone! I've just been here chillin' because your cousin doesn't want to see me right now!" Armando said, his nostrils flaring.

"Yeah, right. You mean to tell me you couldn't find any place else to crash? Ya full of shit, and I'll tell you why: I know that you been creepin' because Karen told me so. Then you had the audacity to lie and bring my name into it!"

Armando turned to face Drake, wishing he would say something to defuse the situation. Drake only stood there with crossed arms and a smile on his face.

"Drake, you tell him that we ain't been doin' nothin'!"

Drake turned his attention to Armando and smiled even more brightly as though he were enjoying the exchange.

"You know, Armando, I love it when you flip between talking ghetto and standard English. That's so cute."

Don rolled his eyes, exasperated at being dragged into this. "See there, what did I tell you, girl? Drake ain't tryin' to take none of y'all fools seriously. Y'all are jokes to him.

Girl, let's go!" Don reached and placed his arms around Cabrien's shoulders to lead him to the door. There was an angry buzz pulsating through Cabrien's body that made Don pull back.

"I beg your pardon," Drake said angrily to Don.

"You heard me, bitch! I warned Cabrien about your ass. I don't appreciate how you've been doggin' my best friend when you know he's caught feelings for you. Cabrien, come on!"

Don went to pull on Cabrien's shirt again, but Cabrien pulled away.

"This ain't over. You best believe this ain't over. You wait until I tell my cousin you've been getting down a man!"

"Listen, you pillow-biting homo, I ain't creeping around fucking dudes, and you better not tell Karen anything!" Armando shouted, moving closer to Cabrien.

Ordinarily, Cabrien might have been alarmed at Armando's threatening stance. But he was angry at being disrespected. "Or what? What's your punk-ass gonna do?" Cabrien stood facing Armando, looking straight at him.

Armando slapped Cabrien, causing him to fall back.

"Hold up, *you're* the punk, nigga! If you say anything to Karen about this, I swear I will kill you! Do you hear me? If you say anything, they won't be able to find you!" Armando's eyes flashed. Grabbing Cabrien by the neck, he lifted Cabrien from the floor and punched him in the nose. Don let out murderous screams for Armando to stop.

"Stop it! You're killing him! Oh, Lawd have mercy!" Don screamed.

"Naw, I'm beatin' that ass!" Armando roared, the veins

in his neck beginning to show and sweat beading on his forehead.

"Your ass is grass, do you hear me? Drake, I'll talk to your bitch-ass later, but Armando—your ass is grass!" Cabrien screamed, staggering away as he put the back of his hand to his bleeding nose.

"Get out of my house!" Drake demanded.

"Yeah, take your faggot-ass on home, Cabrien! And I meant what I said about what you can expect if you say anything to Karen!" Armando called out as Cabrien and Don advanced toward the door.

Tears streamed down Cabrien's face as he allowed himself to be led out of the apartment by Don, who by this point could say nothing.

When Cabrien and Don left, Armando could feel the warmth of anger in his face. Drake unfolded his arms and walked to lock the door.

"He better not say anything," Armando repeated to Drake.

"He won't say anything. Look, he's hurt and he's pissed that you're here and he's not."

"Dude, you better check your boy!"

"All right, fine. I'll call him tomorrow and talk to him."

"You'd better do more than that, Drake, otherwise I'll break *both* of your necks."

"Don't threaten me."

"Whatever, dude. You better put that nigga in his place!" Armando sat back down on the sofa and put his hands over his face. This ordeal was spiraling further out of control. He sat there for a brief moment as Drake decided that he had had enough drama for one evening.

"I'm going to bed," Drake said simply.

"Yeah? Well, I'm leaving."

"You're going to go over there now?"

"I wouldn't have to if he didn't come over here talking shit! I gotta try and fix this, Drake. I love Karen. She's all I have and I'm not going to lose her over this."

"Fine," Drake said. "Turn out the lights when you leave."

Armando went into the bedroom and continued gathering his things, putting them into his bag. He didn't say anything else to Drake. He was angry that he'd allowed his judgment to become corrupted by greed. He was angry he hadn't had enough faith in his relationship with Karen. After all that had happened, hearing her scream at him about losing his job seemed like a better alternative to the mess he created. When it was all said and done, Armando really had no one to blame for this but himself and he knew it.

When Armando left Drake's apartment, he felt freed from prison. As he went downstairs in the elevator, four words kept playing hauntingly in his head like an annoying song that he couldn't get out of his mind... *"Your ass is grass!"*

CHAPTER TWENTY-EIGHT

Gary awoke, having tossed and turned most of the night. He found Wanda sitting at the kitchen island reading the newspaper, glancing up to look at the headlines from the morning news program on TV. She was already on her second cup of coffee as Gary dragged himself to the seat next to her.

"Good morning," Wanda said cheerfully.

"Morning," Gary said, reaching for the coffeepot and pouring himself a cup, making sure he didn't spill any on the marble countertop.

"You look a mess," Wanda said.

"Thank you for your honesty," he replied sarcastically. Gary sipped his coffee, enjoying its rich aroma.

"Gary, what are you doing? You can't drink that. Remember your colonoscopy?"

"Damn, that's right. Okay, I think I've officially become senile." Gary put the mug down and looked at the TV just in time to see the news program break for commercial.

"So how long will you need to be at the office before I pick you up to take you to the hospital?"

"You can wait for me in the car. I'm going to just run

in and leave the letter on Bruce's desk. I figure that way there's less of a chance of him trying to talk me out of it because I'll be long gone by the time he gets it."

"I still think you're making a big mistake," Wanda said.

"Did I ask for the commentary? Can't you just support me?" Gary asked with hurt in his voice.

"You want me to support foolishness? I watched you work hard for years to build a name for yourself. I spent countless nights without a husband, and your daughter went without her father so that you could one day have an opportunity like this. And now you want to throw it away because all of a sudden you can't take the pressure?"

"If it was meant to be then it would've happened for me by now."

"You've wasted so much time shucking and jiving. Before, at least I could say that this chance of a lifetime made it all worth it. Now I don't even have that," Wanda snapped.

"Whoa, was I doing this for me or for *you*?" Gary asked sharply.

"Oh, I suppose you still think this is just about you. Guess your family isn't even worth the consideration," Wanda said, arching one perfect eyebrow.

"You just have to start this morning, don't you?"

"I'm going to take a shower," Wanda said as she took her cup of coffee and newspaper and left the room.

Later, when Wanda drove Gary to the office, there was none of her usual playfulness. The entire ride downtown was set in stony silence. When Gary leaned in to kiss her lips, she quickly turned so that his lips met her cheek. Gary knew she was still angry with him, but he had enough on his mind. She didn't understand where he was coming

from, that was obvious. Did she really care about what this decision had done to him? It hadn't been easy, but it was necessary if he was to maintain his sanity. As far as he was concerned, Wanda would just have to learn to understand that.

After getting out of the car, Gary turned once more to look at Wanda, to perhaps catch a small glint of last minute support, but she turned away, leaving him to make his mistake.

When Gary got to his floor, he was met with a disheveled Stewart McKillen pacing back and forth in front of his office. Bernice looked thankful that Gary arrived when he did.

"Mr. Walsh, he won't leave. He said that it was urgent he speak to you. He had this real crazy look in his eyes. I didn't know if I could trust him," she said, shaking her head as though she had just witnessed something unsightly.

"Bernice, it's all right, I know him." Gary grabbed Stewart by the arm and escorted him into his office.

"You're scaring the staff," Gary said sharply.

"Where in the hell were you last night?" Stewart countered.

"I had some pressing business that I thought was a little more important than your pity party." Gary went to close the door as soon as Stewart was inside the office.

"You promised me that you'd come over and you didn't. That's no way to act; no way to treat your friend."

"Stewart, I don't have time for this shit. You look horrible. You stink like alcohol. Whatever is going on with you is a lot heavier than anything my sitting up with you could ever solve."

"Big deal, I was out all night. Sue me. It was a whole lot better than being cooped up in that hotel room waiting for your black ass to show up!"

"Life is full of disappointment. I'm surprised that after all of these years you've not learned that." Gary stopped for a moment and took a deep breath. "Look, I'm sorry I didn't make it back. Okay? I told you, this isn't the best time for me," Gary said, thinking about his wife sitting out in the car waiting for him.

Stewart spoke quickly. "I'm drowning, Gary. Don't you understand that? Everything is so dark. I feel as though I'm swimming as fast and as hard as I can, and I can see the lighthouse is getting close. But then as soon as I get near it, something makes the darkness grow and I'm start-ing all over again. I can't do it by myself."

Gary stood silent. Never had he seen anyone who seemed so lost.

"I just need someone to help the pain go away. Can't you understand that?" Stewart said, his eyes welling with his tears.

Gary helped Stewart to a chair and sat him down. He knelt and put his arm on Stewart's shoulder. He was being pulled in deeper than he'd expected. *All I wanted to do was give Bruce this damn letter. Now I'm going to have to hear Wanda's mouth,* Gary thought to himself.

"Just let it out. Everything is going to be all right, Stu."

"It's just so hard. Nobody told me that my life was going to be so hard!"

"Life has to be hard sometimes. Otherwise we'd never appreciate all the good that's in it." Gary began to hurt a little for his friend. He was ashamed for being so wrapped up in his own problems that he couldn't see there was

someone obviously going through worse. "I want you to promise me that when you get back to California, you'll go and see a therapist. Only then can you begin to heal, Stu."

Slowly Stewart raised his head and nodded that yes, he would promise to see a therapist. Gary opened the door to signal the end of the conversation. Suddenly, as if cued in a stage direction, Drake Hill appeared at the door.

"Hey, Gary, I have a report for the quarter that you might want to look at."

Gary looked up at Drake with suspicious eyes, his dislike for him barely concealed.

"Just put it down."

Drake came in and set the document down on the corner of Gary's desk, turning to see Stewart. Stewart looked up.

"Drake?" Stewart said, startled.

"Yeah?"

"Don't you remember me?"

Drake's face was blank.

"I met you in New York, in the summer of 1983."

Suddenly Drake's face showed recognition. "Oh, hey, how's it going?"

Stewart folded his arms, glaring at Drake. "Wow. I would've thought you'd remember more readily than that since it was you who turned me gay."

Gary's eyes widened. "Why don't I just leave you two alone?" he said, seizing the opportunity to leave. "I have to stop by Mr. Hedrick's office. Just close the door when you guys are done. Stewart, I meant what I said. You go talk to a professional first thing when you get back to California."

"You mean I won't see you again before I leave?" Stewart asked, puzzled.

"No. I have a doctor's appointment. Wanda's waiting downstairs to take me."

"Are you all right?"

"It's just a colonoscopy." Gary turned to Drake, who was still amazed to find Stewart McKillen in the same room with him. "Oh, by the way, Drake, try not to delete any more files from my computer."

"I don't know what you mean,"

"Why doesn't that surprise me?" Gary said as he left, closing the door behind him.

Drake stood there looking at Stewart, who tried to gather his composure.

"I must look awful," Stewart said, laughing awkwardly.

"You've looked better."

"You might show a little more compassion, Drake. I would still be married if you hadn't seduced me into this lifestyle."

"Lifestyle? That's funny."

"Ruining people's marriages is funny to you?"

"Look, don't put whatever baggage you have on me, okay? You were a grown man and you knew what you wanted. As I remember, you were willing to leave your wife to play house with me, so I think your gayness was what the insurance companies call a preexisting condition. I didn't make you do anything that you didn't want to do."

"Yeah, and I'm still paying for that sin."

"You just let me know when I'm supposed to start feeling sorry for you. I was a kid, okay. I had just graduated college and was out there living my life. We had something going for a while, then it started not to be fun and I ended it, which happens, Stewart."

"I see you haven't changed. You're still the same cold hearted asshole you were then."

"If you haven't made peace with the fact that you like men, then that's your problem, not mine."

"But you could at least apologize for being so cruel to me. After you left the sublet that last time, I never heard from you again. You could've at least told me goodbye."

"Would that make you feel better?" Drake asked, exasperated and angry that Gary had left him alone with Stewart.

"It's a start."

Drake stood there and put on a smile. Then he said, "I'm sorry if you feel I hurt you 25 years ago. I had no idea that I would be confronted with how bad life has treated you, but now that I am, I am so sorry, Stewart."

"Liar," Stewart said, shaking his head.

Drake was silent again. This wasn't how he had anticipated spending his day. Last night was a rocky one, and he didn't want to start his work day with more tension. "If you feel that I offended you, then I apologize. I mean it. Maybe I could have been a little more sympathetic to you during that time. I had no idea it would have affected you like this for so long, so, I'm really sorry."

Stewart studied Drake's face for signs of phoniness and decided that Drake was being sincere.

"Thank you for that, Drake."

"I am sorry," Drake repeated.

The two men were quiet for a moment. Stewart felt as though he'd gotten some closure, but only a little bit.

"So why did you come to Minneapolis?" Drake asked, breaking the silence.

"I wanted to see Gary. I've been going through some

things and he's my best friend. I thought that maybe he could help me through it."

"Wow. You put all of your faith in Gary Walsh? And did he help you through it?"

"He did the best he could," Stewart said carefully.

"I didn't think so," Drake said smugly, folding his arms.

Drake was tired of standing and sat on the corner of Gary's desk, right on top of the document he had put there.

"Are you seeing anyone?" Drake asked, unfolding his arms so that he could balance himself on the desk.

"No. You?" Stewart asked, hoping that Drake would say no.

"Actually I'm working on someone. A straight guy. I must have a magnet that says, 'If you're straight step on up,'" Drake laughed at his joke.

Stewart didn't laugh. "Oh really? So what's the problem?"

"Did I say there was a problem? I'm having the time of my life."

He probably looks like me. Drake can fake the funk all he wants to. He knows perfectly well that he loved me, Stewart thought before asking, "What does he look like?"

"He's got these magnificent gray eyes. I've never seen eyes on a black guy like that before. They're almost cat-like." Drake talked happily on and on about his latest acquisition. But Stewart's throat started to close up and his heart began racing. After hearing the words "magnificent gray eyes," he stopped listening.

"Well, I guess I should be getting back to work," Drake said finally, unaware that Stewart hadn't heard much of what he said.

"Sure, I understand. It was good to see you, Drake. You

seem to have done well for yourself." Stewart rose from his chair and extended his hand to Drake, who looked as though he'd rather not touch it, but smiled politely and shook it. It was then that Stewart realized that Drake had not been sincere about anything he had said.

As Drake turned to walk away, Stewart felt his very essence disintegrating. He followed Drake out of the office, closing Gary's door. Drake walked briskly away, never once looking back to see Stewart watching him. Stewart stood there until Drake was out of sight and then in an instant, the color of the real world began to return. He felt he'd had an out-of-body experience, like when he was in the back room at The Black Out stuffing his dick into the mouth of strangers.

As Stewart walked down the street, he came across a sign that advertised a hotline for depression. As he peered intently at it, a man moved closer to him, and tapped him on the shoulder.

"Hey, dude, how's it going?" the man asked.

"Hey," Stewart said.

"Do you wanna score a little something?"

"What?"

"Do you wanna score something?" The man repeated in a raspy voice.

Stewart looked at the man, who looked to be in his early twenties. He had on baggy jeans and an outdated jean jacket, greasy-looking hair matted to his head. His eyes were dead.

"I got some bangin' coke," the young man said, putting his index finger under his nose and inhaling shallowly.

"No thanks," Stewart said and began to walk away.

The man watched as Stewart made his way done the city block, calling out, "Suit yourself."

Stewart got to the end of the block. He couldn't deny how badly he felt. He felt as though he was being squeezed and his energy was depleted. And he was sad again. Stewart slowly turned back around, and walked back toward the man, who was leering at him.

"How much do you have?" Stewart asked in a conspiratorial whisper.

The man smiled broadly, exposing more gums than teeth. He pulled a small bag of powder from his jacket, dangling it in front of Stewart. "You look so sad. Allow me to fix that."

CHAPTER
TWENTY-NINE

"In the case of three month old Brina, Clark—*You are not the father!*" The fickle studio audience's jeers and boos of condemnation that had antagonized the young man, quickly shifted to Brina's mother. Clark danced a jig of vindication while the humiliated young woman bolted from her seat and ran backstage. The ending to this tale was a common one on these daytime talk shows. And Karen never tired of them. At least Karen had known her baby's father when she'd decided to abort it; Armando never knew about the baby. But her mother did and it was the main reason for the tension between them. Her mother never forgave her for murdering her grandchild, and Karen never forgave her mother for never letting her forget.

Thinking about the abortion depressed her, so she got up and poured herself another cup of coffee. The instant coffee her mother, Thelma, had wasn't the best, but it gave her the early morning jolt she needed.

Thelma walked with a heavy tread into the living room of her ranch-style home. Her posture was somewhat stooped as though she carried everyone's troubles on her shoulders. *Martyr-in-chief*, Karen thought to herself, and

then picked up the latest issue of *Black Hair* from the end table. She admired the regal bearing of one of the models who wore a crown of braids.

"Mama, I'm thinking about getting braids; maybe do like a snake coil braid." Karen made circular motions with her index finger around the crown of her head to give her mother a visual.

"Oh girl, you don't want to put those big ol' things on your head! It'll make your head look so big!" Thelma said, critically. "They don't even use human hair with that. You know the stuff they use for those ropes to anchor boats, that's what they use for that. Don't put that on your head," Thelma warned.

Karen turned her attention back to the show and saw the host consoling the young woman and telling her they could help her find the real father of her child, while on split screen, Clark was still dancing and hamming it up for the studio audience, shaking hands with people who only minutes before were booing him.

"Cut that foolishness off," Thelma snapped.

"C'mon, Mama, I like this show," Karen pleaded like a little girl.

"Then go to your house and watch that stuff. You know how I feel about children born out of wedlock. But at least she *had* the baby."

Thelma, having said all she wanted to on the subject, left the room and went into the kitchen to pour herself coffee. Karen, quietly stung at her mother's words, obediently turned off the TV and followed her.

"Are you going to see Ruby again today?" Karen asked, watching her mother put creamer into her cup.

"Yeah, I'm going back there. You know, it's sad that we

have all of these illegal immigrants here in this country. They were the ones who hit my baby. Neither one of them had a driver's license, nor was it their car. Plus, the guy whose car it is ain't even got any insurance."

"How do you know that?"

"I talked to the police."

"When did you talk to them?"

"It was sometime after you left that first night. I'm just glad they caught the sorry suckers!"

"That's good that they caught them," Karen agreed.

"And to think that they just ran off like that. My baby was laying there half-dead, and they ran off because they didn't want to take responsibility for anything!"

"That's fucked up!"

"Watch your mouth, girl," Thelma snapped. "The Lord resides in this house. I ain't one of your friends. You understand me?"

"Yes, ma'am."

"Where's Armando's no-good butt?"

"I kicked him out, but he's been blowing up my phone."

"And you ain't called him back yet? This must be the end of days!" Thelma chuckled.

Karen was happy that she was able to get a chuckle out of her mother, even if it was at Armando's expense. She loved Armando and missed the way things used to be, but she hated him for lying and for having an affair. The last thing she wanted to do was open a door of opportunity for her mother to say, "I told you so," even though she thought she deserved it.

"Call the boy," Thelma said, looking down at her unopened mail.

"I don't know if I want to."

"Well, then, he will just keep on calling you and leaving you messages. I'd call your father if he was ringing my phone like that." She looked up toward the ceiling and placed her fingers to her lips kissing them and released them, sending love to her deceased husband.

"Don't know why you're doing all that, Daddy cheated on you too," Karen said.

"Call the boy! You're not gonna hear me say that too often, either." Thelma got up, taking her coffee with her.

Karen watched as her mother disappeared around the corner, then she glanced at her cell phone. If Armando called again, she would take the call. But the next call was from someone else.

"Hello?"

"Girl, I'm glad I got a hold of you. Are you at home?" It was Cabrien.

"No, I'm at my mama's house. Why do you sound funny?"

"Girl, we need to talk."

"About what?" Karen asked.

"About your man. Why was he over at Drake's last night?" Cabrien asked in a frenzied voice.

"Who is Drake?"

"You know. That man you met at the bar with me and Armando. You remember him?"

Karen closed her eyes and tried to place the name with a face. There'd been a lot of people there that night, and all she remembered distinctly was dancing with Cabrien and watching that drag queen.

"I don't remember who you're talking about, Cabrien."

"Girl, I'm talking about that man who was trying to talk to Armando," Cabrien responded impatiently.

"Oh, yeah, the one who was making Armando uncomfortable?"

"Yep, that's who I'm talking about. Well, girl, it seems that Drake's found a way to make your man comfortable, because he was over there last night."

Karen felt her mouth become suddenly dry. "What are you trying to say?" Karen asked, her voice agitated

"I'm saying that your man has been creepin,'" Cabrien said, as though it should've been obvious to Karen all along.

"Armando ain't like that! And I can't believe that you of all people would come to me with something like this!"

"I'm dead serious, girl! I know it hurts to hear your man is on the DL, but it hurts me worse to be the one to tell you."

"Cabrien, I'm gonna hang up this phone," Karen said as the feeling of moistness returned to her mouth.

"You know good and well that I wouldn't even come to you with anything like this if it weren't true. I saw him sitting on the couch with my own two eyes, Karen." Cabrien was surprised that Karen wasn't accepting what he was telling her.

"You know what, Cabrien? I should've never brought your faggot-ass around my man. That's why your ass been coming by the apartment, because you've been trying to get with him!" Karen was screaming into her phone.

"You're starting to show your ass now, bitch! You sound like that homophobic mammy of yours!"

"It all makes sense now. Armando said that you came over and took him to the club when I was out there working. Instead of partying and shaking your ass all the damn time, why don't you find your own man?"

Cabrien's voice trembled with emotion. "Okay, fine! If you don't want to believe that your man is out there fucking around on you, then so be it. But you're gonna be a sorry sistah when you have to come crawling back this way wanting to apologize and I tell you to go to hell!"

"I ain't ever going to apologize to you, Cabrien. You're nasty. My mama and everybody else had been trying to tell me that. I can't believe it...my own cousin, trying to get with my man!"

"I don't want your man, Karen. I wanted Drake. That is until I saw your faggot boyfriend over his house. Yes, I called him a faggot. Since you like dropping that word, use it on him!"

Thelma came from the other room. Her face displayed disbelief at the bad language her daughter was using.

"Who are you yelling at?" Thelma asked.

"I'm yelling at your punk-ass nephew!" Karen said, realizing she was probably in for a lecture from her mother.

"Hang up," Thelma said calmly as she took the cell phone from Karen and ended the call.

Karen's throat was raw from screaming. She tried to calm down as her mother gave the phone back to her.

"You had no business talking to him anyway," Thelma said, shaking her head as she left the room again.

Karen knew she'd crossed the line by calling Cabrien a faggot. He had confided in her long ago that his mother and her boyfriends used to call him that when they were drunk and the boyfriends' friends were around. Because he'd been called that word throughout much of his life, he made her promise that no matter how angry they became at each other, she would never call him that.

Karen had broken her promise. But she felt justified. Armando loved women too much to even consider being with another man. She'd spent years as his lover, and she knew how passionate he was with her. If Armando was into men, how could he have maintained an erection all of those times they'd been together? And there was also the night the three of them had gone to Sir Martin's; she remembered how awkward Armando had been. No, there was absolutely no way there could be any truth to what Cabrien said. It was evil for him to say it. He just wanted Armando for himself, she thought. But that wasn't going to happen.

She silently thanked Cabrien for providing her with the reason to patch things up with her man...Better her with Armando than Cabrien.

In the same silence, she shed tears to mourn the passing of her relationship with her favorite cousin. As far as she was concerned, Cabrien LeAnthony Jacobs was dead to her.

There were none of the usual sounds and scents when Armando awoke in his bed. There wasn't the sizzle of bacon, or the aroma of gourmet coffee sifting through its filter. The apartment was cold and empty because Karen wasn't there.

Armando got out of bed uncertain of what lay ahead. But he held steadfastly to the hope that she'd forgive all that he did, and that her love would be stronger than any of the problems they faced. He also knew there was a chance she'd want nothing else to do with him. But he put that thought away for now and proceeded with his day.

After showering and dressing, he went to Bachman's flower shop to find the perfect bouquet of white and red roses as a symbol of his love, and a peace offering. He was going to ask Karen to marry him and buy the ring later when he had more money.

After putting the roses in the car, he dialed Drake's number.

"Did you talk to Cabrien?" Armando asked as soon as Drake said hello.

"Not yet."

"Well, don't you think you better get a move on it?"

"Armando, Cabrien isn't going to say anything. He doesn't want to risk hurting your girlfriend, and he doesn't want to ruin whatever chance he thinks he has with me," Drake said with his typical arrogance.

"Talk to his ass anyway, Drake," Armando said, still unconvinced.

"All right, I'll call him and ask him to meet me for drinks or something. You haven't talked to Karen yet?"

"Nope. She wasn't home last night and she hasn't returned any of my calls. What if he's already gotten to her?"

"Try to calm down. If he hasn't talked to her yet then he probably isn't going to."

"All I wanted to do was give her a better life," Armando murmured into the phone.

"Well, Armando, you know what they say. No good deed goes unpunished."

CHAPTER THIRTY

"Mrs. Walsh?" The figure in the white coat stood over Wanda as she tried to read her magazines.

"Yes?" Wanda said.

"I'm Dr. Fortier and I performed the colonoscopy on your husband. Everything looked pretty good. There was slight inflammation, but nothing I'd be worried about."

A wave of relief washed over Wanda. The tension that had been building in anticipation of bad news slowly dissipated.

"Is he asleep?" she asked, rising.

"No, he's awake. He's in the recovery room." He helped Wanda out of her seat.

"May I see him?"

"Absolutely."

Dr. Fortier walked Wanda toward the recovery room. Her raspberry blouse was a cheerful burst of color under the stark white fluorescent lights.

"Your blouse is beautiful," the doctor said to Wanda. She thanked him. She began to wonder how many people had entered this hospital never to come out alive, and was thankful that her husband wouldn't be one of them anytime soon.

When Wanda got to the recovery room, she looked

across a sea of people. At the end of the room, she saw Gary sitting upright, drinking ginger ale from a straw in a small plastic cup, clutching a graham cracker cookie in his hand as though someone was going to tear it from his grasp. Gary had never looked more worn out. Wanda pulled up a chair to his bed and sat.

"How are you feeling, sweetheart?"

Gary shrugged.

A Latina nurse came by, passing them once and then after checking the clip board, returned.

"Gary Walsh, I'm Yolanda Diaz. I'll be assisting you with your release."

Wanda looked up and noticed how exhausted the woman looked.

"Are you the wife?"

"Yes, I'm his wife."

"Okay, good. He's not going to remember much, so it is important that you fill him in on everything he's going to need to do." The nurse turned to Gary. "How are you feeling, Gary?"

"A little groggy, but mostly I'm hungry. These cookies aren't that good." Gary flicked the crumpled plastic wrap that the crackers had been in into his empty drinking cup.

The nurse, pulling the papers from her clipboard, arranged them neatly inside of a folder bearing the hospital's name. "Okay, your job today is to fart. You'll need to fart like you've never farted before."

Wanda wondered if the nurse had been waiting all day to say that.

"I'm serious. You have a lot of gas built up in you, so don't be afraid of it, just let it all out."

Wanda began to gather up Gary's things. "What else?"

"If he has any blood or discharge then he needs to contact us right away," the nurse said, removing the IV from Gary's hand, then she dabbed the specks of blood that remained after pulling out the IV. Gary winced with discomfort. The nurse handed Wanda the folder.

"Can you remember anything, baby?" Wanda asked stroking Gary's forehead.

"He's not going to remember anything. The Versed *really* fogs people over, so you don't have to worry about him having any memory of the procedure."

"The Versed? What's that?"

"The drug we administered before the procedure." The nurse smiled at Wanda and Gary, and then walked out of the area, forcefully shutting the curtain behind her.

Though the timing was less than ideal, Wanda wanted to know if Gary had gone ahead with his decision to decline the promotion. "You aren't going to work tomorrow, are you?"

"I don't know," Gary said as he repositioned himself to be more comfortable.

"What do you think Mr. Hedrick will say to you when he reads that you're taking yourself from the running?"

Gary stared at her with confusion.

"You *did* deliver your letter, didn't you?"

Again Gary stared at her as though he had no idea what she was talking about.

"That's okay. We can talk about that later."

CHAPTER
THIRTY-ONE

"Cabrien, you didn't!" Drake said in disbelief.

"I sure as hell did!" Cabrien shot back.

"Well, what did she say?"

"The bitch didn't believe me. Can you believe that shit? My own flesh and blood picked her man over me! She's just like my damn mama!"

Drake hadn't given the altercation from the previous evening any more thought, until Armando called him that morning demanding he do something about the situation. As Drake spoke to Cabrien, the prospect of everything working out diminished.

"Don't you realize what you've done? You very well could've killed any chance of Armando and his girlfriend getting back together."

"I told you she didn't believe me. Anyway, why are *you* so worried about whether or not they do? You weren't all that concerned when y'all were up in the bed together!"

Drake decided not to quarrel with Cabrien. He had to do something to get things back to normal if he were to continue his relationship with Armando. What difference would it make if Armando was back with Karen, as long as

he was still able to convince him that the money was too good to turn down? Right now, Cabrien was becoming an irritant.

"I wouldn't assume that Karen didn't believe you. She may not let on that she knows, but I'm sure that she does on an intuitive level," Drake said.

"So why are you calling me with this?"

"Well, I thought about what you said about us being together. I think maybe you were right. I had taken you for granted."

"Oh? All of a sudden you had a change of heart?" Cabrien's voice was drenched in sarcasm.

"Yes. Look, you know I like variety in my life. But I see where it's gotten me, and I hurt people. It's time to stop being selfish for a change."

"What do you want me to do?" Cabrien said, becoming seduced by Drake's phony selflessness.

"I need you to call Karen and tell her it was a mistake. Lie if you have to, but make it good."

"Absolutely not! She called me a faggot, and that's where I draw the line!"

"Just tell her you were drunk last night and mistakenly thought it was Armando," Drake suggested.

"I know what I saw."

Drake put the phone down and began massaging his temples. This was more stress than he needed. He picked the phone up again, in time to hear Cabrien going on about how Karen would need to make the first move if they were ever going to reconcile their differences, and that he was tired of constantly being the one to right the wrongs in his relationships with people.

Drake listened with increasing disinterest, waiting for

an opportunity to respond. "Okay, then do this; why don't you meet me tonight at Sir Martin's? We can sit and have a drink and maybe come up with something together."

"I drank last night."

"So you'll drink again tonight. It's not like it's the first time you had a drink two nights running."

Cabrien began to think about the proposition. He was still angry with Drake for what he did, but maybe when they were together, he would be able to persuade Drake to talk about the possibility of a real relationship between them.

"And then when we've handled all of that other stuff, can we talk about us?"

"Yeah, of course," Drake said as sincerely as he could.

Cabrien beamed from ear to ear. "Good. What time should I meet you?"

"Oh, I don't know. Maybe 5:00 PM?"

"Yeah, I think I can do that," Cabrien responded, his hopes soaring.

"All right, five it is then."

Cabrien hung up the phone and jumped out of bed. Just hearing that Drake would meet him for drinks seemed to bring a burst of sunshine to an otherwise gloomy day. There was still the issue of having to clean up what he told Karen about Armando, but if doing so meant having Drake with him, and the stability of being with someone who actually cared about him, he would swallow his pride and do it.

Cabrien was not entirely foolish. He knew that although Drake seemed to be willing to entertain the idea of a relationship, that didn't lessen his desire for Armando.

Cabrien went into his bathroom and looked inside his

medicine cabinet. He pushed aside the MAC cosmetics and astringents to find a small contact lenses case sitting far in the back. In it soaked a pair of gray lenses that he hadn't worn in some time. He had been through a variety of phases where his look was concerned, and part of that evolution was wearing lighter-colored eye colors to contrast against his dark chocolate complexion. He washed his hands thoroughly and fished the lenses out of the case. He rubbed saline solution from the near-empty bottle he had and carefully put the lenses into his eyes.

Cabrien looked at himself admiringly and said out loud, "If Drake is turned on by gray eyes, then that is what he's gonna get!"

Armando paced back and forth in the living room, hoping Karen would be home soon. When she walked through the door, he wanted everything he said to sound perfect. He was so nervous that he began to talk to himself as though Karen were in the room with him. He practiced getting down on one knee and proposing to her. But then he got up quickly, thinking that perhaps he ought to start out by taking responsibility for the fight in the first place. He wouldn't bring up his previous money making scheme. However, he vowed from this day forward to be honest about everything so there would never again be a rift in their relationship. He was making himself more jumpy than he had been in awhile. Even his sleeping with Drake had not made him as nervous as thinking about proposing to Karen.

Just when Armando thought he was going nuts from

the waiting, Karen walked into the apartment. She had a funny look on her face.

"Karen, baby, I'm so glad you're back."

Seeing Armando again felt good, even though it had only been a day and a half. But, all of a sudden she remembered Cabrien's phone call. "Do you know what that no good cousin of mine did?"

Armando's heart began to pound almost audibly in his chest as he shook his head.

"He called to tell me that he saw you over at that man's house, that you two had been...hell, I can't even repeat what he said," Karen said as she sat next to Armando.

"You must not believe whatever it was he told you," Armando said, studying Karen's face.

"Hell no, I don't believe that. I told Cabrien that you're *all* man, and that you wouldn't do anything like that. I figured he was probably trying to get with you and told me that bullshit in hopes of clearing a path for himself."

Armando began to smile. This was going to be easier than he'd thought. "Well, I didn't want to say anything, but that time that I went to the bar with him, he did try and come on to me."

"See, I knew he was grimy like that. I just didn't expect that he'd do something like that to me. That's why after he called me with that, I decided to come home."

"I'm glad you did, baby," Armando said, taking her hand.

"It's funny. It took someone trying to steal you away from me to make me realize how much you really mean to me." Karen looked at Armando warmly.

"Karen, I'm sorry that I didn't tell you about losing the

job. I should've trusted and believed in us more. I guess it's a male ego thing."

"After all we've been through, Armando, you should've known that I would have your back. Yeah, I may have screamed and yelled, but that's just me. But you should've known that I wasn't going anywhere."

"I'm just glad you're here now. No more secrets. I promise," Armando said, hugging her tightly. He had missed the delicacy of her petite body close to him.

Karen got up, sad that she would no longer have her cousin to confide in, to dish dirt with or share in the happiness of having her man back. Ironically, she wanted to thank him. If he hadn't called her to tell her that Armando was at Drake's, she probably would've stayed miserable at her mother's. Karen turned to walk away, and Armando grabbed her hand. He reached for the flowers on the coffee table.

"I want to do this the right way, Karen. I don't want there to be anything that pushes us apart again."

"Oh, sweetie, they're beautiful," Karen said, lifting the bouquet to her nose to smell them.

"Will you marry me, baby?"

"Don't act stupid, boy. You know damn well that I'll marry you!" She smiled while her eyes teared over.

Later they made love, never taking their eyes from each other until their bodies were exhausted from pleasuring each other. Armando rested well, believing he would be sharing the rest of his life with Karen. They dreamed of only beautiful things that night, innocent of what was to come.

CHAPTER
THIRTY-TWO

Wanda had just given Gary chicken noodle soup, and put him to bed, when the phone rang.

"Well, hello, stranger," Wanda answered cheerfully after noticing Bruce Hedrick's name on the caller ID.

"Ah, Wanda! How are you?"

"Still receiving God's favor."

"And you know there's nothing wrong with a sprinkle of God's favor!"

Both of them chuckled politely. Then Bruce said, "How did everything go with Gary?"

"It went well. Dr. Fortier said there was a little inflammation. Nothing to get bent out of shape about."

"Glad to hear that. I just want to thank God for the good news, and I pray that He keeps Gary healthy."

"Thank you, Mr. Hedrick. Frankly, Gary needs all the prayers and positive energy he can get, generally speaking. But, I know he can handle anything he puts his mind to."

"Oh, I have every faith of that. Working with him as I have, I've seen that fire in him."

"Me, too."

Bruce became quiet for two beats, and then he said,

"Forgive me for saying this because it isn't the most appropriate time, but maybe you could help me wrap my mind around why Gary left this note in my office."

Wanda heard the crinkling of the letter on Bruce's end of the line. "What does it say?"

"Oh, just about how he respects me, and doesn't want to make a mockery out of what I worked so hard to create. Does he really believe that?"

Wanda was silent as her mind began to churn, thinking of something to say.

"Hello?"

"I'll say this: Gary meant what he said about his respect for you. He really does hold you in high esteem. Since he's been working with you, whenever he's had tough decisions to make, the first thing out of his mouth is, 'what would Mr. Hedrick do?'"

"Really?"

"Yes, Gary thinks of you as the father figure he missed out on. He'd been estranged from his father for twenty-five years. Working closely with you inspired him to reconnect with his father, and the two of them have never been closer."

"Wow. Gary never told me that. I'm flattered."

"You should be. You have been a powerful force in my husband's life, and I'd like to thank you for giving him a sense of purpose. And the good news is that just before he went under for his procedure, I could tell he was having second thoughts about writing you that letter."

"Really?"

"Absolutely. All I had to do was look into his eyes and I knew."

"Yes, but what I'd like to know is what would make him start doubting himself in the first place?"

"Gosh, Mr. Hedrick," Wanda said with a cautious, yet, coquettish chuckle. "You're putting me in an awfully uncomfortable spot. Gary's told me some things, but I think maybe you should hear them from him. But I *will* say this, other than what is going on behind your back at the BRC, Gary would have *never* withdrawn himself from the running for this job opportunity."

"Wait a minute. What's going on behind my back?"

"I'm sorry, I shouldn't have said anything."

"Well, can I at least speak to Gary?" Bruce asked.

"That isn't possible. He's resting."

"Wanda, with all due respect, you can't just put certain things out on the table and not explain them."

Wanda sighed. "You're right. But can you at least promise me you won't mention any of this to Gary?"

"Absolutely."

"I mean it. My husband can't know we spoke."

"You have my word as a gentleman."

"Actually, I'm glad to get this off my chest." Wanda paused. "Okay. Gary mentioned some conflict he's been having with Drake Hill. But he didn't really go into much detail except to say he thinks Drake was doing something underhanded."

"Gary didn't go into *any* details?"

"No, if anything I think he was just venting. I didn't really pay it much mind at first. But when Gary told me he was thinking about passing up this opportunity, that's when I started putting two and two together."

"And you're certain he spoke of underhandedness where Drake was concerned? Think carefully. It's impor-

tant that I know if I'm going to move on this. This is a serious allegation."

"All I know is that Gary is certain Drake is up to no good. He even thinks Isaac could've made a deal with Drake to have him do some things. But *please* don't tell Gary I told you that."

"I gave you my word. Thank you, Wanda. You've helped me make some sense out of this mess."

"Gary will be resting for a day or two. I'll have him call you when he's up to it."

"I'll look forward to that."

"Mr. Hedrick, my husband is a strong man. Please don't count him out just yet. At least give him the opportunity to talk to you."

"It's nice to know he's rethinking the whole thing. Gary has just as much right to be considered for the job as anyone else. I'm also glad to hear that he's resting."

"Boy, am I glad we had this talk. Gary was right about you."

"In what way?"

"He said that you're very fair. I can see that for myself."

"I appreciate that. I hope you enjoy the rest of your evening."

"I will. You do the same," she said, hanging up and leaning back into the oversize chair that faced the bay window. She picked up her tea and watched the joggers run around Lake Calhoun that faced the front of their property. She had just bought Gary and herself a second chance. A right-wing nut like Isaac Walterson running the BRC? Not if Wanda could have her way.

She did feel a little guilty about the fib she told Mr. Hedrick, though. Gary's father had been dead for years.

CHAPTER THIRTY-THREE

Stewart returned to his hotel room, took out the baggie of coke, and placed it on the edge of the nightstand. Such an insignificant bit of white powder it seemed, but it was just enough for a coke- induced euphoria this last night in Minneapolis.

The trip had been disappointing to say the least. Seeing Drake again was far more bitter than sweet. Drake was just as self-centered as he had remembered. He also wished he'd had gotten more time with Gary. Instead, he'd gotten little more than a pat on the back and insistence that he seek professional help.

Stewart opened the bag and carefully poured the powder onto a magazine. Taking a credit card from his wallet, he separated the coke into two lines. He took out a dollar bill and rolled it tightly enough to snort.

Gary was right, Stewart needed help. But that would have to wait until tomorrow. Tonight he was going to live out the fantasy of being someone else, someone who would toss caution to the wind, abandoning all sense of good judgment. He'd use this last night of freedom to find a man to spend the evening with.

Taking a deep breath, his heart beating faster in anticipation of the altered state to come, Stewart leaned in and snorted a line—then the other.

Soon Stewart became a brand-new man, bold with the bravado to match. He decided to start the evening at Sir Martin's and then, if there wasn't anyone to his taste there, he'd move into the badlands of The BlackOut. Dressed in all black, with his hair faded close, the handsome, put-together façade Stewart created for the evening was ready to meet the world.

He walked into Sir Martin's with two bulges in his pants. One was his wallet full of money to burn on a good time; the second was his hard dick. There were about twenty people in Sir Martin's when he arrived; all looked to be having a good time.

White men in crisp suits sat alone and in groups, holding martinis or wineglasses with the authority of experienced drinkers. Sitting alone was a young black man with gray eyes that could be seen from across the room, thanks largely to the ray of light that fell on him from the bar. The young man checked his watch anxiously, with a perturbed expression on his face. There was an androgynous sensuality to him. His physique was slender, yet toned. Stewart was attracted to him immediately.

Stewart ordered a drink and sat across the bar so that he could watch this amazing- looking young man. He thought it wise to stay clear, at least until he knew whether or not the man was expecting someone.

Cabrien checked his watch for what seemed to be the millionth time, and with every passing second he became angrier. *It's just like Drake to string me along,* he thought to himself. He ran his index finger along his lash line as

the contacts in his eyes began to ache. He attempted to call Drake at 5:30, but it went immediately to voicemail. And he called every ten minutes after that, leaving just as many messages. Now it was 6:23 PM, and it looked as though Drake didn't want to be bothered. Cabrien finally stopped and decided to return to the old tricks of the trade. If he wasn't going to be able to give his heart to the one he loved, he'd sell his ass to the highest bidder; and since the place was filling up nicely, he'd have plenty to choose from.

Usually Cabrien went for the type of man who looked like he needed to pay for sex: the men too shy to interact with anyone, yet lacking the self-esteem to be okay with going home alone. Cabrien noticed a man watching him from across the bar and was struck at how conventionally handsome he was.

With Kanye West's "Stronger" reverberating in the bar. The man walked confidently over to Cabrien. "Where have you been all my life?"

"Is that the best you can do?" Cabrien asked, exasperated.

"Let me buy you a drink, then," the man said, eyeing the almost finished glass in front of Cabrien, and signaling the bartender over.

"How do you even know I want another one?" Cabrien asked as the bartender approached.

"I've been watching you from over there and you look like you could use another drink, and some company."

"I have someone joining me." Cabrien looked at his watch again.

"Really?" Stewart said, shifting his posture. "You've been waiting a long time, haven't you?"

Cabrien took the refreshed drink without thanking

Stewart for it. He looked at Stewart very closely, and liked what he saw, but didn't want to appear desperate.

"I'm Cabrien." He extended his hand to be shaken.

"I'm Stewart." Stewart took Cabrien's hand and kissed it, making Cabrien laugh.

"What's so funny?"

"I wasn't expecting you to kiss my hand. That's cute, though."

"Listen, Cabrien, why don't we finish these drinks and get the hell out of here?" Stewart said, taking both of Cabrien's hands in his own.

"Whoa, you're moving pretty fast, ain't you? You think that just because you bought me a drink, I'm gonna just give up the cakes to you? It's gonna take more than that, baby, trust!"

"What else is it gonna take? I'm sure we can work something out," Stewart said.

"I told you, I'm waiting for someone."

Stewart wasn't about to sit in a bar all night wasting a good high. His sexual longing had been awakened and it had to be satisfied. He was going to figure out how to get Cabrien to leave with him.

"Who are you waiting for?" Stewart asked, looking at Cabrien's profile.

"Why do you need to know?"

"Because I've watched you from over there, and I saw you look at your watch more times in that short while than I've looked at my own this entire trip."

"It's someone I thought I could reconcile things with, okay?" Cabrien shifted the glass back and forth.

"He's an idiot to let someone as fine as you go!"

Cabrien saw a relentless determination in Stewart's

eyes. "I can't just walk away. We have a history together," Cabrien said.

"Take it from someone who knows—you can't make anyone love you."

Cabrien decided to delight in the moment and see where it took him. The next best thing to a heart filled with love was a pocket filled with cash, and since Stewart seemed so adamant about taking Cabrien home with him, he would have to pay for the pleasure.

"So, why don't we get out of here?" Stewart suggested again.

"Hold on a minute. Why don't you tell me a little about yourself?"

"What do you want to know?" Stewart asked, slightly annoyed.

"Where are you from?"

"Here and there," Stewart replied as he put his hands on either side of Cabrien's face to kiss him.

"Back off. You're moving way too fast!" Cabrien snapped, taking Stewart's hands from his face.

"Oh, yeah right. We can wait till we get to the hotel, when we make love."

"Make love? Don't you have to *be* in love to make love?"

Stewart didn't answer the question. "Hey, do you like to party?" he whispered.

Cabrien became uncomfortable with Stewart's dodging his questions. "You see this?" Cabrien picked up his pack of cigarettes from the bar and showed them to Stewart. "I have my cigarettes and my booze and I'm cool. I don't need anything else. Do you?"

"I've tried it."

"Tried what?"

"I did some coke." Stewart spoke as though he were recalling the most amazing experience he'd had to date.

"Do you have some now?"

"What? No, I don't have any now. But, I can have my driver pick me up some just like that," Stewart lied, snapping his fingers.

"A driver? What do you do for a living?" Cabrien asked, his interest refreshed by the mention of a driver.

"I'm a stockbroker," Stewart lied. He was getting comfortable with his alter ego.

"I see." A warm smile glowed on Cabrien's face.

Stewart leaned in again and tried to kiss Cabrien. Again, Cabrien turned away.

"Why won't you kiss me? Does it really matter if we do it here or in a hotel room, watching porn and drinking champagne?"

Cabrien's ears perked up. "Did you say champagne?"

"I sure did."

But then, Cabrien had thoughts of Drake coming briskly through the door, uttering apologies for being kept late by a meeting, or traffic, even though he worked not too far away from Sir Martin's.

"I don't know, maybe I should wait for my friend to come. He might have been stuck in a meeting or something."

Stewart wanted to finally reel him in. "You're going to just let this son of a bitch call *all* of the shots tonight, aren't you? What happened to forgetting about him?" His tone stunned Cabrien for a moment, who had not expected Stewart to turn so hostile.

"Excuse me? You don't know me like that, okay? I don't even let my mama talk to me like that!" Cabrien shot back.

Stewart began to look around the room as though he were trying to find someone from within the growing crowd of people. He looked like he wasn't paying any attention to Cabrien. His stomach began gurgling as though he felt diarrhea coming.

"Did you hear what I said?" Cabrien asked, miffed.

"Be right back," Stewart whispered into Cabrien's ear. Then he got up and went to the bathroom.

Danny the bartender had been making the rounds and heard most of the exchange. Cabrien looked up at Danny, who looked back disapprovingly.

"What do you want to say to me?" Cabrien asked, shrugging his shoulders.

"He seems desperate and messy. You can do better," Danny said.

"Oh chile, please. I don't see Drake bringing his ass in here."

Danny walked away shaking his head as Stewart came back rubbing his nose.

"Before we go any further, I should tell you that if we leave together, it's gonna cost you."

Stewart blinked. "Oh. I didn't have you pegged for one of those."

"One of what?" Cabrien asked sharply.

"A call boy." He looked at Cabrien, imagining the good time they could have together. "How much?"

"Five hundred."

"Five hundred, huh? You must be pretty good if you can get that much."

"Uh, yeah."

Stewart continued, giving Cabrien a full glance before saying, "I think I can handle that. Come on, let's go."

Cabrien smiled broadly, and then gave Danny a look that said "I'll show you," and got up, leaving with his trick of the night. As soon as they got outside, Stewart walked to the curb and began hailing a taxi.

"What are you doing?" Cabrien asked.

"I'm hailing a cab. Why?"

"I thought you had a driver," Cabrien said.

Stewart shrugged his shoulders and giggled.

"I have my car here. You don't need to hail a cab," Cabrien said, slowing his pace as some of his excitement began to wane.

"Lead the way."

Once they got into Cabrien's car, Stewart grinned as he squeezed Cabrien's leg. Cabrien put the key into the ignition, and noticed Stewart was staring straight ahead. Turning the ignition, Cabrien pasted a smile, saying, "You got the money, right? I don't want to end up someplace and you come talking about you ain't got it."

Stewart said, "Of course I got it." He pulled out a wad of money.

Satisfied, Cabrien pulled his car out into the street and said, "Baby, prepare yourself for one hell of a good time!"

CHAPTER
THIRTY-FOUR

Drake was shutting his computer down for the evening when the red light on his office phone flashed, followed by a ring. He let it ring a second time before answering.

"Hello," Drake said.

"I'd like to see you in my office," Bruce said calmly...too calmly. Drake darted from his desk, and walked briskly toward Bruce Hedrick's office.

"Close the door and have a seat," Bruce instructed.

Drake did so obediently.

"I don't know what kind of organization you think I'm trying to run here, but I will not tolerate sabotage."

"I don't think I understand," Drake said.

"Yes, you do." Bruce began to blot himself with a cloth handkerchief.

"What is this about?"

"I have two of the most qualified men up for an important post, and you want to throw a wrench into it because you're jealous?"

"What did Isaac tell you?"

"I know that you went into Gary Walsh's office and

deleted files that were pertinent to this campaign, and then tried to blackmail Isaac into going along with it."

"That's absurd!"

"Is it? Didn't you go to Isaac and tell him that you did this for him so that Gary wouldn't get voted in? And that he had better change his position on gay rights, and that if he didn't go along with it, you would pin the whole thing on him?"

"I only wanted to help him win. That's what people do," Drake reasoned.

"Let's just cut the crap. You've wanted to promote your lifestyle from the very beginning."

"What?"

"You told Isaac that if you helped to vote him in, he would have to rework some of his points regarding the homosexual agenda."

"I find a lot of what he said in his talking points to be revolting. I think if he's going to speak about gay people, he could at the very least speak to someone who is gay!" Drake shot back.

"Yet, you were willing to align yourself with a supposed bigot? That makes no sense whatsoever, Drake!"

"There's more to it than that."

"Look, Drake, live your life the way you want to. You have to be accountable to God on that but..."

Drake looked Bruce squarely in the eyes and said, "My being gay isn't a morality issue, Mr. Hedrick."

"It is too!"

"Really? Then I suppose you think Isaac carrying on with a mistress is just as deplorable, right?"

"What are you talking about?" Bruce said dismissively.

"What am I talking about? I'm talking about Mr. Fam-

ily Values having a sexual relationship with someone other than his wife. Let's not be selective about what you call out as sin, Mr. Hedrick."

"You have no proof of that!"

"Did you just happen to forget what it is you hired me to do here? You hired me to be your attack dog. Surely you know that if I can dredge up dirt on your opponents then I can do the same on one of your executives."

"Why don't you like Gary?" Bruce asked.

"I have my reasons. It goes back a long way. But I'm not going to tell you because, with all due respect, I'm really not interested in whether or not you approve of them."

"I'm not playing games with you, Mr. Hill. You're done here." Bruce's words were as icy as the expression in his eyes.

Drake's stomach dropped. "I'm what?"

"Pack up your things. You don't work here anymore."

"So, you're going to fire the faggot, but keep the philanderer?"

"No, I'm going to talk with Mr. Walterson again. But I cannot in good faith keep you around, knowing what you've been up to. You're dismissed," Bruce said, pointing to the door.

Drake looked at Bruce, waiting for an indication he'd been joking. But the "just kidding" never came. As Drake sat there trying to figure a way out of this situation, he watched Bruce pick up his phone and call for Isaac Walterson.

Years of hard work and loyalty to this enemy faded in front of him. He realized there would be no scheming or maneuvering his way out of it. He thought about the question Armando posed to him the time they were together:

how could he work for people who clearly didn't have his best interest at heart?

Drake rose slowly from his seat, the weight of defeat draining his energy. When he reached the door, Isaac was there waiting with fear in his eyes. Ordinarily Drake would've smirked, taking pleasure as he always did in the downfall of others. But he'd just faced his own downfall, and it wasn't very funny.

Drake walked back to what was soon to be his former office. Memories of hard won political battles flooded his mind, causing him to swoon briefly. *I have to get the hell out of here,* he thought to himself. He wanted to go home and pull his expensive Egyptian cotton sheets over himself and disappear. Cabrien would be angry, but who cared? Cabrien was *always* angry about something. Drake figured Cabrien had gotten the hint that he wasn't going to show up, and was probably in the embrace of a lonely man who needed Cabrien for that evening more than Drake ever would. As he packed his belongings and his memories, he stopped for a moment. He asked out loud, imitating Bruce Hedrick's drawl, "Why don't you like Gary Walsh?"

"I don't, okay?" Drake replied to no one. "I just don't!"

CHAPTER THIRTY-FIVE

Thursday, September 25, 2008

7:54 PM

Stewart had no intention of bringing Cabrien back to his hotel. Instead, he insisted upon a closer seedy motel located east of the freeway on Lake Street.

Cabrien circled the block trying to find somewhere well lit to park his car. He never liked this part of town, with its derelicts and bums waiting like vampires to taste the blood of their prey.

When they finally stood in front of the motel, Cabrien grimaced at its dinginess. He knew there was no champagne waiting inside. "This is it?" he asked.

"What's wrong with it?" Stewart asked, looking around to see who and what was near them.

"Well, you said we were going to have champagne and watch dirty movies before having sex," Cabrien reminded him.

"I'm sure this place has some kind of porn channel," Stewart assured him.

"What about the champagne?" Cabrien asked.

"Maybe there is a liquor store around here."

Cabrien looked at his watch. "They're closed," he said, his heart sinking.

"Well, there you go."

Cabrien and Stewart walked into the small, run-down lobby of the motel. There were bus transfers all over the floor, and someone had left a Styrofoam box on the ledge with crushed aluminum foil, old French fries, and a half-eaten sandwich in it. They walked over to the front desk, which was a small little space enclosed in heavy glass.

With the exception of a television that was playing in the small office, the place was deathly quiet. An old black man appeared behind the partition.

"Yeah, hi. A room please?" Stewart asked as he fished through his pockets, pulling out crumpled money. He then leaned over and grabbed Cabrien's butt. Cabrien immediately jumped away as the old man gave them a disapproving glance.

"That'll be sixty dollars," the old man said.

Stewart attempted to sort out the denominations of bills. "I ain't countin' all this shit," he said, laughing before sliding a credit card toward the old man.

"Room 302. Go up the stairs, take a right, and go all the way down the hall, way in the back," the old man said with a huff as he slid a key bearing the motel's faded name on it through the partition.

"Stairs? Y'all ain't got an elevator?" Cabrien complained.

"No, we ain't got no elevator," the old man snapped as he slid the credit card and receipt back in their direction.

"That's all right, be glad that you have strength now, because when I'm through with you, you won't be able

to walk," Stewart said, signing the receipt. He pulled at Cabrien's waist.

Cabrien pulled from Stewart, trying to avoid the old man's glare. Stewart ignored the man's hostility. Cabrien snatched the key from Stewart and started in the direction they'd been told. Stewart looked at the old man, shrugged sheepishly and walked away. The man stared at them as far as his view permitted until they were gone from his sight. When they disappeared up the stairs, he shook his head one last time and muttered, "*Fucking faggots!*" and turned back around to watch television again.

By the time they reached the room, both Cabrien and Stewart were panting for breath. Cabrien inserted the key and turned on the lights. The walls were painted white, with heavy mint green curtains thick with dust and grime. The bed was king-size; its bedspread wrinkled as though someone had been sleeping there fairly recently and lazily tried to remake the bed, but didn't quite succeed. The sagging ceiling was popcorn-style with brown stains in the corners.

Cabrien went into the bathroom to look around and saw plaster lying inside of the bathtub, with rust staining the drain. Cabrien wanted to run out screaming about the filth, but he also wanted to make something of this disappointing evening. *I'm gonna kick Drake's ass when I see him!* Cabrien thought to himself.

"I'm gonna need the money upfront," Cabrien said.

"Relax. You know I got the money."

"I don't work like that. No money, no ass."

"Man, you're a bossy one," Stewart said, reaching back into his mound of crumpled cash and began to count to five hundred.

"Not really. I'm just trying to get my money."

Stewart folded the money and handed it to Cabrien, who thumbed through it slowly. When he was satisfied it was all there, he stuffed it into his pocket. Stewart came and stood behind Cabrien and began massaging his shoulders.

"You know, it's a good thing we have a room way in the back. No one will be able to hear you scream," Stewart said, grinning lewdly.

"What does that mean?" Cabrien said, shooting around quickly.

"The screaming you'll be doing while I'm up in it. What did you think I meant? You're too tense. You need to relax." Stewart said, turning Cabrien back around and digging deeply into his shoulders. Cabrien melted at Stewart's touch. Stewart began to kiss Cabrien's neck and brought his tongue out and began to lick the nape of it. Cabrien tingled with pleasure and began to relax.

"Be right back," Stewart said all of a sudden and disappeared into the bathroom.

Cabrien stayed where he was. *He's not so bad. Maybe he's just a little out there. Or maybe he hasn't had sex in awhile.* Cabrien thought to himself. But then he heard the sound of snorting coming from the bathroom. Stewart emerged from the bathroom licking the back of his hand, and a dusting of white powder on his nose.

"I thought you didn't have any coke," Cabrien said.

Stewart giggled, reached over with both of his hands and pulled Cabrien's face gently toward him.

"Come here!" Stewart said lustily. He forced his tongue inside Cabrien's mouth. Cabrien resisted the kiss, squirming with displeasure.

"Dude, slow down," Cabrien yelled. "You told me that you didn't have any coke!"

Stewart raised his hands, palms out, as if to say, *Okay, you got me.* Cabrien stood there in disbelief. Was there anything this man told him that was true?

Stewart looked up into the lights and quickly looked away. "Oh shit! These lights are too bright. I think we should turn the lights out."

"No, I don't think so, buddy," Cabrien said quickly.

As Stewart began to take his clothes off, Cabrien continued to watch, doing nothing.

Soon, Stewart stood before Cabrien in all of his nakedness. He began to stroke himself and then he jumped on top of the bed and stood there, looking down at Cabrien. "Come on," Stewart said. His eyes were intense; he seemed to look through and beyond Cabrien. Cabrien sighed and began to slowly undress. Stewart became impatient, leaping from the bed to assist him.

Soon they were both naked and in bed. Stewart lifted Cabrien's legs onto his shoulders, rubbing his dick back and forth between the crevices of Cabrien's butt. Then, with a hurried, jerked movement, Stewart repositioned himself so they were in alignment to do the 69 position. He began to stuff Cabrien's cock into his mouth while forcing himself into Cabrien's mouth. Stewart sucked Cabrien so hard, it didn't feel good. Cabrien tried to ignore it and go along with it. When he went in to deep throat Stewart, he smelled the remnants of feces all along Stewart's butt area, as though he hadn't properly wiped or had recently gone to the bathroom. Cabrien grimaced at the stench.

Once again in a hurried, jerked movement, Stewart repositioned himself, bored with the previous position,

and this time more forceful and rough. He turned Cabrien on to his stomach and began rubbing himself up and down Cabrien's backside. Cabrien, feeling thrown about like a rag doll, simply went along with it, trying to wait for the right time to leave.

But then, Stewart jumped up and started to pace the room.

"Dude, what is wrong with you?" Cabrien asked, stunned.

"You know, I didn't used to be like this," Stewart said, running his fingers over his own head.

"Like what?" Cabrien said, sitting up.

"Like you. Doing this."

"Uh, do you mean gay?" Cabrien asked, confused.

"He made me this way!" Stewart shouted.

"Nobody can make you gay."

"Drake Hill did this to me! That fucker!"

Cabrien was stunned. "You know Drake?"

Stewart did a double take at Cabrien, remembering what Drake had told him when asked if he were seeing anyone.

"Oh gosh, he's a gorgeous brotha. He has these mag- nificent gray eyes. I've never seen eyes on a black guy like that before. They're almost catlike."

This was the man Drake was talking about, Stewart thought.

"And you're the cocksucker he's seeing now, aren't you?" Stewart said, approaching Cabrien menacingly.

"I have to go," Cabrien said, reaching for his clothes.

"You ain't goin' nowhere," Stewart said, kicking Cabrien's clothes from reach.

"You better get the fuck out of my face, nigga! Or we're gonna be two tusslin' bitches up in here!"

Stewart lunged at Cabrien, pinning him against the wall. Cabrien grabbed for Stewart's throat, pushing him to arm length, but still holding his grasp.

"Naw, bitch, naw!" Cabrien yelled, squeezing tightly. He hit Stewart in the temple with his free hand.

Stewart head-butted Cabrien, knocking him senseless. Then, with a balled fist, he hit Cabrien to the floor. Stewart stood over him, his pupils large. He licked his lips harshly as he began kicking Cabrien in the chest and stomach, knocking the wind out of him.

"No, please stop!"

"Shut the fuck up!" Stewart kicked Cabrien in the face.

Cabrien tried to protect his head, but...as Stewart opened up on him, kicking and punching wildly...Cabrien's arms and hands went wherever he was being struck next. He thought about the old man downstairs and how he would never bother to help.

He's gonna kill me! Cabrien's mind screamed to him.

Stewart reached in with both hands around Cabrien's thin neck and squeezed. Cabrien balled his fists and tried hitting Stewart's hands with his own, and then tried to pry Stewart's hands from his neck. He became lightheaded. Tingling sensations passed through his body as he began to lose consciousness.

"Please," Cabrien pleaded, now with barely a whisper escaping his badly bruised and cut mouth. And suddenly Stewart let go of his grasp. Cabrien slumped over, gasping for needed air, clawing at his own throat as though the air would come to him more quickly. His chest rose and fell with pain from having been repeatedly kicked. Blood

stained his body and the carpet. He was dizzy and looked up through blurred vision.

Stewart paced the room again, slapping the top of his head, and clenching his teeth as though the internal battle in his mind was tearing through to the outside world.

Cabrien was deathly afraid, not knowing what was going to happen next. Was he still going to die? Had he been given a reprieve? Should he try to will the strength to attempt some sort of escape? He was too weak to even fight back, and as he lifted his head and looked downward he noticed the blood mark on the carpet expanding.

Stewart sat on the bed and looked at Cabrien's body, watching the rising and falling of Cabrien's collapsed chest, listening to his labored whimper. Then Cabrien coughed, spewing bits of teeth and more blood onto the carpet. Then Stewart stood over Cabrien's torn body, waiting for it to move again.

Stewart went over to the lamp on the end table by the bed and snatched it from the outlet. He went back to where Cabrien lay, and waited. He looked at himself from the mirror across the room, seeing the unfamiliar image of a man holding a lamp over his head with someone else's blood splattered on his nude, male form. He saw himself looking every bit like a barbarian out in the wild. Looking again at Cabrien's body, again seeing the rising and falling of his chest and hearing labored breathing, he smashed the lamp down on Cabrien's head.

Cabrien began to sob softly, never thinking this could happen to him. He thought about Karen, and his mother. He thought about Armando. He thought about Drake...until his consciousness became lost in blackness.

Fragments of ceramic lay all around Cabrien's motion-

less body. The cord from the lamp was completely ripped from it; the bulb broken into millions of pieces, and the lampshade bent, never to be used again. Stewart spit on Cabrien's body as the pool of blood spread so far that it touched the tip of his toes, causing him to inch back onto the bed. The rising and falling of Cabrien's chest had stopped.

He picked up his clothes and dressed quickly. After putting his shoes on, he went over to Cabrien's pants that had been kicked into a corner and dug around the pockets until he found his money.

"Your raggedy-bitch ass won't be needing this after all," he said with panted breath. Then he lifted the musty, heavy comforter from the bed and tossed it on top of Cabrien's body, turned out the light and left.

When Stewart arrived back in the lobby, with Cabrien's car keys in his hand, he was about to leave when the old man called to him from behind the partition. "Hey! Where's the other one that was with you?" the old man asked.

"Oh, him? He looked so peaceful, I didn't want to wake him. I think I wore him out," Stewart said, smiling.

The old man didn't smile. "He can't just sleep up there all night, ya know. I need more money!"

"Well, here's sixty bucks. How long does that give him?"

"The same as before. Then, I'm gonna go and rouse him up and kick his ass out!"

"Do what you need to do, sir," Stewart said, this time sliding three crumpled twenty-dollar bills toward the old man. "But I should tell you, he's in such a deep sleep, you might think he's dead."

Friday, September 26, 2008

12:01 AM

"All right, sir. Talk to me." Officer McLean stood behind the old man as they watched the security video.

"Well, sir, you can see there was two of 'em. One was older than the other."

"And which one came downstairs?"

"The older one, sir."

"When did you discover the young man?"

"Well, to be honest, I knew what they had been up there doin', so I wasn't lookin' forward to havin' to go up there and get him."

"Wait a minute. You knew there was an altercation taking place?"

"No, sir. I meant I knew they had been up there, well, I ain't got to tell you what they were doin'. You look pretty smart to me, sir."

"You mean they had been having sex," Officer McLean suggested.

The old man's face twisted at the thought. "Yes, sir. And I think the older one was payin' for it. I could tell by the body language. The younger guy was with him, but you could tell they didn't know each other that well."

"Okay, so when did you go up there?"

"We ain't sold out, so I waited a good while before I went up there. Like I said, I guess I was tryin' to avoid havin' to deal with the situation. I'd say it was about eleven when I finally got the spirit to kick him out. I knocked about three times and there was no answer. I had to let myself into the room." He ejected the VHS security video.

Officer McLean smiled. "Don't suppose you ever thought to update your technology, huh?"

"Naw, sir. I wouldn't know what to do with it. This here system I got been workin' just fine."

"Now, you're sure there weren't any other visitors to that room?"

"Yes, sir. I'm as sure as I am my name is Harold Jenkins." He handed the officer the security video and credit card receipt Stewart had left.

Officer McLean nodded his appreciation as he picked up the telephone. "Yeah, Dopps, I need you to do a check on a Stewart McKillen. I got a credit card receipt of possibly his last transaction, see if you can pick up anything else." Then he hung up the phone, facing Mr. Jenkins. "Don't worry, we'll get him."

CHAPTER
THIRTY-SIX

Friday, September 26, 2008

8:00 AM

Wanda went over to the dresser and pulled her cell phone from her purse. She scowled at the name that appeared next to all seventeen missed calls from the previous evening. Hearing Gary stirring in bed behind her, she turned to face him.

"Morning, darling," she said, dropping the phone back into her purse.

"Morning."

"You slept like a baby."

"I slept okay. The inside of my ass hurts."

"I bet it does. But at least you've got a free pass to lay around all day."

"No. I think I should try and go into the office."

"Uh, no, you're going to stay in bed and rest. And pass as much gas as your behind can muster. Nurse's orders."

Gary sighed wearily. "I barely remember anything from it."

"That's because they pumped you full of drugs. Do you

want to remember having instruments put up your rectum?"

Gary grimaced at the mental picture.

"Yeah, I didn't think so," she said, leaning down to kiss him on the forehead.

"I suppose I could use the relaxation. I deserve it."

"You sure do."

Wanda's cell phone rang loudly. She glanced in its direction, rolling her eyes.

"Aren't you going to get that?"

"It's probably just the girls at the salon. Whatever it is, I'm sure they can wait until I get there."

Gary shrugged lazily. "You look pretty." He marveled at her effortless beauty. He especially liked the gray business pantsuit she was wearing. Made her look both chic and in charge.

"Okay, let me get out of here. I'll come home around lunchtime and fix you something to eat."

"You could just come home and jump into this bed with me."

"We'll see," she said with a wink. "I love you."

"Love you more."

Friday, September 26, 2008

12:15PM

Wanda left the salon to return home to prepare something for Gary. When she reached her car, the ringing from her phone began again, seemingly relentless. She picked up. "Clearly you don't take hints very well," she said.

"Meet me behind the bandstand at Lake Harriet...right

now. And you *better* show up, too." Then the caller hung up.

Wanda sighed, turned her car around and headed in the opposite direction. When she pulled into the parking lot directly behind the bandstand, she sat for a moment, watching him pace back and forth. Finally, she got out of her car and marched over to him, like a soldier going off to a war.

Isaac turned around, visibly angry. "Why aren't you answering my phone calls all of a sudden?"

"I was with my husband. He had his colonoscopy yesterday, remember?" she snapped.

"I don't give a damn about Gary. I'm out of a job!"

Wanda paused. "What are you talking about?"

"Maybe if you answered your goddamned phone you would've known that I got fired!"

"What happened?"

"It was that cocksucker, Drake! He told Bruce that I'd been keeping a mistress." Isaac sneered. "Needless to say, Bruce didn't think that would fit with the Family Values image of the organization. What I want to know is how Drake found out?"

Wanda stood, looking at her watch, unfazed by what Isaac said. The more casual she appeared to him, the angrier he grew.

"I can see you care deeply."

"I was going to tell you this; I suppose now is not the best time, but I should tell you anyway." She said, looking out at the lake.

"Tell me what?" Isaac asked, coming in closer to her.

"I've really had an opportunity to reevaluate things and I've decided that we can't keep doing this—*especially now.*

It was wrong for us to even begin seeing each other. I just think we need to break it off." Wanda continued staring at the lake.

"Right. So not only do I lose my job, but I lose you too?"

"Did you really think you had me? Look, Isaac, we're both married. Our sleeping together never changed those basics."

"So that's it? You're going to walk out on me?"

"You didn't think this would go on forever, did you?" Wanda asked coldly. She began to walk to her car, leaving Isaac Walterson more confused than he was before she had arrived. She turned to him once more. "Go home to your wife, and stop acting stupid."

Isaac was amazed at how coldly Wanda was behaving. "You set me up, didn't you? This was your plan all along. Use me to get your piece-of-shit husband a job he can't handle. Well fuck you *and* your dried-up pussy!"

"Do you kiss the bitch you got at home with that mouth? How did you ever get to be the poster boy for Christianity anyway?"

"We're not done talking yet!" Isaac said, grabbing Wanda's arm.

"I think we are done," Wanda said, pulling away. "Oh and about the sex? Not great. Your wife has my sympathies."

"Where do you think you're going?" Isaac called out to her as she moved toward her car. He felt angry at being abandoned.

"Well, I was going to go home to fix my husband a grilled cheese sandwich, but now, thanks to you, I think I'll pay Drake a visit."

"Black bitch," Isaac muttered as she sped away, leaving

him where she found him. Instead of her scent of lingering perfume, Isaac was treated to the smell of car exhaust.

Wanda headed downtown feeling exuberant. When she reached Drake's door, she knocked at it. Drake scowled when he saw her standing there.

"What do *you* want?" Drake said, letting Wanda in.

"Now, Drake, is that any way to speak to your benefactor? After all, I think a thank-you is in order," she said, grinning.

"*This* is how you thank me? I don't recall losing my job being part of the deal, Wanda!"

"Oh come now, my dear. I did you a favor. So, in actuality, *you* should be thanking me."

"Yeah right. Some favor," Drake said, sitting down on his couch.

"Great. Now both you *and* Isaac are angry with me," Wanda said in a hurt voice, although all Drake had to do was look in her eyes to know that Wanda was far from hurt.

"He's not too happy with you, by the way," she quipped.

"I don't give a shit," he muttered.

Wanda took her checkbook from her purse, along with her favorite expensive pen.

She signed a check for $150,000 and handed it to Drake as though she did it on a regular basis.

"Great, I've got $50,000 and no job, thanks to you," Drake said glumly. He folded the check without looking at it.

"Uh, I think you'd better take a good look at that check. I just added a little cherry on top. That should take off some of the sting from being fired, shouldn't it? Don't think of this as an ending. Think of it as a new beginning.

I know it's a new beginning for me," Wanda said, her voice full of gleeful satisfaction.

"What are you talking about?"

"I broke it off with Isaac today."

"What do you mean 'broke it off'?"

"I had to break up with him. Gary is going to head one of the most promising political organizations in the Midwest. I had to let my relationship with Isaac end." Wanda spoke as though Drake should have expected as much from her.

"But you told me that Isaac had a mistress; you said to use that against him if necessary."

"Yes, I did."

"And it was *you* the entire time?"

"Yes, it was."

"And you didn't tell me?"

"And give you something that you could hold over me? Drake, you better stop playing. Besides, you're very good at digging up dirt on people, I'm sure you would've found out had you bothered to look."

"But you told me not to."

"And now you know why," Wanda said, pleased with her own craftiness.

Drake had genuinely been outfoxed for the first time in his life.

"Look, all I asked you to do was steal some of Gary's files, and make it look as though Isaac did it. In the meantime, I had to mess around with Isaac so it would give believability to your allegation that he was cheating on his wife. So when you threatened him, he knew that it was something real. You didn't have to necessarily know *who* he was cheating with."

"Does Gary know?" Drake asked, still mystified as to how he could have been tricked.

"Don't be ridiculous! I love Gary, but you and I both know he'd be crushed by the news."

"You're a smart lady, Wanda Walsh. You got fucked and actually got something to show for it." Drake said, looking at the check in his hand.

"Well, a wise woman once told me that sometimes we ladies have to do strange things to get what we want. I'm just glad it paid off," she said simply. "Okay, so you're $150,000 richer, not that you even need the money," Wanda said, her eyes darting about the apartment. Then her eyes settled back on Drake. "Maybe you can use it to pay for the services of those men you're so fond of." Her glance turned knowing.

"How do you know about that?" Drake asked, doing a double take.

"I have to know everything about those I do business with. Just in case it gets, well, *tricky*." Wanda put the checkbook and pen back inside of her purse. She walked over to Drake and extended her hand to him.

"It was a pleasure doing business with you." The look in her eyes was warm and sincere. Drake stood up and met her hand with his own.

"Likewise," he said with a smile.

"What are you going to do with yourself now?"

"I was thinking about taking some time off and going to New York."

"Mmm, New York sounds good."

"How is Gary doing?"

"Oh, he's fine. The procedure went well." Then Wanda became serious and looked Drake directly in his eyes.

"Drake, besides the money, why did you help Gary? I know you don't like him very much."

"Because Isaac is the bigger asshole," Drake said, laughing.

"No, seriously. Why did you help Gary when you don't like him?"

"I don't know, Wanda. It's like, you know how there are circumstances that look worse to the other person than they actually are? I think that's what happened with Gary and me. I did an interview a long time ago for a newspaper and I kind of insinuated that the reason he married you was..."

"So he could get his hands on my money when I became successful. I heard that before," Wanda interrupted.

"No, that was only part of it. The other part was that I thought you were his beard."

"His what?" Wanda asked puzzled.

"His beard. That's what you call a woman who is seen out with a gay man. I thought that Gary was gay."

Wanda laughed.

"Not only that, but we've really never liked each other. It happens."

"I'm just glad that you got over that enough to help me pull this off."

"What's past is past, Anyway, he and I won't have to see each other ever again, so it all worked out. But I couldn't stand for that bigot Isaac to be in a position to be able to write into law legislation that would make me a second-class citizen."

"I understand," Wanda said, walking toward the door and opening it.

Drake followed her. "What are you going to do with yourself now?" Drake wanted to know.

"I'm going back home to be with my husband."

"I wish him well," Drake said.

"And you, what are you going to do now?"

"I'm going to call someone I stood up last night. With any luck, he'll still talk to me."

"Then I'll say goodbye, Drake. Take care."

Drake went over to his phone and began dialing. As he listened to the ringing of the phone, he practiced what he would say. "Hello Cabrien, it's me...I want to apologize."

CHAPTER
THIRTY-SEVEN

Friday, September 26, 2008

1:30 PM

Officer McLean cautiously poked his head into the hospital room. "Excuse me, folks. Are you the Jacobs family?"

There was a collective yes, followed by quizzical glances.

"I'm David McLean. I was one of the responding officers to the scene last night." Entering the room, he caught a full glance of Cabrien, who looked like a mound of bruised flesh. "No improvement?"

Karen stepped away from Armando's embrace. "No. He's still unconscious. Will you please tell us what happened?"

"I responded to a call at about midnight. Cabrien was in the company of a man named Stewart McKillen. It appears that Cabrien was acting as a sex worker-for-hire. At some point in the evening Mr. McKillen assaulted Cabrien, but was apprehended this morning at his hotel before he could flee to California."

Karen's mother, Thelma, rose to her feet, and threw her hands in the air, exclaiming, "Lord Jesus! Rock of Ages!"

"So, you mean to tell me that my cousin is a prostitute?"

Armando bit his bottom lip and averted his eyes as he put his arm back around Karen.

The officer nodded and said, "Damn shame the kid felt he had to sell himself just to make ends meet."

Tears came to Karen's eyes. "You know, he asked me a couple months back if I'd help him with his rent money. I shoulda gave it to him."

"Now, you stop that foolish talk. We all know ain't nothing good gonna come from that lifestyle. He did that because he wanted to," Thelma said.

"Well, does anyone have any questions for me?" the officer asked.

"What did the guy say when you arrested him?" Armando asked.

"What's interesting is that there is record of him doing this same kind of thing in California. Not sure why he was out walking around if that's the case. Anyway, when I asked him about this instance, he didn't even deny it. Said he didn't know why he'd done it. But the important thing is we got him, and unlike last time, he's going away for a long time."

"Well, thank you, mister," Karen said, extending a hand to Officer McLean.

"It was my pleasure. Here are Cabrien's clothes and cell phone," he said, handing a bag to Karen. "If I can just get you to sign for them."

Karen signed the form and gave it back to the officer.

"You folks feel free to give me a call in the event you have any more questions." Then Officer McLean left.

Thelma stood in silence, exhausted from having prayed since the early morning hours that Cabrien would regain consciousness. Thelma had her beliefs, and she had her reasons for believing what she did. And although she didn't want him to die, she wasn't going to change those feelings or beliefs because Cabrien was clinging to life. These were the wages of sin as far as she was concerned, but she was there to be supportive of her daughter.

Armando felt pangs of guilt for having kept Cabrien's secret to himself. It wasn't any of his business, he kept telling himself. Still, he wondered if things would've been different if he had told Karen what Cabrien was doing.

Karen felt awful for allowing the last conversation she had with Cabrien to be one of anger and mistrust. If God would spare his life, she vowed, she would be good and kind to him forever. She was sorry for having called him a faggot. She wished she'd simply lent him money when he needed it, so he wouldn't have had to sell himself to pay the rent.

If only God would let him come out of this okay.

The hospital room smelled the way one imagined death to smell like. Not the smell of decomposition, but of emptiness, and of a spirit freeing itself from its physical body.

Karen took Cabrien's phone out of the bag and left the room. When she returned several minutes later, she tearfully knelt before Cabrien, grasping hold of his cool hand. Armando came and tried to raise her up and away, but she wouldn't move. She squeezed Cabrien's hand tightly, hoping the small shock of pain would wake him. She'd never

seen him look like this. There was none of the usual life-light in his face.

Friday, September 26, 2008

2:00PM

When Drake walked in, Armando froze, remembering the confrontation from the last time he'd seen Cabrien. Drake walked past everyone and looked at Armando. Their eyes met, and although Armando was afraid of the truth of his relationship with Drake exposed, he knew that it was essential for Drake to be there.

"Y'all, who is this man?" Thelma asked suspiciously.

"That's Drake, uh, one of Cabrien's friends. He called Cabrien's phone, and I answered it," Karen said, nodding in Drake's direction.

"You have Cabrien's phone?" Armando asked.

"You didn't see the cop give it to me?"

"Oh yeah," Armando said, nervously looking at Drake.

"Anyway, I took the phone downstairs to scroll the numbers and while I had it on Drake called and I told him everything."

"How long has he been like this?" Drake asked, genuinely concerned, but he didn't wait for an answer. He rushed to Cabrien's side. "Cabrien, I'm sorry. I'm so sorry for being such an asshole. I'm sorry that I didn't meet you last night. If I had, you wouldn't be in this hospital bed. I'm sorry that this happened to you."

As Drake reached for Cabrien's hand, Karen let go of her grasp to let Drake have his moment. Thelma shook her head and walked out of the room.

"You have to pull out of this, Cabrien," Drake's voice became emotional, his eyes teary. "At least come back to your family!"

Drake repositioned his hand beneath Cabrien's. He bent down, kissing Cabrien gently on the lips. A few seconds later he felt a slight squeeze of his hand. Slowly, Cabrien's bruised eyes opened.

"Mama, get in here!" Karen shouted as she witnessed the miracle.

Thelma came back in the room, and began to cry out, "Praise the Lord!"

Karen pushed past them all. "Can you hear me?" she asked.

Cabrien nodded slowly.

"He's gonna be all right. Do you hear me? He's gonna be all right!"

Tears began to well in Cabrien's eyes. Drake leaned in, wiping them away with his finger.

"You're absolutely right! He's going to be just fine," Drake said, smiling at Cabrien.

As Karen reached over and impulsively put her hands on Drake's shoulders, Cabrien raised his hand feebly, motioning that he wanted to speak. He swallowed hard, trying to moisten his mouth. But nothing came out. It hurt too much.

"Yeah, he's gonna be all right," Karen said encouragingly, blotting tears from her own eyes with a tissue.

Drake watched as Cabrien's family gathered around him. Thelma turned around and noticed Drake in the corner. She approached him.

"Look, I appreciate you being here and all, but this is a

time for his family, and frankly, you ain't no family I know of," Thelma said.

Drake blinked at her directness. "You're right, Madame. I certainly mean no disrespect. I'll come back at a better time," he said, turning to leave.

Seeing both Karen and her mother engrossed with Cabrien, Armando followed Drake out. "Yo, Drake. Wait up, man," Armando called out.

Drake stopped.

"Listen, I know it's jacked up to talk about this while they're in there, but, I thought you should know that Karen and I are getting married."

"She took you back after she found out you made a homo?"

"Karen didn't believe him."

"Well, aren't you lucky? But I think it's more that she *chose* not to believe him."

"Yeah, maybe. Either way you're not gonna say anything, are you?" Armando asked.

Drake looked at Armando, his face turning serious. "I don't know what you're talking about."

Armando studied Drake's face, not knowing if this was yet another game.

"So, is that a 'no'?"

"Like I said, I don't know what you're talking about. We're just two guys who spent some time together and got to know each other. What's to talk about?" Then he smiled. "Congratulations."

"Thanks, man," Armando said, smiling awkwardly. He was relieved.

"Better get back in there. You don't want to rouse suspicion, do you?"

The smile faded from Armando's lips. He looked as though he had suddenly become aware of the risk. He nodded almost involuntarily as he turned to leave. Drake remained where he was, staring as Armando left. It would take a little time, but he knew he'd have to go on with his life, without Armando. He thought about what he said to Armando the night Cabrien caught them, when he told him that Cabrien would just have to learn the lesson that some people don't always get what they want. Today, Drake laughed at the irony of becoming one of those people.

Monday, September 29, 2008

1:00 PM

After lunch, Drake took a chance and went back to the hospital, hoping Cabrien's family wasn't there, or would at least allow him to visit. Cabrien, who was sitting up, looked in pain.

"Hey you," Drake said cheerily, expecting Cabrien's face to light up upon seeing him. "How are you?"

"You mean, how am I doing considering I'm laying up in this hospital bed? Peachy."

"I guess that was a dumb question. You look like you're in pain."

"That's because I am." Cabrien folded his arms.

"You know, I was thinking. When you're ready to be released, why don't I come by and bring you home?" Drake asked.

"That's all right. Karen will come and pick me up."

"No, I was talking about bringing you home with me. So you can recuperate. I think I'd like that very much."

Cabrien's stomach fluttered despite his pain. "And what happens after I'm all better?"

"I don't know."

"What kind of answer is that, Drake?"

Drake smiled at Cabrien's feistiness. He rubbed Cabrien's forearm gently and said, "Let's just take it one day at a time, shall we?"

Cabrien chuckled and shook his head. "You know what, Drake? You're a hot mess."

"Excuse me?"

"Did I stutter? You think you can just come up in here and offer me a place to stay for a few days, tell me we can work it out and then toss me out on my black ass when I'm better?"

"No, I meant it."

"Yeah, right. Bullshit never suited you."

"This isn't bullshit, Cabrien. I feel bad that this happened to you."

"Good, I'm glad that you feel bad. You *should* feel bad. It's because of your stupid ass that I'm laying in this bed. So what, you thought you'd make your little announcement and that would make everything all right? Be honest about the shit, Drake, you didn't come here for me, you came here for yourself!"

"Cabrien, look, you're upset. I don't blame you. But I didn't stand you up that night to be cruel. I had a lot of shit going on. I couldn't..."

"Let's not even go there. You couldn't be bothered. That's all it was."

"No, I was getting fired, Cabrien. I know you remember what that was like when you got fired," Drake said in a huff.

"Good. That's what your ass gets. See, the problem with people like you, Drake, is that you have no soul. That's why it's so easy to do the grimy things you do!"

Drake stood there silently. He understood Cabrien's anger, but didn't understand why Cabrien couldn't see that he was being sincere.

"It's quite all right, baby. You're not the settling-down type, I know that now. But what *you* need to know, is that the day is gonna come when your ass is gonna get older, and if karma does what it's supposed to, I hope you're home alone when you drop dead. And it'll be months before anybody even finds your sorry ass!"

Drake's eyes widened with disbelief. "Whoa, that's harsh even for you, Cabrien."

"Yeah, but I mean it. You're selfish, Drake. That's your sickness."

"Boy, it's been a real treat knowing you," Drake hissed. "I've bailed you out I don't know how many times, Cabrien. Since you're feeling so self-righteous, I hope you remember all of this when you're better and have to come crawling to me to ask for more money."

"If I have to work five jobs so that I can have the satisfaction of not having to ask your trifling ass for anything, it would be worth it."

Drake's eyes narrowed; a smirk formed on his lips, "Oh? Honest pay for an honest day's work? Armando had a hell of a time finding a job. What makes you think it'll be any easier for you?"

"The fact that I'm alive after that son of a bitch nearly stomped me to death lets me know that I'm blessed. My Heavenly Father will make a way for me, trust!"

Drake burst into a fit of laughter that Cabrien had never heard before. "We'll see, my friend." And he left.

Cabrien turned his head weakly toward the hospital room's window. He allowed the many tears he hadn't wanted Drake to see to stream down his face. The dream he had that they would be together stubbornly faded. Yet, despite his physical pain and weakness he was pleased with himself for having closed the Drake Hill chapter of his life. He knew however, that nothing he'd said to Drake had gotten through to him. In the end, Drake would go on being Drake.

As the evening came, Cabrien became tired and began to fall asleep. Twenty minutes before the end of visiting hours, he received one last visitor. He was awakened by a soft touch to his shoulder.

"Hey, Boo. Your May-May is here."

Cabrien opened his eyes to see Don standing there. As his eyes adjusted, the light surrounding Don gave him an angelic glow.

"You're just now coming to see me?"

"No, I came by three days ago after your cousin called me from your phone to tell me you were here. But when I got here, some nasty-ass old woman told me that only family was seeing you. Was that your mama?"

Cabrien tried to sit up. Don helped him readjust the pillow behind him. "Boy, please! That was *not* my mama. Wasn't no man at stake for her to trouble herself to see her only son. It must've been my auntie."

"Chile, she a mess!"

"I know it."

"Did you have any fans come by today, diva?" Don asked.

"Yeah, Drake brought his goofy ass by."

"He had the nerve to show up here?"

"He called himself feeling guilty."

"That's the least he could do."

"Don't worry, I told him about himself. I don't think he'll be coming back anytime soon."

"Good. I'm glad you read his ass for filth. I told you, girl, he ain't no damn good."

"Yeah, well, I guess it took me a minute to figure that one out."

Don touched Cabrien's cheek. It reminded Cabrien of his mother when he was little. "So, have you figured out what you're going to do when they release you?"

"I already told Drake, I'll work five jobs if it means being rid of him."

"I meant, where are you going to go when the hospital lets you out?"

"Karen said she'll come and pick me up."

"Honey, I got a sofa bed. It ain't much, but it's comfortable and it's yours if you want it. I can't have my best friend staying all by himself."

Cabrien smiled sadly. It was an appreciated kind gesture. "That'll work." Then, as he rubbed his eyes with one hand, he extended the other to Don, who took it readily.

"I think it's written somewhere that I'm supposed to be unlucky in love."

"Baby, you'll find a man. You just have to do *you* for a while, and get to appreciate yourself for who you are. The right guy will come around, and I guarantee he won't pull any stunts and shows like that bastard Drake."

"It just hurts, you know?"

"Yeah, but, you'll be all right. Like I said, you'll meet

somebody. Even I'll meet somebody. But until then, like my girl Joy Behar from *The View* says, 'So what? Who cares?'" Don said, imitating Joy's Brooklyn accent.

"Don't make me laugh, Don. It hurts," Cabrien said, wincing from laughter.

"I'm sorry, Cabrien. I'm going to leave you be. You look like you could use some rest."

"Don't go. Stay until they kick you out."

Don pulled up a chair and sat with Cabrien, the two of them sitting in silence, occasionally looking toward the window. When Cabrien finally drifted off to sleep, the nurse came to tell Don that visiting hours were over. He nodded, rising to leave. Before leaving, he turned to look at Cabrien as he slept peacefully. "You don't need that jive ass Drake, Cabrien," Don said softly. "I'll take care of you. Cuz' *that's* what a true friend is supposed to damn do."

Acknowledgments

I'm thankful to God for placing this gift in my hands. It's taken me nine years to create this book. In that time, the story evolved into something I never would have expected, yet am very proud of. I'd like to credit and thank two great editors who brought their expertise to this project and helped me find my way: Jerry Gross and Cherise Fisher. I'd like to thank Nira A. Hyman for her copy editing services; Peter and Caroline at Bespoke Book Covers for killing it with the book cover; and Hugh and his team at Pressbooks for delivering top notch converted files.

I'd like to thank the following people for their friendship, but also for lending their eyes by reading multiple drafts of this book, and offering their support: Nancy Roberts, you have probably been one of the biggest supporters since the very beginning. I remember when you called me up at work to see how my NYU fiction writing class had gone. When we've had rough days at work, you would always say, "You better get writing!" And it was that support that helped me keep going, especially when I second guessed myself. Robin DeFelice, thanks for understanding why I had to go away, but still offering your friendship. You're the absolute best; Melissa Buccheri, thanks for helping me stay true to character motivation

when it seemed I was getting lost in over-the-top story-telling. Your friendship is everything to me!

To my sister-in-law, Lois, who always asked how the writing was coming along and when would it go on sale. Lois, thanks so much for your encouragement and enthusiastic support!

To Karen Masi, thank you for allowing me a safe place to dream, and for sharing your dreams with me. This fuel will keep us going. Our comets are on fire! We'll get there! Trust and believe!

I'd like to shout out to M.T. Pope, a very talented author who in my opinion has defined a genre. You have been both gracious and generous with what you know about the book game. You are who I'd like to be! May God bless you with continued success!

I'd like to thank my brother, Philip Trueblood, who despite being eleven years my junior can give the best advice and tell me when I need to get over myself. Love you, bro!

I want to thank Rose McHugh for offering me television and keeping it real. And I'd like to thank the Schmitt family for twenty-two years of friendship and fellowship. Grace, thank you for always being the one to show interest in my writing. You are what is good about humanity. There is no one else I'd rather kill a bottle of wine with!

I want to thank the love of my life, Lyle, for supporting me and loving me as only you can, and for giving me twenty-two years of wonderful!

And of course, I'd like to thank my readers. I am eternally grateful that you read my books and allow me to entertain you. I do this for you.

About the Author

Lloyd is a Minnesota native, currently living in New England. He rediscovered his passion for writing in 2004, and has been working on his craft ever since. Lloyd enjoys telling stories without being pinned to any one genre. He is currently working on his fourth novel.

If you are a book reviewer or just an ardent reader who loves Lloyd's books, he would love to hear from you. Please drop him a line!

www.authorlloydjohnson.com

Facebook: Author Lloyd Johnson

Twitter: @lloydjohnson19